Four Novels
by Marguerite Duras

Four Novels
by Marguerite Duras

INTRODUCTION BY
GERMAINE BRÉE

Grove Press, Inc.
New York

The Square copyright © 1959 by John Calder (Publishers) Ltd. Originally published in France by Librairie Gallimard as *Le Square*, © 1955.

Moderato cantabile copyright © 1960 by Grove Press, Inc. Originally published in France by Les Editions de Minuit as *Moderato cantabile*, © 1958.

Ten-thirty on a Summer Night copyright © 1962 by Marguerite Duras. Originally published in France by Librairie Gallimard as *Dix heures et demie du
soir en été*, © 1960.

The Afternoon of Mr. Andesmas copyright © 1965 by Grove Press, Inc., Originally published in France by Librairie Gallimard as *L'après-midi de Monsieur Andesmas*, © 1962.

First Evergreen Edition 1982
First Printing 1982
ISBN: 0-394-17987-0
Library of Congress Catalog Card Number: 65-14208

Manufactured in the United States of America

GROVE PRESS, INC., 196 West Houston Street, New York, N.Y. 10014

INTRODUCTION

by Germaine Brée

No ONE WHO HAS SEEN and liked Alain Resnais' film *Hiroshima, Mon Amour* is likely to forget the moment when the voices of the man and woman rise alternately slow, calm, almost impersonal. They come, one feels, from a long inner distance, far beyond the immediacy of the two tightly-clasped bodies on the screen: " 'You saw *nothing* of Hiroshima. Nothing.' 'I saw everything. *Everything.* For instance, the hospital. I saw the hospital. I'm sure of that. How could I miss it?' 'You did not see the Hiroshima hospital. You saw nothing of Hiroshima.' " Unpredictable, dogged, and strangely persuasive, the dialogue between the man and woman begins to unfold.

On the whole, the movie-going public is more sensitive to the flow of images on the screen than to the words spoken, more attentive to the acting or the direction than to the script. That is why the name of Marguerite Duras, who gave the dialogue of *Hiroshima* its haunting, unobtrusive beauty, has remained relatively unknown to so many people indirectly stirred by the intensity of feeling she was able to enclose in words.

The script of Resnais' film is an excellent introduction to her writing, except that she is not usually concerned with great historical events. Rather, she concentrates on individual situations, which over the years she has tended to simplify, isolating in her stories brief but intense moments of awareness when, for an instant, two lives, or sometimes three, unpredictably act one upon the other, and an inner event seems to be taking shape. These are moments when, coming out of their isolation, her characters are willing to communicate, or to make an attempt at communication. To speak one to the other is in essence to relate. That is why dialogue is the key to Marguerite Duras's world and why, no doubt, her stories move so easily from narrative to stage or

v

scenario. Of the four novels included in this volume, *The Square* was staged in Paris and *Moderato Cantabile* adapted for the screen, both successfully.

Fiction, drama, cinema: these are her media, though her ten novels to date point to her greater involvement with the first; yet the hold the cinema has always had on her imagination is great and visibly affects her narrative techniques. Unlike the best known of the "experimental" novelists in France—Robbe-Grillet, Butor, Sarraute—Marguerite Duras has never been an essayist, an exponent of esthetic theories and ideas. But she shares with her contemporaries the desire to discard many of the rather worn-out conventions of the traditional novel, conventions which she put to effective use in her first works. *Barrage against the Pacific* (1950), the best-known of these, is a Hemingway-type story based on Marguerite Duras's memories of South Indochina where she lived until she was seventeen. The very title of the story suggests a dogged, unequal battle against a superhuman force. This was to remain one of Duras's basic themes: barrage against the immense solitude of human beings, barrage against the pain of all involvements, barrage against despair. In two of the stories, *Moderato Cantabile* and *Ten-thirty on a Summer Night*, alcohol is just such a barrage and, at the same time, ambiguously a kind of overwhelming Pacific.

The group of four short novels presented here and written between 1955 and 1962 are the works of a mature writer. They all reflect Duras's major esthetic preoccupation: to shape a story so that it achieves an emotional intensity and unity that goes beyond the limits of the outer events related. Each is a particular embodiment of a fundamental human feeling. Certainly the famous description of the modern novel as "dehumanized" does not apply to Marguerite Duras's, whose characters are pathetically and humanly vulnerable, humbly aware of the pain involved in human affections, yet dependent upon them, drawing from them the joys and disasters of living. Marguerite Duras's world is nothing if not intensely, vibrantly human. Were it not for the strict formal control she imposes on it, it might almost appear sentimental.

Duras's control is apparent in the manner in which she delimits situation and event. Each of the four novels unfolds in what resembles a stage set, or a series of clearly delineated sets. Each, as in drama, is carefully plotted within certain units of time. In *The Square*, a twenty-year-old girl and a man sit side by side on a park bench, in early summer, on a certain Thursday, from 4:30 P.M. to nightfall. It is on a

vi

Friday afternoon, in June, that in *Moderato Cantabile* Anne Desbaresdes hears the scream of a murdered woman, and on Saturday, at the same hour, she enters the bar where, for a little over one week, as spring moves into summer, she returns almost every day. In *Ten-thirty on a Summer Night*, the main set is the overcrowded hotel of a small Spanish town, where Maria, her husband Pierre, their daughter Judith, and a friend Claire spend one night, unexpectedly, because of the storm, and the entire story lasts barely twenty-four hours. The whole story of *The Afternoon of Mr. Andesmas* takes place on a terrace, one Saturday in early summer, between four o'clock and six. Though Marguerite Duras thus isolates what might appear as a fragment of existence, she does not present fragments of experience, but within the limits set by the molding of the narrative, she reaches toward an essential moment when, in a flash of awareness, the inner truth of a situation comes to light in the form of pure emotion.

In each story, mood, setting, and encounter are thematically developed and blended to achieve a certain pitch of emotional intensity bearable only because of the control Marguerite Duras maintains over her medium. To create her effect, she makes a flexible and unobtrusive use of point of view. Her stories at first seem to have no end or beginning, no central focus. A child comes up to the bench in the park; a child refuses to answer his piano teacher; a woman drinks manzanilla in a Spanish bar as a deluge of rain comes down; a dog appears at the corner of a terrace. As in films, the viewer, or listener, is not immediately described; only what is seen, or heard, and the narrative guided by the storyteller shifts, often without transition, from character to character, from the world inside to the world outside. The reader must, to a certain extent, yield to the narrative, allow himself to be drawn into its rhythms and tempo. Rhythm, tempo, silence, pause, repetition, modulation, a contrapuntal use of descriptive passages alternating with dialogue replace the habitual analysis, motivation, the logical sequence of events and rationally substantiated conflicts of the run of the mill novel.

All four novels are dominated, though to a different extent, by the human voice. *The Square* is almost entirely a dialogue; in *Moderato Cantabile* the dialogue—picked up, repeated, broken, ambiguous —dominates the narrative flow; less prominent in *Ten-thirty on a Summer Night* and *Mr. Andesmas*, the successive sequences of words spoken are none the less climactic. The words spoken are punctuated by the changing play of light and shadow; the shifting patterns of scenery glimpsed at different moments, in different lights. Light and shadow mark the slowly moving, steady pattern of outer time, in contrast to the long-drawn-out moments of suspense, the sudden speeded-up moments of awareness that give its tempo to the characters' inner life. Recurrence, leitmotiv, tempo are the stylistic devices whereby Marguerite Duras establishes the continuous yet shifting patterns of her stories. The dialogue moves freely between mere comment on the outer surface of things and the expression of inner moods and aspiration, usually voiceless. Certainly, it is not Marguerite Duras's intention to give us a plausible reconstruction of characteristic speech patterns, but rather, through carefully patterned speech, to bring to light inner unexpressed tensions, hopes, modes of being as felt by specific individuals. An unexpected remark, an unfinished sentence, an apparent *non sequitur* are often the key to the emotion from which it draws its cogency, a key to the inner event in the making which it is the novelist's intention to track down, disclose, and make clear.

Very little is necessary to start her stories moving. The story of Mr. Andesmas was born, Marguerite Duras indicates, of a few "words overheard": "I have just bought a house. A very beautiful spot. Almost like Greece. The trees around the house belong to me. One of them is enormous and, in summer, will give so much shade that I'll never suffer from the heat. I am going to build a terrace. From that terrace at night you'll be able to see the lights of G." Simple words overheard, from which it would seem was born the massive figure of seventy-eight-year-old Mr. Andesmas, seated in his creaking wicker chair overlooking the sea. "Words overheard": for example the name of Rodrigo Paestra repeated by an entire town, or, more incongruously in another case, a rending scream attacking the placid peace of French provincial life, are sufficient to project two of Duras's most pathetic characters, Maria and Anne, out of middle-class banality into a strangely macabre adventure.

Marguerite Duras is endowed with the novelist's gift to pursue, track down, and develop the fictional potentialities of the most simple situations, and she generously shares that gift with the characters that dominate her imagination: Anne will live vicariously the passion of another woman; Maria will almost literally, from the intensity of her involvement in his story, bring Rodrigo Paestra to life before she drives him to his death; and Mr. Andesmas, for a short while, will be so obsessed by the presence of Michel Arc's dark-haired wife that he will

viii

forget his own obsessive preoccupation with his golden-haired daughter Valérie.

Each novel concentrates on one central relationship that gives it its dramatic cogency, but it is not an isolated relationship, for implacably it draws all other relationships into its orbit, modulating them as it were. In each case, the inner and outer fluctuations of the dominant relationship draw together or tear apart the two people involved, as in a *pas de deux*. Dancing, like music, is a fundamental Duras theme: the maid and the salesman, Anne and Chauvin, Maria and Pierre, Mr. Andesmas and Michel Arc's wife are all partners in rhythmical motion. But each movement involves the entire person, the entire inner fabric of the maid's or the salesman's life; Anne's relation to her son, to her world; the relation of Pierre, Maria's husband, with Claire; the relation of Valérie, Mr. Andesmas's daughter, with Michel Arc. "He" and "she," timidly approaching each other as in *The Square*; haunted by an impossible desire in *Moderato Cantabile;* torn apart by nascent sexual attraction in *Ten-thirty on a Summer Night;* confronting the end of an exclusive possession in *Mr. Andesmas*. Within the limitations of the narrative forms she has developed, Marguerite Duras deals in stark, basic human emotions—desire, dread, suspense, solitude, happiness, as they pertain to the one basic "ocean" of feeling for others, which is love. It is the hope, the possibility of love that the dialogue of *The Square* uncovers, the saving grace for two inconsequential lives. In the bar, in the small town, Anne Desbaresdes discovers the destructive, intoxicating desire to love unto death, a desire thwarted, but not before it has devastated her life. The rescue and death of Rodrigo Paestra are connected to Maria's discovery, at ten-thirty on a summer night, of the silhouettes of Pierre and Claire in each other's arms. What seventy-eight-year-old Mr. Andesmas discovers is "the knowledge" of his love for his eighteen-year-old daughter Valérie, and that he must relinquish her to Michel Arc.

Love, the fierceness of love, the happiness, the pain, the compelling and destructive power of love is Marguerite Duras's essential theme, and not, as is too often stressed, solitude. Of all human bonds, none is more subtly described than the bond between parent and child. In all four stories, the child appears, untouched by the adult world, which only Valérie is about to enter. The child playing in the park, although not theirs, is benignly looked upon by maid and salesman; the first scene of *Moderato Cantabile* is a small gem of humor and delight—the delight of Anne in her rebellious little boy. We see Judith, happily skipping in the muddy stream of water alongside her mother, who is befuddled by alcohol; Valérie, at fifteen, caught in the glow of sunlight as she stuffs candy in her mouth. By their presence, these children illuminate the stories, somehow saving even Anne and Maria—the two women destroyed, doubly, by thwarted love and alcohol—from the macabre.

The sixth of Marguerite Duras's novels, *The Square* (1955) is the first in which she experimented with a new stylized form of storytelling which, without being analytical, would bring to light certain fundamental patterns of human feeling. In the fifties, as Nathalie Sarraute ironically observed in her essay *An Age of Suspicion,* no sophisticated French novelist could pronounce the word "psychology" without blushing. The novel of psychological analysis, long held in high esteem in France, was considered played out. The American "behaviorist" novel, so popular in the forties, had yielded all it could; the existentialist novel, as practiced by the post-Sartrean writers, was weighted down by outworn techniques and earnest stereotypes. The fifties brought in the highly articulate "new" novelists, all experimentally inclined. With *The Square,* Marguerite Duras took front rank among these new novelists. Yet, in a sense, it was with the human psyche exclusively that Marguerite Duras was concerned, with the psychological event. In her hands, the chance encounter of a girl and a man who, socially, think of themselves as "the lowest of the low," becomes a kind of paradigm of one of the basic polarities in human experience. The dialogue form she adopted to deal with the encounter—the basic ingredient of all "romances"—recalls the stylized work of the English novelist Ivy Compton-Burnett, and was particularly well-suited to Duras's theme. *The Square* tends toward equilibrium, stasis, and the complete, carefully spoken paragraphs give the requisite impression of weight and balance.

In the exchange of words, the girl and the man disclose, through the scrutiny of their own individual positions, two ways of coping with one's position in life, two approaches to life. Immersed at first in solitude, the two speakers win their way into a differently organized sensibility, complementary to their own. Each, responding to the other's reality, speaks the words appropriate to a fundamental role, as woman, as man. The biological and the emotional are fused, as are the individual and the basically human. The girl's stubborn, reiterated hope

—that a man will choose her to be his wife—is the simple transcription of her grasp of what will give her fulfillment. Not that her life, in its outer harsh pattern, will necessarily change. Marguerite Duras does not deal in the glossy myths of the commercially advertised "happy couple." But the girl on the park bench knows that it is in her relation to a man that she will pass from her state as maid, as instrument or object, to her status as an individual person, free within her own sphere of existence. As for the man, his semi-understanding of her desperate need and hope is a first step out of insignificance toward a human responsibility and involvement.

In the facts that the dialogue quietly brings to light there is no sugar-coating, no deprecation of or recoil from truth. The sordid outer limitations of the girl's position, the insignificance of the man's occupations are clearly stated. Yet the words hope, beauty, happiness, unhappiness, and, more persistently, "understanding" are woven into the fabric of their language without sentimentality or emotional fakery. The dialogue—like the dance so dear to the girl—is esthetically designed in terms of approach, retreat, pause, re-engagement as the two partners reach within themselves, as each opens the way toward the other. The attitudes they describe seem at first to exclude any possible involvement. The girl's passionate refusal to come to terms with her situation is, in fact, a form of heightened dramatic suspense. The man's indifference, solitude, and detachment is accompanied by a poetic receptivity to the present—to a gleam of sunlight in a public garden, to a passing conversation on a park bench. Hence the tension in the dialogue, its urgency, and the sense that, at the end, perhaps fleetingly, perhaps more durably—the conclusion is uncertain—an event has taken place. Between the girl and the man there has been a measure of understanding, an exchange of truth, unambiguous, untainted by self-pity, recrimination, or sentimentality. Each has approached the other with integrity. The quasi-ceremonial patterning of the dialogue in *The Square* creates a sense of the dignity inherent in the encounter and the exchange.

In form and mood, *Moderato Cantabile* (1958) is quite different from *The Square*, more fluid and musical, and apparently less coherent in its development. Again the situation chosen is basic in romance, but in this instance it has a macabre melodramatic appeal: a man brutally kills a woman in the street and then, desperately and in the sight of all, covers her dead body with kisses and caresses—a "true confession" episode.

The originality of this short eight-part novel lies in Marguerite Duras's use of this initial design to set the theme of a story concerned entirely with another couple—Anne Desbaresdes and Chauvin, a man encountered by chance on the scene of the crime. The simplicity and clarity of the narrative design, coupled with its surface incoherence, may at first appear disconcerting. But the incoherence and simplicity prove to be entirely deceptive. Marguerite Duras's design has a good deal in common with Robbe-Grillet's techniques in *Last Year at Marienbad*. *Moderato Cantabile* is the story of an auto-intoxication, a seduction desired and lived on two levels. At its origin the crime is witnessed, perpetually retold by the second couple and mutely relived, but only emotionally, not in actuality—an artist's translation of a violent reality.

As in the case of the two protagonists in *The Square*, the outer facts concerning Anne Desbaresdes and Chauvin—the social facts that, in more conventional novels set the framework and determine the events —here emerge only incidentally. And they are incidental. Anne Desbaresdes, it is slowly revealed, is the wife of a wealthy provincial industrialist, who lives in a large house surrounded by a garden in the residential section of a small town by the sea. During her ten years of married life, not a breath of scandal has touched her. All we know of Chauvin is that he was formerly employed by Anne's husband and once caught sight of her at a party given for the employees. But the scandal inherent in that ten-day adventure is not the banal scandal of a socially reprehensible affair. There is, in fact, no affair; only five confrontations in a bar, a hand placed on hers, a brief kiss on Anne's ice-cold lips. The scandal is in Anne's total alienation from society, the alienation of intoxication, and the revelation of an obsessive sexual desire lived to the limit of annihilation. *Moderato Cantabile* is a modern restatement of the incompatibility of individual passion with the orderly mechanism of social decorum.

What the novelist first exposes in the overture of the novel, in the music lesson scene, is the emotional center of Anne Desbaresdes' life. With quiet, poetic humor Marguerite Duras weaves into the familiar situation—music teacher, recalcitrant boy, mother—two conflicting themes: the theme of quiet provincial living kept within orderly bounds, and the tremulous unbounded capacity for passion latent in Anne Desbaresdes' shy yet delighted complicity with the stubborn little boy, her son, who so resolutely refuses to do as he is bidden. As the Diabelli Sonatina, with its "moderato cantabile" tempo, stops and starts sporadically, and then is played to the end, the sound of the sea, the throbbing of the engine, the mute exchanges between mother and son set up the dimensions of another, larger world. In a few brief pages Marguerite Duras gives Anne Desbaresdes an elusive poetic presence, in harmony with that outer world and incompatible with the restrictions and strictures of bourgeois respectability. The scream of the dying woman, drowning out the sonatina, is the signal of her temporary escape and passion, a fierce passion relentlessly lived beyond all human contact and aid.

Fascinating, in contrast to the stark violence of the theme, is the manner in which it is handled. "Moderato cantabile" suggests a tempo and lyrical mode that are in direct contradition with the violence of the crime, with the fierce desire that engulfs Anne and Chauvin, and with the strange new detached mode of perception Anne acquires in her state of intoxication. The description of the formal dinner, in the seventh section of the story, as Anne teeters between two worlds, an object of scandal in the eyes of her set, an object of wild desire for the man outside circling the garden railings—until she vomits up both the wine he poured and the "strange food" served at her table—is a fine example of a controlled musical interweaving of themes, of a formal simplicity and dignity that envelops and protects Anne's "fall."

The Diabelli Sonatina, in the narrative pattern, seems to emphasize, by contrast, the gravity and depth of the relationship between Anne and Chauvin, who between them play out the variations inherent in the shaping of the initial episode, the crime they have witnessed. Unlike the girl and the man in *The Square*, they do not speak in carefully constructed sentences and coherent paragraphs. They speak in snatches, hesitantly, restating fragments of the theme, their exchange of words revolving around a hidden center, which is their urge to relive the passion of the couple that has died. In their five encounters in the bar, Anne and Chauvin, like two musical instruments, must repeat and relive, in a kind of purity and eternity, the movements inherent in the initial design, until they confront the stark, sexual, destructive nature of their desire and the design is totally interiorized and completed: " 'I wish you were dead,' Chauvin said. 'I am,' Anne Desbaresdes said." Relinquishing the very core of her former life, her relation with her child, Anne has re-enacted to the end the tragic modulations of absolute passion which Marguerite Duras holds within the formal confines of melody and rhythm.

The strange, acute, yet different modes of perception reached through intoxication—another form of alienation—give *Ten-thirty on a Summer Night* (1960) its strange double structure. The poetic intensity and incongruity of vision that shape Maria's encounter with Rodrigo Paestra underscore the contrapuntal development of her suffering as she witnesses the desire magnetically and visibly drawing Pierre toward her friend, Claire. A number of events, held in suspense, coincide to give the story its unique pattern. Maria's acute apprehension of each moment of time imposes a distinctive tempo on the story. Suspense is an atmospheric component of the storm that hangs over the small Spanish town, halting all normal plans and activity. Suspense is inherent in the outer situation Maria discovers, the hunt for Rodrigo Paestra, who has killed his wife and his wife's lover. It is because her life is held in suspense that Maria has the power to sense the suspense loose in the small town and feels the urge to intervene in Paestra's fate and, vicariously, to partake of it.

Only two people were directly involved in *The Square*; two couples, essentially, in *Moderato Cantabile*. In *Ten-thirty on a Summer Night*, two groups of three are involved. Paestra, his wife and her lover; Maria, her husband Pierre, and Claire. And in both cases, the theme is murder. Paestra has already killed the lovers when the novel begins; at the end, Maria knows the love she and Pierre had shared is dead. Paestra's lonely vigil on the rooftops deflects, as it were, Maria's lonely vigil on the balcony; as he waits for his inevitable capture and death at dawn, so she waits for the inevitable moment of consummation of desire for which Pierre and Claire are waiting. At ten-thirty on that summer night, the three vigils come together in Maria's perception. She sees Paestra's figure dimly outlined against the chimney tops as the silhouettes of Pierre and Claire, entwined, appear on the balcony over her head. Her bid to save Paestra is a "barrage" against her fate, a useless, heroic struggle against fate. Here, more visibly than in *Moderato Cantabile*, in the baroque setting evoked, outer and inner events fuse, merge, and develop with a poetic inevitability. Death, love, desire, and violence mold the most banal of events: a man's infidelity to his wife. Extraordinarily moving and pure is the account of Maria's suffering, free from personal animosity with regard to Claire, humble in its recognition of the overwhelming authority of sexual desire. That, in time, all lovers are bound to live emotionally the modulations of suspense, is an abstract and commonplace statement. The story of

Maria's night of anguish and revelation is told in an atmosphere of intoxication and nightmare, visually reconstructed as in a film, each moment sharply etched in darkness or light, without any recourse to explanation, extraneous comment, or moral judgment. More markedly than in *Moderato Cantabile*, the intensely subjective yet quasi-impersonal vision of intoxication shapes the strange sequence of events that fills Maria's night.

Mr. Andesmas (1962), like *Ten-thirty on a Summer Night*, is a story of suspense, but a suspense that evolves toward a disengagement from the passion of living—and thereby from time—that human relationships reveal. Thematically, the narrative is built on two contrasting moods and tempos: the gay mood of the village dance with its leitmotiv "When the lilac blooms my love . . ."; the empty hours of solitary waiting on the terrace of the house above, punctuated by three encounters: the passage of a dog; the arrival of a child "not like the others"; then the arrival of her mother, whose fate, like Valérie's—the daughter Mr. Andesmas cherishes, with the singleness of mind typical of old age—is being sealed that afternoon. "There are moments here," the epigraph says, "when the light is absolute, accentuating everything, and at the same precise, relentlessly shining on one object." The object, Valérie, is in this case absent, except as she appears in the mind of others. Her father and Michel Arc's wife—the woman abandoned for her sake—both vicariously live two distinct moments of Valérie's fate, and simultaneously suffer their own. Like Anne and Maria, Mr. Andesmas and Michel Arc's wife are dispossessed; they are like the child whose hands let go of her possessions, then pick them up again. But in this instance, the story being recounted indirectly, it is suggested by Mr. Andesmas himself, and differs from the others. He will not, like the child, like Michel Arc's wife, close his hands again over some other treasure. Mr. Andesmas, in the slow hours of his solitude, passes into the realm of extreme old age and in part, lives his own removal from a duration inwardly apprehended; he in fact lives a form of his own death. The thematic pattern of the story, its clarity and serenity, offer a striking contrast to the tormented, baroque design of the two preceding works.

Seen in relation to one another, these four short novels of Marguerite Duras, published over a seven-year period, offer a remarkable range and variety in mood and situation. They share, too, a unique, elusive, poetic quality, the hallmark of Duras's originality. All the characters she describes are, in a sense, living vicariously events which they both retell and relive in another key; someone else's story, always relived in different modes, yet always the same. Desire and love, as in all romances, well up within them and fatally encounter the hard boundaries of a reality that inevitably circumscribes, limits, modifies, and destroys. As storyteller, within the limitations she sets herself, Marguerite Duras establishes, in terms of form and style an ever fluid interchange and relationship between the inner aspiration and the outer bounds, between the self and the desired other. Each story suggests a mode of being "in love," and culminates in a recognition of the nature of human bonds. This recognition emerges from the depths of experiences suffered, and fully accepted by the central characters, possessed and esthetically dominated by the writer.

THE SQUARE

TRANSLATED BY

SONIA PITT-RIVERS & IRINA MORDUCH

One

THE CHILD CAME OVER quietly from the far side of the Square and stood behind the girl.

"I'm hungry," he announced.

The man took this as an opportunity to start a conversation.

"I suppose it is about tea-time?"

The girl was not disconcerted: on the contrary she turned and smiled at him.

"Yes, it must be nearly half past four, when he usually has his tea."

She took two sandwiches from a bag beside her on the bench and handed them to the child, then skillfully knotted a bib around his neck.

"He's a nice child," said the man.

The girl shook her head as if in denial.

"He's not mine," she remarked.

The child moved off with his sandwiches. It was afternoon and the Park was full of children: big ones playing marbles and hide-and-seek, small ones playing in the sand pits, while smaller ones still sat patiently waiting in their prams for the time when they would join the others.

"Although," the girl continued, "he could be mine and, indeed, is often taken for mine. But the fact is he doesn't belong to me."

"I see," said the man. "I have no children either."

"Sometimes it seems strange, don't you think, there should be so many children, that they are everywhere one goes and yet none of them are one's own?"

"I suppose so, yes, when you come to think of it. But then, as you said, there are so many already."

"But does that make any difference?"

"I should have thought that if you are fond of them anyway, if you enjoy just watching them, it matters less."

"But couldn't the opposite also be true?"

3

"Probably. I expect it depends on one's nature: I think that some people are quite happy with the children who are already there, and I believe I am one of them. I have seen so many children and I could have had children of my own and yet I manage to be quite satisfied with the others."

"Have you really seen so many?"

"Yes. You see, I travel."

"I see," the girl said in a friendly manner.

"I travel all the time, except just now of course when I'm resting."

"Parks are good places to rest in, particularly at this time of year. I like them too. It's nice being out of doors."

"They cost nothing, they're always gay because of the children and then if you don't know many people there's always the chance of starting a conversation."

"That's true. I hope you don't mind my asking, but do you sell when you travel?"

"Yes, you could call that my profession."

"Always the same things?"

"No, different things, but all of them small. You know those little things one always needs and so often forgets to buy. They all fit into a medium-sized suitcase. I suppose you could call me a traveling salesman if you wanted to give what I do a name."

"Like those people you see in markets selling things from an open suitcase?"

"That's right. I often work on the outskirts of markets."

"I hope you don't think it rude of me to ask, but do you manage to make a living?"

"I've nothing to complain of."

"I'm glad. I thought that was probably the case."

"I don't mean to say that I earn a lot of money because that would not be true. But I earn something each day and in its way I call that making a living."

"In fact you manage to live much as you would like?"

"Yes, I think I live about as well as I want to: I don't mean that one day is always as good as another. No. Sometimes things are a little tight, but in general I manage well enough."

"I'm glad."

"Thank you. Yes, I manage more or less and have really nothing to worry about. Being single with no home of my own I have few worries and the ones I have are naturally only for myself—sometimes for instance I find I have run out of toothpaste, sometimes I might want for a little company. But on the whole it works out well. Thank you for asking."

"Would you say that almost anyone could do your work? I mean is it the kind of work which practically anybody could take up?"

"Yes, indeed. I would even go so far as to say that simply through being what it is it is one of the ways of earning a living most open to everybody."

"I should have thought it might need special qualifications?"

"Well, I suppose it is better to know how to read, if only for the newspaper in the evenings at the hotel, and also of course to know which station you are at. It makes life a little easier but that's all. It's not much of a qualification as you can see, and yet one can still earn enough money to live."

"I really meant other kinds of qualification: I would have thought your work needed endurance, or patience perhaps, and a great deal of perseverance?"

"I have never done any other work so I could hardly say whether you are right or not. But I always imagined that the qualifications you mention would be necessary for any work; in fact that there could hardly be a job where they are not needed."

"I am sorry to go on asking you all these questions but do you think you will always go on traveling like this?"

"I don't know."

"I'm sorry. Forgive me for being so curious, but we were talking. . . ."

"Of course and it's quite all right. But I'm afraid I don't know if I will go on traveling. There really is no other answer I can give you: I don't know. How does one know such things?"

"I only meant that if one traveled all the time as you do, I would have thought that one day one would want to stop and stay in one place. That was all."

"It's true I suppose that one should want to stop. But how do you stop doing one thing and start another? How do people decide to leave one job for another, and why?"

"If I've understood you, the fact that you travel depends only on yourself, not on anything else?"

"I don't think I have ever quite known how such things are decided. I have no particular attachments. In fact I am a rather solitary person and unless some great piece of luck came my way I cannot really see how I could change my work. And somehow I can't imagine where any luck would come from: there doesn't seem much about my life which would attract it. Of course I don't mean that some luck could not come my way —after all one never knows—nor that if it did I would not accept it very gladly. But for the moment I must confess I cannot see much luck coming my way helping me to a decision."

"But couldn't you just simply want it? I mean just decide you wanted to change your work?"

"No, I don't think so. Each day I want to be clean, well fed and sleep well, and I also like to feel decently dressed. So you see I hardly have time for wanting much more. And then, after all, I don't really dislike traveling."

"Can I ask you another question? How did all this start?"

"How could I begin to tell you? Things like that are so long and so complicated, and sometimes I really think they are a little beyond me. It would mean going so far back that I feel tired before I start. But on the whole I think things happened to me as they do to anyone else, no differently."

A wind had risen, so light it seemed to carry the summer with it. For a moment it chased the clouds away, leaving a new warmth hanging over the city.

"How lovely it is," the man said.

"Yes," said the girl, "almost the beginning of the hot weather. From now on it will be a little warmer each day."

"You see, I had no special aptitude for any particular work or for any particular kind of life. And so I suppose I will go on as I am. Yes, I think I will."

"So really your feelings are only negative? They are just against any particular work or any particular life?"

"Against? No. That's too strong a word. I can only say that I have no very strong likes. I really just came to be as I am in the way that most people come to be as they are: there is nothing special about my case."

"But between the things that happened to you a long time ago and now, wasn't there time for you to change—almost every day in fact —and start liking things? Anything?"

"I suppose so. I don't deny it. For some people life must be like that and then again for others it is not. Some people must get used to the idea

6

of never changing and I think that really is true of me. So I expect I will just go on as I am."

"Well, for me things will change: they will not go on being the same."

"But can you know already?"

"Yes, I can, because my situation is not one which can continue: sooner or later it must come to an end, that is part of it. I am waiting to marry. And as soon as I am married my present life will be quite finished."

"I understand."

"I mean that once it is over it will seem so unimportant that it might as well never have been."

"Perhaps I too—after all it's impossible to foresee everything, isn't it?—might change my life one day."

"Ah, but the difference is that I want to change mine. What I do now is hardly a job. People call it one to make things easier for themselves, but in fact it is not. It's something different, something with no meaning outside itself like being ill or a child. And so it must come to an end."

"I understand, but I've come back from a long journey and now I'm resting. I never much like thinking of the future and today, when I'm resting, even less: that's why I am so bad at explaining to you how it is I can put up with my life as it is and not change it, and what is more, not even be able to imagine changing. I'm sorry."

"Oh no, it is I who should apologize."

"Of course not. After all we can always talk."

"That's right. And it means nothing."

"And so you are waiting for something to happen?"

"Yes. I can see no reason why I should not get married one day like everybody else. As I told you."

"You're quite right. There is no reason at all why you should not get married too."

"Of course with a job like mine—one which is so looked down upon —you could say that the opposite would be more true and that there is no reason at all why anyone should want to marry me. And so somehow I think that to make it seem quite ordinary and natural, I must want it with all my might. And that is how I want it."

"I am sure nothing is impossible. People say so at least."

"I have thought about it a great deal: here I am, young, healthy and truthful just like any woman you see anywhere whom some man has

7

settled for. And surely it would be surprising if somewhere there isn't a man who won't see that I am just as good as anyone else and settle for me. I am full of hope."

"I am sure it will happen to you. But if you were suggesting that I make the same sort of change, I can only ask what I would do with a wife? I have nothing in the world but my suitcase and it is all I can do to keep myself."

"Oh no, I did not mean to say that you need this particular change. I was talking of change in general. For me marriage is the only possible change, but for you it could be something else."

"I expect you are right, but you seem to forget that people are different. You see, however much I wanted to change, even if I wanted it with all my might, I could never manage to want it as much as you do. You seem to want it at all costs."

"Perhaps that is because for you a change would be less great than it would for me. As far as I am concerned I feel I want the greatest change there could be. I might be mistaken but still it seems to me that all the changes I see in other people are simple and easy beside the one I want for myself."

"But don't you think that even if everyone needed to change, and needed it very badly indeed, that even so they would feel differently about it according to their own particular circumstances?"

"I am sorry but I must explain that I am quite uninterested in particular circumstances. As I told you I am full of hope and what is more I do everything possible to make my hopes come true. For instance every Saturday I go to the local Dance Hall and dance with anyone who asks me. They say that the truth will out and I believe that one day someone will take me for what I am, a perfectly marriageable young woman who would make just as good a wife as anyone else."

"I don't think it would help me to go dancing, even if I wanted to change, and wanted it less than you do. My profession is insignificant: in fact it can hardly even be called a profession since it only just provides enough for one person, or perhaps it would be nearer the truth to say a half-person. And so I couldn't, even for an instant, imagine that anything like that would change my life."

"But then perhaps, as I said before, it would be enough for you to change your work?"

"Yes, but how? How does one change a profession, even such a miserable one as mine? One which doesn't even allow me to marry? All

8

I do is to go with my suitcase through one day to the next, from one night to another and even from one meal to the next meal, and there is no time for me to stop and think about it as perhaps I should. No, if I were to change then the opportunity must come to me: I have no time to meet it halfway. And then again I should, perhaps, explain that I never felt that anyone particularly needed my services or my company—so much so that quite often I am amazed that I occupy any place in the world at all."

"Then perhaps the change you should make would be just to feel differently about things?"

"Of course. But you know how it is. After all, one is what one is and how could anyone change so radically? Also I have come to like my work, even if it could hardly be called that: I like catching trains, and sleeping almost anywhere no longer worries me much."

"You must not mind my saying this, but it seems to me that you should never have let yourself become like this."

"You could perhaps say I was always a little predisposed to it."

"For me it would be terrible to go through life with nothing but a suitcase full of things to sell. I think I should be frightened."

"Of course that can happen, especially at the beginning, but one gets used to little things like that."

"I think in spite of everything I would rather be as I am, in my present position rather than in yours. But perhaps that is because I am only twenty."

"But you mustn't think that my work has nothing but disadvantages. That would be quite wrong. With all the time I have on my hands for instance, on the road, in trains, in Squares like this, I can think of all manner of things. I have time to look around and even time to work out reasons for things."

"But I thought you said you had only enough time to think of yourself? Or rather of managing to keep yourself and of nothing else?"

"No. What I lack is time to think of the future, but I have time to think of other things, or perhaps I should say I make it. Because, after all, if one can face struggling a little more than others do, just to get enough to eat, it is only possible on condition that once a meal is over one can stop thinking about the whole problem. If immediately one meal is finished you had to start thinking about the next one it would be enough to drive you mad."

"I imagine so. But you see, what would drive me mad would be going from city to city as you do with no other company than a suitcase."

"Oh, one is not always alone you know. I mean so alone that one might go mad. No, there are boats and trains full of people to watch and observe and then, if one ever feels one is really going mad, there is always something to be done about it."

"But what good would it do me to make the best of things since all I want is to finish with my present position? In the end all your attitude does for you is to give you more reasons for not finishing with yours."

"That is not completely true, because should an opportunity arise for me to change my work I would certainly seize it: no, my attitude helps me in other ways. For example it helps me to see the advantages of my profession, such as traveling a great deal and possibly of becoming a little wiser than I was before. I am not saying I am right. I could easily be wrong and, without realizing it, have become far less wise than I ever was. But then, since I wouldn't know, it doesn't really matter, does it?"

"And so you are continually traveling? As continually as I stay in one place?"

"Yes. And even if sometimes I go back to the same places they can be different. In the spring for instance cherries appear in the markets. That is really what I wanted to say and not that I thought I was right in putting up with my life as it is."

"You're right. Quite soon, in about six weeks, the first cherries will be in the markets. I am glad for your sake. But tell me what other things you see when you travel?"

"Oh, a thousand things. One time it will be spring and another winter; either sunshine or snow, making the place unrecognizable. But I think it is really the cherries which change things the most: suddenly there they are, and the whole marketplace becomes scarlet. Yes, they will be there in about six weeks. You see, that is what I wanted to explain, not that I thought my work was entirely satisfactory."

"But apart from the cherries and the sunshine and the snow, what else do you see?"

"Sometimes nothing much: small things you would hardly notice, but a number of little things which added together seem to change a place. Places can be familiar and unfamiliar at the same time: a market which once seemed hostile can, quite suddenly, become warm and friendly."

"But sometimes isn't everything exactly the same?"

10

"Yes. Sometimes so exactly the same that you can only think you left it the night before. I have never understood how this could happen because after all it would seem impossible that anything could remain so much the same."

"Tell me more about other things you see."

"Well, sometimes a new block of flats which was half built when last I was there is finished and lived in: full of people and noise. And the odd thing is that although the town had never seemed overcrowded before, there it suddenly is—a brand new block of flats, completed and inhabited as if had always been utterly necessary."

"All the things you describe and the changes you notice are there for anyone to see, aren't they? They are not things which exist for you alone, for you and for no one else?"

"Sometimes there are things which I alone can see, but only negligible things. In general you are right: the things I notice are mostly changes in the weather, in buildings, things which anyone would notice. And yet sometimes, just by watching them carefully, such things can affect one just as much as events which are completely personal. In fact it feels as though they were personal, as if somehow one had put the cherries there oneself."

"I see what you mean and I am trying to put myself in your place, but it's no good, I still think I should be frightened."

"That does happen. It happens to me sometimes when I wake up at night. But on the whole it is only at night that I feel frightened, although I can also feel it at dusk—but then only when it's raining or there's a fog."

"Isn't it strange that although I have never actually experienced the fear we are talking about, I can still understand a little what it must be like."

"It is not the kind of fear you might feel if you said to yourself that when you died no one would care. No, it's another kind of fear, a general one which affects everything and not just you alone."

"As if you were suddenly terrified of being yourself, of being what you are instead of different, almost instead of being some quite other kind of thing."

"Yes. It comes from feeling at the same time like everyone else, exactly like everyone else, and yet being oneself. In fact I think it is just that: being one kind of thing rather than another. . . ."

"It's complicated, but I understand."

"As for the other kind of fear—the fear of thinking that no one would notice if you died—it seems to me that sometimes this can make one happier. I think that if you knew that when you died no one would suffer, not even a dog, it makes it easier to bear the thought of dying."

"I am trying to follow you, but I am afraid I don't understand. Perhaps because women are different from men? All I do know is that I could not bear to live as you do, alone with that suitcase. It is not that I would not like to travel, but unless there was someone who cared for me somewhere in the world I don't think I could do it. In fact I can only say that I would prefer to be where I am."

"But could you not think of traveling while waiting for what you want?"

"No. I don't believe you know what it is to want to change one's life. I must stay here and think about it, think with all my might, or else I know I will never manage to change."

"Perhaps. I don't really know."

"How could you know? Because, however modest a way of life you have, it is at least yours. So how could you know what it is like to be nothing?"

"Am I right in thinking that no one would particularly care if you died either?"

"No one. And I've been twenty now for two weeks. But one day someone will care. I know it. I am full of hope. Otherwise nothing would be possible."

"You are quite right. Why shouldn't someone care about you as much as about anyone else?"

"That's just it. That's just what I say to myself."

"You're right, and now I'd like to ask you a question. Do you get enough to eat?"

"Yes, thank you, I do. I eat as much as and even more than I need. Always alone, but one eats well in my job since after all one does the cooking; and good things too. Even if I have to force myself I always eat a great deal because sometimes I feel I would like to be fatter and more impressive so that people would notice me more. I think that if I were bigger and stronger I would stand a better chance of getting what I want. You may say I'm wrong, but it seems to me that if I were radiantly healthy people would find me more attractive. And so you see, we are really very different."

"Probably. But in my own way I am also someone who tries. I must have explained myself badly just now. I assure you that if I should ever want to change, why then I would set about it like everyone else."

"You know, it is not very easy to believe you when you say that."

"Perhaps, but you see while I have nothing against hope in general, the fact is that there has never seemed much reason for it to concern me. And yet I feel that it would not take a great deal for me to feel that hope is as necessary to me as it is to others. It might only need the smallest bit of faith. Perhaps I lack the time for it, who knows? I don't mean the time I spend in trains thinking of this or that, or passing the time of day with other people, no, I mean the other kind of time: the time anyone has, each day, to think of the one that follows. I just lack the time to start thinking about that particular subject and so discovering that it might mean something to me too."

"And yet it seems to me, as I think you yourself said, that there was a time when you were like everyone else?"

"Yes, but almost so much so that I was never able to do anything about it. I could never make up my mind to choose a profession. No one can be everything at once or, as you said, want everything at once, and personally I was never able to get over this difficulty. But after all I have traveled, my suitcase takes me to a great many places and once I even went to a foreign country. I didn't sell much there but I saw it. If anyone had told me some years ago that I should want to go there I would never have believed them, and yet you see one day when I woke up I suddenly felt I would like to visit it and I went; and although very little has happened to me in my life at least I managed that—I went to that country."

"But aren't people unhappy in this country of yours?"

"Yes."

"And there are girls like me, waiting for something to happen?"

"I expect so, yes."

"So what is the point of it?"

"Of course it's true that people are unhappy and die there and there are probably girls like you waiting hopefully for something to happen to them. But why not know that country as well as just this one where we are, even if some things are the same. Why not see another country?"

"Because . . . and I am sure I am wrong, and I am sure you will tell me I am, but the fact is that it is a matter of complete indifference to me."

"Ah, but wait. There for instance the winters are less harsh than here: in fact you would hardly know it was winter."

"But what use is a whole country to anyone, or a whole city or even the whole of one warm winter? It's no use, you can say what you like but you can only be where you are, when you are and so what is the point?"

"But that is exactly the point. The town where I went ends in a big square surrounded by huge balustrades which seem to go on for ever. . . ."

"I am afraid I simply don't want to hear about it."

"The whole town is built in white limestone: imagine, it is like snow in the heart of summer. It is built on a peninsula surrounded by the sea."

"And the sea I suppose is blue. It is blue isn't it?"

"Yes, very blue."

"Well, I am sorry, but I must tell you that people who talk of how blue the sea is make me sick."

"But how can I help it? From the Zoo you can see it surrounding the whole town. And to anybody it must seem blue. It's not my fault."

"No. For me, without those ties of affection I was talking about, it would be black. And then, although I don't want to offend you in any way, you must see that I am much too preoccupied with my desire to change my life to be able to go away or travel or see new things. You can see as many towns as you like but it never gets you anywhere. And once you have stopped looking, there you are, exactly where you were before."

"But I don't think we are talking about the same thing. I'm not talking of those huge events which change a whole life, no, just of the things which give pleasure while one is doing them. Traveling is a great distraction. Everyone has always traveled, the Greeks, the Phoenicians: it has always been so, all through history."

"It's true that we're talking of different things. Travel or cities by the sea are not the things I want. First of all I want to belong to myself, to own something, not necessarily something very wonderful, but something which is mine, a place of my own, maybe only one room, but mine. Why sometimes I even find myself dreaming of a gas stove."

"You know it would be just the same as traveling. You wouldn't be able to stop. Once you had the gas stove you would want a refrigerator

14

and after that something else. It would be just like traveling, going from city to city. It would never end."

"Excuse me, but do you see anything wrong in my wanting something further perhaps after I have the refrigerator?"

"Of course not. No, certainly not. I was only speaking for myself, and as far as I am concerned I find your idea even more exhausting than traveling and then going on traveling, moving as I do from place to place."

"I was born and grew up like everyone else and I know how to look around me: I look at things very carefully and I can see no reason why I should remain as I am. I must start somehow, anyhow, to become of consequence. And if at this stage I began losing heart at the thought of a refrigerator I might never even possess the gas stove. And anyway, how am I to know if it would weary me or not? If you say it would, it might be because you have given the matter a great deal of thought or perhaps even because at some time you very much disliked one particular refrigerator."

"No, it is not that. Not only have I never possessed a refrigerator, but I have never had the slightest chance of doing so. No, it's only an idea, and if I talked of refrigerators like that it was probably only because to someone who travels they seem especially heavy and immobile. I don't suppose I would have made the same remarks about another object. And yet I do understand, I assure you, that it would be impossible for you to travel before you had the gas stove, or even perhaps, the refrigerator. And I expect I am quite wrong to be so easily discouraged at the mere thought of a refrigerator."

"It does seem very strange."

"There was one day in my life, just one, when I no longer wanted to live. I was hungry, and as I had no money it was absolutely essential for me to work if I was to eat. It was as if I had forgotten that this was as true of everyone as of me. That day I felt quite unused to life and there seemed no point in going on living because I couldn't see why things should go on for me as they did for other people. It took me a whole day to get over this feeling. Then, of course, I took my suitcase to the market and afterwards I had a meal and things went on as they had before. But with this difference, that ever since that day I find that any thought of the future—and after all thinking of a refrigerator is thinking of the future—is much more frightening than before."

"I would have guessed that."

15

"Since then, when I think about myself, it is simply in terms of one person more or one person less, and so you see that a refrigerator more or less can hardly seem as important to me as it does to you."

"Tell me, did this happen before or after you went to that country you liked so much?"

"After. But when I think about that country I feel pleased and I think it would have been a pity for one more person not to have seen it. I don't mean that I imagine I was especially made to appreciate it. No, it just seems to me that since we are here, it is better to see one country more rather than one less."

"I can't feel as you do and yet I do understand what you are saying and I think you are right to say it. What you really mean is that since we are alive anyhow it is better to see things than not to see them. It was that you meant, wasn't it? And that seeing them makes the time pass quickly and more pleasantly?"

"Yes, it is a little like that. Perhaps the only difference between us is that we feel differently about how to spend our time?"

"Not only that, because as yet I have not had the time to become tired of anything, except of waiting of course. I don't mean that you are necessarily happier than I am, but simply that if you were unhappy you could imagine something which would help, like moving to another city, selling something different, or even . . . even bigger things. But I can't start thinking of anything yet, not even the smallest thing. My life has not begun except, of course, for the fact that I am alive. There are times, in summer for example when the weather is fine, when I feel that something might have begun for me even without there being any proof of it, and then I am frightened. I become frightened of giving in to the fine weather and forgetting what I want even for a second, of losing myself in something unimportant. I am sure that if at this stage I started thinking of anything except the one big thing, I would be lost."

"But it seemed to me for instance that you were fond of that little boy?"

"It makes no difference. If I am I don't want to know it. If I started finding consolation in my life, if I was able, to however small a degree, to put up with it then I know I would be lost. I have a great deal of work to do, and I do it. Indeed I am so good at my work that each day they give me a little more to do, and I accept it. Naturally it has ended by them giving me the hardest things to do, dreadful things, and yet I do them and I never complain. Because if I refused it would mean that I imagined that my situation, as it stands, could be improved, that it could be made somehow bearable, and then, of course, it would end up one day by becoming bearable."

"And yet it seems strange to be able to make one's life easier and refuse to do so."

"I suppose so, but I must do whatever they ask. I have never refused anything although it would have been easy at the beginning and now it would be easier still since I am asked to do more and more. But for as long as I can remember it has always been like this: I accepted everything quite quietly so that one day I would be quite unable to accept anything any more. You may say that this is a rather childish way of looking at things, but I could never find another way of being sure that I would get what I wanted. You see, I know that people can get used to anything and all around me I see people who are still where I am, but ten years later. There is nothing people cannot get accustomed to, even to a life like mine, and so I must be careful, very careful indeed, not to become accustomed to it myself. Sometimes I am frightened, because although I am aware of this danger, it is still so great that I am afraid that even I, aware as I am, might give in to it. But please go on telling me about the changes you see when you travel, apart from the snow, the cherries and the new buildings?"

"Well, sometimes the hotel has changed hands and the new owner is friendly and talkative where the old one was tired of trying to please and never spoke to his clients."

"Tell me, it is true isn't it that I must not take things for granted: that each day I must still be amazed to be where I am or else I shall never succeed?"

"I think that everyone is amazed, each day, to be still where they are. I think people are amazed quite naturally. I doubt if one can decide to be amazed at one thing more than at another."

"Each morning I am a little more surprised to find myself still where I am. I don't do it on purpose: I just wake up and, immediately, I am surprised. Then I start remembering things . . . I was a child like any other: there was nothing to show I was different. At cherry time we used to go and steal fruit in the orchards. We were stealing it right up to the last day, because it was in that season that I was sent into service. But tell me more about the things you see when you travel?"

"I used to steal cherries like you, and there was nothing which seemed to make me different from other children, except perhaps that even then I loved them very much. Well, apart from a change of proprietor in a hotel, sometimes a radio has been installed. That's a big change, when a café without music suddenly becomes a café with music: then of course they have many more customers and everyone stays much later. And that makes an evening to the good."

"You said to the good?"

"Yes."

"Ah, I sometimes think: if only we had known. . . . My mother simply came up to me and said, 'Well, you must come along now.' And I just let myself be led away like an animal to the slaughterhouse. If only I had known then, I promise you I would have fought. I would have saved myself. I would have begged my mother to let me stay. I would have persuaded her."

"But we don't know."

"The cherry season went on that year like all the others. People would pass under my window singing and I would be there behind the curtains watching them, and I got scolded for it."

"I was left free to pick cherries for a long time. . . ."

"There I was behind the window like a criminal and yet my only crime was to be sixteen. But you? You said you went on picking them for a long time?"

"Longer than most people. And yet you see. . . ."

"Tell me more about your cafés full of people and music."

"I like them very much. I don't really think I could go on living without them."

"I think I would like them too. I can see myself at the bar with my husband, listening to the radio. People would talk to us and we would make conversation. We would be with each other and with the others. Sometimes I feel how nice it would be to go and sit in a café, but if you are a single young woman you can hardly afford to do so."

"I forgot to add that sometimes someone looks at you."

"I see, and comes over?"

"Yes, they come over."

"For no reason?"

"For no particular reason, but then the conversation somehow becomes less general."

"And then?"

"I never stay longer than two days in any town. Three at the most. The things I sell are not so essential."

18

"Alas."

The wind, which had died down, rose again scattering the clouds, and once more the sudden warmth in the air brought thoughts of approaching summer.

"But the weather is really wonderful today," the man said again.

"It is nearly summer."

"Perhaps the fact is that one never really starts anything: perhaps things are always in the future?"

"If you can say that, it is because each day is full enough for you to prevent you thinking of the next. But my days are empty, a desert."

"But don't you do anything of which you could say later that at least it was something to the good?"

"No, nothing. I work all day, but I never do anything of which I could say what you have just said. I cannot even think in those terms."

"Please don't think I want to contradict you, but you must see that whatever you do, this time you are living now will count for you one day. You will look back on this desert as you describe it and discover that it was not empty at all, but full of people. You will not escape it. You think this time has not begun, and it has begun. You think you are doing nothing and in reality you are doing something. You think you are moving towards a solution and when you look round you find it's behind you. In just this sense I did not fully appreciate that city I mentioned. The hotel wasn't first class, the room I had reserved in advance had already been rented, it was late and I was hungry. Nothing was awaiting me in this city, except the city itself, and imagine for a moment what an enormous city, completely preoccupied with its own affairs, can be for a weary traveler seeing it for the first time."

"No, I can't imagine."

"All you find is a bad room overlooking a dirty, noisy courtyard. And yet thinking back I know that this trip changed me, that much of what I had seen before making it was leading up to it and illuminated by it. You're well aware that only after it's all over does one know he has visited this or that town."

"If that is the way you understand it, then perhaps you are right. Perhaps it has already started, perhaps it started on that particular day when I first wished it would start."

"Yes, you think that nothing happens, and yet, don't you see, it seems to me that the most important thing that has happened to you is precisely your will not to live yet."

"I understand you, I really do, but you must also try and understand me. Even if the most important part of my life is over, I can't know it as yet and I haven't the time to understand it. I hope one day I will know, as you did with your journey, and that when I look back everything behind me will be clear and fall into place. But now, at this moment, I am too involved to be even able to guess at what I might feel one day."

"I know. And I know that probably it is impossible for you to undertand things you have not yet felt, but all the same it is hard for me not to try and explain them to you."

"You are very kind, but I am afraid that I am not very good yet at understanding the things I am told."

"Believe me that I do understand all you have said, but even so, is it absolutely necessary to do all that work? Of course I am not trying to give you any advice, but don't you think that someone else would make a little effort and still manage, without quite so much work, to have as much hope for the future as before? Don't you think that another person would manage that?"

"Are you frightened that one day, if I have to wait too long and go on working a little more each day without complaining, I might suddenly lose patience altogether?"

"I admit that your kind of will power is a little frightening, but that's not why I made my suggestion. It was just because it is difficult to accept that someone of your age should live as you do."

"But I have no alternative, I assure you. I have thought about it a great deal."

"Can I ask you how many people there are in the family you work for?"

"Seven."

"And how big is the house?"

"Average."

"And rooms?"

"Eight."

"It's too much."

"But no. That's not the way to think. I must have explained myself very badly because you haven't understood."

"I think that work can always be measured and that, no matter what the circumstances, work is always work."

"Not my kind. It's probably true of the kind of work of which it is better to do too much than too little. But if in my kind of work there was time left over to think or start enjoying oneself then one would really be lost."

"And you're only twenty?"

"Yes, and as they say I've not yet had time to do any wrong. But that seems beside the point to me."

"On the contrary, I have a feeling that it is not and that the people you work for should remember it."

"After all, it's hardly their fault if I agree to do all the work they give me. I would do the same in their place."

"I should like to tell you how I went into that town, after leaving my suitcase at the hotel."

"Yes, I should like to hear that. But you mustn't worry on my account: I would be most surprised if I let myself become impatient. I think all the time of the risk I would run if that should happen and so, you see, I don't think it will."

"I did not manage to leave my suitcase until the evening. . . ."

"You see people like me do think too. There is nothing else for us to do, buried in our work. We think a great deal, but not like you. We have dark thoughts, and all the time."

"It was evening, just before dinner, after work."

"People like me think the same things of the same people and our thoughts are always bad. That's why we are so careful and why it's not worth bothering about us. You were talking of jobs, and I wonder if something could be called a job which makes you spend your whole day thinking ill of people? But you were saying it was evening, and you had left your suitcase?"

"Yes. It was only towards the evening, after I had left my suitcase at the hotel, just before dinner, that I started walking through that town. I was looking for a restaurant and of course it's not always easy to find exactly what one wants when price is a consideration. And while I was looking I strayed away from the center and came by accident to the Zoo. A wind had risen. People had forgotten the day's work and were strolling through the gardens which, as I told you, were up on a hill overlooking the town."

"But I know that life is good. Otherwise why on earth should I take so much trouble."

"I don't really know what happened. The moment I entered those gardens I was a man overwhelmed by a sense of living."

"How could a garden, just seeing a garden, make a man happy?"

"And yet what I am telling you is quite an ordinary experience and other people will often tell you similar things in the course of your life. I am a person for whom talking, for example, feeling at one with other people, is a blessing, and suddenly in that garden I was so completely at home, so much at my ease, that it might have been made specially for me although it was an ordinary public garden. I don't know how to put it any better, except perhaps to say that it was as if I had achieved something and become, for the first time, equal to my life. I could not bear to leave it. The wind had risen, the light was honey-colored and even the lions whose manes glowed in the setting sun were yawning with the pure pleasure of being there. The air smelt of lions and of fire and I breathed it as if it were the essence of friendliness which had, at last, included me. All the passers-by were preoccupied with each other, basking in the evening light. I remember thinking they were like the lions. And suddenly I was happy."

"But in what way were you happy? Like someone resting? Like someone who is cool again after having been very hot? Or happy as other people are happy every day?"

"More than that I think. Probably because I was unused to happiness. A great surge of feeling overwhelmed me, and I did not know what to do with it."

"A feeling which hurt?"

"Perhaps so, yes. It hurt because there seemed to be nothing which could ever appease it."

"But that, I think, is hope."

"Yes, that is hope, I know that really is hope. And of what? Of nothing. Just the hope of hope."

"You know if there were only people like you in the world, no one would get anywhere."

"But listen. You could see the sea from the bottom of each avenue in that garden, every single one led to the sea. Actually the sea really plays very little part in my life, but in that garden they were all looking at the sea, even the people who were born there, even, it seemed to me, the lions themselves. How can you avoid looking at what other people are looking at, even if normally it doesn't mean much to you."

"The sea couldn't have been as blue as all that since you said the sun was setting?"

"When I left my hotel it was blue but after I had been in that garden a little while it became darker and calmer."

22

"But you said a wind had come up: it couldn't have been as calm as all that?"

"But it was such a gentle wind, if you only knew, and it was probably only blowing on the heights: on the town and not on the plain. I don't remember exactly from which direction it came, but surely not from the open sea."

"And then again, the setting sun couldn't have illuminated all the lions. Not unless all the cages faced the same way on the same side of the garden looking into the sun?"

"And yet I promise you it was like that. They were all in the same place and the setting sun lit up each lion without exception."

"And so the sun did set first over the sea?"

"Yes, you're quite right. The city and the garden were still in sunshine although the sea was in shade. That was three years ago. That's why I remember it all so well and like talking about it."

"I understand. One thinks one can get by without talking, but it's not possible. From time to time I find myself talking to strangers too, just as we are talking now."

"When people need to talk it can be felt very strongly, and strangely enough people in general seem to resent it. It is only in Squares that it seems quite natural. Tell me again, you said there were eight rooms where you worked? Big rooms?"

"I couldn't really say since I don't suppose anyone else would see them in quite the same way as I do. Most of the time they seem big, but perhaps they're not as big as all that. It really depends. On some days they seem endless and on others I think I could stifle they seem so tiny. But why did you ask?"

"It was only out of curiosity. For no other reason."

"I know that I must seem stupid to you, but I can't help it."

"I would say you are a very ambitious person, if I have really understood you, someone who wants everything that everyone else has, but wants it so much that one could almost say your desire is heroic."

"That word doesn't frighten me, although I had not thought of it in that way. You could almost say I have so little that I could have anything. After all I could want to die with the same violence as I want to live. And is there anything, any one little thing in my life to which I could sacrifice my courage? And who or what could weaken it? Anyone would do the same as I do: anyone, I mean, who wanted what I want as much as I do."

"I expect so. Since everyone does what he has to do. Yes, I expect there are cases where it is impossible to be anything else but heroic."

"You see, if just once I refused the work they give me, no matter what it was, it would mean that I had begun to manage things, to defend myself, to take an interest in what I was doing. It would start with one thing, go on to another, and could end anywhere. I would begin to defend my rights so well that I would take them seriously and end by thinking they existed. They would matter to me. I wouldn't be bored any more and so I would be lost."

There was a silence between them. The sun, which had been hidden by the clouds, came out again. Then the girl started talking once more.

"Did you stay on in that town after being so happy in that garden?"

"I stayed for several days. Sometimes I do stay longer than usual in a place."

"Tell me, do you think that anyone can experience the feelings you had in that garden?"

"There must be some people who never do. It's an almost unbearable idea but I suppose there are such people."

"You don't know for certain do you?"

"No. I can easily be mistaken. The fact is I really don't know."

"And yet you seem to know about these things."

"No more than anyone else."

"There's something else I want to ask you: as the sun sets very quickly in those countries, surely, even if it set first on the sea, the shade must have reached the town soon afterwards? The sunset must have been over very soon, perhaps ten minutes after it had begun."

"You are quite right, and yet I assure you it was just at that moment that I arrived; just at the moment when everything is alight."

"Oh, I believe you."

"It doesn't sound as though you do."

"But I do, completely. And anyway you could have arrived at any other moment without changing all that followed, couldn't you?"

"Yes, but I did arrive then, even if that moment only lasts for a few minutes a day."

"But that isn't really the point?"

"No, that isn't really the point."

"And afterwards?"

"Afterwards the garden was the same, except that it became night. A coolness came up from the sea and people were happy for the day had been hot."

"But even so, eventually you had to eat?"

"Suddenly I was no longer very hungry. I was thirsty. I didn't have dinner that evening. Perhaps I just forgot about it."

"But that's why you had left your hotel, to eat I mean?"

"Yes, but then I forgot about it."

"For me, you see, the days are like the night."

"But that is a little because you want them to be like that. You would like to emerge from your present situation just as you were when you entered it, as one wakes up from a long sleep. I know, of course, what it is to want to create night all around one but it seems to me that however hard one tries the dangers of the day break through."

"Only my night is not as dark as all that and I doubt if the day is really a threat to it. I'm twenty. Nothing has happened to me yet. I sleep well. But one day I must wake up and for ever. It must happen."

"And so each day is the same for you, even though they may be different?"

"Tonight, like every Thursday night, there will be people for dinner. I will eat chicken all alone in the kitchen."

"And the murmur of their conversation will reach you the same way? So very much the same that you could imagine that each Thursday they said exactly the same things."

"Yes, and as usual, I won't understand anything they talk about."

"And you will be all alone, there in the kitchen, surrounded by the remnants of food in a sort of drowsy lull. And then you will be called to take away the meat plates and serve the next course."

"They will ring for me, but they won't waken me. I serve at table half-asleep."

"Just as they are waited on, in absolute ignorance of what you might be like. And so in a way you are quits: they can neither make you happy nor sad, and so you sleep."

"Yes. And then the guests will leave and the house will be quiet till the morning."

"When you will start ignoring them all over again, while trying to wait on them as well as possible."

"I expect so. But I sleep well! If you only knew how well I sleep. There is nothing they can do to disturb my sleep. But why are we talking about these things?"

"I don't know, perhaps just to make you remember them."

"Perhaps it is that. But you see one day, yes one day, I shall go into the drawing room and I shall speak."

"Yes, you must."

"I shall say: 'This evening I shall not be serving dinner.' Madam will turn round in surprise. And I will say: 'Why should I serve dinner since as from this evening . . . as from this evening' . . . but no, I cannot even imagine how things of such importance are said."

The man made no reply. He seemed only attentive to the softness of the wind, which once more, had risen. The girl seemed to expect no response to what she had just said.

"Soon it will be summer," said the man and added with a groan, "We really are the lowest of the low."

"It's said that someone has to be."

"Yes, indeed and that everything has its place."

"And yet sometimes one wonders why this should be so."

"Why us rather than others?"

"Yes. Although sometimes, in cases like ours, one wonders whether its being us or someone else makes any difference. Sometimes one just wonders."

"Yes, and sometimes, in certain instances, that is a consoling thought."

"Not for me. That could never be a consoling thought. I must believe that I myself am concerned rather than anyone else. Without that belief I am lost."

"Who knows? Perhaps things will soon change for you. Soon and very suddenly: perhaps even this very summer you will go into that drawing room and announce that, as from that moment, the world can manage without your services."

"Who knows indeed? And you could call it pride, but when I say the world, I really mean the whole world. Do you understand?"

"Yes, I do."

"I will open the door of that drawing room and then, suddenly, everything will be said and forever."

"And you will always remember that moment as I remember my journey. I have never been on so wonderful a journey since, nor one which made me so happy."

"Why are you suddenly so sad? Do you see anything sad in the fact that one day I must open that door? On the contrary doesn't it seem the most desirable thing in the world?"

"It seems utterly desirable to me, and even more than that. No, if I felt a little sad when you talked of it—and I did feel a little sad—it was only because once you have opened that door it will have been opened forever, and afterwards you will never be able to do it again. And then, sometimes, it seems so hard, so very hard to go back to a country which pleased me as well as that one did, that occasionally I wonder if it would not have been better never to have seen it at all."

"I wish I could, but you must see I cannot understand what it is like to have seen that city and to want to go back to it, nor can I understand the sadness you seem to feel at the thought of waiting for that moment. You could try as hard as you liked to tell me there was something sad about it, I could never understand. I know nothing, or rather I know nothing except this: that one day I must open that door and speak to those people."

"Of course, of course. You mustn't take any notice of what I say. Those thoughts simply came into my mind when you were talking, but I didn't want them to discourage you. In fact quite the opposite. I'd like to ask you more about that door. What special moment are you waiting for, to open it? For instance why couldn't you do it this evening?"

"Alone I could never do it."

"You mean that being without money or education you could only begin in the same way all over again and that really there would be no point to it?"

"I mean that and other things. I don't really know how to describe it, but being alone I feel as if I had no meaning. I can't change by myself. No. I will go on visiting that Dance Hall and one day a man will ask me to be his wife. Then I will open that door. I couldn't do it before that happened."

"How do you know if it would turn out like that if you have never tried?"

"I have tried. And because of that I know that alone . . . I would be, as I said, somehow meaningless. I wouldn't know any more what it was to want to change. I would simply be there, doing nothing, telling myself that nothing was worthwhile."

"I think I see what you mean: in fact I believe I understand it all."

"One day someone must choose me. Then I will be able to change. I don't mean this is true for everyone. I am simply saying it is true for

27

me. I have already tried and I know. I don't know all this just because I know what it is like to be hungry, no, but because when I was hungry I realized I didn't care. I hardly knew who it was in me who was hungry."

"I see all that: I can see how one could feel like that: in fact I can guess it, although personally I have never felt the need to be singled out as you want to be; or perhaps I really mean that if such a thought ever did cross my mind I never attached much importance to it."

"You must understand: you must try to understand that I have never been wanted by anyone, ever, except of course for my capacity for housework; and that is not choosing me as a person but simply wanting something impersonal which makes me as anonymous as possible. And so I must be wanted by someone, just once, and even if only once. Otherwise I shall exist so little even to myself that I would be incapable of knowing how to want to choose anything. That is why, you see, I attach so much importance to marriage."

"Yes, I do see and I follow what you are saying, but in spite of all that, and with the best will in the world, I cannot really see how you hope to be chosen when you cannot make a choice for yourself?"

"I know it seems ridiculous but that is how it is. Because you see, left to myself, I would find any man suitable: any man in the world would seem suitable on the one condition that he wanted me just a little. A man who so much as noticed me would seem desirable just for that very reason, and so how on earth would I be capable of knowing who would suit me when anyone would, on the one condition that they wanted me? No, it's impossible. Someone else must decide for me, must guess what would be best. Alone I could never know."

"Even a child knows what is best for him."

"But I am not a child, and if I let myself go and behaved like a child and gave in to the first temptation I came across—after all I am perfectly aware that it is there at every street corner—why then I would follow the first person who came along, the first man who just wanted me. And I would follow him simply for the pleasure I would have in being with him, and then, why then I would be lost, completely lost. You could say that I could easily make another kind of life for myself, but as you can see I no longer have the courage even to think of it."

"But have you never thought that if you leave this choice entirely to another person it need not necessarily be the right one and might make for unhappiness later?"

"Yes, I have thought of that a little, but I cannot think now, before

28

my life has really begun, of the harm I might possibly do later on. I just say one thing to myself and that is: if the very fact of being alive means that we can do harm, however much we don't want to, just by choosing or making mistakes, if that is an inevitable state of affairs, why then, I too will go through with it. If I have to, if everyone has to, I can live with harm."

"Please don't get so excited: there will be someone one day who will discover that you exist both for him and for others, you must be sure of that. And yet you know one can almost manage to live with this lack of which you speak."

"Which lack? Of never being chosen?"

"If you like, yes. As far as I am concerned I should be so surprised if anyone chose me, that I should simply laugh."

"While I should be in no way surprised, I am afraid I would find it perfectly natural. It is just the contrary which astonishes me, and it astonishes me more each day. I cannot understand it and I never get used to it."

"It will happen. I promise you."

"Thank you for saying so. But are you saying that just to please me, or can people tell these things? Can you guess it already just from talking to me?"

"I expect such things can be guessed, yes. To tell you the truth, I said that without thinking much, but not at all because I thought it would please you. It must have been because I could see it."

"And you? How are you so sure the opposite is true of you."

"Well, I suppose it is because. . . . Yes, just because I am not surprised. I think it must be that. I am not at all surprised that no one has chosen me, while you are so amazed that you have not yet been singled out."

"In your place, you know, I would force myself to want something, however hard it might be. I would not remain as you are."

"But what can I do? Since I don't feel this same need it could only come to me. . . . Well, from the outside. How else could it be?"

"You know you almost make me wish I was dead."

"Is it I in particular who has that effect, or were you just speaking in general?"

"Of course I was only speaking in general. In general about us both."

"Because there is another thing I would not really like, and that is to have provoked in anyone, even if only once, a feeling as violent as that."

"Oh, I'm sorry."

"It doesn't matter."

"And I would like to thank you too."

"But for what?"

"I don't really know. For your niceness."

Two

THE CHILD CAME OVER quietly from the far side of the Park and stood beside the girl.

"I'm thirsty," he announced.

The girl took a thermos and a mug from the bag beside her.

"I can well imagine," said the man, "that he must be thirsty after eating those sandwiches."

The girl uncorked the thermos. Warm milk gleamed in the sunshine.

"But as you see," she said, "I have brought him some milk."

The child drank the milk greedily, then gave the mug back to the girl. A milky cloud stayed round his lips. The girl wiped them. The man smiled at the child.

"If I said what I did," he remarked, "it was only to try and make myself clear. For no other reason."

Completely indifferent the child contemplated this man who was smiling at him. Then he went back to the sand pit. The girl's eyes followed him.

"His name is James," she said.

"James," the man repeated.

But he was no longer thinking of the child.

"I don't know if you've noticed," he went on, "how a trace of milk stays round a child's mouth when he has drunk it? It's strange. In some ways they are so grown up: they seem to talk and walk like everyone else and then when it comes to drinking milk, one realizes. . . ."

"He doesn't say 'milk,' he says 'my milk.'"

"When I see something like that milk I suddenly feel full of hope although I could never say why. As if some pain was deadened. I think perhaps that watching these children reminds me of the lions in that Garden. I see them as minute lions, but lions all the same."

"Yet they don't seem to give you the same kind of happiness as those lions did in their cages facing the sun?"

"They give me a certain happiness but you are right, not the same one. Somehow children always make one feel obscurely worried, and it is not that I particularly like lions; it would be untrue to say that. It was just a way of putting things."

"I wonder if you attach too much importance to that town with the result that the rest of your life suffers by comparison? Or is it just that never having been there I can hardly be expected to understand the happiness it gave you?"

"And yet it is probably to someone like you that I should most like to talk about it."

"Thank you. It was kind of you to say that. But you know I didn't want to imply that I was particularly unhappy, more unhappy I mean than anyone else would be in the same position. I was speaking of something quite different, something which I am afraid could not be solved by seeing any country, anywhere in the world."

"I'm sorry. You see when I said that I should like to talk most about that country to someone like you I did not mean for a second that you were unhappy without knowing it, and that telling you certain things would make you feel better. I simply meant that you seemed to me to be a person who might understand what one was trying to say better than most people. That's all. But I expect I have talked too much about that town and it is natural that you should have misunderstood."

"No, I don't think it is that. All I wanted was to put you right in case you had made the mistake of thinking I was unhappy. Of course there are times when I cry, naturally there are, but it's only from impatience or irritation. I am not old enough yet to be profoundly sad about my life. That stage is to come."

"Yes, I really do see, but don't you think it is just possible that you might be wrong, that you don't know which stage you have reached?"

"No, that would not be possible. Either I shall be unhappy in the same way as everyone else is, or I shall not be unhappy at all. I want to be exactly like everyone else and I shall go on trying as much as I can. I want to find out for myself if life is terrible. I shall die as I mean to and someone will care. But let's forget all that. Please tell me more of how you felt in that town."

"I am afraid I will tell it badly. I had no sleep and yet I was not tired."

"And. . . ."

32

"I did not eat and I wasn't hungry."

"And then. . . ."

"All the minor problems of my life seemed to evaporate as if they had never existed except in my imagination. I thought of them as belonging to a distant past and laughed at them."

"But surely you must have wanted to eat and sleep in the end? It would have been impossible for you to go on without feeling tired or hungry."

"I expect so, but I didn't stay long enough there for those feelings to come back to me."

"And were you very tired when they did come back?"

"I slept for a whole day in a wood by the roadside."

"Like a tramp?"

"Yes, just like a tramp with my suitcase beside me."

"I understand."

"No, I don't think you can, yet."

"I mean I am trying to understand and one day I will. One day I shall understand what you have been saying to me completely. After all, anybody could, couldn't they?"

"Yes, I think one day you will understand them as completely as possible."

"Ah, if only you knew how difficult the things I was telling you about can be. How difficult it is to get for yourself, completely by yourself, just the things which are common to everyone. I think I really mean how hard it is to fight the apathy which comes from wanting just the ordinary things which everyone else seems to have."

"I expect it is just that which prevents so many people from trying to achieve them. I admire you for being as you are."

"Ah, if only will power were enough! There have been men who found me attractive from time to time, but so far none of them has asked me to be his wife. There is a great difference between liking a young girl and wanting to marry her. And yet that must happen to me. Just once in my life I must be taken seriously. I wanted to ask you something: if you want a thing all the time, at every single moment of the day and night, do you think that you necessarily get it?"

"Not necessarily, no. But it still remains the best way of trying and the one with the greatest chance of success. I can really see no other way."

"After all, we're only talking. And as you don't know me or I you, you can tell me the truth."

"Yes, that's quite true, but really and truly I can see no other way. But perhaps I haven't had enough experience to answer your question properly."

"Because I once heard that quite the opposite was true. That it was by trying not to want something that it finally happened."

"But tell me, how could you manage not to want something, when you want it so much?"

"That is exactly what I say to myself, and to tell you the truth I never felt that the other was a very serious idea. I think it must apply to people who want little things, to people who already have something and want something else, but not to people like us—I didn't mean that, I mean not to people like me who want everything, not just a part of something but . . . I don't know how to say it. . . ."

"A whole."

"Perhaps it is that. But please tell me more about your feelings for children. You said you were fond of them?"

"Yes. Sometimes when I have no one else to talk to I talk to them. But you know how it is, one can't really talk to children."

"Oh, you're right. We are the lowest of the low."

"But you mustn't think either that I am unhappy simply because sometimes I need to talk so badly that I talk to children. That's not true, because after all I must in some way have chosen my life or else I am just a madman indulging in his folly."

"I'm sorry. I don't mean what I said. I simply saw the fine weather and the words came out of their own accord. You must try to understand and not mind, because sometimes fine weather makes me doubt everything: but it never lasts for more than a few seconds. I'm sorry."

"It doesn't matter. When I sit in Squares like this it is generally because I have been for some days without talking: when there have been no opportunities for conversation except with the people who buy my goods and they have been so rushed or standoffish that I could say nothing to them except the things that go with the sale of a reel of cotton. Naturally you mind this after some time and suddenly you want to talk and be listened to so badly that it can even produce a feeling of illness like a slight fever."

"I know how you feel. You feel you could do without everything

34

else, without eating, sleeping, anything rather than be silent. But in that town you were telling me about you didn't have to talk to children?"

"Not in that town, no. I was not with children then."

"That is what I thought."

"I used to see them in the distance. There were lots of them in the streets: they are left very free there and from about the age of the one you look after they cross the whole town on their own to visit the Zoo. They eat at any hour and sleep in the shadow of the lions' cages. Yes, I saw them in the distance sleeping in the shadow of those cages."

"Children have all the time in the world and they'll talk to anyone and always be ready to listen, but one hasn't very much to say to them."

"That's the trouble. It's true they don't despise solitary people: in fact they like almost anyone, but then, as you said, there is so little to say to them."

"But tell me more."

"Oh, as far as children go one person is as good as another, provided they talk about airplanes and trains. There is never any difficulty in talking to children about that sort of thing. It can become a little monotonous, but that's how it is."

"They can't understand other things, unhappiness for example, and I don't think it does much good to mention them."

"If you talk to them of things that don't interest them they simply stop listening and wander off."

"Sometimes I have conversations on my own."

"That has happened to me too."

"I don't mean I talk to myself. I speak to a completely imaginary person, not just anybody, but to my worst enemy. You see, although I haven't any friends yet, I invent enemies."

"And what do you say to them?"

"I insult them: and always without the slightest explanation. Why do I do this?"

"Who knows? Probably because an enemy never understands one and I think you would be hard put to it to accept being understood and to give in to the particular comfort it brings."

"After all, my insults are a form of talking aren't they? And I never mention my work."

"Yes, it is talking; and since no one hears you and it gives you some satisfaction it seems better to go on."

"When I spoke of the unhappiness which children cannot understand

I was talking of unhappiness in general, the unhappiness everyone knows about, not of a particular kind of personal unhappiness."

"I knew that. The fact is we could not bear it if children could understand unhappiness. Perhaps they are the only people we cannot stand to see unhappy."

"There are not many happy people are there?"

"I don't think so. There are some who think it important to be happy and believe that they are, but at bottom are not really as happy as all that."

"And yet I thought it was a duty for people to be happy, an instinct like going to the sun rather than to the dark. Look at me for instance; at all the trouble I take over it."

"But of course it's like a duty. I feel that too. But if people feel the need for the sun it is because they know how sad the dark can be. No one can live always in the dark."

"I make my own darkness but since other people seek the sun, I do so too, and that is what I feel about happiness. Everything I do is for my happiness."

"You are right and that is probably why things are simpler for you than for other people: you have no alternative, while people who have a choice can long for things they know nothing about."

"You would think the gentleman where I am in service would be happy. He is a businessman with a great deal of money and yet he always seems distracted as if he were bored. I think sometimes that he has never looked at me, that he recognizes me without ever having seen me."

"And yet you are a person people would look at."

"But he doesn't see anyone. It is as if he no longer used his eyes. That is why he sometimes seems to me less happy than one might think. As if he were tired of everything, even of looking."

"And his wife?"

"His wife too. One could take her for being happy but I know she is not."

"Do you find that the wives of such men are easily frightened and have the tired, shaded look of women who no longer dream?"

"Not this one. She has a clear look and nothing catches her off her guard. Everyone thinks she has everything she could want and yet I know it is not so. You learn about these things in my work. Often in the evening she comes into the kitchen with a vacant expression which doesn't deceive me, as if she wanted my company."

"It is just what we said: in the end people are not good at happiness. They want it of course but when they have it they eat themselves away with dreaming."

"I don't know if it is that people are not good at happiness or if they don't understand what it is. Perhaps they don't really know what it is they want or how to make use of it when they have it. They may even get tired of trying to keep it. I really don't know. What I do know is that the word exists and that it was not invented for nothing. And just because I know that women, even those who appear to be happy, often start wondering towards evening why they are leading the lives they do, I am not going to start wondering if the word is meaningless. That is all I can say on the subject."

"Of course it is. And when I said that happiness is difficult to stand I didn't mean that because of that it should be avoided. I wanted to ask you: is it around six o'clock when she comes into your kitchen?"

"Yes, always around that time. I know what it means, believe me. I know it is a particular time of day when many women long for things they haven't got: but for all that I refuse to give up."

"It's always the same: when everything is there for things to go right people still manage to make them go wrong. They find happiness sad."

"It makes no difference to me. I can only say again that I want to experience that particular sadness."

"If I said what I did, it was for no special reason. I was only talking."

"One could say that without wanting to discourage me you were, all the same, trying to warn me."

"Oh, hardly at all. Or only in the smallest degree, I promise you."

"But since my work has already shown me the other side of happiness you need not worry. And in the end what does it matter if I find happiness or something else as long as it is something real I can feel and deal with. Since I am in the world I too must have my share of it. There is no reason why I should not. I will do just as everyone else does. You see, I cannot imagine dying without having had the look that my employer has in her eyes when she comes to see me in the evening."

"It is hard to imagine you with tired eyes. You may not know it, but you have very fine eyes."

"They will be fine when they need to be."

"I can't help it, but the thought that one day you might have the same look as that woman is sad, that's all."

"Who can tell how things will turn out? And I will go through whatever is necessary. That is my greatest hope. And after my eyes have been fine they will become clouded like everyone else's."

"When I said that your eyes were fine I meant that they had a wonderful expression."

"I am sure you are wrong and even if you were right I couldn't be satisfied with it."

"I understand and yet I find it hard not to tell you that for other people your eyes are very beautiful."

"Otherwise I would be lost. If for one moment I was satisfied with my eyes as they are I would be lost."

"And so you said this woman comes into the kitchen?"

"Yes, sometimes. It is the only moment of the day when she does and she always asks the same thing, how am I getting on?"

"As if things could go differently for you from one day to another?"

"Yes, as if they could."

"Such people have strange illusions about people like us. What else can you expect? And perhaps it is part of our job to preserve their illusion."

"Have you ever been dependent on a boss? It seems as if you must have to understand so well."

"No. But it is a threat which hangs over people like us so constantly that it is easier to imagine than most things."

There was a silence between the girl and the man and one would have thought them distracted, attentive only to the softness of the air. Then once again the man started to speak. He said:

"We really agree, you know. You see, when I talked of this woman and of people who managed not to be entirely happy I did not mean that it was a reason for not following their example, for not trying in one's own turn and in one's own turn failing. Nor that one should deny longings such as you have for a gas stove, which would be to reject in advance all that might follow from it, such as a refrigerator or even happiness. I don't doubt the truth of your hopes for a moment. On the contrary I think they are exactly what they should be. I really do."

"Must you go? Is that why you said all that?"

"No, I have no need to go. I just didn't want you to misunderstand me, that's all."

38

"The way you talked like that, all of a sudden drawing conclusions from everything we had said, made me think that perhaps you had to go."

"No, I have nothing to go for. I just wanted to say that I understood you and like everything about you. And I was going to add that if there was one thing I didn't quite understand, and I hate being a bore on this subject, it is still the fact that you take on so much extra work and that you always agree to do whatever they ask. Don't blame me for coming back to it, but I can't agree with you on this point even if I do understand your reasons. I am afraid. . . . What I am really afraid of is that you might feel that if you accept all the worst things that come your way you will one day have earned the right to be finished with them forever. . . ."

"And if that was the case?"

"Ah, no. I cannot accept that. I don't believe that anything or anyone exists whose function it is to reward people for their personal merits, and certainly not people who are obscure or unknown. We are abandoned."

"But if I told you it was not for that reason but so that I should never lose my horror for my work, so that I should go on feeling all the disgust I felt for it as much as ever."

"I am sorry but even then I could not agree. I think you have already begun to live your life and even at the risk of repeating this endlessly to you and becoming a bore I really must say that I think things have already started for you, that time passes for you as much as for anyone else, and that even now you can waste it; as you do when you take on work which anyone else in your place would refuse."

"I think you must be very nice to be able to put yourself into other people's places and think for them with so much understanding. I could never do that."

"You have other things to do; if I can think about other people it is only because I have the time for it, and as you said yourself, it is not the best kind of time."

"Perhaps you're right. Perhaps the fact that I have decided to change everything is a sign that things have begun for me. And the fact that I cry from time to time is probably also a sign and I expect I should no longer hide this from myself."

"Everyone cries, and not because of that, but simply because they are alive."

"But one day I checked up on my position and I discovered that it was quite usual for maids to be expected to do most of the things I have to do. That was two years ago. For instance there's no reason why I shouldn't tell you that sometimes we have to look after very old women, as old as eighty-two, weighing two hundred pounds and no longer quite right in their minds, making messes in their clothes at any hour of the day or night and whom nobody wants to bother about."

"Did you really say two hundred pounds?"

"Yes, I am looking after one now; and what's more, last time she was weighed she had gained. And yet I would have you appreciate the fact that I haven't killed her, not even that time two years ago after I had found out what was expected of me. She was fat enough then and I was eighteen. I still haven't killed her and I never will, although it becomes easier and easier as she gets older and frailer. She is left alone in the bathroom to wash and the bathroom is at the far end of the house. All I would have to do would be to hold her head under water for three minutes and it would all be over. She is so old that even her children wouldn't mind her death, nor would she herself since she hardly knows she is there any more. But I look after her very well and always for the reasons I explained, because if I killed her it would mean that I could imagine improving my present situation, making it bearable, and that would be contrary to my plan. No, no one can rescue me except a man. I hope you don't mind my telling you all this."

"Ah, I no longer know what to say to you."

"Let's not talk about it any more."

"Yes, but still! You said it would be easy to get rid of that old woman and no one, not even she herself, would mind. I am still not giving you advice but it seems to me that in many cases other people could do something of that nature to make their lives a little easier and still be able to hope for their future as much as before?"

"It's no good talking to me like that. I would rather my horror became worse. It is my only chance of getting out."

"After all, we were only talking. I just wondered whether it might not be almost a duty to prevent someone from hoping so much."

"There seems no reason why I shouldn't tell you that I know someone like me who did kill."

"I don't believe it. Perhaps she thought she had killed someone but she couldn't really have done it."

"It was a dog. She was sixteen. You may say it is not at all the same thing as killing a person, but she did it and says it is very much the same."

"Perhaps she didn't give it enough to eat. That's not the same as killing."

"No, it was not like that. They both had exactly the same food. It was a very valuable dog and so they had the same food: of course it was not the same as the things the people in the house ate and she stole the dog's food once. But that wasn't enough."

"She was young and longed for meat as most children do."

"She poisoned the dog. She stayed awake a long time mixing poison with its food. She told me she didn't even think about the sleep she was losing. The dog took two days to die. Of course it is the same as killing a person. She knows. She saw it die."

"I think it would have been more unnatural if she had not done it."

"But why such hatred for a dog? In spite of everything he was the only friend she had. One thinks one isn't nasty and yet one can do something like that."

"It is situations like that which should not be allowed. From the moment they arise the people involved cannot do otherwise than as they do. It is inevitable, quite inevitable."

"They knew it was she who killed the dog. She got the sack. They could do nothing else to her since it is not a crime to kill a dog. She said that she would almost have preferred them to punish her, she felt so guilty. Our work, you know, leads us to have the most terrible thoughts."

"Leave it."

"I work all day and I would even like to work harder but at something else: something in the open air which brings results you can see, which can be counted like other things, like money. I would rather break stones on the road or work steel in a foundry."

"But then do it. Break stones on the road. Leave your present work."

"No, I can't. Alone, as I explained to you, alone I could not do it. I have tried, without success. Alone, without any affection, I think I should just die of hunger. I wouldn't have the strength to force myself to go on."

"There are women roadmenders. I've seen them."

"I know. I think about them every day. But I should have started in that way. It's too late now. A job like mine makes you so disgusted with yourself that you have even less meaning outside it than in it. You don't even know that you exist enough for your own death to matter to you. No, from now on my only solution is a man for whom I shall exist; only then will I get out."

"But do you know what that is called . . .?"

"No. All I know is that I must persist in this slavery for some time longer before I can enjoy things again, things as simple as eating."

"Forgive me."

"It doesn't matter. I must stay where I am for as long as I have to. Please don't think that I lack good will because it is not that. It is just that it is not worthwhile trying to make me hope less—as you put it —because if I tried to hope less than I do, I know that I would no longer hope at all. I am waiting. And while I wait I am careful not to kill anything, neither a person nor a dog, because those are serious things and could turn me into a nasty person for the rest of my life. But let's talk a little more about you: you who travel so much and are always alone."

"Well, yes, I travel and I am alone."

"Perhaps one day I will travel too."

"You can only see one thing at a time and the world is big, and you can only see it for yourself with your own two eyes. It is little enough and yet most people travel."

"All the same, however little you can see, I expect it is a good way of passing the time."

"The best, I think, or at least it passes for the best. Being in a train absorbs time as much as sleeping. And a ship even more: you just look at the furrows following the ship and time passes by itself."

"And yet sometimes time takes so long to pass that you feel almost as if it was something which had been dragged out of your own insides."

"Why not take a little trip for eight days or so? For a holiday. You need only want to. Couldn't you do that? While still waiting of course."

"It's true that waiting seems very long. I joined a political party, not because I thought it would help my personal problems but I thought it might make the time pass more quickly. But even so it is very long."

"But that is it exactly! Since you are already doing something outside your job, and you go to this Dance Hall, since in fact you are doing everything you can to be able to leave your present job one day, then surely you could also make a short journey while waiting for your life to take the turning you want it to?"

42

"I did not mean anything more than I said: that sometimes things seem very long."

"All you need to do is change your mood just a fraction and then you could take a little voyage for eight days or so."

"On Saturday when I come back from dancing I cry sometimes as I told you. How does one make a man desire one? Love cannot be forced. Perhaps it is the mood that you were talking about which makes me so undesirable: a feeling of rancor, and how could that please anyone?"

"I meant nothing more about your mood than that it prevented you from taking a holiday. I wouldn't advise you to become like me, a person who finds hope superfluous. But you must see that from the moment you decided it was best to let that old woman live out her days, and that you must do everything they ask of you, so as one day to be free to do something quite different, then it seems to me that as a kind of compensation you could take a short holiday and go away. Why, even I would do it."

"I understand, but tell me what would I do with a holiday? I wouldn't know what to do with myself. I would simply be there looking at new things without them giving me any pleasure."

"You must learn, even if it is difficult. From now on as a provision against the future you must learn that. Looking at new things is something one learns."

"Yes, but tell me again: how could I ever manage to learn how to enjoy myself in the present when I am worn out with waiting for the future? I wouldn't have the patience to look at anything new."

"It doesn't matter. Forget about it. It wasn't very important."

"And yet if you only knew, I would so much like to be able to look at new things."

"Tell me, when a man asks you to dance with him, do you immediately think he might marry you?"

"Yes. You see I'm too practical. All my troubles come from that. But how could I be anything else? It seems to me that I could never love anyone before I had some freedom and that can only come to me through a man."

"And another question: if a man doesn't ask you to dance do you still think he might marry you?"

"I think less then because I am at the Dance. When I dance I get carried away by the movement and the excitement and at those moments I think a man might most easily forget who I am, and even if he did find out he would mind it less under those circumstances than at any other time. I dance well. In fact I dance very well and when I am dancing I feel quite different from my usual self. Ah, sometimes I don't know what to do any more."

"But do you think about it while you are at the Dance Hall?"

"No. There I think of nothing. I think before or afterwards. There it is as if I were asleep."

"Everything happens, believe me. We think that nothing will ever happen but it does. There is not a man among all the millions who exist, not a single one, who hasn't known the things you are waiting for."

"I am afraid you don't really understand what it is I am waiting for."

"I am talking, you see, not only of the things you know you want but also of the things you want without knowing. Of something less immediate, something of which you are still unaware."

"Yes, I follow what you are saying. And it is true that there are things I don't know of now. But all the same I would so like to know how those things happen."

"They happen like anything else."

"Just as I know I am waiting?"

"Exactly. It is difficult to talk to you of things you know so little. I think that those things either come about suddenly, all at once, or else so slowly that one scarcely notices them. And when they have happened and are there they don't seem at all surprising: it feels as if they had always been there. One day you will wake up and there it will all be. And it will be the same for the gas stove: you will wake up one day and not even be able to explain how it came to be there."

"But what about you? You who are always traveling and who seem, if I have understood you, to attach so little importance to events."

"But the same things can happen anywhere without any warning. In places like trains. And the only difference between the things which happen to me and those you want for yourself are that in my case they are without a future: there is nothing one can do with them."

"I don't know what to say but I think it must be very sad to live as you do, always with events which can have no future. I think that from time to time you must cry too."

"But no. One gets used to it like everything else. And good gracious me everyone has cried at least once, every single one of all the millions of people on earth. That proves nothing in itself. Perhaps I should also explain that as far as I am concerned the tiniest thing can make me happy. I like waking up in the morning for instance and quite often I find myself singing while I shave."

"Oh, but surely singing proves nothing to someone who talks as you do?"

"But you must understand: I like being alive and I should have thought that was the one point on which no one could make a mistake."

"I don't know what it feels like. Perhaps that is why I understand you so badly."

"Whatever the cause of your unhappiness—and I really can find no other word for it—you must, you really must, show a little good will."

"But I am worn out with waiting and yet I go on waiting. It is more than I can do to wash that old woman and yet I go on washing her. I do all the things which are really too much for me. What more do you ask?"

"By good will I mean that you could, perhaps, wash her as you would wash anything else—a saucepan for example."

"No, I tried that but it was no good. She smiles, she smells bad. She is human."

"Alas. What can one do?"

"Sometimes I don't know myself. I was sixteen when this life began for me. At the beginning I didn't pay too much attention and now look where I am. I am twenty and nothing has happened to me, nothing, and that old woman never manages to die and is still there. And nobody has asked me to be his wife. Sometimes I even think I must be dreaming, that somehow I must be inventing so many difficulties."

"Why not work for another family? One where there are no old people? Find a place with some advantages—although naturally I know they could only be relative."

"That wouldn't help. Whatever the family was like it would always treat me as something apart. In my kind of work changing jobs means nothing, since the only real change would be for such jobs to be abolished. If I did manage to find a family such as you describe I wouldn't really be able to put up with them any better than I do with my present one. And then just through changing and changing, without changing anything I would end by believing in, I hardly know what, some sort of fate and that would be worse than anything. No. I must stay where I am right up to the moment when I can leave forever. Sometimes I believe in it so much. I can hardly tell you how much. As much as I know I am sitting here."

"Well, then, while staying where you are, you could still take that little journey. I believe you could."

"Yes, perhaps. Perhaps I could make that journey."

"Of course you could."

"But from all you said that city you talked about must be very far away. Immensely far."

"I reached it by little stages, taking fifteen days in all, stopping off here and there for a day at a time. But someone who could afford to do so could reach it by one night in the train."

"You can be there in a night?"

"Yes, and already it is full summer there. Of course I couldn't be certain that someone else would find it as beautiful as I did. I suppose it is quite possible that someone else might not like it at all. I imagine I didn't see it with the same eyes as a person who found nothing there but the place itself."

"But if one knew in advance that another person had been happy there I think one would look at it with different eyes. We're only talking. . . ."

"Yes."

They were silent. Imperceptibly the sun was sinking and once more a memory of winter lay over the city. It was the girl who started the conversation again.

"What I meant," she began, "was that something of that happiness must remain in the air. Don't you agree?"

"I don't know."

"I would like to ask you something more. Could you tell me more about those things we were discussing—the things that could take place in a train for example?"

"Not really. They happen, that's all. You know, few people would put up with a traveling salesman of my status."

"But I am only a maid and I still hope. You mustn't talk like that."

"I am sorry. I explained myself badly. You will change but I don't think I will, or rather I don't think so any more. And whichever way you look at it there is nothing to be done about it. Even if I could have wished that things had been different I can never forget the traveling salesman I have become. When I was twenty I was smart and gay and played tennis. That is how my life started. I mean a life can begin anyhow—a fact we do not appreciate enough. And then time passes and we discover that life has very few solutions: and things become established until one fine day we find they are so established that the very idea of changing them seems absurd."

"That must be a terrible moment."

"No. It passes unnoticed as time passes. But you mustn't be sad. I am not complaining about my life and to tell you the truth I don't think about it much. The least thing amuses me."

"And yet you give the impression of not having told the whole truth about your life."

"I assure you I am not someone to be pitied."

"I too know that life is terrible. I am not as stupid as that. I know it is as terrible as it is good."

Once more a silence fell between the man and the girl. The sun was sinking even lower.

"Although I only took the train in small stages," the man said, "I don't think it can be very expensive."

"I spend very little money," said the girl, "in fact the only expenses I have are connected with dancing. So you see even if the train was expensive I could still afford the journey if I wanted to. But I am afraid that wherever I was I would feel I was wasting my time. I would say to myself: what are you doing here instead of being at that Dance Hall? For the moment your place is there and nowhere else. Wherever I was I would think of it. If it interests you the Dance Hall is called the Mecca: by the station. A lot of soldiers go there and unfortunately they never think of marrying, but there are other people too and one never knows."

"Thank you. But you know they also have dances in that town and if you did decide to make the journey you could go to them. And no one would know who you were there."

"Are they held in the Garden?"

"Yes, in the open air. On Saturdays they last all night."

"I see. But then I would have to lie about what I am. I know you will say that it's not my fault that I have to do the job I do, but it still makes me feel as if I had a crime to conceal."

"But since you want to change so much surely concealing it would only be a half-lie?"

"I think I could only lie about something for which I was responsible, but not about anything else. And although it sounds strange I feel almost as if I had chosen that particular Dance Hall and that what I want must happen there. It's a small one but it suits me as I really have no illusions about what I am or what I might become. I would feel strange and out of

47

place anywhere else. If you were to come there we could have a dance while waiting for someone else to ask me. I mean if you would like to, of course. I dance well and I've never been taught."

"I dance well too."

"Don't you find that strange? Why should we dance well? Why us rather than anyone else?"

"Us rather than the people who dance badly you mean?"

"Yes, I know some. If you could only see them. They have no idea at all. It's double dutch to them. . . ."

"But you're laughing."

"What else can I do? People who dance badly always make me laugh. They try, they concentrate and there's nothing to be done about it: they simply can't manage."

"It must be because dancing is something which cannot entirely be learned. Do the ones you know hop or shuffle?"

"She hops and he shuffles with the result . . . I can hardly describe it to you. And yet it's obviously not their fault."

"No, it's not their fault. And yet it's difficult not to feel that somehow there is a certain justice in the fact that they can't dance."

"We may be wrong."

"Yes, we may be and after all it doesn't matter so much whether one dances well or badly."

"No, it's of no great importance. Yet all the same it's as if we had a secret strength concealed in us. Oh, nothing very much of course. . . . And yet don't you think I'm right?"

"But they could just as easily have been good dancers?"

"Yes, that's true, but then there would be something else, although I can't imagine what, which we would have and they would not: I don't know what it would be but it would be something."

"I don't know either, but I think you're right."

"I love dancing. It is probably the only thing I do now which I would like to go on doing for the rest of my life."

"I feel the same. I think everyone likes dancing, even people like us, and perhaps we would not be such good dancers if we didn't enjoy it so much."

"But perhaps we don't know exactly how much we do enjoy it? How could we know?"

"I don't think it matters. If it suits us so well we should go on not knowing."

48

"But the dreadful part is that when the Dance is over I start remembering. Suddenly it's Sunday and I mutter 'Old Bitch' as I wash her. I don't think I'm a nasty person, but of course I have no one to reassure me on this point and so I can only believe myself. When I say 'Bitch' she smiles."

"I can tell you that you are not a nasty person."

"But when I think about the people I work for my thoughts are so evil, if you only knew, just as if my wretchedness was their fault. I try to reason with myself but I can never manage to think in any other way."

"Don't worry about those thoughts. You are not a nasty person."

"Do you really think so?"

"I do. One day you will be very giving, with yourself and with your time."

"You really are nice."

"But I didn't say that out of niceness."

"But you, what will happen to you?"

"Nothing. As you can see I am no longer very young."

"But you. . . . You who once thought of killing yourself—because you did say that."

"Oh, that was only laziness at the thought of having to go on feeding myself: nothing serious really."

"But that's impossible. Something will happen to you or else it will only be because you don't want anything to happen."

"Nothing happens to me except the things that happen to everyone, every day."

"You say that, but in that town?"

"There I was not alone. And then, afterwards, I was alone again. I think it was just luck."

"No. When someone is without any hope at all, as you are, it is because something happened to him: it's the only explanation."

"One day you will understand. There are people like me, people who get so much pleasure from just being alive that they can get by without hope. I sing while I shave—what more do you want?"

"But were you unhappy after you left that town?"

"Yes."

"And did you think of staying in your room and never leaving it again?"

"No, not then. Because then I knew that it is possible not to be alone, even if only by accident."

"Tell me what else you do, apart from singing while you shave?"

"I sell my goods, then I eat, then I travel, then I read the newspapers. I can't tell you how much I enjoy the newspapers. I read them from cover to cover including the advertisements. I get so absorbed in a newspaper that when I put it down I have to think for a minute who I am."

"But I meant other things: what do you do apart from all the obvious things, apart from shaving and selling your goods and taking trains and eating and reading the newspapers? I mean those things which no one appears to be doing, but which everyone is doing all the same."

"I see what you mean. . . . But I really don't know what I do apart from the things I mentioned. I don't deny that sometimes I do wonder what I am doing, but just wondering doesn't seem to be enough. I probably don't wonder hard enough and I think it's perfectly possible that I shall never know. You see I believe that it is quite usual to be like me and that a great many people go through life without ever exactly knowing why."

"But it seems to me that one could try to know a little harder than you do."

"But I hang by a thread. I even hold on to myself by the merest thread. So you see life is easier for me than it is for you, which explains everything. And then too I can manage to live without having to know certain things."

Once more they were silent. Then the girl went on:

"I still can't understand. Forgive me for going back to the subject, but I still can't understand how you came to be as you are, nor even how you came to do the work you do."

"But as I told you, little by little. My brothers and sisters are all successful people who knew what they wanted. And I can only say once again that I didn't know. They can't understand either how I managed to come down so much in the world."

"That seems an odd way of putting it: I would rather say, how did you come to be so discouraged? And it's still beyond me to understand how you came to do such wretched work."

"Perhaps it comes from the fact that the idea of success was always a little vague in my mind. I never quite understood what it had to do with me. And after all I don't find my work quite so wretched."

50

"I am sorry to have used that expression, although I thought it would have been all right from me since my own work can hardly even be described as work. I only said that to try and make you tell me more. I wanted you to see that I found you mysterious, not that I was blaming you."

"I understand that and I'm sorry I took you up. I know there are people in the world who can judge what I do on its own merits and not necessarily despise it. I didn't mind anything you said. To tell you the truth I was only half aware of what I was saying myself. I am afraid it always bores me to talk of myself in the past."

Again they were silent. This time the memory of winter became insistent. The sun would no longer reappear: it had reached the stage where it was hidden by the mass of the city's buildings. The girl remained silent. The man started to talk to her again:

"I wanted to say," he went on, "that I would be very unhappy if you thought, even for an instant, that I was trying to influence you in any way. Even when we talked about that old woman we were, after all, only talking. . . ."

"Please let's not talk about that any more."

"All right, let's not talk about it any more. All I meant was that by understanding people, by trying at least to put yourself in their place, by trying to determine what might make their waiting easier you make certain suppositions and hypotheses. But from there to giving advice is quite a step to take, and I regret having taken it unconsciously. . . ."

"Please let's not talk about me any more."

"All right."

"But I wanted to ask you something. What happened after you left that town?"

The man was silent and the girl did not try to break his silence. Then, when she no longer seemed to expect a reply, he said:

"I told you. I was unhappy."

"But how unhappy?"

"I believe as unhappy as it is possible to be. I thought I had never been unhappy before."

"Did that feeling go eventually?"

"Yes, in the end."

"You were never alone in that town?"

"Never."

"Neither during the day nor the night?"

"Never, not by day nor by night. It lasted eight days."

"And then you were alone again? Completely alone?"

"Yes. And I have been alone ever since."

"I suppose it was tiredness that made you sleep all day in the wood with your suitcase beside you?"

"No, it was unhappiness."

"Yes, you did say you were as unhappy as it was possible to be. Do you still believe that?"

"Yes."

It was the girl's turn to be silent.

"Please don't cry, I beg you," the man said, smiling.

"I can't help myself."

"Things happen like that. Things that cannot be avoided, that no one can avoid."

"Oh, it is not that. Those things hold no terrors for me."

"You want them to?"

"Yes, I want them."

"You are right, because nothing is so worth living as the things which make one so unhappy. Don't cry."

"I'm not crying any more."

"You will see. Before the summer is out you will open that door and it will be forever."

"Sometimes it almost doesn't seem to matter any more."

"But you will see. You will see. It will happen quite quickly."

"It seems to me you should have stayed in that town. You should have tried to stay by all possible means."

"I stayed as long as I could."

"No, I don't believe you did everything. I cannot believe it."

"I did everything I thought could be done. Perhaps I didn't go about it in the right way. Don't think about it any more. You will see, before the summer is out things will have turned out all right for you."

"Perhaps. Who knows? Sometimes I wonder if it is all worth so much trouble?"

"Of course it is. And after all, as you said yourself, since we are here —we didn't ask to be but here we are—we must take the trouble. There is nothing else we can do, and you will do it. Before the summer is out you will have opened the door."

"Sometimes I think I will never do it. That when I am ready to open it I will draw back."

"No. You will open it."

"If you say that it must be because you think I have chosen the best way of getting what I want, of ending my present life and finally becoming something?"

"Yes, I do think so. I think the way you have chosen is the best for you."

"If you say that it must be because you think there are other ways which other people would have taken?"

"I expect there are other ways but I also believe they would suit you less well."

"Are you sure of what you are saying?"

"I believe what I am saying, but neither I nor anyone else could tell you with complete certainty."

"I ask because you said you understood things through traveling and seeing so many different places and people."

"Perhaps I understand less well where hope is concerned. I think that if I understand anything it's probably more than the small, ordinary things of everyday life: little problems rather than big ones. And yet I can say this: even if I am not absolutely and entirely sure of the means you have chosen, that before this summer is out you will have opened that door."

"Thank you all the same, very much. But tell me once again, what about you?"

"Spring is on its way and the fine weather. I will be off again."

They were silent one last time. And one last time it was the girl who took up the conversation:

"What was it that made you get up and start off again after sleeping in the wood?"

"I don't really know. Probably simply that one just had to get up and go on."

"A short while ago you said it was because from then on you knew it was possible not to be alone, even if only by accident?"

"It was later that I knew that. Some days later. At the time it was different. I knew nothing at all."

"You see how different we really are. I think I should have refused to get up."

"But of course you would not. What or who would you have refused?"

"Nothing or no one. I would have simply refused."

"You're wrong. You would have done as I did. It was cold, I was cold, and I got up."

"But we are different all the same."

"Oh, doubtless we are different in the way we take our troubles."

"No, I think we are even more different than that."

"I don't think so. I don't think we are more different than anyone is different from anyone else."

"Perhaps I am mistaken."

"Since we understand each other. Or at least we try to. And we both like dancing. You said you went to the Mecca?"

"Yes. It is a well-known place. A lot of people like us go there."

Three

THE CHILD CAME OVER quietly from the far side of the Square and stood beside the girl.

"I'm tired," he announced.

The man and the girl looked around them. It was darker than it had been. It was evening.

"It is true, it is late," said the girl.

This time the man made no comment. The girl wiped the child's hands, picked up his toys and put them into her bag, all without rising from the bench. Tired of playing, the child sat down at her feet to wait.

"Time seems shorter when one is talking," said the girl.

"And then afterwards, suddenly, much longer."

"Yes, like another kind of time. But it does one good to talk."

"Yes, it does one good. It is only afterwards that it is rather sad: after one has stopped talking. Then time becomes too slow. Perhaps one should never talk."

"Perhaps," said the girl after a pause.

"Only because of the slowness afterwards: that was all I meant."

"And perhaps because of the silence to which we are both returning."

"Yes, it is true that we are both returning to silence. It seems as though we are already there."

"No one will talk to me again this evening: I will go to bed in silence. And I am only twenty. What have I done to the world that my life should be like this?"

"Nothing. There are no answers to be found in thinking in that direction. You should be thinking rather of what you will do to the world. Yes, perhaps one should never talk. When one starts it is like picking up a delightful habit one had abandoned: even if it is a habit one had never quite acquired."

"Yes, that is right. As if we knew how wonderful it was to talk. It must be very deep instinct to be so strong."

"And to be talked to is as deep and as natural an instinct."

"I expect so, yes."

"Later you will understand how much. At least for your sake I hope that you will."

"I have talked so much that I feel ashamed."

"Oh, that is the very last thing you should worry about, if indeed there is any need for you to worry at all."

"Thank you."

The girl rose. The child got up and took her hand. The man remained seated.

"It is getting quite cold," the girl said.

"Yes, it is not yet summer although sometimes, during the day, one has the illusion that it is already here."

"Yes, one forgets that it is still too soon. It is rather like going back into silence after talking."

"Yes, it is the same thing."

The child tugged at the girl's hand.

"I'm tired," he repeated.

The girl did not seem to have heard the child.

"I really must go back," she said at last.

The man made no move. His eyes rested vaguely on the child.

"And you, are you not leaving?" asked the girl.

"No. I will stay here until the Square closes and go then."

"Have you nothing to do this evening?"

"No. Nothing in particular."

"I must go back," said the girl after a moment's hesitation.

The man rose slightly from the bench, and very lightly blushed.

"Could you not, just for once I mean, go back a little later?"

For a space the girl hesitated, and then she pointed at the child:

"I wish I could, but I cannot."

"I only meant that it seems to me that it does you good to talk. Particularly you. That was all I meant."

"Oh, I understood that, but I cannot stay. I am late already."

"Well then, I must say good-bye. You said it was on Saturdays that you went to that Dance Hall?"

"Yes. Every Saturday. If you came there we could have a dance together. If you would like to, I mean."

"Yes, perhaps we could. If you would allow me to invite you?"

"I simply meant for the fun of it."

"That is how I understood you. Well, perhaps we shall meet again. On Saturday perhaps, one never knows."

"Perhaps. Well, good-bye."

"Good-bye."

The girl took two steps and then turned back:

"I wanted to say . . . all I wanted to say was, why don't you go for a walk . . . instead of sitting there waiting for the Square to close?"

"It is kind of you, but I think I would prefer to remain here until it shuts."

"But just a little walk, for no particular reason. Just to look at things."

"No, thank you. I really prefer to remain here. A walk means nothing to me."

"It is going to become colder . . . and if I am so insistent it is only because . . . because perhaps you do not know what Squares are like toward closing time, how sad they can be. . . ."

"I do know. But I would rather stay here."

"Do you always do that? Always wait for Squares to close?"

"No. Generally I am like you: it is a moment I avoid. But today I want to wait for it."

"Perhaps you have your own reasons," said the girl reflectively.

"I am a coward, that is why."

The girl moved back a step towards him.

"Oh, if you say that," she said, "it must be because of me, because of what I said."

"No. It is because somehow this time of day always makes me want to recognize and to speak the truth."

"Please don't say things like that."

"But surely my cowardice was clear in every word I said, ever since we started talking."

"No. It is not the same thing as saying it all at once, in one word. You are wrong."

The man smiled.

"Believe me, it is not such a very serious matter."

"But I cannot understand why the fact that the Square is closing should suddenly make you discover that you are a coward."

"Because I do nothing to avoid . . . despair. On the contrary."

"But in that case what difference could a walk make?"

"To do anything to avoid it would be courageous. To create any diversion, however small."

"I beg of you. Just take a little walk."

"No. It would not be possible. My whole life is like this."

"But try just once! Try."

"No. I don't want to start to change."

"Ah! I see that I have talked far too much."

"On the contrary. It was the great pleasure I had in listening to you that made me understand so well what I am really like: how submerged in cowardice. It is not your fault: I am no worse than I was yesterday, for example, and no better."

"I am afraid I do not understand cowardice very well, but I know that yours suddenly seems to make my courage a little despicable."

"And to me, you see, your courage makes my cowardice appear more dreadful still. That is what it means to talk."

"It is as if, after knowing you, courage became slightly useless, a thing which, finally, one could do without."

"In the end we only do what we can, you with your courage and me with my cowardice, and that is all that matters."

"You are probably right, but why is it that courage seems so unattractive and cowardice so appealing? For it is like that, isn't it?"

"It is all cowardice. If you only knew how facile it was."

The little boy pulled at the girl's hand.

"I'm tired," he said again.

The man raised his eyes and seemed troubled.

"Do you think I am wrong?"

"Completely."

"I am sorry."

"Ah, if only you knew how little it mattered. It is as if someone other than I were involved."

They waited a few moments in silence. The Square was emptying. At the ends of the streets the sky showed pink.

"It is true," the girl said, and her voice was almost the voice of sleep, "that we do what we can, you with your cowardice and I with my courage."

"And yet we manage to earn our livings. We have at least managed that."

"Yes, that is true, we have managed that as well as anyone else."

"And from time to time we even manage to talk."

"Yes, even if it makes us unhappy afterwards."

"Everything, no matter what, makes one unhappy. Sometimes even eating."

"You mean eating after one has been hungry for too long?"

"Yes, just that."

The child started to whimper. The girl looked at him as though for the first time.

"I must go," she said.

She turned again to the child.

"Just for once," she said to it gently, "just for once you must be good."

And she turned again to the man.

"And so I will say good-bye."

"Good-bye. Perhaps we will meet again at that Dance Hall."

"Perhaps. You do not know yet if you will go there?"

The man made an effort to reply.

"Not yet, no."

"How strange that is."

"If you only know what a coward I am."

"But you mustn't let going to the Dance Hall depend on your cowardice. If you go, let it be for fun; for no other reason."

The man made a further effort to reply.

"It is very difficult for me to know yet whether I will go. I cannot, no I cannot know now whether I will or not."

"But you do go dancing from time to time?"

"Yes, without knowing anyone."

It was the girl's turn to smile.

"But just for the fun of it, that is all you must think of. And you will see how well I dance."

"Believe me, if I went it would be for fun."

The girl smiled even more. But it was a smile the man could ill support.

"I thought, if I understood you correctly, that you reproached me for allowing too little place for pleasure in my life?"

"It is true, yes."

"You said I should be less suspicious of it than I am?"

"You know so little about it, if you only knew how little."

"You must excuse me for saying this, but I have the feeling that perhaps you know less about it than you imagine. I was talking of the pleasure of dancing of course."

"Yes, of dancing with you."

The child started whimpering again.

"We are going," the girl said to him, and to the man, "I must say good-bye. Perhaps then we shall meet again this coming Saturday?"

"Perhaps, yes, perhaps. Good-bye."

The girl turned and went off rapidly with the child. The man watched her going, watched her as hard as he could. She did not turn back. And he took this as a sign of encouragement to go to that Dance Hall.

MODERATO CANTABILE

TRANSLATED BY

RICHARD SEAVER

One

"WILL YOU PLEASE READ what's written above the score?" the lady asked.

"Moderato cantabile," said the child.

The lady punctuated his reply by striking the keyboard with a pencil. The child remained motionless, his head turned towards his score.

"And what does moderato cantabile mean?"

"I don't know."

A woman, seated ten feet away, gave a sigh.

"Are you quite sure you don't know what moderato cantabile means?" the lady repeated.

The child did not reply. The lady stifled an exasperated groan, and again struck the keyboard with her pencil. The child remained unblinking. The lady turned.

"Madame Desbaresdes, you have a very stubborn little boy."

Anne Desbaresdes sighed again.

"You don't have to tell me," she said.

The child, motionless, his eyes lowered, was the only one to remember that dusk had just exploded. It made him shiver.

"I told you the last time, I told you the time before that, I've told you a hundred times, are you sure you don't know what it means?"

The child decided not to answer. The lady looked again at the object before her, her rage mounting.

"Here we go again," said Anne Desbaresdes under her breath.

"The trouble is," the lady went on, "the trouble is you don't want to say it."

Anne Desbaresdes also looked again at this child, from head to toe, but in a different way from the lady.

"You're going to say it this minute," the lady shouted.

The child showed no surprise. He still didn't reply. Then the lady struck the keyboard a third time, so hard that the pencil broke. Right next to the child's hands. His hands were round and milky, still scarcely formed. They were clenched and unmoving.

"He's a difficult child," Anne Desbaresdes offered timidly.

The child turned his head towards the voice, quickly towards his mother, to make sure of her existence, then resumed his pose as an object, facing the score. His hands remained clenched.

"I don't care whether he's difficult or not, Madame Desbaresdes," said the lady. "Difficult or not, he has to do as he's told, or suffer the consequences."

In the ensuing silence the sound of the sea came in through the open window. And with it the muffled noise of the town on this spring afternoon.

"For the last time. Are you sure you don't know what it means?"

A motorboat was framed in the open window. The child, facing his score, hardly moved—only his mother noticed it—as the motorboat passed through his blood. The low purr of the motor could be heard throughout the town. There were only a few pleasure craft. The whole sky was tinted pink by the last rays of the sun. Outside, on the docks, other children stopped and looked.

"Are you really sure, for the last time now, are you sure you don't know what it means?"

Again, the motorboat passed by.

The lady was taken aback by such stubbornness. Her anger abated, and she so despaired at being so unimportant to this child who, by a single gesture, she could have made to answer her, that she was suddenly aware of the sterility of her own existence.

"What a profession, what a profession," she lamented.

Anne Desbaresdes made no comment, but tilted her head slightly as if, perhaps, agreeing.

The motorboat had finally passed from the frame of the open window. The sound of the sea arose, boundless, in the child's silence.

"Moderato?"

The child opened his fist, moved it, and lightly scratched his calf. His gesture was unconstrained, and perhaps the lady admitted its innocence.

"I don't know," he said, after he had finished scratching himself.

The color of the sunset suddenly became so magnificent that it changed the gold of the child's hair.

"It's easy," the woman said a bit more calmly.

She blew her nose.

"What a child," Anne Desbaresdes said happily, "really, what a child! How in the world did I happen to have such an obstinate . . ."

The lady decided that such pride deserved no comment.

"It means," she said to the child, as though admitting defeat, "for the hundredth time, it means moderately and melodiously."

"Moderately and melodiously," the child said mechanically.

The lady turned around.

"Really. I mean *really*."

"Yes, it's terrible," Anne Desbaresdes said, laughing, "stubborn as a goat. It's terrible."

"Begin again," the lady said.

The child did not begin again.

"I said begin again."

The child still did not move. The sound of the sea again filled the silence of his stubbornness. The pink sky exploded in a final burst of color.

"I don't want to learn how to play the piano," the child said.

In the street downstairs a woman screamed, a long, drawn-out scream so shrill it overwhelmed the sound of the sea. Then it stopped abruptly.

"What was that?" the child shouted.

"Something happened," the lady said.

The sound of the sea moved in again. The pink sky began to fade.

"No," said Anne Desbaresdes, "it's nothing."

She got up and went to the piano.

"You're so nervous," the lady said, looking at both of them with a disapproving air.

Anne Desbaresdes took her child by the shoulders, shook him, and almost shouted:

"You've got to learn the piano, you've got to."

The child was also trembling, for the same reason, because he was afraid.

"I don't like the piano," he murmured.

Scattered shouts followed the first, confirming an already established fact, henceforth reassuring. So the lesson went on.

"You've got to," Anne Desbaresdes insisted.

The lady shook her dead, disapproving such tenderness. Dusk began to sweep over the sea. And the sky slowly darkened, except for the red in the west, till that faded as well.

"Why?" the child asked.

"Because music, my love . . ."

The child took his time, trying to understand, did not understand, but admitted it.

"All right. But who screamed?"

"I'm waiting," said the lady.

He began to play. The music rose above the murmur of a crowd that was beginning to gather on the dock beneath the window.

"There now, there you are," Anne Desbaresdes said happily, "you see."

"When he wants to," the lady said.

The child finished the sonatina. The noise from the street grew more insistent, invading the room.

"What's going on?" the child asked again.

"Play it again," the lady replied. "And don't forget: moderato cantabile. Think of a lullaby."

"I never sing him songs," Anne Desbaresdes said. "Tonight he's going to ask me for one, and he'll ask me so sweetly I won't be able to refuse."

The lady didn't want to listen. The child began to play Diabelli's sonatina again.

"B flat," the lady said sharply, "you always forget."

The growing clamor of voices of both sexes rose from the dock. Everyone seemed to be saying the same thing, but it was impossible to distinguish the words. The sonatina went innocently along, but this time, in the middle of it, the lady could take no more.

"Stop."

The child stopped. The lady turned to Anne Desbaresdes.

"I'm sure something serious has happened."

They all went to the window. To their left, some twenty yards from the building, a crowd had already gathered on the dock in front of the café door. From the neighboring streets people were running up to join the crowd. Everyone was looking into the café.

"I'm afraid this part of town . . ." the lady said.

She turned and took the boy's arm. "Start again, one last time, where you left off."

"What's happened?"

"Your sonatina."

The child played. He played it at the same tempo as before, and as the

66

end of the lesson approached he gave it the nuances she wanted, moderato cantabile.

"It upsets me when he does as he's told like that," Anne Desbaresdes said. "I guess I don't know what I want. It's a cross I have to bear."

The child went on playing well.

"What a way to bring him up, Madame Desbaresdes," the lady said almost happily.

Then the child stopped.

"Why are you stopping?"

"I thought . . ."

He began playing the sonatina again. The noise of the crowd grew increasingly loud, becoming so powerful, even at that height, that it drowned out the music.

"Don't forget that B flat in the key," the lady said, "otherwise it would be perfect."

Once again the music crescendoed to its final chord. And the hour was up. The lady announced that the lesson was finished for today.

"You'll have plenty of trouble with that one, I don't mind telling you," she said.

"I already do. He worries me to death."

Anne Desbaresdes bowed her head, her eyes closed in the painful smile of endless childbirth. Below, a welter of shouts and orders proved the consummation of an unknown incident.

"Tomorrow we'll know it perfectly," the lady said.

The child ran to the window.

"Some cars are coming," he said.

The crowd blocked both sides of the café entrance, and was still growing, but the influx from the neighboring streets had lessened. Still, it was much larger than one might have suspected. The people moved aside and made a path for a black van to get through. Three men got out and went into the café.

"Police," someone said.

Anne Desbaresdes asked what had happened.

"Someone's been killed. A woman."

She left her child in front of Mademoiselle Giraud's door, joined the body of the crowd, and made her way forward till she reached the front row of silent people looking through the open windows. At the far end of the café, in the semi-darkness of the back room, a woman was lying motionless on the floor. A man was crouched over her, clutching her shoulders, and saying quietly:

"Darling. My darling."

He turned and looked at the crowd; they saw his eyes, which were expressionless, except for the stricken, indelible, inward look of his desire. The patronne stood calmly near the van and waited.

"I tried to call you three times."

"Poor woman," someone said.

"Why?" Anne Desbaresdes asked.

"No one knows."

In his dilirium the man threw himself on the inert body. An inspector took him by the arm and pulled him up. He did not resist. It seemed that all dignity had left him forever. He looked absently at the inspector. The inspector let go of him, took a notebook and pencil from his pocket, asked for the man's identity, and waited.

"It's no use. I won't say anything now," the man said.

The inspector didn't press the matter, and went over to join his colleagues who were questioning the patronne at the last table in the back room.

The man sat down beside the dead woman, stroked her hair and smiled at her. A young man with a camera around his neck dashed up to the café door and took a picture of the man sitting there smiling. By the glare of the flashbulb the crowd could see that the woman was still young, and that blood was coming from her mouth in thin trickles, and that there was blood on the man's face where he had kissed her. In the crowd, someone said:

"It's horrible," and turned away.

The man lay down again beside his wife's body, but only for a moment. Then, as if he were tired, he got up again.

"Don't let him get away," the patronne shouted.

But the man had only got up in order to find a better position, closer to the body. He lay there, seemingly resolute and calm, holding her tightly in his arms, his face pressed to hers, in the blood flowing from her mouth.

But the inspectors had finished taking the patronne's testimony and slowly, in single file, walked over to him, an identical air of utter boredom on their faces.

The child, sitting obediently on Mademoiselle Giraud's front steps, had almost forgotten. He was humming the Diabelli sonatina.

"It was nothing," Anne Desbaresdes said. "Now we must go home."
The child followed her. More policemen arrived—too late, for no reason. As they passed the café the man came out, flanked by the inspectors. The crowd parted silently to let him through.

"He's not the one who screamed," the child said. "He didn't scream."

"No, it wasn't he. Don't look."

"Why did she . . . ?"

"I don't know."

The man walked meekly to the van. Then, when he reached it, he shook off the inspectors, and, without a word, ran quickly back towards the café. But just as he got there the lights went out. He stopped dead, again followed the inspectors to the van, and got inside. Then, perhaps, he was crying, but it was already too dark to see anything but his trembling, blood-stained face. If he was crying, it was too dark to see his tears.

"Really," Anne Desbaresdes said as they reached the Boulevard de la Mer, "you might remember it once and for all. Moderato means moderately slow, and cantabile means melodiously. It's easy."

Two

IT WAS THE FOLLOWING day. At the other end of town the factory chimneys were still smoking, and it was already later than when they went to the port every Friday.

"Come along," Anne Desbaresdes said to her child.

They walked along the Boulevard de la Mer. Some people were already out for a stroll. There were even a few in swimming.

The child was used to taking a daily walk through town with his mother, so that she could take him anywhere. But once they had passed the first breakwater and reached the place where the tugboats were moored just below Mademoiselle Giraud's house, he became frightened.

"Why did we come here?"

"Why not?" said Anne Desbaresdes. "Today we're only going for a walk. Come along. Here or somewhere else."

The child gave in, and followed her blindly.

She went straight to the bar. A man was there alone, reading a newspaper.

"A glass of wine," she ordered.

Her voice trembled. The patronne looked surprised, then composed herself.

"And for the child?"

"Nothing."

"This is where the scream came from, I remember," the child said.

He went over to the sun in the doorway, took a step down, and disappeared onto the sidewalk.

"A nice day," the patronne said.

She saw that the woman was trembling, and she avoided looking at her.

"I was thirsty," Anne Desbaresdes said.

"The first warm days, that's the reason."

"In fact, I think I'll have another glass of wine."

From the persistent trembling of the hands gripping the glass, the patronne realized that it would take a while to get the explanation she wanted, but that, once the emotion had passed, it would come of its own accord.

It came faster than she had expected. Anne Desbaresdes drank the second glass of wine without pausing.

"I was just passing," she said.

"It's nice weather for a walk," the patronne said.

The man had stopped reading his paper.

"At this time yesterday I was at Mademoiselle Giraud's."

Her hands were steadier, and the expression on her face was almost normal.

"I recognize you."

"There was a murder," the man said.

Anne Desbaresdes told a lie.

"I see . . . I was just wondering."

"That's natural enough."

"Of course," said the patronne. "I had a regular procession of people in here this morning."

The child outside was hopping on one foot.

"Mademoiselle Giraud is teaching my little boy to play the piano."

The wine must have helped, for her voice had also become more steady. A smile of deliverance slowly appeared in her eyes.

"He looks like you," said the patronne.

"That's what they say." The smile broadened.

"The eyes."

"I don't know," said Anne Desbaresdes. "You see . . . since I was taking him for a walk, I thought I might as well come here today. So . . ."

"Yes, a murder."

Anne Desbaresdes lied again.

"Ah . . . I didn't know."

A tugboat eased away from the dock, and got underway with a hot, even clatter of its engines. The child stood still on the sidewalk while the tugboat was maneuvering, then turned to his mother.

"Where's it going?"

She said she didn't know. The child left again. She picked up the empty glass in front of her, realized her mistake, set it down on the counter, and waited, her eyes lowered. Then the man came over.

"May I?"

She was not surprised, which upset her all the more.

"It's just that I'm not used to drinking, Monsieur."

He ordered some wine, and took another step towards her.

"The scream was so loud it's really only natural for people to try and find out what happened. I would have found it difficult not to, you know."

She drank her wine, the third glass.

"All I know is that he shot her through the heart."

Two customers came in. They recognized this woman at the bar and were surprised.

"And I don't suppose you can tell me why?"

It was obvious that she was not used to drinking wine, and that at this hour of the day she was generally doing something quite different.

"I wish I could, but I'm not really sure of anything."

"Perhaps no one knows?"

"He knew. He's gone out of his mind, been locked up since yesterday evening. As for her, she's dead."

The child ran in from outside and snuggled against his mother with a movement of happy abandon. She stroked his hair absent-mindedly. The man watched her more closely.

"They loved each other," he said.

She started, almost imperceptibly.

"Well, now do you know what the scream was about?" asked the child.

She did not answer, but shook her head no. The child moved again towards the door, her eyes following him.

"He worked at the dockyard. I don't know about her."

She turned towards him, moved closer.

"Perhaps they had problems, what they call emotional problems."

The customers left. The patronne, who had overheard, came to the corner of the bar.

"And she was married," she said, "three children, and she drank. It makes you wonder."

"But maybe it was like I said?" suggested Anne Desbaresdes, after a pause.

72

The man did not acquiesce. She was embarrassed. And then her hands began to shake again.

"I really don't know . . ." she said.

"No," the patronne said, "take it from me, and generally I'm not one to meddle in other people's affairs."

Three new customers came in. The patronne moved away.

"Still, I think it might have been what you said," the man smiled. "Yes, they must have had emotional problems. Maybe that's why he killed her. Who knows?"

"Yes. Who knows?"

Mechanically the hand reached for the glass. He made a sign to the patronne for some more wine. Anne Desbaresdes did not protest; on the contrary, she seemed to expect it.

"From the way he acted with her," she said softly, "as if it didn't matter to him any more whether she was alive or dead, do you think that it's possible for anyone to reach such a . . . state . . . except . . . through despair?"

The man hesitated, looked directly at her, and said sharply:

"I don't know."

He handed her her glass; she took it and drank. Then he brought her back to topics that were doubtless more familiar.

"You often go for walks through town?"

She drank a little wine, a smile came back to her face like a mask, more pronounced than before. She was becoming slightly drunk.

"Yes, I take my child for a walk every day."

He glanced at the patronne, who was talking to the three customers. It was Saturday. People had plenty of time to kill.

"But in this town, small as it is, something happens every day, as you well know."

"I know, but no doubt on some days . . . something happens to shock you," she stammered. "Usually I go to the parks or the beach."

And all the time, because of her growing intoxication, she brought herself to look more directly at the man in front of her.

"You've been taking him on these walks for a long time?"

The eyes of this man, who was talking to her and watching her at the same time.

"I mean you've been going to the parks and the beach for a long time," he went on.

She felt uncomfortable. Her smile vanished into a pout, which left her face brutally exposed.

"I shouldn't have drunk so much wine."

A siren wailed, announcing the end of work for the Saturday shift. Immediately afterwards the radio started to blare unbearably.

"Already six o'clock," the patronne said.

She turned the radio down, and busied herself setting up lines of glasses on the counter. Anne Desbaresdes remained looking dumbly at the docks for a minute, as if she were unable to decide what to do with herself. Then, as the distant noise of approaching men was heard from the port, the man spoke to her again.

"I was saying that you've been taking your child for walks to the beach or the parks for a long time now."

"I've thought about it over and over again since yesterday evening," said Anne Desbaresdes, "ever since my child's piano lesson. I couldn't help coming here today, you know."

The first men came in. The child, his curiosity aroused, made his way through them, and went up to his mother, who pulled him against her with a mechanical movement of protection.

"You are Madame Desbaresdes. The wife of the manager of Import Export et des Fonderies de la Côte. You live on the Boulevard de la Mer."

Another siren sounded, more faintly than the first, at the other end of the docks. A tugboat arrived. The child pulled himself brusquely away and ran off.

"He's learning to play the piano," she said. "He's talented enough, but he doesn't apply himself, I must admit."

In order to make room for the men who kept coming into the café in large numbers, he moved closer and closer to her. The first customer left. Others were still arriving. Between them, as they came and went, one could see the sun setting on the sea, the flaming sky, and the child who, on the other side of the dock, was playing all alone those games whose secret could not be discerned at that distance. He was jumping over imaginary hurdles and seemed to be singing.

"I want so many things for the child all at once that I don't know how to go about it, where to start. And I make a mess of it. I must be getting back because it's late."

"I've often seen you. I never imagined that one day you would come here with your child."

74

The patronne turned the radio up a little for the late-comers who had just come in. Anne Desbaresdes turned towards the bar, made a wry face, accepted the noise, forgot it.

"If you only knew how much happiness you really want for them, as if it were possible. Perhaps it would be better if we were separated from each other once in a while. I can't seem to understand this child."

"You have a beautiful house at the end of the Boulevard de la Mer. A big walled garden."

She looked at him quizzically, then came back to reality.

"But I get a lot of pleasure from these piano lessons," she said.

The child, trailed by twilight, came back towards them. He stayed there looking at the people, the customers. The man made a sign to Anne Desbaresdes to look outside. He smiled at her.

"Look," he said, "the days are getting longer and longer . . ."

Anne Desbaresdes looked, adjusted her coat, carefully, slowly.

"Do you work here in town, Monsieur?"

"Yes, in town. If you came back here, I'd try to find out some more and tell you."

She lowered her eyes, remembered, and went pale.

"Blood on her mouth," she said, "and he was kissing her, kissing her." She went on: "Did you really believe what you said?"

"I said nothing."

The sun was now so low in the sky that it shone on the man's face. His body, leaning lightly against the bar, had been bathed in it for some time.

"Since you saw what happened, it wasn't possible to stop it, was it? It was almost inevitable?"

"I said nothing," the man repeated. "But I think he aimed at her heart, just as she asked him to."

Anne Desbaresdes sighed. A soft, almost erotic sigh.

"It's strange, I don't feel like going home," she said.

Suddenly he took his glass, emptied it, made no answer, looked away from her.

"I must have drunk too much," she said. "That must be it."

"Yes, that must be it," the man said.

The café was nearly empty. Not many people were coming in now. The patronne watched them out of the corner of her eye while she washed glasses, intrigued to see them staying so late. The child, back at the door, gazed at the now silent docks. Standing before the man, her

75

back to the port, Anne Desbaresdes said nothing for a long time. He seemed not to notice her presence.

"It would have been impossible for me not to come back," she said finally.

"And I came back too for the same reason as you."

"She's often out for a walk," the patronne said, "with her little boy. Every day in good weather."

"The piano lessons?"

"Once a week, on Fridays. Yesterday. This trouble actually gave her a reason for coming out today."

The man jingled the money in his pocket. He looked at the docks in front of him. The patronne did not press the matter further.

Past the breakwater the Boulevard de la Mer stretched out, perfectly straight to the edge of town.

"Lift your head," Anne Desbaresdes said. "Look at me."

The child, who was used to her ways, obeyed.

"Sometimes I think I must have invented you—that you don't really exist, you know."

The child lifted his head and yawned. His mouth was flooded with the last rays of the setting sun. Every time she looked at this child, Anne Desbaresdes was just as astonished as the first time she had seen him. But this evening her astonishment was greater than ever.

Three

THE CHILD PUSHED THE railing, his little school satchel bouncing up and down on his back, then he stopped at the entrance to the garden. He looked at the grass around him, tiptoed slowly, on the lookout, you never know, for the birds that he would have frightened away ahead of him. Just then a bird flew away. He watched it for a time, till it landed in a tree in the garden next door, then continued on his way till he was beneath a certain window behind a beech tree. He looked up. Every day at this time there was a smile for him at this window. The smile was there.

"Come on," shouted Anne Desbaresdes, "let's go for a walk."

"By the seashore?"

"By the seashore, everywhere. Come on."

Again they walked along the Boulevard de la Mer towards the breakwater. The child was quick to understand, and was not overly surprised.

"It's such a long way," he complained—then he resigned himself, and hummed a tune.

It was still early when they passed the first dock. The southern horizon was darkened by black streaks, ocher clouds spewed skyward by the foundries.

It was early, the café was empty, except for the man at the far end of the bar. As soon as she went in, the patronne got up and came over to Anne Desbaresdes. The man did not move.

"What'll it be?"

"I'd like a glass of wine."

She drank it as soon as it was served. She was trembling more than she had three days ago.

"I suppose you're surprised to see me again."

"Oh, in this business . . ." the patronne said.

She glanced surreptitiously at the man—he had also grown pale—sat down, then shifting her position, turned, and with a quick movement switched on the radio. The child left his mother and went out on the sidewalk.

"As I said, my little boy is taking piano lessons from Mademoiselle Giraud. You probably know her."

"Yes, I know her. For more than a year I've been seeing you go by, once a week, on Friday, right?"

"Yes, Friday. I'd like another glass of wine."

The child had found a friend. They stood motionless at the end of the dock watching the sand being unloaded from a barge. Anne Desbaresdes drank half of her second glass of wine. Her hands were a little steadier.

"He's a child who's always alone," she said, looking towards the end of the dock.

The patronne picked up her red sweater, and didn't answer. Another tugboat, loaded to the gunwales, entered the port. The child shouted something unintelligible. The man came over to Anne Desbaresdes.

"Won't you sit down?" he said.

She followed him without a word. As she knitted, the patronne followed the tugboat's every maneuver. It was obvious that in her opinion things were taking an unfortunate turn.

"Here."

He pointed out a table. She sat down across from him.

"Thank you," she murmured.

The room had a cool, dark air of early summer.

"I came back, you see."

Outside, not far away, a child whistled. She started.

"I'd like you to have another glass of wine," the man said, his eyes on the door.

He ordered the wine. The patronne silently obliged, no doubt already past worrying about the strangeness of their ways. Anne Desbaresdes sat back in her chair, momentarily relaxed. Unafraid.

"It's been three days now," the man said.

She made an effort to sit up, and again drank her wine.

"It's good," she said quietly.

Her hands were steady now. She sat up straighter and leaned slightly forward towards the man, who was looking at her.

"I meant to ask you, you're not working today?"

"No, I need some free time for the moment."

Her smile was timidly hypocritical.

"Time to do nothing?"

"That's right, nothing."

The patronne was stationed at her post behind her cash register. Anne Desbaresdes spoke in an undertone.

"It's difficult for a woman to find an excuse to go into a café, but I told myself that I could surely think of something, like wanting a glass of wine, being thirsty . . ."

"I tried to find out something more. But I couldn't."

Anne Desbaresdes made an effort to remember again.

"It was a long, high-pitched scream, that stopped when it was at its loudest," she said.

"She was dying," the man said. "The scream must have stopped when she could no longer see him."

A customer came in, scarcely noticed them, and leaned on the bar.

"I think I must have screamed something like that once, yes, when I had the child."

"They met by chance in a café, perhaps even here, they both used to come here. And they began to talk to each other about this and that. But I don't know. Was it very painful when you had your child?"

"I screamed . . . You have no idea."

She smiled as she remembered, leaned back in her chair, suddenly completely free of her fear. He moved closer and said dryly:

"Talk to me."

She tried to find something to say.

"I live in the last house on the Boulevard de la Mer, the last one as you leave town. Just before the dunes."

"The magnolia tree in the left-hand corner of the garden is in bloom."

"Yes, there are so many flowers at this time of year that you can dream about them and be ill all the next day because of them. You shut your window, it's unbearable."

"It was in that house that you were married, some ten years ago?"

"Yes. My room is on the second floor, to the left, overlooking the sea. You told me last time that he had killed her because she had asked him to, to please her in fact?"

He waited before answering her, at last able to see the outline of her shoulders.

"If you shut your window at this time of year," he said, "you must be too hot to sleep."

Anne Desbaresdes became more serious than his remark seemed to call for."

"The scent of magnolias is overpowering, you know."

"I know."

He raised his eyes from the line of her shoulders and looked away.

"Isn't there a long hallway on the second floor, a very long hallway into which your and everyone else's room opens, so that you're together and separated at the same time?"

"There's a hallway," Anne Desbaresdes said, "just as you say. But please tell me, how did she come to realize that that was what she wanted from him, how did she know so clearly what she wanted him to do?"

His eyes returned to hers, and he stared at her wearily.

"I imagine that one day," he said, "one morning at dawn she suddenly knew what she wanted him to do. Everything became so clear for her that she told him what she wanted. I don't think there's any explanation for that sort of discovery."

Outside the children were playing quietly. The second tug had reached the dock. In the silence after its motors had stopped, the patronne pointedly rattled some objects under the bar, reminding them that it was getting late.

"You were saying that it's necessary to go through this hallway to get to your room?"

"Yes, through the hallway."

The child ran in and laid his head on his mother's shoulder. She paid no attention to him.

"Oh, I'm having a lot of fun," he said, and raced out again.

"I forgot to tell you how much I wish he were already grown up," Anne Desbaresdes said.

He poured her some wine, handed her her glass, and she immediately drank it.

"You know," he said, "I suspect that he would have done it of his own accord one day, even without her asking. That she wasn't the only one to discover what she wanted from him."

She returned from her daydreams to her insistent, methodical questions.

80

"I'd like you to tell me about the very beginning, how they began to talk to each other. It was in a café, you said . . ."

The two children were running in circles, still playing at the end of the dock.

"We don't have much time," he said. "The factories close in a quarter of an hour. Yes, I'm almost sure it was in a café that they began to talk to each other, although it might have been somewhere else. Maybe they talked about the political situation, or the chances of war, or maybe something totally different from anything we can imagine, about everything and nothing. Perhaps we could drink one more glass of wine before you go back to the Boulevard de la Mer."

The patronne served them, still without a word, perhaps a trifle hastily. They paid no attention to her.

"At the end of this long hallway"—Anne Desbaresdes chose her words carefully—"there's a large bay window overlooking the boulevard. The wind lashes it like a whip. Last year, during a storm, the windows were smashed. It was at night."

She leaned back in her chair and laughed.

"To think that it happened here in this town . . . Really, it's hard to believe."

"Yes, it's a small town. Hardly enough people for the three factories."

The wall at the far end of the room was lighted by the setting sun. In the middle their two shadows were fused in black.

"And so they talked," said Anne Desbaresdes, "they talked for a long time, a very long time, before it happened."

"Yes, I think they must have spent a lot of time together to reach that stage. Talk to me."

"I don't know what else to say," she admitted.

He gave her an encouraging smile.

"What difference does it make?"

She began again, very slowly, with obvious effort and concentration.

"It seems to me that this house we were talking about was built somewhat arbitrarily, if you see what I mean, but nevertheless in such a way that it's convenient for everybody."

"On the ground floor there are rooms where receptions are given every year at the end of May for the people who work in the foundries."

The siren blasted unmercifully. The patronne got up, put her red sweater away, and rinsed the glasses that squeaked under the cold water.

"You were wearing a black dress with a very low neck. You were looking at us pleasantly, indifferently. It was hot."

This did not surprise her, and she cheated.

"It's an exceptionally lovely spring," Anne Desbaresdes said, "everybody's talking about it. You think it was she who first brought it up, who first dared mention it, and that then they talked about it together as they talked about other things?"

"I don't know any more about it than you do. Maybe they only talked about it once, maybe every day. How will we ever know? But somehow they both reached exactly the same stage, three days ago, where they no longer knew what they were doing."

He lifted his hand, let it fall close to hers on the table, and left it there. For the first time she noticed these two hands side by side.

"I've drunk too much wine again," she complained.

"Sometimes there's a light on till late at night in the hallway you mentioned."

"Sometimes I can't fall asleep."

"Why do you also keep the hall light on and not just a light in your room?"

"A habit of mine. I really don't know."

"Nothing happens there, nothing at night."

"Yes, behind one of the doors my child is sleeping."

She brought her arms back towards the table and, as if she were cold, pulled her coat around her shoulders.

"Perhaps I ought to be getting back. See how late it is."

He raised his hand as if asking her to stay. She stayed.

"The first thing in the morning, you go and look out of the big bay window."

"In summer the workers at the dockyards begin passing about six o'clock. In the winter most of them take the bus because of the wind and cold. It only lasts a quarter of an hour."

"At night, no one ever goes by—ever?"

"Yes, sometimes a bicycle, one wonders where it came from. Is it the grief of having killed her, of her being dead, that drove him mad, or something else from his past added to that grief, something no one knows about?"

82

"I suspect there was indeed something else, something we don't know about yet."

She straightened up, slowly, as if she were being raised, and adjusted her coat again. He didn't help her. She still sat facing him, saying nothing. The first men came in, were surprised, gave the patronne a questioning look. The patronne gave a barely perceptible shrug, indicating that she herself didn't much understand what was going on.

"Perhaps you won't come back again."

When he in turn stood up, Anne Desbaresdes must have noticed that he was still young, that the setting sun was reflected in his eyes as clearly as in a child's. She looked past his gaze into his blue eyes.

"I hadn't thought that I might never come back here."

He detained her one last time.

"You often watch those men on their way to the dockyards, especially in summer, and at night, when you have trouble sleeping, they come back to you."

"When I wake up early enough," Anne Desbaresdes admitted, "I watch them. And you're right, sometimes at night the memory of some of them comes back to me."

As they left, some other workers emerged onto the docks. They were probable workers from the Fonderies de la Côte, which was farther from town than the dockyards. It was lighter out than it had been three days before. There were some seagulls in the sky, which was now blue again.

"I had fun playing," the child said.

She let him talk about his games till they had passed the first breakwater, from which the Boulevard de la Mer stretched straight as far as the dunes, where it ended.

The child grew impatient.

"What's the matter?"

As twilight fell the wind began to rise. She was cold.

"I don't know. I'm cold."

The child took his mother's hand, opened it and clasped it implacably, resolutely in his. She was overwhelmed by the gesture, and almost shouted:

"Oh, my love!"

"But you're going again."

"I expect so."

They passed some people on their way home who were carrying folding chairs. The wind lashed them in the face.

"What are you going to buy me?"

"A red motorboat. Would you like that?"

The child weighed the thought in silence, then sighed happily.

"Yes, a big red motorboat. How did you think of it?"

She took him by the shoulders, and held him as he tried to squirm loose to run on ahead.

"You're growing up, oh, you're getting so big, and I think it's wonderful."

Four

AGAIN THE NEXT DAY Anne Desbaresdes took her child to the port. The lovely weather persisted, only a little cooler than the day before. The sky was increasingly clear, overcast only at rare intervals. The whole town was talking about the unseasonably good weather. Some voiced the fear that it would end the next day, it had already lasted so unusually long. Others felt sure that the brisk wind sweeping the town would keep the sky clear, and prevent any clouds from forming for a while yet.

Anne Desbaresdes braved this weather, this wind, and reached the port after having passed the first breakwater and anchorage where the sand barges were moored, where the industrial section of the city began. She stopped again at the bar; the man was already in the room waiting for her, no doubt still bound by the ritual of the first meetings, which she instinctively adhered to. She ordered some wine, still terribly afraid. The patronne, who was behind the bar knitting her red wool, noticed they did not acknowledge each other's presence for a long time after she had come in, a sham that lasted longer than on the previous day. It lasted even after the child had joined his new-found friend outside.

"I'd like another glass of wine," Anne Desbaresdes said.

She was served with obvious disapproval. And yet, when the man got up, went over to her, and took her back into the semi-darkness of the back room, her hands had already stopped shaking, the color had returned to her face.

"I'm not used to going so far away from home," she explained. "But it's not because I'm afraid. I think it's more surprise, or something like it."

"It could be fear. People will get to know about this in town, like they get to know everything," the man added with a smile.

Outside the child shouted happily, because two tugboats were coming in side by side towards the anchorage. Anne Desbaresdes smiled.

"That I drink wine with you," she finished, suddenly exploding into a laugh. "Now why do I keep wanting to laugh today?"

He moved his face close to hers, placed his hands against hers on the table, and stopped laughing when she stopped.

"The moon was almost full last night. You could see your garden very clearly, how well kept it is, smooth as glass. It was late. The light was still on in the hallway on the second floor."

"I told you, sometimes I have trouble sleeping."

He pretended to turn his glass in his hand to make things easier for her, put her at her ease, as he suspected she wanted him to, so she could look at him more closely. She looked at him more closely.

"I'd like a little wine," she said plaintively, as if she were hurt. "I didn't know you could acquire the habit so quickly. I've almost acquired it already."

He ordered the wine. They drank it together avidly, but this time nothing made Anne Desbaresdes drink except her nascent desire to become intoxicated from the wine. She drank, then paused, and in a soft, half-guilty voice began to question the man again.

"I'd like you to tell me now how they came not to speak to each other any more."

The child appeared in the doorway, saw that she was still there, and ran off again.

"I don't know. Perhaps through the long silences that grew up between them at night, then at other times, silences they found more and more difficult to overcome."

The same trouble that had closed Anne Desbarcsdcs' eyes the day before now made her hunch her shoulders forward dejectedly.

"One night they pace back and forth in their rooms, like caged animals, not knowing what's happening to them. They begin to suspect what it is, and are afraid."

"Nothing can satisfy them any longer."

"They're overwhelmed by what is happening, they can't talk about it yet. Perhaps it will take months. Months for them to know."

He paused for a moment before going on. He drank a full glass of wine. While he was drinking the sun was reflected in his eyes with all the exactitude of chance. She saw it.

"In front of a certain window on the first floor," he said, "there's a beech tree, one of the most beautiful trees in the garden."

"That's my room. It's a big room."

His mouth was moist from having drunk and, in the soft light, it too seemed implacably exact.

"They say it's a quiet room, the best room in the house."

"In summer this beech tree hides my view of the sea. One day I asked to have it removed, cut down. I must not have insisted enough."

He glanced above the bar to try to see what time it was.

"In a quarter of an hour work will be over, and very soon after that you'll be going home. We really have very little time. I don't think it matters one way or the other whether the beech tree is there or not. If I were you I'd let it go on growing, let its shadow grow a little every year on the walls of the room that is called—wrongly, I believe—yours."

She leaned way back in her chair, displaying her bust in a movement that was almost vulgar, and turned away from him.

"But sometimes its shadow is like black ink," she said softly.

"I don't think that matters."

He laughed as he handed her a glass of wine.

"That woman had become a drunkard. At night people found her in the bars out beyond the dockyards, stone drunk. There was a lot of bad talk."

Anne Desbaresdes feigned astonishment, but overdid it.

"I suspected something, but nothing as bad as that. Maybe in their case it was necessary?"

"I don't know any more than you do. Talk to me."

"Yes." She dug deep. "Sometimes, on Saturday, one or two drunks also come along the Boulevard de la Mer singing at the top of their voices or making speeches. They go as far as the dunes, to the last lamppost, and come back, still singing. Generally it's late when they come, when everyone else is asleep. I think they're brave to wander around in that section of town, it's so deserted."

"You're lying in bed in that big, quiet room, and you hear them. The room has a disorderly air about it that's not like you. You were lying there, you were."

Anne Desbaresdes stiffened and, as was sometimes her custom, went limp. Her voice deserted her. Her hands began to tremble slightly.

"They're going to extend the boulevard beyond the dunes," she said, "They're talking about doing it sometime soon."

"You were lying in bed. No one knew. In ten minutes it will be quitting time."

"I know it," said Anne Desbaresdes, "and . . . these last years at whatever time it was, I always knew, always . . ."

"Whether you were asleep or awake, dressed or naked, they passed outside the pale of your existence."

Anne Desbaresdes resisted, guilty, and yet she accepted it.

"You shouldn't," she said. "I remember, anything can happen . . ."

"Yes."

She kept staring at his mouth, which was the only thing still lighted by the dying rays of day.

"It would be easy to mistake that garden from a distance, since it's enclosed and overlooks the sea. Last June—in a few days it will be a year ago—you were standing facing him on the steps, ready to receive us, the workers from the foundries. Above your breasts, which were half bare, there was a white magnolia. My name is Chauvin."

She resumed her usual position facing him, leaning on the table. Her face was already unsteady from the wine.

"I knew it. And I also knew that you left the foundries without reason and that you'll soon have to go back, because no other company in town has a job for you."

"Keep talking to me. Soon I won't ask you anything more."

Anne Desbaresdes began mechanically, like a schoolchild reciting a lesson she had never learned.

"When I came to this house the privet hedges were already there. When a storm approached they grated like steel. When you get used to it, it's like . . . like listening to your own heart. I got used to it. What you told me about that woman was a lie, about their finding her dead drunk in the bars by the dockyards."

The siren went off, right on time, deafening the whole town. The patronne checked the time and put her red sweater aside. Chauvin spoke as calmly as if he had not heard.

"Lots of women have already lived in that same house and listened to the hedges at night, in place of their hearts. The hedges have always been there. They all died in their room behind that beech tree which, by the way, you're wrong about: it has stopped growing."

"That's as much a lie as what you told me about their finding that woman dead drunk every night."

"Yes, that's a lie too. But this house is enormous. It covers hundreds of square yards. And it's so old that you can conjecture endlessly about it. It must be frightening."

She was seized by the same emotion, and closed her eyes. The patronne got up, moved around, began rinsing some glasses.

"Hurry up and say something. Make it up."

She made an effort; her voice was almost loud in the café, which was still empty.

"People ought to live in a town where there are no trees trees scream when there's a wind here there's always a wind always except for two days a year in your place don't you see I'd leave this place I wouldn't stay all the birds or almost all are seagulls you find them dead after a storm and when the storm is over the trees stop screaming you hear them screaming on the beach like someone murdered it keeps the children from sleeping no I'll leave."

She paused, her eyes still shut with fear. He looked at her attentively.

"Perhaps we're wrong," he said, "perhaps he wanted to kill her right away, the first time he saw her. Talk to me."

She couldn't. Her hands began to shake again, but for reasons other than fear and the turmoil that any allusion to her existence threw her into. So he talked instead, his voice calm again.

"It's true that it's so rare for the wind to stop in this town that when it does you feel stifled. I've already noticed it."

Anne Desbaresdes wasn't listening.

"Dead," she said, "even after she was dead she was still smiling happily."

The children's shouts and laughter exploded outside, greeting the evening as if it were dawn. From the south other shouts—of grown-ups, of men released from work—rose above the dull humming of the foundries.

"The wind never fails," Anne Desbaresdes went on wearily, "it always comes back and—I don't know whether you've ever noticed it —it varies from day to day. Sometimes it comes all of a sudden, especially at sundown, and sometimes very slowly, but then only when it's terribly hot, and in the wee hours of the morning, at dawn. The privet hedges shout, you know what I mean, that's how I know."

"You know everything about this one garden, which is almost exactly like all the other gardens on the Boulevard de la Mer. In summer, when the privet hedges shout, you close your window to shut them out, and you're naked because of the heat."

"I'd like some wine," Anne Desbaresdes pleaded. "I keep wanting more wine . . ."

He ordered some wine.

"The siren went ten minutes ago," the patronne warned when she served them.

The first man arrived, and drank the same wine at the bar.

"In the left corner of the garden," Anne Desbaresdes went on in a near whisper, "there's an American copper beech to the north. I don't know why, I don't know at all why . . ."

The man at the bar recognized Chauvin, and nodded to him in a slightly embarrassed way. Chauvin didn't see him.

"Tell me more," Chauvin said, "you can tell me anything at all."

The child appeared, out of breath, his hair all mussed. The streets leading to the docks resounded with men's footsteps.

"Mother," the child said.

"In two minutes," Chauvin said, "she's leaving in two minutes."

The man at the bar tried to pat the child's head as he passed, but the boy broke away savagely.

"One day," Anne Desbaresdes said, "I had that child."

A dozen or so workers burst noisily into the café. Some of them recognized Chauvin. Again Chauvin didn't see them.

"Sometimes at night, when the child is sleeping," Anne Desbaresdes went on, "I go downstairs and walk in the garden. I go to the railings and look at the boulevard. It's very peaceful there at night, especially in winter. Sometimes in summer a few couples pass with their arms around each other, that's all. We picked that house because it's quiet, the quietest house in town. I must be going."

Chauvin leaned back in his chair, taking his time.

"You go to the railings, then you go away and walk around the house, then you come back again to the railings. The child is sleeping upstairs. You have never screamed. Never."

She put her suitcoat back on without replying. He helped her. She got up and once again remained standing beside him near the table, staring past the men at the bar. Some of them tried to make a sign of recognition to Chauvin, but to no avail. He was looking at the dock.

Anne Desbaresdes finally shook off her torpor.

"I'll be back," she said.

"Tomorrow."

He accompanied her to the door. Several groups of men arrived, in a

90

hurry. The child was in their wake. He ran to his mother, took her by the hand, and led her resolutely away. She followed him.

He told her that he had a new friend, and wasn't surprised that she didn't answer him. He stopped beside the empty beach—it was later than the day before—to watch the waves, which were rougher than usual that night. Then he started off again.

"Come on."

She let him lead, and started after him.

"You're walking slowly," he whined, "and it's cold."

"I can't go any faster."

She walked as fast as she could. The night, fatigue, and childhood made him cling to her, to his mother, and they walked on together. But since she was too drunk to see very far, she avoided looking towards the end of the boulevard, so as not to be discouraged by such a long distance.

Five

"YOU'LL REMEMBER NOW," Anne Desbaresdes said, "it means moderately and melodiously."

"Moderately and melodiously," the child repeated.

As they climbed the steps, the cranes rose in the sky to the south of town, turning with identical movements but at different speeds.

"I don't want her to scold you, I can't stand it."

"I don't want her to either. Moderately and melodiously."

A giant steam shovel, slobbering wet sand, swung into view through the last window on the floor, its teeth like those of a hungry beast gripping its prey.

"Music is necessary, and you have to learn it. Do you understand?"

"I understand."

Mademoiselle Giraud's apartment was high enough—it was on the sixth floor—so that its windows overlooked a wide expanse of ocean. Aside from the flight of the gulls, there was nothing to distract the child's attention.

"Well, did you learn what happened? A crime of passion. Please sit down, Madame Desbaresdes."

"What was it?" the child asked.

"All right now, quickly, the sonatina," Mademoiselle Giraud said.

The child sat down at the piano. Mademoiselle Giraud sat down beside him, the pencil in her hand. Anne Desbaresdes sat down on the other side of the room, near the window.

"The sonatina. Go ahead, Diabelli's pretty little sonatina. What is the tempo of this pretty little sonatina? Tell me."

The child cringed at the sound of her voice. He seemed to reflect, took his time, and perhaps lied.

"Moderately and melodiously," he said.

Mademoiselle Giraud crossed her arms, looked at him, and sighed.

"He does it deliberately. There's no other explanation."

The child did not bat an eyelash. His two little hands lay clenched on his knees, waiting for his torture to end, smug in the ineluctability of his own act, repeated over and over again.

"You can see the days are getting longer," Anne Desbaresdes said softly.

"They are indeed," said Mademoiselle Giraud.

The sun was noticeably higher in the sky than last week at the same time. And besides, it had been such a lovely day that the sky was covered with a haze, a light haze to be sure, but unusual for that time of year.

"I'm still waiting for your answer."

"Perhaps he didn't hear."

"He heard perfectly well. One thing you'll never understand, Madame Desbaresdes, is that he does it deliberately."

The child turned his head slightly towards the window, and looked obliquely at the watery mark on the wall made by the reflection of the sun on the sea. His mother was the only one who could see his eyes.

"Shame on you, darling," she whispered.

"In four-four time," the child said listlessly, without moving.

That evening his eyes were almost the same color as the sky, except that they sparkled with flecks of gold the color of his hair.

"Some day," his mother said, "some day he'll know it, and he'll say it without hesitating, it's inevitable. Even if he doesn't want to he'll know it."

She laughed gaily, silently.

"You ought to be ashamed, Madame Desbaresdes," said Mademoiselle Giraud.

"So they say."

She unfolded her arms, struck the keyboard with her pencil, just as she had been doing for the thirty years she had been teaching, and shouted:

"Scales. Ten minutes of scales. To teach you a lesson. Begin with C major."

The child turned back to the piano, raised both hands and placed them on the keyboard with triumphant meekness.

A C major scale rose above the sound of the surf.

"Again. Again. That's the only way to teach boys like you."

The child began again at the point he had started the first time, the

93

exact and mysterious point of the keyboard where it was necessary to start. A second, then a third C major scale rose amid Mademoiselle Giraud's anger.

"Again. I said ten minutes."

The child turned and looked at Mademoiselle Giraud, his hands resting quietly on the keyboard.

"Why?"

A look of such ugly rage filled Mademoiselle Giraud's face that the child turned back to the piano and froze in a pose of seemingly academic perfection. But he did not play.

"Really, he's impossible."

"They don't ask to come into this world," Anne Desbaresdes said with another laugh, "and then we force them to take piano lessons. What can you expect?"

Mademoiselle Giraud shrugged her shoulders, and without replying directly to Madame Desbaresdes, without replying to anyone in particular, composed herself and said for her own benefit:

"Strange how children end up by making you lose your temper."

"But one day he'll know his scales too,"—Anne Desbaresdes made an effort to placate her—"he'll know them as well as his tempo, I'm sure of it, he'll even be bored from knowing them so well."

"The way you bring that boy up is absolutely appalling, Madame," Mademoiselle Giraud shouted.

She seized the child's head with one hand and twisted it around, forcing him to look at her. He lowered his eyes.

"You'll play them because I told you to. And impertinent to boot. G major three times, if you please. And C major once more."

The child began playing the C major scale again. He played it a little more carelessly than the preceding times. Then he waited again.

"I said G major now. G major."

He dropped his hands from the keyboard. Stubbornly, he lowered his head. His little dangling feet, still a long way from the pedals, rubbed angrily against each other.

"Perhaps you didn't hear what I said?"

"You heard," his mother said, "I'm sure you heard."

The child was seduced by the tenderness of the voice. Without answering, he again placed his hands on the keyboard at exactly the right spot. One, then two G major scales were encompassed by the mother's love. The siren from the dockyards signalled the end of

94

the working day. The light was fading. The scales were so perfect the lady acknowledged them.

"It's good for the fingers as well as the character," she said.

"You're quite right," his mother said sadly.

But the child balked at playing the third G major scale.

"I said three times. Three."

This time the child withdrew his hands from the keyboard, placed them on his knees, and said:

"No."

The sun began to dip in such a way that suddenly, obliquely, the sea was illuminated. Mademoiselle Giraud grew utterly calm.

"The only thing I can say to you, Madame Desbaresdes, is that I pity you."

The child glanced surreptitiously at his mother, who was so much to be pitied and who was laughing. Then he sat rigidly at his post, his back necessarily to the sea. Twilight was falling, the rising wind crossed the room in little eddies, rustling the stubborn child's hair like grass. In silence his little feet began dancing jerkily under the piano.

"You don't mind playing it once more," his mother said laughingly, "just once more."

The child turned to her, ignoring his teacher.

"I don't like scales."

Mademoiselle Giraud watched both of them, first one then the other, not listening to what they were saying, too discouraged even to be indignant.

"I'm waiting."

The child turned back to the piano, but swung as far away as he could from the lady.

"Darling," his mother said, "just once more."

Her words made him blink. And yet he still hesitated.

"No scales then."

"Yes," she said, "you must play the scales."

He still hesitated; then, just as they were about to give up, he made up his mind and began to play. But Mademoiselle Giraud was too disturbed and frustrated to be placated.

"You know, Madame Desbaresdes, I don't know whether I can go on giving him lessons."

The G major scale was again perfect, perhaps faster than the time before, but only a trifle.

"I admit he's not really trying," his mother said.

When he had finished the scale the child, completely unperturbed by the passage of time, raised himself on the piano stool and tried to see what was going on below on the docks, but it was impossible.

"I'll explain to him that he'll have to apply himself," his mother said with false penitence.

Mademoiselle Giraud looked upset and said pompously:

"You shouldn't explain anything to him. It's not up to him to decide whether or not he's going to take piano lessons, Madame Desbaresdes. That's what is called education."

She struck the piano. The child gave up trying to see out the window.

"And now your sonatina. In four-four time."

The child played it as he had played the scales. He knew it perfectly. And although his heart was not in it, he played it musically, there was no denying.

"There's no getting around it," Mademoiselle Giraud went on above the music, "there are some children you have to be strict with. Or else they'll drive you to distraction."

"I'll try," Anne Desbaresdes said.

She listened to the sonatina. It came from the depths of the ages, borne to her by her son. Often, as she listened to it, she felt she was on the verge of fainting.

"The trouble is, don't you see, he thinks he can decide for himself he doesn't like to study the piano. But I know perfectly well I'm wasting my breath saying that to you, Madame Desbaresdes."

"I'll try."

The sonatina still resounded, borne like a feather by this young barbarian, whether he liked it or not, and showered again on his mother, sentencing her anew to the damnation of her love. The gates of hell banged shut.

"Begin again, and this time play it a little more slowly."

The child did as she said, playing more slowly and subtly. Music flowed from his fingers as if, in spite of himself, it seemed to make up its mind, and artfully crept out into the world once again, overwhelming and engulfing the unknown heart. Down below, on the docks, they listened to it.

"He's been working on it for a month," the patronne said. "It's a pretty piece."

A first group of men was heading towards the café.

96

"Yes, at least a month," she added. "I know it by heart."

Chauvin, at the end of the bar, was still the only customer. He looked at the time, stretched and hummed the sonatina in time to the child's playing. The patronne kept an eye on him as she arranged the glasses under the counter.

"You're young," she said.

She estimated how long it would take the first group of men to reach the café. She spoke quickly, but her words were well-meaning.

"Sometimes, you know, when the weather's good, I seem to remember that she goes the long way around, by the second dock. She doesn't always come this way."

"No," the man laughed.

The group of men passed the door.

"One, two, three, four," Mademoiselle Giraud counted, "that's the way."

Beneath the child's hands the sonatina flowed on, although he was unconscious of it—it built and rebuilt, borne by his indifferent clumsiness to the limits of its power. And as the music built, the light visibly declined. A huge peninsula of flaming clouds rose on the horizon, its frail and fleeting splendor compelling other thoughts. In ten minutes all the color of day would have vanished. For the third time the child finished his task. The sounds of the sea, mingled with the voices of the approaching men, rose to the room.

"By heart," said Mademoiselle Giraud. "Next time I want you to know it by heart, do you understand?"

"All right. By heart."

"I promise you he will," his mother said.

"Because it can't go on like this. He's making fun of me. It's outrageous."

"I promise."

Mademoiselle Giraud reflected, not listening.

"We might try having someone else come with him to his lessons," she said. "We could see if it did any good."

"No," the child shouted.

"I don't think I could bear that," Anne Desbaresdes said.

"And yet I'm afraid that's what it will have to come to," said Mademoiselle Giraud.

When the door was closed, the child stopped on the staircase.

"You saw how awful she was."

"Do you do it deliberately?"

The child gazed at the cluster of cranes, now motionless in the sky. The lights in the suburbs were coming on.

"I don't know," the child said.

"I love you so much."

The child began slowly descending the stairs.

"I don't want to take any more piano lessons."

"I never could learn the scales," Anne Desbaresdes said, "but how else can you learn?"

Six

ANNE DESBARESDES DID NOT go in, but paused at the door of the café. Chauvin came over to her. When he reached her she turned towards the Boulevard da la Mer.

"There are so many people here now," she said softly. "These piano lessons finish so late."

"I heard the lesson," Chauvin said.

The child let go of her hand and fled to the sidewalk, wanting to run, as he ran every Friday evening at that time. Chauvin raised his head towards the dark blue sky, which was still faintly lighted, and moved closer to her. She did not move back.

"It'll soon be summer," he said. "Come on."

"But here you can hardly tell the difference."

"Sometimes you can. If you know how. Like tonight."

The child jumped over the rope barriers, singing the Diabelli sonatina. Anne Desbaresdes followed Chauvin. The café was full. The men dutifully drank their wine as soon as it was served, and hurried home. Others, arriving from more distant factories, replaced them at the bar.

When she entered Anne Desbaresdes lost her nerve and drew back near the door. Chauvin turned and gave her an encouraging smile. She went to the end of the bar, which was fairly secluded, and, like the men, downed her glass of wine quickly. The glass in her hand was still shaking.

"It's been seven days now," Chauvin said.

"Seven nights," Anne said casually. "How wonderful wine is."

They left the bar, and he took her to the back of the room and had her sit down at the place he had picked out for her. The men at the bar still looked at this woman but distantly, and were still surprised. The room was quiet.

"So you heard the lesson? And all those scales she made him play?"

"It was early. I was the only customer. The windows overlooking the docks must have been open. I heard everything, even the scales."

She smiled gratefully at him, and drank some more. Her hands, holding the glass, were almost calm now.

"I had somehow got the idea that he had to learn music, you know. He's been studying for two years."

"Sure, I understand. So, the grand piano, to the left as you go into the room?"

"Yes." Anne Desbaresdes clenched her fists and struggled to maintain her composure. "But he's still so little, such a little child, you have no idea. When I think about it, I wonder whether I'm not wrong."

Chauvin laughed. They were still the only ones seated at the back of the room. There were fewer customers at the bar now.

"Do you know that he knows his scales perfectly?"

Anne Desbaresdes laughed, this time wholeheartedly.

"Yes, he knows them. Even his teacher had to admit that, you see . . . sometimes I get strange ideas . . . They make me laugh to think of them now."

As her laughter began to subside Chauvin spoke to her in a different way.

"You were leaning on this grand piano. Your breasts were naked under your dress, and between them there was that magnolia flower."

Anne Desbaresdes listened to his story with rapt attention.

"Yes."

"When you lean forward this flower brushes against the outline of your breasts. You'd pinned it carelessly, too high up. It's a huge flower, too big for you, you picked it at random. Its petals are too hard, it has already reached full bloom the night before."

"I'm looking outside?"

"Have a little more wine. The child is playing in the garden. Yes, you're looking outside."

Anne Desbaresdes did as she was asked, and drank some more wine, trying to remember, then returned from the depths of her surprise.

"I can't remember having picked that flower. Or having worn it."

"I only glanced at you, but long enough to see the flower too."

She concentrated on holding the glass very tightly, and her voice and gestures seemed slow and wooden.

"I never really knew how much I liked wine."

"Now, talk to me."

"Oh, let me alone," Anne Desbaresdes begged.

"I can't, we probably have so little time."

Twilight was so far advanced that only the café ceiling reflected the last pale light of day. The bar was brightly lighted, the room in shadow. The child came running up, not surprised at how late it was, and announced:

"The other little boy's arrived."

In the moment following his departure, Chauvin's hands moved closer to hers. All four lay flat on the table.

"As I told you, sometimes I have trouble sleeping. I go into his room and stand there looking at him."

"And other times?"

"And other times it's summer, and there are people strolling along the boulevard. Especially on Saturday evening, no doubt because people don't know what to do with themselves in this town."

"No doubt," Chauvin said. "Especially the men. You often watch them from that hallway, or from your garden, or from your room."

Anne Desbaresdes leaned forward and finally said to him:

"Yes, I think I often must have watched them, either from the hallway or from my room, on nights when I didn't know what to do with myself."

Chauvin murmured something to her. Her expression slowly dissolved at the insult, and softened.

"Go on."

"Apart from these walks, the day has a fixed routine. I can't go on."

"There's very little time left. Go on."

"There's the endless round of meals. And the evenings. One day I got the idea of these piano lessons."

They finished their wine. Chauvin ordered another. There were even fewer men at the bar now. Anne Desbaresdes drank again as if she were terribly thirsty.

"It's already seven o'clock," the patronne warned.

They didn't hear her. It was dark out. Four men, obviously there to kill time, came to the back room. The radio was announcing the weather for the following day.

"I was saying that I had the idea of these piano lessons for my darling —at the other end of town—and now I can't do without them. It's seven o'clock, you know."

"You're going to arrive home later than usual, maybe too late, you can't avoid it. You'd better resign yourself to the idea."

"How can you avoid a fixed routine? I could tell you that I'm already late for dinner, counting the time it will take me to walk home. And besides, I forgot that I'm supposed to be home for a party tonight."

"You know that there's no way you can avoid arriving home late. You know that, don't you?"

"Yes, I know it."

He waited. She spoke to him in a quiet, offhand manner.

"I could tell you that I told my child about all those women who lived behind that beech tree, and are dead now, and he wanted to know if he could see them, the darling. See, I've just told you all I can tell you."

"As soon as you'd told him about the women you were sorry you had, and you told him about the vacation he's going to spend this year—a few days from now—at another seashore?"

"I promised him a vacation at the seashore, somewhere where it's hot. In two weeks time. He was terribly upset about the death of those women."

Anne Desbaresdes drank some more wine, and found it strong. She smiled, but her eyes were glassy.

"It's getting late. And you're making yourself later and later," Chauvin said.

"When being late becomes as serious a matter as it is now for me," Anne Desbaresdes said, "I think that a little while longer isn't going to make it any more serious."

There was only one customer left at the bar. The four others in the room were talking intermittently. A couple came in. The patronne served them, and resumed knitting her red sweater, which she had put aside as long as the bar was crowded. She turned down the radio. The tide was running high that night, breaking loudly against the docks, rising above the songs.

"Once he had realized how much she wanted him to do it, I'd like you to tell me why he didn't do it, say, a little later or . . . a little sooner."

"Really, I know very little about it. But I think that he couldn't make up his mind, couldn't decide whether he wanted her alive or dead. He must have decided very late in the game that he preferred her dead. But that's all pure conjecture."

Anne Desbaresdes was lost in thought, her pale face lowered hypocritically.

"She hoped very much that he would do it."

"It seems to me that he must have hoped so just as much as she did. I don't know really."

"As much as she did?"

"Yes. Don't talk any more."

The four men left. The couple was still sitting there in silence. The woman yawned. Chauvin ordered another bottle of wine.

"Would it be impossible if we didn't drink so much?"

"I don't think it would be possible," Anne Desbaresdes murmured. She gulped down her glass of wine. He let her go on killing herself. Night had completely occupied the town. The lampposts along the docks were lighted. The child was still playing. The last trace of pink had faded from the sky.

"Before I leave," Anne Desbaresdes begged, "if you could tell me I'd like to know a little more. Even if you're not very sure of your facts."

Chauvin went on, in a flat, expressionless voice that she had not heard from him before.

"They lived in an isolated house, I think it was by the sea. It was hot. Before they went there they didn't realize how quickly things would evolve, that after a few days he would keep having to throw her out. It wasn't long before he was forced to drive her away, away from him, from the house. Over and over again."

"It wasn't worth the trouble."

"It must have been difficult to keep from having such thoughts, you get into the habit, like you get into the habit of living. But it's only a habit."

"And she left?"

"She left when and how he wanted her to, although she wanted to stay."

Anne Desbaresdes stared at that unknown man without recognizing him, like a trapped animal.

"Please," she begged.

"Then the time came when he sometimes looked at her and no longer saw her as he had seen her before. She ceased to be beautiful or ugly, young or old, similar to anyone else, even to herself. He was afraid. It was the last vacation. Winter came. You're going back by the Boulevard de la Mer. It will be the eighth night."

The child came in and snuggled for a moment against his mother. He was still humming the Diabelli sonatina. She stroked his hair, which

103

was very close to her face. The man avoided looking at them. Then the child left.

"So the house was isolated," Anne Desbaresdes said slowly. "It was hot, you said. When he told her to leave she always obeyed. She slept under the trees, or in the fields, like . . ."

"Yes," Chauvin said.

"When he called her she came back. And when he told her to go, she left. To obey him like that was her way of hoping. And even when she reached the threshold she waited for him to tell her to come in."

"Yes."

In a daze, Anne Desbaresdes brought her face close to Chauvin's, but he moved back out of reach.

"And it was there, in that house, that she learned what you said she was, perhaps even . . ."

"Yes, a bitch," Chauvin interrupted her again.

Now it was her turn to draw back. He filled her glass and offered it to her.

"I was lying," he said.

She arranged her hair, which was completely disheveled, and wearily trying to restrain her compassion, got hold of herself.

"No," she said.

Chauvin's face looked inhumanly harsh under the neon light, but she could not take her eyes off him. Again the child ran in from the sidewalk.

"It's dark out now," he announced.

He looked out the door and yawned, then turned back to her and stood beside her, humming.

"See how late it is. Quckly, tell me the rest."

"Then the time came when he thought he could no longer touch her except to . . ."

Anne Desbaresdes raised her hands to her bare neck in the opening of her summer dress.

"Except to . . . this. Am I right?"

"Yes. That."

Her hands let go and slipped from her neck.

"I'd like you to leave," Chauvin murmured.

Anne Desbaresdes got up from her chair and stood motionless in the middle of the room. Chauvin remained seated, overwhelmed, no longer aware of her. Unable to resist, the patronne put her knitting aside, and

104

openly watched them both, but they were oblivious of her stare. It was the child who came to the door and took his mother's hand.

"Come on, let's go."

The lights were already on along the Boulevard de la Mer. It was much later than usual, an hour later at least. The child sang the sonatina one last time, then grew tired of it. The streets were almost deserted. People were already eating supper. After they had passed the first breakwater, the Boulevard de la Mer stretched endlessly before them. Anne Desbaresdes stopped.

"I'm too tired," she said.

"But I'm hungry," the child whined.

He saw that his mother's eyes were filled with tears. His whimpering ceased.

"Why are you crying?"

"For no reason. Sometimes people just cry."

"Please don't."

"It's all over, darling. I think it's all over."

He forgot and ran on ahead, then retraced his steps, revelling in this unaccustomed freedom after dark.

"At night," he said, "the houses are far away."

Seven

THE SALMON, CHILLED IN its original form, is served on a silver platter that the wealth of three generations has helped to buy. Dressed in black, and with white gloves, a man carries it like a royal child, and offers it to each guest in the silence of the nascent dinner. It is proper not to talk about it.

At the northern end of the garden the scent of magnolias arises, drifting from dune to dune till it disappears. Tonight the wind is from the south. A man prowls along the Boulevard de la Mer. A woman knows he is there.

The salmon passes from guest to guest, following a ritual that nothing can disturb, except everyone's hidden fear that such perfection may suddenly be marred or sullied by some excessively obvious absurdity. Outside, in the garden, the magnolias' funereal flowering continues in the dark night of early spring.

The wind ebbs and flows like the surf, striking the urban obstacles, then moving on, wafting the scent to the man, then whisking it away again.

In the kitchen the women, their honor at stake, sweat to put the finishing touches to the next course, smothering a duck in its orange-shrouded coffin. Meanwhile the pink, succulent, deep-sea salmon, already disfigured by the brief moments just past, continues its ineluctable advance towards total annihilation, slowly dispelling the fear of an unsuccessful evening.

A man, facing a woman, looks at her as though he does not recognize her. Her breasts are again half exposed. She hastily adjusts her dress. A drooping flower lies between them. There are still flashes of lucidity in her wildly protruding eyes, enough for her to succeed in helping herself to some of their salmon when it comes her turn.

In the kitchen, now that the duck is ready and put into the oven to keep warm, they finally find a moment of peace to put their thoughts to words, saying that she is really going a bit too far. Tonight she arrived later than the night before, well after her guests had arrived.

Fifteen people had waited for her in the main living room on the ground floor. She had entered that glittering assembly without so much as the slightest apology. Someone apologized for her.

"Anne is late. Please forgive Anne."

For ten years she has never been the subject of any gossip. If she is bothered by her incongruity, she is unaware of it. A fixed smile makes her face acceptable.

"Anne didn't hear what you said."

She puts her fork down, looks around, tries to grasp the thread of conversation, fails.

"That's true," she says.

They ask again. Her blond hair is mussed, and she runs her fingers listlessly through it, as she had done a little while before in a different setting. Her lips are pale. Tonight she forgot to make herself up.

"I'm sorry," she says, "right now a sonatina by Diabelli."

"A sonatina? Already?"

"That's right."

Silence moves in again around the question, and the fixed smile returns to her face. She is a wild animal.

"He didn't know what moderato cantabile meant?"

"No, he didn't."

Tonight the magnolias will be in full bloom. Except for the one she is wearing, the one she picked tonight on her way home from the port. Time moves monotonously past this forgotten flowering.

"Darling, how could he have guessed?"

"He couldn't."

"He's sleeping, I suppose."

"Yes, he's sleeping."

Slowly the digestion of what was a salmon begins. The osmosis of the species that ate it was carried out like a perfect ritual. Nothing upset the solemnity of the process. The other waits, snug and warm, in its orange shroud. And now the moon rises on the sea, and on the man lying on the ground. Through the white curtains you now could barely distinguish the shapes and forms of night. Madame Desbaresdes contributes nothing to the conversation.

"Mademoiselle Giraud told me that story yesterday. She gives my little boy lessons also, you know."

"Is that so?"

People laugh. A woman somewhere around the table. Little by little the chorus of conversation grows louder and, with considerable effort and ingenuity, some sort of society emerges. Landmarks are discovered, cracks open, allowing familiarities to slip in. And little by little a generally biased and individually noncommittal conversation builds up. It will be a successful party. The women bask in their own brilliance. The men have covered them with jewels according to their bankrolls. Tonight one of them suspects he may have made a mistake.

In the sequestered garden the birds sleep peacefully, for the weather is still fine. The same sort of sleep as the child's. The remains of the salmon are offered around again. The women will devour it to the last mouthful. Their bare shoulders have the gloss and solidity of a society founded and built on the certainty of its rights, and they were chosen to fit this society. Their strict education has taught them that they must temper their excesses in the interest of their position. They stuff themselves with mayonnaise, specially prepared for this dish, forget themselves, and lap it up. The men look at them and remember that therein lies their happiness.

Tonight one of them does not share the others' appetite. She comes from the other end of town, from beyond the breakwaters and oil depots at the other end of the Boulevard de la Mer, from beyond the limits imposed upon her ten years before, where a man had offered her more wine than she could handle. Full of this wine, an exception to the general rule, she could not bring herself to eat. Beyond the white blinds lay darkness, and in this darkness a man, with plenty of time to kill, stands looking now at the sea, now at the garden. Then at the sea, at the garden, at his hands. He doesn't eat. He cannot eat either, his body obsessed by another hunger. The capricious wind still bears the scent of magnolias to him, taking him by surprise, tormenting him as much as the scent of a single flower. A light in the second story was turned out a little while ago, and was not turned back on. They must have closed the windows on that side of the house, to shut out the oppressive odor of the flowers at night.

Anne Desbaresdes keeps on drinking. Tonight the champagne has the annihilating taste of the unknown lips of the man outside in the street.

The man has left the Boulevard de la Mer and circled the garden, keeping watch from the dunes which bound it on the north, then he has retraced his steps and descended the slope to the beach. And there he lay down again in the same place. He stretches, stares for a moment out to sea, then turns and looks again at the bay windows with their white blinds. Then he gets up, picks up a pebble, aims at the windows, turns back again, tosses the pebble into the sea, lies down, stretches again, and says a name out loud.

Two women, alternately and cooperatively, prepare the second course. The other victim is waiting.

"As you know, Anne is defenseless when it comes to her child."

Her smile broadens. The remark is repeated. Again she runs her fingers through the blond disorder of her hair. The circles under her eyes are deeper than before. Tonight she cried. By now the moon has risen above the town, and above the man lying on the beach.

"That's true," she says.

Her hand falls from her hair, and pauses at the wilting magnolia at her breast.

"We're all alike really."

"Yes," Anne Desbaresdes says.

The petals of the magnolia are smooth. Her fingers crumple it, pierce the petals, then stop, paralyzed, lie on the table, wait, affecting an attitude of nonchalance, but in vain. For someone has noticed it. Anne Desbaresdes tries to smile apologetically, as if to imply that she couldn't help it, but she is drunk, and her expression shamelessly betrays it. He scowls, but remains impassive. He has already recovered from his surprise. He has always expected as much.

With half-closed eyes, Anne Desbaresdes drinks another glass of wine in one swallow. She has reached the point where she can't help it. She derives from drink a confirmation of what was till then her hidden desire, and a base consolation for that discovery.

Other women drink in turn, raising their bare arms, their enticing, irreproachable, matronly arms. The man on the beach is whistling a tune heard that afternoon in a café at the port.

The moon has risen, and as the night advances it begins to grow cold. Perhaps the man is cold.

They begin to serve the pressed duck. The women help themselves generously, fully capable of doing justice to the delicacy. They murmur softly in admiration as the golden duck is passed around. The sight of it makes one of them grow faint. Her mouth is desiccated by another hunger that nothing, except perhaps the wine, can satisfy. A song she cannot sing comes back to her, a song heard that afternoon in a café at the port. The man is still alone on the beach.

He has just spoken the name again, and his mouth is still half open.

"No thank you."

The man's closed eyes are caressed by the wind, and, in powerful, impalpable waves, by the scent of the magnolias, as the wind ebbs and flows.

Anne Desbaresdes has just declined to take any of the duck. And yet the platter is still there before her, only for a brief moment, but long enough for everyone to notice. She raises her hand, as she has been taught to do, to emphasize her refusal. The platter is removed. Silence settles around the table.

"I just couldn't. I'm sorry."

Again she raises her hand to her breast, to the dying flower whose scent slips beyond the garden and drifts to the sea.

"Perhaps it's that flower," someone suggests, "the scent is so strong."

"No, I'm used to it. It's nothing really."

The duck continues on its course. Someone opposite her looks on impassively. And again she tries to force a smile, but succeeds only in twisting her face into a desperate, licentious grimace of confession. Anne Desbaresdes is drunk.

Again she is asked if she is not ill. She is not ill.

"Perhaps that flower," the voice insists, "is making you nauseous without your knowing it."

"No, I'm used to the scent of magnolias. I just don't happen to be hungry."

They leave her alone, and begin to devour the duck. Its flesh will be digested in other bodies. A man in the street closes his eyes, his eyelids fluttering from such willful patience. His body is chilled to the bone, and nothing can warm him. Again his mouth has uttered a name.

In the kitchen they announce that she has refused the pressed duck, that she is ill, there is no other explanation for it. Here they are talking of other things. The meaningless shapes of the magnolias caress the eyes of the solitary man. Once again Anne Desbaresdes takes her glass, which has just been refilled, and drinks. Unlike the others, its warmth fires her witch's loins. Her breasts, heavy on either side of the heavy flower, suffer from its sudden collapse, and hurt her. Her mouth, filled with wine, encompasses a name she does not speak. All this is accomplished in painful silence.

The man has left the beach and approached the garden railings. He seizes them and grips them tightly. The lights are still on in the bay windows. How come it has not yet happened?

The pressed duck is passed around again. With the same gesture as before Anne Desbaresdes implores him not to serve her. She is passed by. She returns to the silent agony of her loins, to their burning pain, to her lair.

The man has let go of the garden railings. He looks at his empty hands, distorted by the strain. There, at arm's length, a destiny was decided.

The sea wind blows cooler through the town. Most people are already asleep. The second story windows are dark and closed, to keep the scent of the magnolias from disturbing the child's sleep. Red motorboats sail through his innocent dreams.

Some of the guests have taken a second helping of duck. The conversation flows more and more easily, increasing the distance of the night with every passing minute.

Bathed in the brilliant light of the chandeliers, Anne Desbaresdes continues to smile and say nothing.

The man has decided to leave the garden and walk to the edge of town. As he goes, the scent of the magnolias grows fainter, giving way to the smell of the sea.

Anne Desbaresdes will accept a little coffee ice cream, for the sake of appearances.

In spite of himself the man will retrace his steps. Again he sees the magnolias, the railings, the bay windows in the distance, still lighted, still lighted. On his lips, the song heard that afternoon, and the name that he will utter a little louder this time. He will come.

She knows it. The magnolia at her breast is completely wilted. In one hour it has lived through a whole summer. Sooner or later the man will pass by the garden. He has come. She keeps torturing the flower at her breast.

"Anne didn't hear what you said."

She tries to smile more broadly, but it is useless. The words are repeated. One last time she runs her fingers through her blond hair. The circles under her eyes are even darker than before. Tonight she cried. They repeat the words for her benefit alone, and wait.

"Yes," she says, "we're going on vacation. We're taking a house by the sea. It will be hot there. In a house off by itself at the seashore."

"Darling," someone says.

"Yes."

While the guests pass from the dining room into the main living room, Anne Desbaresdes will go upstairs. From the big bay window of the long corridor of her life she will look at the boulevard below. The man will already have left. She will go into the child's room, and lie down on the floor at the foot of the bed, paying no attention to the magnolia crushed to pieces between her breasts. And to the inviolable rhythm of her child's breathing she will vomit forth the strange nourishment that had been forced upon her.

A shadow will appear in the doorway leading into the hall, deepening the shadow of the room. Anne Desbaresdes will run her hand through her disheveled hair. This time she will offer an apology.

The shadow will not reply.

Eight

THE GOOD WEATHER CONTINUED. It had lasted longer than anyone had dared hope. People talked about it now with a smile, as of a completely unseasonal phenomenon whose very persistence concealed some irregularity that would soon be discovered, thus reassuring everyone that the seasons were indeed following their normal course.

Today, even compared to the previous days, the weather was so lovely, at least for that time of year, that when the sky was not too overcast, when the sun shone through for a while, it would have been easy to believe that the weather was better, more precocious, more summery, than ever. In fact it took so long for the clouds to cover the sun that today was almost more beautiful than the preceding days had been. Even the seawind was balmy, much like the wind of certain summer days still far away.

Some people declared that the day had been hot. Others—and they were the majority—did not deny it had been a beautiful day, but claimed that it had nevertheless not been hot. Still others had no opinion.

Anne Desbaresdes did not return to the port till the second day following her previous visit. She arrived only slightly later than usual. As soon as Chauvin saw her—she was still a good distance away, beyond the breakwater—he went back into the café to wait for her. The child was not with her.

Anne Desbaresdes entered the café during one of those moments when the sun was out from behind the clouds for a long time. The patronne, seated in the shadow behind the counter, did not lift her eyes from her knitting when she came in. The knitting was progressing nicely. Anne Desbaresdes joined Chauvin at their usual table in the back of the room. Chauvin had not shaved that morning, but only the day

113

before. Anne Desbaresdes' face was not as carefully made up as usual. Neither of them seemed to notice it.

"You're alone," Chauvin said.

It took her a long time to acknowledge that obvious fact. She tried to evade it, and was again surprised to find she could not.

"Yes."

To escape the stifling simplicity of this confession she turned towards the café door, towards the sea. To the south the foundries were humming. There, in the port, the sand and coal were being unloaded as usual.

"It's a nice day," she said.

Chauvin followed her gaze and looked outside, squinting at the weather, at what kind of weather it was out today.

"I wouldn't have believed it could happen so quickly."

In the ensuing silence the patronne turned around and switched on the radio, with no show of impatience, rather almost tenderly. In a foreign town, a woman sang. It was Anne Desbaresdes who moved closer to Chauvin.

"Starting this week someone else is taking my child to Mademoiselle Giraud for his lesson. I finally agreed that someone else should take him."

She sipped her wine, till she had emptied her glass. Chauvin forgot to order more.

"That's no doubt a better arrangement."

A customer came in, obviously to kill time, obviously lonely, very lonely, and also ordered some wine. The patronne served him, then went over and served the others in the room, without waiting to be asked. They said nothing to her, but immediately began to drink the wine. Anne Desbaresdes' words came out in a rush.

"I threw up the wine I drank last time," she said. "It was only a few days ago I started drinking . . ."

"It doesn't matter now."

"Please . . ." she begged.

"I suppose we'd really better decide whether to talk or say nothing. Whichever you like."

She looked around the café, then at him, then around again, then at him, looking for help that was not forthcoming.

"I've been sick before, but never from drinking. For very different reasons. I was never used to drinking so much wine at once. I mean in

114

such a short time. It made me sick. I couldn't stop. I thought I would never be able to stop. But then all of a sudden I had to stop, however hard I tried not to. It wasn't any longer a question of wanting or not wanting to."

Chauvin put his elbow on the table and held his head in his hands. "I'm tired."

Anne Desbaresdes filled her glass and passed it to him. He didn't refuse.

"I can keep quiet," she said apologetically.

"No."

He laid his hand beside hers on the table, in the shadow cast by his body.

"The garden gate was locked as usual. The weather was lovely, almost no wind. The bay windows on the ground floor were lighted."

The patronne put her red sweater aside, rinsed some glasses, and, for the first time, did not seem concerned about whether they would stay on for a while or not. It was close to quitting time.

"We don't have much time left," Chauvin said.

The sun began to set. He watched it draw slow, fawn-colored patterns on the back wall.

"My child," Anne Desbaresdes said, "I didn't have time to tell you . . ."

"I know," Chauvin said.

She withdrew her hand from the table, and kept staring at Chauvin's hand which was still there. It was shaking. Then, in her impatience, she moaned softly—so softly that the sound of the radio covered it, and he alone heard it.

"Sometimes," she said, "I think I must have invented him."

"I know all I want to about your child," Chauvin said harshly.

Anne Desbaresdes moaned again, louder than before. Again she put her hand on the table. His eyes followed her movement and finally, painfully, he understood and lifted his own leaden hand and placed it on hers. Their hands were so cold they were touching only in intention, an illusion, in order for this to be fulfilled, for the sole reason that it should be fulfilled, none other, it was no longer possible. And yet, with their hands frozen in this funereal pose, Anne Desbaresdes stopped moaning.

"One last time," she begged, "tell me about it one last time."

Chauvin hesitated, his eyes somewhere else, still fixed on the back wall. Then he decided to tell her about it as if it were a memory.

"He had never dreamed, before meeting her, that he would one day want anything so badly."

"And she acquiesced completely?"

"Wonderfully."

Anne Desbaresdes looked at Chauvin absently. Her voice became thin, almost childlike.

"I'd like to understand why his desire to have it happen one day was so wonderful?"

Chauvin still avoided looking at her. Her voice was steady, wooden, the voice of a deaf person.

"There's no use trying to understand. It's beyond understanding."

"You mean there are some things like that that can't be gone into?"

"I think so."

Anne Desbaresdes' expression became dull, almost stupid. Her lips had turned pale, they were gray and trembled as though she were on the verge of tears.

"She does nothing to try and stop him?" she whispered.

"No. Have a little more wine."

She sipped her wine. He also drank, and his lips on the glass were also trembling.

"Time," he said.

"Does it take a long time, a very long time?"

"Yes, a very long time. But I don't know anything." He lowered his voice. "Like you, I don't know anything. Nothing at all."

Anne Desbaresdes forced back her tears. Her voice was normal, momentarily awake.

"She will never speak again," she said.

"Of course she will. Suddenly one day, one beautiful morning, she'll meet someone she knows and won't be able to avoid saying good morning. Or she'll hear a child singing, it will be a lovely day and she'll remark how lovely it is. It will begin again."

"No."

"You can think whatever you like about it, it doesn't matter."

The siren went off, a loud wail that quickly spread to the far corners of the town and even beyond, into the suburbs, and to certain neighboring villages, borne by the sea wind. The sunset was a welter of even brighter yellow on the far wall. As often at sunset, the clouds billowed in fat clusters in the still sky, revealing the last fiery rays of the sun. That evening it seemed that the siren would never stop. But it finally did.

"I'm afraid," Anne Desbaresdes murmured.

Chauvin moved closer to the table, searched for her, searching for her, then gave up.

"I can't."

Then she did what he had been unable to do. She moved close enough to him for their lips to meet. They lingered in a long embrace, their lips cold and trembling, so that it should be accomplished, performing the same mortuary ritual as their hands had performed a moment before. It was accomplished.

From the nearby streets a subdued murmur reached them, punctuated by calm, carefree shouts. The dockyards nearby had opened their gates to eight hundred men. The patronne turned on the neon light above the bar, although the place was flooded with sun. After a moment's hesitation she went over to the now silent couple and solicitously served them some wine, although they had not asked for it. Then she remained there after she had served them, close to their table, hunting for something to say, but she found nothing and moved away.

"I'm afraid," Anne Desbaresdes said again.

Chauvin did not reply.

"I'm afraid," Anne Desbaresdes almost shouted.

Still Chauvin did not reply. Anne Desbaresdes doubled over, her forehead almost touching the table, and accepted her fear.

"So we're going to leave things just as they are," Chauvin said. "That happens sometimes," he added.

A group of workers, who had already seen them there before, entered the café. Like the patronne and everyone else in town, they knew what was going on, and avoided looking at them. The café resounded with the chorus of various conversations.

Anne Desbaresdes raised her head, and tried to reach Chauvin across the table.

"Maybe I won't be able to," she murmured.

Perhaps he wasn't listening any longer. She pulled her suitcoat tightly around her, and buttoned it. Again she moaned, and was surprised to hear herself.

"That's impossible," she said.

Chauvin heard that.

"Wait a minute," he said, "and we'll be able to."

Anne Desbaresdes waited a minute, then she tried to stand up. She succeeded in getting to her feet. Chauvin was not looking at her. The men still kept their eyes turned away from this adulteress. She stood there.

"I wish you were dead," Chauvin said.

"I am," Anne Desbaresdes said.

Anne Desbaresdes moved around her chair so as to avoid having to sit down again. Then she took one step back and turned around. Chauvin's hand fluttered and fell to the table. But she was already too far away to see him.

She passed the cluster of men at the bar and found herself again moving forward into the fiery red rays of the dying day.

After she had left, the patronne turned the radio up louder. Some of the men complained that in their opinion it was too loud.

TEN-THIRTY on a SUMMER NIGHT

TRANSLATED BY

ANNE BORCHARDT

"HIS NAME IS PAESTRA. Rodrigo Paestra."

"Rodrigo Paestra."

"Yes. And the man he killed is Perez. Toni Perez."

"Toni Perez."

On the square, two policemen were walking by in the rain.

"When did he kill Perez?"

The customer didn't know exactly, at the beginning of the afternoon that was coming to an end. At the same time that he killed Perez, Rodrigo Paestra had also killed his wife. Both victims had been found two hours earlier, at the back of a garage belonging to Perez.

In the café, it was already getting dark. Candles had been lit on the wet counter in the back, and their yellow light mingled with the blueness of the dying day. The shower stopped suddenly, as it had started.

"How old was she, Rodrigo Paestra's wife?" Maria asked.

"Very young. Nineteen."

There was a look of regret on Maria's face.

"I would like another glass of manzanilla," she said.

The customer ordered it for her. He was also having a manzanilla.

"I wonder why they haven't caught him yet," she went on, "the town is so small."

"He knows the town better than the police. Quite a man, Rodrigo."

The bar was full. Everyone was talking about Rodrigo Paestra's crime. They all agreed about Perez, but about his young wife they didn't. A child. Maria was drinking her manzanilla. The customer looked at her with surprise.

"Do you always drink like that?"

"It depends," she said, "more or less, yes, almost always like that."

"Alone?"

"At the moment, yes."

The café wasn't directly on the street but on a square arcade, divided, split right through by the town's main avenue. This arcade was bordered by a stone balustrade, with a top that was wide and strong enough to hold children who sometimes jumped over it and sometimes lay flat on it while watching the rain come down or the police walk by. Among them was Judith, Maria's daughter. Leaning against the balustrade, she was looking at the square, with only her head showing above it.

It must have been between six and seven in the evening.

Another shower started and the square became empty. A group of palmettos in the middle of the square were bending under the wind, crushing the flowers between them. Judith came back from the arcade and huddled against her mother. But her fear had vanished. The strokes of lightning came so close together that they seemed like one, and the noise in the sky was continuous. It was a noise that sometimes burst like metal fireworks, but which would immediately rise again, its modulation less and less defined as the shower let up. In the arcade there was silence. Judith left her mother and went to take a closer look at the rain, and the square that was dancing in the streaks of rain.

"This will last all night," the customer said.

All of a sudden the shower stopped. The customer left the counter and pointed at the dark blue sky, patched with large spots of dark gray, and so low that it brushed the rooftops.

Maria wanted to go on drinking. He ordered the manzanillas without saying anything. He was also going to have one.

"It's my husband who wanted us to spend our vacation in Spain. I would have preferred somewhere else."

"Where?"

"I haven't thought about it. Everywhere at once. Including Spain. Don't pay attention to what I say. Actually, I'm quite happy to be in Spain this summer."

He picked up her glass of manzanilla and handed it to her. He paid the waiter.

"You got here around five, didn't you?" the customer asked. "Weren't you in the little black Rover that stopped on the square?"

"Yes," Maria answered.

"It was still very light," he went on. "It wasn't raining yet. There were four of you in the black Rover. There was your husband, driving.

Were you next to him? Yes? And in the back there was a little girl"—he pointed at her—"that one. And another woman."

"Yes. We had been running into thunderstorms since three o'clock, out in the country, and my daughter was afraid. That's why we decided to stop here instead of going on to Madrid."

During the conversation, the customer was watching the square, and the police who had come out again with the end of the rain; and, through the noise of the storm, he listened hard to the whistles which rang out from every street corner.

"My friend was also afraid of the storm," Maria added.

The sun set at the end of the main avenue. The hotel was in that direction. It wasn't quite as late as it seemed. The storm had scrambled the hours, pushed them on, but here they were again, reddening the sky.

"Where are they?" the customer asked.

"At the Hotel Principal. I must go and join them."

"I remember. A man, your husband, got half out of the black Rover and asked some young people how many hotels there are in town. And you left in the direction of the Hotel Principal."

"There were no rooms left, naturally. Already, there were none left."

The sunset was covered again. A new phase of the storm was getting ready. The afternoon's dark blue, oceanlike mass moved slowly over the town. It was coming from the east. There was just enough light left to see its threatening color. They must still be at the threshold of the balcony. There, at the end of the avenue. Look, now your eyes are blue, Pierre is saying, this time because of the sky.

"I can't go back yet. Look what's coming."

Judith, this time, wasn't coming back. She was watching children playing barefoot in the gutter around the square. The water that ran between their feet was filled with clay. The water was dark red, like the stones of the town and the earth around it. All the young people were outside, on the square, under the lightning and the constant grumbling of the sky. You could hear songs whistled by some youngsters, so sweet they pierced the thunder.

Another shower. The ocean spilled onto the town. The square disappeared. The arcades filled with people. In the café they had to talk louder to be heard. Some screamed at times. And the names of Rodrigo Paestra and Perez.

"Leave Rodrigo Paestra alone," the customer said.

He pointed at the police who had taken shelter in the arcade and who were waiting for the shower to end.

"He was married six months," the customer went on. "He found her with Perez. Who wouldn't have done the same. He'll be acquitted, Rodrigo."

Maria kept on drinking. She made a face. The time of day had come when liquor turned her stomach.

"Where is he?" she asked.

The customer leaned toward her. She could smell the thick, lemony odor of his hair. His lips were smooth, beautiful.

"On one of the roofs."

They smiled at each other. He moved away. She could still feel the warmth of his voice on her shoulder.

"Drowned?"

"No," he was laughing, "I'm just repeating what I heard. I don't know."

At the back of the café, a very noisy argument about the crime had started, which made the other conversations stop. Rodrigo Paestra's wife had thrown herself into Perez's arms, was it Perez's fault? Can you push away a woman who falls into your arms like that?

"Can you?" asked Maria.

"It's hard. But Rodrigo had forgotten that."

Perez had some friends who were mourning him that night. His mother was there, alone, next to his body in the town hall. And Rodrigo Paestra's wife? Her body was also in the town hall. But she didn't come from here. No one was with her tonight. She came from Madrid, she had come here for the wedding, in the autumn.

The shower was over and with it the nerve-racking noise of the rain.

"Once she was married, she wanted every man in the village. What was there to do? Kill her?"

"What a question," Maria said and she pointed to a spot on the square, a big, closed door.

"That's where it is, that's right," said the customer, "that's the town hall."

A friend came back into the café. Again they talked about the crime.

Once more, with the end of the shower, the square filled with children. It was hard to see the end of the avenue, where the town ends, and the white shape of the Hotel Principal. Maria noticed that Judith was among the children in the square. She inspected the paving carefully and finally stepped into the red, muddy water. The customer's friend offered Maria a manzanilla. She accepted. How long had she been in Spain? Nine days, she said. Did she like Spain? Of course. She knew it from before.

"I have to go back," she said. "With this storm, you don't know where to go."

"My place," said the customer.

He was laughing. She laughed, but not as much as he would have liked.

"One more manzanilla?"

No, she didn't want to drink any more. She called Judith who came in with red boots dyed onto her by the muddy water.

"Will you be back? Tonight?"

She didn't know, it was possible.

They took the sidewalk leading to the hotel. Stable smells and smells of hay were blowing through the town. The night was going to be good, sea-like. Judith was walking in the puddles of red water. Maria let her. They met the police who were guarding every street corner. It was nearly night. There was still no electricity, and there probably wouldn't be any for some time. On the rooftops there was the glimmering of the sunset for those who could see it. Maria took Judith's hand and talked to her. Judith, as usual, was not listening.

They were there, sitting opposite each other, in the dining room. They smiled at Maria and Judith.

"We waited for you," Pierre said.

He looked at Judith. On the road, she too had been very afraid of the storm. She had cried. She still had rings under her eyes.

"The thunderstorm hasn't stopped yet," Pierre said. "It's a shame. We could have been in Madrid tonight."

"It was to be expected," said Maria. "They still have no rooms? No one dared to leave?"

"None. Not even for the children."

"Tomorrow will be much less hot," Claire said, "that's one consolation."

Pierre promised Judith they would stay.

"We shall eat," Claire told her. "And they'll put blankets in the halls for little girls like you."

There wasn't one free table in the dining room.

"And they're all French," Claire said.

In the candlelight her beauty was even more obvious. Had someone told her he loved her? She was there, smiling, ready for a night that wouldn't happen. Her lips, her eyes, her uncombed hair, her hands spread apart, open, loose in anticipation of happiness growing closer, none of this proved that tonight they had set aside for the silent fulfillment of the promise of approaching happiness.

The rain again. It made so much noise on the skylight above the dining room that the guests had to shout their orders. Children were crying. Judith hesitated, did not cry.

"What rain," Claire said—she stretched with impatience—"it's crazy how it's raining, crazy, crazy; listen, Maria, how it's raining."

"Remember how afraid you were, Claire?"

"Yes."

Everything in the hotel had been upside down. It hadn't been raining yet, but the storm was always present, threatening. When Maria had joined them, they were in the hotel lobby. They were talking, next to each other in the hotel lobby. She stopped, filled with hope. They hadn't seen Maria. That's when she noticed their hands, discreetly linked together, their bodies close. It was early. You might have thought that evening had come, but it was the storm darkening the sky. There wasn't a trace of fear left in Claire's eyes. Maria had decided that she had enough time—enough time—to go to the square, to the café they had seen when they arrived.

So as not to look at Pierre, they watched the waiters juggling trays of manzanilla and other sherries. Claire caught a waiter on his way by and asked him for manzanillas. You had to shout because of the noise of the rain on the skylight. They shouted louder and louder. The dining room door opened every minute. People were still coming in. The storm was huge, very spread out.

"Where were you, Maria?" Pierre asked.

"In a café, with a friend of that man Rodrigo Paestra."

Pierre leaned toward Maria.

"If you really want to," he said, "we can go on to Madrid tonight."

Claire was listening.

"Claire?" Maria questioned.

"I don't know."

She almost moaned. Pierre's hands moved toward hers and then pulled back. Earlier he had made the same gesture, in the car when she was afraid of the storm, the sky rolling over on itself, hanging over the

126

wheat fields; Judith screaming; the day dark like twilight. Claire had become pale, so much so that her paleness was even more surprising than the fear it revealed.

"You don't know, Claire, you don't know this type of inconvenience, sleepless nights spent in hotel corridors."

"Of course I do. Who doesn't know?"

She was struggling, immersed in the thought of Pierre's hands on her, only a few hours ago under Maria's blinded eyes. Did she grow pale again? Did he notice she was getting pale again?

"We'll stay here tonight," he said. "Just this time."

He smiled. Did he ever smile before?

"Just this time?" Maria asked.

Pierre's hands, this time, reached their goal and touched the hands of his wife, Maria.

"I meant that I wasn't used to these inconveniences enough to be as frightened as you, Maria."

Maria moved away from the table and, clutching at the chair while speaking, closed her eyes.

"Once, in Verona," she said.

She didn't see what was going on. It was Claire's voice which, through the noise of the other voices, cut a bright path.

"In Verona? What happened there?"

"We slept badly," Pierre said.

The meal had started. The smell of the candles was so strong that it overpowered the smell of the food which perspiring waiters were carrying in big loads. There were shouts and complaints. The hotel manager asked that she be forgiven, she was in a difficult spot that night, because of the storm.

"Did I drink," Maria announced. "Again, did I drink!"

"It always surprises you," said Claire.

The rain had stopped. In moments of unforeseen silence, you could hear the gay streaming of rain on the skylight. Judith, who had gone off to the kitchen, was brought back by a waiter. Pierre was talking about Castile. About Madrid. He found out that in this town there were two Goyas in the church of San Andrea. The church of San Andrea is on the square they crossed when they arrived. The waiter brought the soup. Maria served Judith. And Judith's eyes filled with tears. Pierre smiled at his child. Maria gave up hope of getting Judith to eat.

"I'm not hungry tonight," Claire said, "you know, I think it's the storm."

"Happiness," said Maria.

Claire concentrated on what was going on in the dining room. Behind her suddenly thoughtful expression there was a smile. Pierre, wincing, raised his eyes on Maria—the same eyes as Judith's—and Maria smiled at those eyes.

"Everyone has been waiting so much for this storm, for this coolness," Maria explained.

"Yes," Claire said.

Maria was again hoping to get Judith to eat. She succeeded. Spoonful by spoonful, Judith ate. Claire told her a story. Pierre was listening too. The disorder in the dining room was straightening out a little. Yet, you could still hear thunder, more or less loud, depending on whether the storm was coming closer or moving farther away. Every time the skylight was lit up by lightning, a child would cry.

While dinner was being served, people spoke of Rodrigo Paestra's crime. Some laughed. Who would ever have the chance to kill with such simplicity, like Rodrigo Paestra?

Police whistles continued in the night. Whenever they were heard very close to the hotel, conversations would die down, people would listen. Some were hoping and waiting for Rodrigo Paestra to be captured. A difficult night was ahead.

"He's on the rooftops," Maria said very softly.

They didn't hear her. Judith was eating fruit.

Maria got up. She walked out of the dining room. They were left alone. She had said she was going to see what the hotel looked like.

There were many corridors. Most of them were circular. Some had a view of the wheat fields. Others, a vista of the avenue which crossed the square. No one was sleeping in the corridors yet. Still others led to balconies overlooking the rooftops of the city. Another shower was in the making. The horizon was lurid. It seemed very far away. The storm had become even bigger. There seemed to be little hope that it would die down during the night.

"Storms go as they come," Pierre had said. "Just like that. You mustn't be afraid, Claire."

That's what he had said. Maria didn't yet know the irresistible perfume of her fear, of her frightened youth. Just a few hours ago.

The rooftops were empty. They would probably always be, whatever hope you might have of seeing them, just for once, filled with people.

The rain was light but it covered the empty rooftops, and the town disappeared. You couldn't see anything any more. There remained only the memory of a dream of loneliness.

When Maria came back to the dining room the manager was announcing the arrival of the police.

"As you probably know," she said, "a crime was committed in our town this afternoon. We are very sorry."

NO ONE HAD TO identify himself. The manager vouched for her guests.

Six policemen rushed through the dining room. Three others walked over to the circular corridors surrounding it. They were going to search the rooms off these corridors. They were just going to search these rooms, the manager said. It wouldn't take long.

"I was told he's on the rooftops," Maria said again.

They heard. She had spoken softly. But they weren't surprised. Maria left it at that. The confusion in the dining room had reached a new peak. All the waiters came from this village and knew Rodrigo Paestra. The policemen also came from the village. They questioned one another. The waiters stopped serving.. The manager intervened. Be careful not to say anything bad about Perez. The waiters went on talking. The manager shouted orders that no one heard.

And then, little by little, everything having been discussed by the waiters, the customers slowly regained their wits and asked for the rest of their meal. The waiters went back to work. They spoke to the customers. All the customers listened carefully to what the waiters were saying, watched the police coming and going, worried, gained or lost hope as to the outcome of the search, some were still smiling at Rodrigo Paestra's naïveté. Some women talked about how horrible it is to be killed at nineteen, and to be left like Rodrigo Paestra's wife, alone, so alone, that night, in the town hall, a mere child. But all were eating, more or less heartily, in the midst of the confusion, eating the food brought in by the waiters in the midst of anger and confusion. Doors slammed in the corridors, and the policemen crossed the dining room, with Tommy guns, wearing boots and belts, unalterably serious, giving off a nauseating smell of wet leather and sweat. At the sight of them, children always start to cry.

Two of the policemen must have gone to the corridor, on the left of the dining room, where Maria had just been.

Judith, in a state of terror, stopped eating her fruit. There were no longer any policemen in the dining room. The waiter who had been taking care of them came back to their table shaking with anger; he was muttering insults against Perez and paying tribute to Rodrigo Paestra's lasting patience; and Judith, pieces of orange dripping between her fingers, was listening all the time.

They must have reached the balcony at the end of the circular corridor where Maria had just been. It wasn't raining any more, and Maria could hear their footsteps fading away in that corridor alongside the dining room, through the noise of streaming rain on the skylight, of which no one in the dining room seemed to be aware now.

Everything was quiet again. The quiet of the sky. The quiet streaming of the rain on the skylight punctuated by the policemen's steps in that last corridor—once the rooms, the kitchens, the courtyards will have been searched—will they forget him? Some day? No.

If they reached the balcony, then it was certain that Rodrigo Paestra was not on the rooftops.

"Why was I told such a thing?" Maria went on again very softly.

They heard. But neither one was surprised.

She had seen these rooftops. A moment before they were stretched out, evenly strewn under the sky, entangled, bare, right under the balcony, bare and consistently empty.

Calls could be heard from outside. From the street? From the courtyard? Very close. The waiters stopped and listened, their hands full of dishes. Nobody complained. The calls went on. They bore gaps of terror into the sudden silence. Listening, you could hear that these calls were always the same. His name.

"Rodrigo Paestra."

In long, plaintive, rhythmical, nearly tender tones, they begged him to answer, to surrender.

Maria stood up. Pierre took her by the arm and forced her to sit down. She sat down obediently.

"But he is on the rooftops," she said very softly.

Judith didn't hear.

"It's funny," Claire said very softly, "I don't care at all."

"But," Maria said, "it's just that I know."

Pierre gently called Maria.

131

"Please, Maria," he said.

"It's those calls," she said, "that get on one's nerves, it's nothing."
The calls stopped. And another shower began. The police were back.
The waiters went back to their work, smiling, their eyes lowered. The
manager stayed at the dining room door, she kept an eye on her staff,
she smiled too, she too, she knew Rodrigo Paestra. A policeman went
into the hotel office and made a phone call. He called the neighboring
town to ask for reinforcements. He was shouting because of the noise of
the rain on the skylight. He said that the village had been thoroughly
surrounded as soon as the crime had been discovered and that there were
ten chances out of ten they would find Rodrigo Paestra at dawn, they
had to wait, the search was difficult because of the storm and the power
failure, but it was probable that the storm, as usual, would end at
daybreak, and what they had to do was to guard, all night, the roads
leading from the town, for that they needed more men, so that as soon
as it was light Rodrigo Paestra would be caught like a rat. The
policeman had made himself understood. He was waiting for an answer
that came at once. Around ten, in an hour and a half, the reinforcements
would be there. The waiter came back to their table, trembling, and
spoke to Pierre.

"If they catch him," he said, "if they manage to catch him, he won't
let them take him to jail."

Maria was drinking wine. The waiter left. Pierre leaned toward
Maria.

"Don't drink so much Maria, please don't."

Maria raised her arm, pushed away the potential obstacle this voice
seemed to be, again and again. Claire had heard Pierre speaking to
Maria.

"I'm not drinking much," Maria said.

"It's true," Claire said, "tonight Maria is drinking less than usual."

"You see," Maria said.

As for Claire, she wasn't drinking anything. Pierre got up and said
that he too was going to take a look at the hotel.

There were no longer any policemen in the hotel. They had left, in
single file, by the staircase next to the office. It wasn't raining. The
whistling kept on, but far away, and in the dining room the chatter had
started again, the complaints, especially about the bad Spanish food
which the waiters were still serving to late-comers with triumphant
gusto because Rodrigo Paestra had not yet been caught. Judith was calm

and started to yawn. When the waiter came back to their table he spoke to Claire, to Claire's beauty, and stopped to look at her again after speaking.

"One chance they don't catch him," he said.

"Did she love Perez?" Claire asked.

"Impossible to love Perez," the waiter said.

Claire laughed and the waiter gave way to laughter also.

"Still," Claire said, "what if she loved Perez?"

"Why do you want Rodrigo Paestra to understand?" the waiter asked.

He left. Claire began to nibble some bread. Maria was drinking and Claire let her.

"Pierre isn't coming back?" Maria said.

"I don't know. Any more than you do."

Maria moved toward the table, straightened up, then leaned very close to Claire.

"Listen, Claire," Maria said, "listen to me."

Claire leaned back in the opposite direction. She looked past Maria, staring at the back of the dining room without seeing it.

"I'm listening to you, Maria," she said.

Maria fell back into her chair and said nothing. Some time passed. Claire had stopped nibbling bread. When Pierre came back he told them that he had picked the best corridor in the hotel for Judith, he had seen the sky, he had seen the storm petering out little by little; it would probably be nice tomorrow and very early, if they wanted, they could reach Madrid, after looking at the two Goyas in San Andrea. Since the storm had started again, he spoke a little louder than usual. His voice was beautiful, always precise, with a precision, this evening, that was almost oratorical. He was talking about the two Goyas it would be a shame not to see.

"Without this storm, we would have forgotten them," Claire said.

She said this like anything else and yet she never would have said it like that before this evening. Where, in the half darkness Maria had given them earlier, in what part of the hotel, did they first wonder and then marvel at having known each other so little until then, at the wonderful agreement that had grown between them, and then at last come to light behind this window? or on that balcony? or in this corridor? in this surging warmth of the streets after the showers, behind the sky so dark, Claire, that your eyes, at that very moment, were the very color of rain. How could I have noticed it before? Your eyes, Claire, are gray.

She told him that the light always had something to do with it and that he was probably mistaken that evening because of the storm.

"It seems to me, if I remember correctly," Maria said, "that before leaving France we had talked about these two Goyas."

Pierre remembered. Not Claire. The shower stopped and they could hear one another. The dining room was getting emptier. The humming picked up in the corridors. They were probably dividing up beds. Children were being undressed. The time had come for Judith to go to sleep. Pierre was quiet. Finally Maria said it.

"I'm going to put Judith to sleep in the corridor."

"We'll wait for you," Pierre said.

"I'll be back."

Judith didn't object. In the hall there were many children, some already asleep. Maria didn't undress Judith that night. She wrapped her in a blanket, against the wall, half-way down the corridor.

She waited for Judith to fall asleep. She waited a long time.

Three

So MUCH TIME WENT by that no trace of twilight was left in the sky.

"Don't expect any electricity tonight," the manager of the hotel had said. "Usually around here the storms are so violent that there's no electricity all night."

There was no electricity. There were going to be more storms, more sudden showers throughout the night. The sky was still low and small, still whipped by a very strong wind, toward the west. The sky could be seen, perfectly arched up to the horizon. And the limits of the storm could be seen too, trying to take over more of the clearer part of the sky.

From the balcony where she was standing, Maria could see the whole expanse of the storm. They remained in the dining room.

"I'll be back," Maria had said.

Behind her, in the corridor, all the children were now sleeping. Among them was Judith. When Maria turned around she saw her asleep, her body outlined in the soft light of the oil lamps hooked up on the walls.

"As soon as she's asleep, I'll come back," Maria had told them.

Judith was asleep.

The hotel was full. The rooms, the corridors, and later on this hall, would be still more crowded. There were more people in the hotel than in a whole district of the town. The town, beyond which stretched deserted roads, all the way to Madrid, toward which the storm was moving since five o'clock, bursting here and there, its clouds breaking and then mending again. To the point of exhaustion. Until when? It was going to last all night.

There was no longer a single café open.

"We'll wait for you, Maria," Pierre had said.

The town was small, it covered about five acres, all of it was crowded into an irregular, but full, neatly outlined shape. Beyond it, whichever way you turned, open country stretched out, bare, rolling (this was hardly noticeable that night, and yet, in the east, there seemed to be a sudden drop). A stream previously dried out, would overflow in the morning.

If you looked at the time it was ten o'clock. In the evening. It was summer.

Policemen were walking under the hotel balconies. They must have been tired from searching. They dragged their feet in the muddy streets. The crime had been committed a long time ago, hours ago, and they were talking about the weather.

"Rodrigo Paestra is on the rooftops."

Maria remembered. The rooftops were there, they were empty. They were shining dimly under the balcony where she was standing. Empty.

They were waiting for her in the dining room, in the midst of cleared tables, oblivious of her, looking at each other, motionless. The hotel was full. There was no other place for them to look at each other except there.

Whistling started again at the other end of the town, well beyond the square, in the direction of Madrid. Nothing happened. Policemen gathered at the street corner, on the left, stopped, moved off again. It was just a break in the waiting period. The policemen walked by under the balcony, and turned into another street.

It wasn't much later than ten. It was later than when she should have gone back to the dining room, entered, moved in between them, sat down, and told them once more the surprising news.

"I've been told that Rodrigo Paestra is hiding on the rooftops."

She left the balcony, entered the hall and lay down next to her sleeping child, her own, the body which, among all the other children in the hall, belonged to her. She kissed her hair lightly.

"My life," she said.

The child didn't wake up. She barely moved, sighed, and fell back into a calm sleep.

And the town was like her, already locked in sleep. Some still talked about Rodrigo Paestra whose wife was found naked next to Perez, both asleep after hours of love. And then dead. The nineteen-year-old body was in the town hall.

If Maria were to get up, if she were to go to the dining room, she could ask for a drink. She thought of the first sip of manzanilla in her mouth and the peace in her body that would follow. She didn't move.

Beyond the hall, through the yellow and vacillating screen of the oil lamps, you could imagine the rooftops, covered with the moving sky, its darkness deepening. The sky was there, against the frame of the open balcony.

Maria got up, hesitant about going back to the dining room where they would still be immersed in the wonder of their overpowering desire, still alone in the midst of cleared tables and exhausted waiters who were waiting for them to leave, and whom they didn't see.

She walked back to the balcony, smoked a cigarette. The rain hadn't returned yet. It was slow. The sky was still brooding, it would still be a while. In the back of her, there were couples coming into the hall. They were speaking softly because of the children. They lay down. They kept quiet at first, hoping for sleep that did not come, and then they talked again. From everywhere, particularly from the crowded rooms, came the muted sound of voices, regularly interrupted by the fateful passing of the police.

After each passing, the conjugal hum started again, in the rooms, in the circular corridors, the everyday sound, slow and tired. Behind the doors, in the twin beds, in the embraces born in the cool of the storm, there was talk of the summer, of this summer storm, and of Rodrigo Paestra's crime.

At last the shower. In a few seconds it filled the streets. The earth was too dry and couldn't drink up so much rain. The trees on the square were twisted by the wind. Maria could see their tops appear and disappear behind the angle of the roofs and, when lightning lit up the town and the open country, in its livid illumination, she could at the same time see Rodrigo Paestra's motionless and drowned shape clutching a dark stone chimney.

The shower lasted a few minutes. Calm returned as the strength of the wind weakened. A vague glimmering, so long hoped for, descended from the appeased sky. And in this glimmering, which increased as you hoped it would, but which you knew would quickly fade with the beginnings of another phase of the storm, Maria could see the indefinite shape of Rodrigo Paestra, Rodrigo Paestra's dazzling, shrieking and indefinite shape.

Again the police started their search. They returned as the storm subsided. They marched through the mud again. Maria leaned over the railing of the balcony and saw them. One of them laughed. At regular intervals, the whole town rang with the sound of whistling. Just more pauses in the waiting period, which was going to last until morning.

In addition to the balcony where Maria was standing, there were others on the north side of the hotel. They were empty, except one, just one, on Maria's right, one flight above. They must have been there for a very short time. Maria hadn't seen them arrive. She moved back slightly into the corridor where people were now asleep.

This must have been the first time they had kissed. Maria put out her cigarette. She could see them fully outlined against the moving sky. While Pierre kissed her, his hands touched Claire's breasts. They were probably talking. But very softly. They must have been speaking the first words of love. Irrepressible, bursting words which came to their lips between two kisses.

The lightning made the town look livid. It was unforeseeable, striking irregularly. But every time it made their kisses livid too, as well as their single, nearly blinding shape. Was it on her eyes, behind the screen formed by the dark sky, that he had first kissed her? How could one know. Your eyes were the color of your fear in the afternoon, the color of rain at that very moment, Claire, your eyes, I could hardly see them, how could I have noticed it before, your eyes must be gray.

Opposite these kisses, a few yards away, Rodrigo Paestra wrapped in his brown blanket was waiting for the infernal night to end. At dawn, it would be all over.

A new phase of the storm was coming up that was going to separate them and prevent Maria from seeing them.

As he did it, so did she, bringing her hands to her lonely breasts, then her hands fell and, useless, grasped the balcony. While she had moved too far out onto the balcony while they were merging into a single, nearly blinding shape, she now moved back a little from the balcony, toward the corridor where the new wind was already sweeping into the lamp chimneys. No, she couldn't help seeing them. She could still see them. And their shadows were on that roof. Now their bodies broke apart. The wind raised her skirt, and, in a flash, they laughed. The same wind that had raised her skirt, again crossed the whole town, bumping up against the edges of the rooftops.

Two more minutes, and the storm would come, sweeping over the whole town, emptying the streets, the balconies. He must have stepped back in order to hold her better, to be reunited with her for the first time, their happiness intensified by the suffering he created by holding her far from him. They didn't know, they were still unaware that the storm would separate them for the night.

More waiting. And the impatience of the waiting grew so intense it reached its climax, and at last calm set in. One of Pierre's hands was moving all over another woman's body. His other hand held her close against him. It was done now, forever.

It was ten-thirty. And summer.

And then it was a little later. Night had come at last, completely. There was no room that night, in that town, for love. Maria lowered her eyes before this reality: their thirst for love would remain unfulfilled, the town was bulging, in this summer night made for their love. The flashes of lightning kept lighting up the shape of their desire. They were still there, folded in each other's arms, and motionless, his hand now resting on her hip, hers forever, while she, she, her hands unable to move as they clung to his shoulders, her mouth against his mouth, she was devouring him.

The same flashes, at the same time, lit up the roof opposite them and on its top, around a chimney, the shrouded shape of Rodrigo Paestra, the murderer.

The wind increased, swept into the hallway and moved over the sleeping children. A lamp had gone out. But nothing would wake them. The town was dark and asleep. In the rooms there was silence. Judith was good.

They had disappeared from the balcony as suddenly as they had come. He must have led her away without letting go of her—how could he—into the shadow of the sleeping corridor. The balcony was deserted. Maria looked at her watch once again. It was almost eleven. Because of the wind that was still growing stronger, one of the children —it wasn't that one—uttered a cry, isolated, turned over and fell back to sleep.

The rain. And again its ineffable smell, its lifeless smell of muddy streets. Just as it did on the fields, the rain was falling on the dead shape of Rodrigo Paestra, dead of sorrow, dead of love.

Where could they have found a place to be toegther that night, in that hotel? Where would he take off her light skirt, that very night? How beautiful she is. How beautiful you are, God how beautiful. With the rain, their shapes had vanished from the balcony.

Summer was everywhere, in the rain, in the streets, in the courtyards, in the bathrooms, in the kitchens, summer, everywhere, summer was everywhere for their love. Maria stretched, went back in, lay down in the hallway, stretched again. Was it done now? Perhaps there was no one in another dark, stifling corridor—could anyone know all of them? —the corridor extending from their balcony, for example, right above this one, in this miraculously forgotten corridor, along the wall, on the floor, was it done?

Tomorrow would be there in a few hours. You had to wait. The shower was longer than the previous one. It kept coming down with force. And also on the skylight, echoing horribly throughout the hotel.

"We waited for you, Maria," Pierre said.

They appeared with the end of the shower. She saw their two shadows move toward her while she was lying next to Judith, two huge shadows. Claire's skirt had risen above her knees, bulging around her hips. The wind in the corridor. Too fast. They hadn't had much time between leaving the balcony and arriving there, next to Maria. They were smiling. So that hope had been foolish. Love hadn't been fulfilled that night in the hotel. More waiting. The rest of the night.

"You said you would be back, Maria," Pierre said again.

"Well, I was tired."

She had seen him looking for her on the floor of the corridor carefully, almost walk past her, and stop in front of her; she was the last one, just where the corridor ended, engulfed in the darkness of the dining room. Claire was following him.

"Well," Maria repeated—she was pointing at Judith—"she would have been afraid."

Pierre smiled. He stopped looking at Maria and discovered an open window leading onto a balcony at the end of the corridor.

"What weather," he said.

He brushed away his discovery of the window at the very moment he made it. Was it fear?

"And it will last all night," he said. "It will end by daybreak."

She could have told just from his voice, trembling, shaky, affected by desire for that woman.

Then Claire also smiled at Judith. At the small, lopsided shape, wrapped in a brown blanket. Her hair was still wet from the rain on the balcony. Her eyes in the yellow light of the oil lamp. Your eyes, blue stones. I'll eat your eyes, he was telling her, your eyes. The youthfulness of her breasts showed clearly under her white sweater. Her blue gaze was haggard, paralyzed by frustration, by the very fulfillment of frustration. Her gaze left Judith and moved back to Pierre.

"Did you go back to a café, Maria?"

"No. I stayed here."

"A good thing we didn't leave for Madrid," Pierre said. "You see." He turned again toward the open window.

"A good thing, yes."

In the street alongside the hotel, a whistle rang out. Was it over? There was no second whistle. The three of them waited. No. Once more, just a pause in the waiting period. Steps made heavy by the mud in the streets moved toward the northern part of town. They didn't talk about it.

"She isn't warm tonight," Claire said.

Maria stroked Judith's forehead.

"Not really. Less than usual. It's comfortable."

Maria could have told just from Claire's breasts that they were in love. They were going to lie down there, next to her, separated while torn and tortured by desire. And both were smiling, equally guilty, terrified and happy.

"We waited for you," Pierre repeated.

Even Claire raised her eyes. Then she lowered them and only a vague, indelible smile remained on her face. Maria would have known just from seeing her eyes lowered on that smile. What glory. On what glory were those eyes closing? They must have looked, looked all over the hotel for a spot. It had been impossible. They had had to give up. Pierre had said Maria is waiting for us. What a future ahead of them, the days to come.

Pierre's hands were dangling beside him. For eight years they had caressed her body. Now Claire was stepping into the misfortune that flowed straight from those hands.

"I'm going to sleep," she announced.

She took a blanket that had been put on a table. She wrapped herself in it, still laughing, and, with a sigh, stretched out below the oil lamp. Pierre did not move.

"I'm sleeping," Claire said.

Pierre also took a blanket, then lay down next to Maria, on the other side of the corridor.

Did Rodrigo Paestra still exist, there, twenty yards from them? Yes. The police had again walked by in the street. Claire sighed again.

141

"Ah, I'm already asleep," she said. "Good night, Maria."

"Good night, Claire."

Pierre lit a cigarette. The sound of regular breathing rose in the freshness of the corridor, in its odor of rain and of Claire.

"It's very pleasant," Pierre said softly.

Some time went by. Maria should have told Pierre again: "You know, it's crazy, but Rodrigo Paestra is really there, on the roof. Opposite. And with daybreak, he'll be caught."

Maria said nothing.

"You're tired, Maria?" Pierre asked even more softly.

"Less than usual. The storm I suppose. It feels better."

"Yes," Claire said, "we're less tired than the other nights."

She wasn't sleeping. A gust of wind put out the last light. Lightning again at the end of the corridor. Maria turned slightly, but you couldn't see the roof from where they were.

"It will never stop," Pierre said. "Do you want me to put the light back on, Maria?"

"It's not worth it. I like it like that."

"I like it too," Claire went on again.

She stopped talking. Maria knew it: Pierre was hoping she would fall asleep. He was no longer smoking and lay motionless against the wall. But Claire was talking again.

"Tomorrow," she said, "we'll have to reserve rooms in Madrid by noon."

"We should, yes."

She yawned. Pierre and Maria were waiting for her to fall asleep. It was raining hard. Can you die if you want to from having to bear the brunt of a storm? Maria seemed to remember that it was Rodrigo Paestra's dead shape that she had seen on the roof.

Maria knew that Pierre wasn't sleeping, that he was aware of her, Maria, his wife, and that the desire he felt for Claire was becoming corrupted by the memory of his wife; that he was becoming gloomy for fear she had guessed something; that he was disturbed at the thought of Maria's new loneliness, tonight, compared to what had been before.

"Are you sleeping?"

"No."

They had spoken very softly once more. They were waiting. Yes, this time, Claire was asleep.

"What time is it?" Maria asked.

With the end of the rain, there came the policemen whom Rodrigo Paestra must have also heard. Pierre looked at his watch in the light of the cigarette he had just started.

"Eleven twenty. Do you want a cigarette?"

Maria did.

"It's already lighter," Pierre said. "Maybe it's clearing up now. Here, Maria."

He handed it to her. They sat up a little, just long enough for him to light it, then they lay down again. At the end of the corridor, Maria saw the dark blue screen of the balcony.

"Nights like this are so long," Pierre said.

"Yes. Try to sleep."

"And you?"

"I would like a manzanilla. But it's impossible."

Pierre waited before answering. A last cloudburst, very light, fell on Rodrigo Paestra. You could hear singing and laughing in the street. The police, once again. But in the corridor all was quiet.

"Won't you try to drink a little less, Maria? Just once?"

"No," Maria said. "No more."

The earthy smell came up from the street, endless, the smell of tears along with its complement, the smell of wet, fully ripened wheat. Was she going to tell him: "It's crazy, Pierre, but Rodrigo Paestra is there. There. Right there. And with daybreak he will be caught."

She said nothing. It was he who spoke.

"You remember? Verona?"

"Yes."

If he reached out, Pierre would touch Maria's hair. He had spoken of Verona. Of love all night, the two of them, in a bathroom in Verona. A storm too, and it was summer, and the hotel was full. "Come, Maria." He was wondering. "When, when will I have enough of you?"

"Give me another cigarette," Maria said.

He gave it to her. This time she didn't sit up.

"If I spoke to you about Verona, it's because I couldn't help it."

The smell of mud and wheat came in whiffs into the corridor. The hotel was bathed in this odor, as well as the town, Rodrigo Paestra and his dead, and the inexhaustible but perfectly vain memory of a night of love in Verona.

Claire was sleeping soundly. Then she turned suddenly and moaned because of the recent stir of Pierre's hands, that night, on her body.

Pierre also heard Claire's moan. It was over. Claire grew quiet. And Maria next to Pierre only heard the sound of children breathing, and the police kept marching by more and more regularly as morning came closer.

"You're not asleep?"

"No," said Maria. "What time is it?"

"A quarter to twelve"—he was waiting. "Here, have another cigarette."

"All right. At what time is dawn in Spain?"

"Very early at this time of year."

"I wanted to tell you, Pierre."

She took the cigarette that he was holding out to her. Her hand trembled a little. He waited until he was lying down again before asking her.

"What do you want to tell me, Maria?"

Pierre waited a long time for an answer which didn't come. He didn't insist. Both of them were smoking, lying on their backs because of the tiles that bruised their hips. You had to suffer this bruise as best you could. She couldn't remove the free end of Judith's blanket that was covering her without being exposed to Pierre's look. She could only try to close her eyes between each puff of her cigarette, open them again, without moving at all, keeping quiet.

"Lucky we found this hotel," Pierre said.

"Lucky, yes."

He was smoking faster than she. He had finished his cigarette. He put it out in the narrow space between him and Maria, in the middle of the corridor, between the sleeping bodies. The showers lasted only a short length of time now, the length of one of Claire's sighs.

"You know Maria. I love you."

Maria also was through with her cigarette, she put it out, just like Pierre, on an empty tile in the corridor.

"Yes, I know," she said.

What was happening? What was in the air? Was this really the end of the storm? Whenever there were showers, it was like pails of water spilled on the skylight and the roofs. A sound of showering that would only last a few seconds. They should have fallen asleep before this phase of the storm. Have accepted the idea of this last night before this moment.

"You must sleep, Maria."

"Yes. But the noise," she said.

She could do it, she could turn over and find herself right against him. They would get up. They would go away together far from Claire's sleep whose memory would grow dimmer with the passing of night. He knew it.

"Maria, Maria. You are my love."

"Yes."

She hadn't moved. In the street, more whistling announced that dawn was close, always closer. There was no more lightning, except weak and far away. Claire moaned again because of the memory of Pierre's hands clasping her hips. But that too you became accustomed to like the soft scraping noise of the children breathing. And the smell of rain engulfed the uniqueness of Claire's desire, mixing it with the sea of desire which, that night, raged through the town.

Maria sat up quietly, hardly turned toward him, stopped moving and looked at him.

"It's crazy, but I saw Rodrigo Paestra. He is there on the roof."

Pierre was asleep. He had just fallen asleep, as suddenly as a child. Maria remembered that it had always been like that.

He was sleeping. Her need to be sure was funny. Hadn't she been sure?

She sat up a little more. He didn't move. She got up completely, brushed against his body, freed, lonely, abandoned in its sleep.

When Maria reached the balcony, she looked at the time she carried with her on her wrist, her time. It was half past midnight. In about three hours, at this time of year, it would be dawn. Rodrigo Paestra, the same statue of death she had seen earlier, was waiting for this dawn, and to be killed.

Four

THE SKY HAD RISEN above the town, but in the distance, it was still flush with the wheat fields. But this was the end. The lightning was weaker. And the rumbling of the thunder was weaker. In two and a half hours it would be dawn whatever the weather. A bad, veiled dawn, a bad dawn for Rodrigo Paestra. Now everyone was asleep in the hotel and in the town, except Maria, and Rodrigo Paestra.

The police whistles had stopped. They were keeping watch around the town, guarding all exits, waiting for the bright daylight when they would catch Rodrigo Paestra. In two and a half hours.

Perhaps Maria would fall asleep. Her desire to drink was so strong. Perhaps it was too much for her to wait for dawn. The time of night had arrived when, already, each hour pushed you into the weariness of the next, unavoidable day. The mere anticipation of its coming weighs down on you. During this next day, their love would grow still stronger. Wait.

Maria stayed on the balcony, even when a new shower split the sky again. The shower was light, and warm.

The pointed roof opposite her was washed by the rain. On top of it, around a square chimney, where the two sides of the roof met, was this thing whose shape had remained identical to what Maria had seen at ten-thirty, in a flash of lightning. The thing was wrapped in darkness. The rain fell on it just as it fell on the roof. Then it stopped. And the shape was there. It fitted the shape of the chimney so perfectly that, if you looked at it long enough, you might doubt it was human. Perhaps it was cement, propping up the chimney, darkened over the years. And yet at the same time, whenever lightning lit up the roof, it was the shape of a man.

"What weather," Maria said. She had spoken as if she had said it to Pierre. Then she waited.

146

The shape remained identical. One chance in a lifetime that it was a man. Silent, tired policemen walked by in the street, their boots splashing. Then they were gone.

This time Maria called.

"Rodrigo Paestra."

The possibility that he might answer, move, abandon this inhuman position was enough to make her imagination leap with joy.

"Hey," Maria called out. She gestured toward the roof.

Nothing moved. Little by little Maria woke up. She still felt like drinking. She remembered that there was a bottle of brandy in the car. A while ago, when she mentioned it to Pierre, this desire to drink was slight, hardly noticeable, but now it had become violent. She looked into the corridor, and beyond, to see if some light in the dining room would offer her hopes of getting a drink. None. If she asked Pierre, he would do it. Tonight, he would do it, he would go and wake up one of the waiters. But she wasn't going to do it, she wasn't going to wake up Pierre. "You know, Maria, I love you." He was sleeping near Claire ever since she left the corridor. So let him sleep near Claire. Let him sleep, let him sleep. If this was Rodrigo Paestra, this night in particular, what luck for Maria. What relief from boredom. This time it was because of Claire.

"Hey there," Maria shouted again.

Wait. Why should this shape be a man? Once in a lifetime it was possible that this would be he, a man. But it was possible. Why not then accept this possibility?

"Hey," Maria shouted again.

Once more the slow, dull sound of the police moving closer toward dawn. Maria was silent. Could it be Rodrigo Paestra? It was within the realm of possibility that it was he. As long as she was Maria. It was in the realm of possibility that he should have happened on her, Maria, the night. Wasn't the proof right there in front of her? The proof was urgent. Maria had just invented that this was Rodrigo Paestra. No one else knew it but this woman who was eleven yards away from him, away from this man wanted by the police, the storm murderer, this treasure, this monument of suffering.

Again the rain fell softly on him. And on everything else too, the other roofs, the wheat, the streets. The shape hadn't moved. It was waiting to be caught, death for the dawn of the coming day. At dawn, little by little, the roofs would be lit. When the storm would have blown over the wheat fields, dawn would be pale red.

"Rodrigo Paestra, Rodrigo Paestra," Maria called.

Did he want to die? Again the police. Respectful of the people's sleep, they made their rounds without speaking, without calling, sure of themselves. They turned into the swampy streets, on the right, and their footsteps disappeared without echoes. Maria called a bit louder.

"Answer, Rodrigo Paestra. Answer me."

She was against the iron railing of the balcony. The railing beat. It was Maria's heart. He didn't answer. Hope was getting thinner, became minute, disappeared. She would know at dawn if it was he. But then it would be too late.

"I beg you, Rodrigo Paestra, answer me."

It wasn't he? Nothing was sure. Except that Maria wanted it.

Someone coughed in the corridor. Moved. Pierre. Yes, Pierre.

Within the next two days, Pierre and Claire would come together. They would devote themselves to this purpose. They would have to find where. What would follow was still unknown, unpredictable, an abyss of time. A length of time not yet known to them, nor to Maria, which was already spreading beyond the storm. Madrid would be its beginning. Tomorrow.

What words should she use? What words?

"Rodrigo Paestra, trust me."

It was already one in the morning. In two hours Rodrigo Paestra would be trapped like a rat if nothing happened until dawn but the passage of time.

Maria leaning over the balcony was looking at the man. Above him the sky was clear. The rain had to stop now, it had to. It seemed there was some blue, and moons, appearing in the light, endless sky. Around the chimney, nothing, nothing moved. The rain that had already fallen, flowed down, murmuring, from the shape as well as from the roofs. Fire, as well, could burn it. He wasn't going to surrender at dawn. It was certain that he was waiting to be crushed right there by the city's licensed snipers.

Maria, her body bent over the balcony, started to sing. Very softly. A tune from that summer, that he should know, that he should have danced to with his wife on Saturday nights.

Maria stopped singing. She waited. Yes, the sky had cleared. The storm had moved away. Dawn would be beautiful. Pale red. Rodrigo

Paestra didn't want to live. The song had brought no change to his shape. To this shape that had become less and less identifiable with anything but him. A sharp, without sharp angles, long and supple enough to be human, with this sudden roundness on top, the small surface of the head surging from the mass of the body. A man.

Maria complained for a long time, in the night. It was like dreaming. The shape did not move. It was like dreaming that it did not move from the moment it could be Rodrigo Paestra. To the shape, Maria was complaining about her fate.

The town became abstract like a jail. No longer the smell of wheat. It had rained too much. It was too late. You could no longer talk about the night. But about what then, about what?

"Oh, I beg you, I beg you, Rodrigo Paestra."

She would have turned him in for a sip of brandy that she didn't go and get. Maybe we can do something, Rodrigo Paestra. Rodrigo Paestra, in two hours it will be light.

She now said words that meant nothing. The difficulty was so great. She called him, called this beastliness of pain.

"Hey there, hey there."

Without stopping, softly as she would with an animal. Louder and louder. She had closed the balcony windows behind her. Somebody had moaned, then fallen asleep.

Then the police came. There they were. These men had just arrived there, they were probably fresh troops, they were talking. They were talking more than the others. Reinforcements for dawn. There had been a rumor in the hotel that they would come. They talked about the weather. Maria, leaning over the railing of the balcony, could see them, one of them raised his eyes, looked at the sky, didn't see Maria, and said that the storm had definitely vanished from these parts. On the square, in the distance, a light appeared. The truck bringing reinforcements? Or a café that they had had opened that night, so early, because of the murder and so the police could drink and eat there while waiting to surround the town at dawn? They were talking of thirty men, reinforcements that had arrived at the hotel. Rain, from Maria's wet hair, turned into sweat. The patrol had left.

"Hey, hey," Maria called again as she would call an animal.

The moon disappeared behind a cloud, but it wasn't going to rain again. He didn't answer. It was a quarter past one. She couldn't see him while the cloud moved in the sky. Then the sky freed itself from this

149

cloud. It hadn't rained. There he was again around the chimney, still motionless, unalterable, there for eternity.

"You're an idiot," Maria shouted.

No one had waked up in the town. Nothing happened. The shape had remained wrapped in its stupidity. In the hotel nothing had moved. But a window lit up in the house next to the hotel. Maria moved back a little. She had to wait. The light went out. No more shouting. The shout had come from the hotel, from a tourist. Therefore people went back to sleep. Again the deadly silence. And in this silence, Maria insulted him again.

"Idiot, idiot," she said softly, being careful.

The patrol came again. Maria stopped shouting insults. The patrol passed. They had been talking about their families, about jobs. If Maria had a weapon she would shoot at the shape. So it would be done. The rain which would not dry made Maria's blouse stick to her shoulders. She must wait for dawn and Rodrigo Paestra's death.

She wasn't calling any more. He knew it. Again she opened the corridor door. She saw, she could see them, the others, sleeping, cruelly separated. She looked at them for a long time. It hadn't been fulfilled yet, this love. What patience, what patience, she didn't leave the balcony. Rodrigo Paestra knew that she was there. He was still breathing, he existed still in this dying night. He was there, in the same place, geographically related to her.

As often happens in summer, a climatic miracle occurred. The fog had disappeared from the horizon and then little by little from the whole sky. The storm dissolved. It no longer existed. Stars, yes stars, in the pre-dawn sky. Such a long time. The stars could make you cry.

Maria wasn't calling any more. She wasn't shouting insults any longer. She hadn't called him ever since she had insulted him. But she stayed on this balcony, her eyes on him, on this shape which fear had reduced to animal idiocy. Her own shape as well.

A quarter of an hour passed, shortening by that much the time that moved toward a green dawn; the dawn which would start by poking its nose into the wheat fields, and then would sweep this roof, opposite her, and would reveal him, and his terror, to the eyes of everyone. No, Maria wasn't calling any more. Time was getting old, buried. She wasn't going to call any more. Never again.

The night moved at a dizzy speed, without ever halting in its course.

Without events acting as relays. None but the bitter duration of failure. Maria recognized it.

There was one chance left. If he could see, through his shroud, that she was still there, at her post, waiting for him. And if, in his turn, he thought he should display a last act of kindness, and signal to her. One chance that he should remember that time was passing while she was waiting uncomfortably, on this balcony, where perhaps she would stay until dawn. One chance that, because of her, he should step for a short instant out of the artlessness of despair, that he should remember certain general principles of human behavior, of war, of flight, of hatred. That he should remember the pale red dawn moving over his land; the ordinary reasons for living, in the long run, until the end, even when these reasons have disappeared.

A blue light now fell from the sky. It wasn't possible that he didn't see this woman's shape leaning toward him—as no other ever had—on the hotel balcony. Even if he wanted to die, even if he wanted this particular fate, he could answer her one last time.

Again the policemen of hell. They went by. Then there was silence. Behind Maria, the blue sky lit up the hallway where Claire and Pierre were sleeping, apart. An indescribable difference brought on by sleep, was keeping them apart for a few more hours. Tomorrow, their love would be fulfilled, unparalleled, screaming, in the hotel, in Madrid. Oh, Claire. You.

Did he lose hope of seeing her again while she had turned?

Something had emerged from the black shroud. Something white. A face? or a hand?

It was he, Rodrigo Paestra.

They confronted each other. It was a face.

The renewal of time asserted itself. They were face to face and looked at each other.

Suddenly, in the street, below, the police went by, already in the talkative, happy mood of the approaching killing.

Maria had fallen prey to happiness. They became bolder. While the police were passing by they kept looking at each other. The waiting finally burst open, released. From every corner of the sky, from all the streets and from those who were lying there. Just from the sky Maria would have guessed that this was Rodrigo Paestra. It was now ten to two. An hour and a half before his death, Rodrigo Paestra had accepted to see her.

151

Maria raised her hand to say hello. She waited. A slow, slow hand came out of the shroud, rose and also made the gesture, of mutual understanding. Then both of the hands fell down.

At last, the horizon was completely cleared by the storm. Like a blade it was cutting the wheat fields. A warm wind rose and began to dry the streets. The weather was beautiful, just as it would be beautiful during the day. The night was still whole. Perhaps solutions could be found to the problems of conscience. Perhaps.

Serenely Maria raised her hand, again. He answered, again. Oh, how marvelous. She raised her hand to tell him that he must wait. Wait, her hand was saying. Did he understand? He did. His head had completely emerged from the black shroud, as white as snow. They were eleven yards away from each other. Did Rodrigo Paestra understand that she wanted to help him? He had understood. Maria started again, patiently, reasonably. Wait, wait Rodrigo Paestra. Wait a little longer, I'm going down, I'm coming to you. Who knows, Rodrigo Paestra?

The patrol arrived. This time Maria entered the corridor. The head too had heard and had covered itself again with the shroud. But they couldn't see anything from down below. The idea would never occur to them. Again they spoke about their work, about their low pay, of how hard it is to be a policeman. Like the previous patrol. Just wait. They were gone.

On its own the head had again come out of the shroud, and looked toward the balcony where this woman was waiting. Again she signaled that he should wait. The head nodded. Yes, he had understood that he should wait, that she was going down, coming to him.

Everyone in the corridor was sleeping. Maria took off her shoes to walk around the sleeping bodies. Her little girl was there, in a position of blissful tranquility, lying on her back. There was Claire too, asleep. And Pierre. Two steps away from her, wanted by Claire but unaware. Claire, this beautiful fruit of the slow degradation of their love.

Maria had gone beyond the corridor. She was holding her shoes in her hand. Through the skylight the brightness of the sky shone on the tables and made the tablecloths look blue, as well as the air. The tables were half cleared. Bodies were lying on the benches: the waiters had probably given their rooms to the tourists. The whole staff was still asleep.

Maria again crossed this area of sleep. It was summer. The staff was exhausted. The back doors must have been left open. It had been a crime of passion, just a one-time murderer. Why would they have locked the doors? On the right there was the manager's office, where Claire and Pierre, last night, had at last been alone, without her, for a long time. The office was dark. Maria looked through the glass pane. Nobody was sleeping there. If Maria wanted to leave by this side of the hotel, she would have to cross a short glass-enclosed passage adjoining the corridor.

The door to this passage was locked.

Maria tried again. Sweat covered her face. The door was locked. There was no other exit to the street besides the stairs leading from this passage. The only other way of leaving was through the servants' hall.

Maria walked back through the dining room. Toward the doors in the rear. One of them was open. Leading to the kitchen. First there was a pantry. Then a long, immense kitchen. Everything was in complete disorder. This was noticeable because a big bay window let in more light there than in the dining room. Could it be dawn? It was impossible that it was dawn. Maria looked through the bay window. It was just a lamp in the courtyard where the cars were parked. The heat from the ovens could still be felt, sticky, heavy, nauseating.

There in the kitchen, near the exit, a young man was sleeping on a camp bed.

A door had been left open in the back; where the walls narrowed, between the bay window and a cupboard. Maria pulled it toward her. The young man turned over and groaned. Then he was quiet and Maria opened the door. The door opened on a spiral staircase. Had Rodrigo Paestra kept on hoping? The stairs were made of wood. They creaked under Maria's footsteps. It was as hot there as during the day. Sweat was running down from Maria's hair. Two floors. The staircase went on for two floors and was completely dark.

The glazed door was unlocked. It opened onto the garage, and the courtyard within the hotel. Maria hadn't thought of that. But probably there was a watchman there too. He couldn't have heard Maria calling Rodrigo Paestra. The courtyard was far from the street. Perhaps there was no one there. And in that case the gate would be locked. Maria looked at her watch. It was five past two. Pierre had driven the car into the garage. Maria didn't know where it was. She went out. The courtyard seemed sandy, white. The cars were in the back, many of them under a shed, in the dark.

Maria was near the door. She closed it. The door made a long, shrill sound, but apparently no one heard it. No one? Wait. No, apparently no one had heard the door complain.

Between this door and the shed, the courtyard was empty, wide and empty. She had to cross this space. A quarter moon lit up the courtyard. In the middle of this courtyard, the shadow of a roof. The roof of the last house in the town, before the wheat fields. Yes, the light which shone in the kitchen through the bay window came from a storm lamp hanging from the shed, very high, and dancing in the light night wind. The cars were shining. There probably was a reliable watchman. But where?

Just as Maria decided to cross the courtyard, the police went by in the street behind the courtyard gate. They were coming straight from the other street, the one where Rodrigo Paestra was. Maria recognized their soft footsteps in the mud of the street: the last one before the wheat fields. They were still talking. She looked at her watch. And noticed that thirteen minutes had gone by since she had left the balcony, in other words, since the previous patrol. She had put her shoes back on before opening the glazed door at the bottom of the staircase. She went on through the courtyard. And she reached the shed. Already the patrol was in the distance.

It was probably best to make a noise. There was the black Rover. Maria opened the door. Then she waited. A familiar perfume came out of the car: Claire's perfume. Maria noisily slammed the door shut.

Someone coughed in the shed. Then someone asked what was the matter. Maria opened the door again, left it open, and walked toward the voice.

The man hadn't moved. He had sat up on his camp bed, against the wall, in the corner of the shed that was farthest away from the gate.

"I'm a guest at the hotel," Maria said. "I was looking for the little black Rover."

She took out her cigarettes from her skirt pocket. She offered him one, lit it for him. He was about thirty. Very casually he took the cigarette. He probably had been asleep. He was covered with the same brown blanket as Rodrigo Paestra.

"You're already leaving for Madrid?"

He was surprised. Maria pointed to the sky.

"No," she said. "The weather is so nice. I couldn't sleep in the corridor. I'm going for a ride."

The man got up completely. He stood in front of her. She smiled at

154

him. There were still men who would look at her. Both of them were smoking and could see each other in the light of their cigarettes.

"I disturbed you, I'm sorry. But it's because of the gate."

"It doesn't matter. It's not locked. It's the same every summer."

He pulled himself together. Spoke about the weather, about the coolness which, every night, comes about that same time.

"You should go back to sleep," Maria said. "I'll close the gate."

He lay down on his bed, went on looking at her. And as she moved away, all of a sudden he became bolder.

"You're going for a ride, like that, alone? I could come along if you want. If you don't take too long." He laughed.

Maria also laughed. She could hear her laughter in the empty courtyard. The man didn't insist.

Maria took her time. She lowered the top, fastened it. The man heard her. He cried out softly, already half asleep.

"The storm is over," he said. "Tomorrow will be beautiful."

"Thanks," Maria said.

She got into the Rover, backed up, and drove to the gate without headlights. She idled. She had to wait for the next patrol which was due in two minutes. She could see the time.

There it came. The patrol stopped in front of the gate, was silent, and moved on. Tourists, they must have thought, leaving for Madrid at night to take advantage of the cool temperature.

When Maria opened the gate, the patrol had vanished. She had to get out of the Rover again, but this time, very fast. Maria got out, then closed the gate. Still this heat in her hair. Why be so scared? Why?

Once, the surface of a lake had been as calm as this night. The weather was sunny. Maria remembered the reflection of the sun on the lake and, suddenly, from the boat, through the calm water, you could see the depth of the lake shining also. The water was clear. Shapes appeared. Normal shapes, but raped by the sun.

Pierre was in the boat with Maria.

Maria got back into the Rover. The watchman hadn't followed her. She looked at her watch. Dawn would be there in less than an hour and a half. Maria took the brandy bottle and drank. A long, enormous gulp. It burned so much that she had to close her eyes with pleasure.

Five

SHE HAD TO ENTER the street the patrol had just left. Their paths went in different directions at the end of that street. They had gone to the right, taking the last street in the town, the one along the wheat fields. She would move toward the main square, driving parallel to the front of the hotel. From the balcony she had been able to see clearly the layout of the town. It was possible. Two perpendicular streets bound Rodrigo Paestra's roof.

She started very slowly, up to the turn, a few yards from the gate. Then she had to speed up. Only ten minutes left before the next patrol. Unless her calculations were wrong. If they were, it was probable that Maria would give Rodrigo Paestra to the town police two hours before dawn.

The Rover was making a dull noise, but it drowned out the sound of the patrol's footsteps, dimmed by the mud. Still, she had to move forward. She reached the corner of the two streets from which you could see their whole length. They were still deserted. In just an hour people would be getting up to go to the fields. But these people were still asleep.

The noise of the engine didn't wake anyone at that time of night.

Maria didn't get out of the Rover. Could he hear her? She sang softly.

From where she was, she couldn't see him. She could only see the sky and, in the sky, the clearly outlined mass of the chimney. The section of the roof on Maria's side was plunged in the darkness of night.

She went on singing the song she had been singing earlier, when she was losing hope that he was there. And she went on singing as she got out of the Rover. She opened the back door, put away the numerous objects Judith always picked up wherever they stopped and then left behind on the back seat. There were also newspapers. One of Pierre's jackets. Claire's scarf, even her own scarf, there. Newspapers, more newspapers.

There were about eight minutes left before the next patrol.

A shadow broke up the neat angle of the roofs against the clear sky. It was he. He had gone around the chimney. Maria kept singing. Her voice clutched at her throat. You can always sing. She couldn't stop singing once she had started. He was there.

The warm wind was again blowing all over. It made the palm trees on the square cry out. It alone was moving through the deserted streets.

He had gone around the chimney, still wrapped in the black shroud in which she had seen him earlier. He was down on all fours. He had become a mass more shapeless than before, monstrously inapt. Ugly. He crawled over the tiles while Maria sang.

Probably six more minutes before the police would come by.

He must have been barefoot. He made no noise except a sound like the wind when, in its course, it blows against trees, houses, street corners.

He was slow. Did he know there was so little time left? Did he know? His legs, stiff after such a long wait, were clumsy. His face was exposed and his whole body, enormous, on the ridge of the roof, was spread out like an animal in a butcher's stall. With both hands, while singing, Maria signaled him to roll over, down the slope of the roof. And then she pointed to the Rover. Showing him that he would, at the end of his fall, land in the Rover. She sang faster, still faster, more and more softly. The wall was blind for twenty yards on this side of the town. Nobody could hear Maria.

He was doing it. He got ready to do it, his legs raised at first and then falling down, and he was doing it. Again his face had disappeared in the black shroud and a bundle of rags worn by time, its color nondescript like soot, moved toward Maria.

Still no one in the streets. He now rolled cleverly, trying not to make the tiles of the roof squeak under him. Maria made more noise with the engine. She was still singing, not realizing that she was singing for nothing. He was there, he was coming, he was getting there. She sang.

He had covered a yard. She was still singing, still the same song. Very softly. Another yard covered. He had covered three yards. In the street, there still was no one, not even the watchman who must have gone back to sleep.

A patrol should have left the square and gone northward, in the direction of the Hotel Principal. That was their route. Voices were coming from there, loud at first, then becoming dimmer. There were probably four minutes left before these voices would burst out at the end of the street alongside the hotel. Rodrigo Paestra had to cover one more yard to reach Maria.

Just as she thought her calculations were wrong because, before the four minutes were up, steps were already echoing that would turn up in the street alongside the hotel balconies, just as she thought that she wasn't hearing right, that it was impossible, Rodrigo Paestra must have thought so too because he covered the one yard that was left and fell into the Rover, rolling more quickly, flexible, his body like a spring. He had hurled himself forward. He had fallen into the Rover. A bundle of soft, black laundry had fallen into the Rover.

That was it. Just as Maria started, the patrol must have turned into the street. He had fallen on the seat. And he must have rolled onto the floor. Nothing moved. And yet he was there, close to her, on the floor, wrapped in his blanket.

A window lit up. Someone shouted.

Whistles rang out through the town, taking turns endlessly. Maria was approaching the main square. When he had fallen from the roof, the gutter had broken under his weight and had made a catastrophic noise, an obscene racket. One window lit up? Yes. Two, three windows lit up. Things crying out. Doors of the night.

Was it the warm wind that had just risen? Was it Rodrigo Paestra? The whistling went on. The patrol on the hotel street had sounded the alarm. But it hadn't seen the Rover taking off fifty yards away, in another street. The wind had carried its noise toward the fields. Those squares of light over the countryside were windows. The electricity still wasn't working and the windows were slow to light up. After making a turn, Maria was about a hundred yards from where the police must have been searching the roofs.

A patrol was coming toward her on the double. She stopped. The patrol slowed down in front of her, looked at the empty car and went on. It stopped further on, under a window, and called out. No one answered. It went on to the end of the street.

She had to go more slowly. Why would the Rover have been where the gutter was still vibrating, broken, in the wind? The black Rover belonged to a guest at the hotel, a guest who was free, alone, disturbed by this difficult night. What should Maria be afraid of?

Was she no longer afraid? Her fear had practically disappeared. It had left only a fresh, just matured, flowering memory of what it had been. Less than a minute had gone by. Fear became as inconceivable as the heart's jumbled adolescence.

Maria had to make up her mind to cross the square. She did it. She knew now that behind her nothing could be seen of Rodrigo Paestra. The seat was empty. It was impossible to leave the town without crossing the square, where the two roads leading out of the town started, one going to Madrid, the other to Barcelona and France.

At that time of night, only one car, it had to start at some point, was driving toward Madrid. The first tourist, people would say.

About twenty policemen were standing opposite the café where Maria had had her manzanillas the day before. They were listening to the whistles, were answering, waiting for orders to move on. One of them stopped Maria.

"Where are you going?"

He looked at the empty car, was reassured, smiled at her.

"I'm staying at the hotel. We didn't get a room and I can't sleep," she added, "with all the noise you're making. I'm going for a ride. What's going on?"

Did he believe her? Yes, he looked at her carefully, then glanced away from her and pointed toward the hotel, in the distance. He explained: "They must have found Rodrigo Paestra on a roof, but I am not sure."

Maria turned around. Spotlights swept the rooftops just before the hotel. The policeman said nothing else.

She started off slowly. The road to Madrid was right opposite her. You had to turn around a clump of palmettos. She remembered very clearly that it was there, the road to Madrid. There couldn't be any doubt.

The engine of the car worked smoothly. Claire's black Rover took off, then moved in the direction Maria wanted, toward Madrid. Maria was at the wheel and, carefully and methodically, she drove around the square. The whistling went on in the part of town where the gutter was still yelping. A jackal. The young policeman, puzzled and smiling, watched Maria drive away. She was driving around him, around the square. Was she smiling at him? She would never know. She drove into the main street, the westward extension of the hotel street. She didn't look whether any balconies, adjacent to corridors she knew, were lit up.

It was the road to Madrid. The biggest road in Spain. Straight ahead, monumental.

True, this was still the town. One patrol, two patrols, empty-handed, saw and looked at the black Rover with foreign license plates which was moving toward Madrid so early in the day. But the recent storm, and this sudden youthfulness of the night, made several of them smile.

One called out to the woman who was driving alone.

There were two garages. And then some kind of a shop, quite large, and isolated. And then very small houses. Maria no longer knew what time it was. It was just any time before dawn. But dawn wasn't there yet. It needed its usual amount of time to get there. It wasn't there yet.

After the houses, the shacks, there were the wheat fields. And nothing but wheat under the blue light. Blue was the wheat. It went on and on. Maria was driving slowly, but moving ahead. At some point in the night, at a turn, she saw a sign, clearly lit up by her headlights, and noticed that she was eight miles out of the town she had just left, Rodrigo Paestra's town.

She went on, up to a dirt road that looked dark next to the light wheat field. She turned into it, went on for about a third of a mile, and stopped. On both sides of this road there was the same wheat as before, and the night was just as full. There was no village in sight. And there was total silence as soon as Maria turned off the engine.

When Maria turned around, Rodrigo Paestra was getting out of his shroud.

He sat down on the back seat and looked around him. His face looked blurred in the blue light of the night.

If there were birds in this plain, they were probably still sleeping in the sodden clay, between the blades of wheat.

Maria took some cigarettes out of her pocket. She pulled one out and handed it to him. He pounced on it and when she lit it for him she noticed that Rodrigo Paestra was shivering with cold. He smoked the cigarette with both hands so as not to let it fall. It is cold in Spain, on stormy nights, an hour before dawn.

He was smoking.

He hadn't looked at this woman.

But she was looking at him. His name is Rodrigo Paestra. While looking at the wheat, she could see him.

160

His hair was glued to his scalp. His clothes were stuck to his body as if he had drowned. He probably was tall and robust. Was he about thirty? He was still smoking. What was he looking at? The cigarette. Most likely, as he looked at it, his eyes were black.

Maria unfolded the blanket next to her and held it out to him. He took it and put it on the back seat. He hadn't understood. He was smoking again. Then he looked at both sides of the car. He was the first to speak.

"Where are we?"

"The road to Madrid."

He didn't say anything else. Maria didn't either. She turned again, facing the windshield. They were both smoking. He finished first. She gave him another one. He was still shaking. In the light of the match, his expression was vacant, reduced to his concentrating on not shaking.

"Where do you want to go?" Maria asked.

He didn't answer immediately. He was probably looking at her for the first time, from very far away, without caring. Anyway, this was a glance from him. Maria didn't see his eyes, but she saw his glance as clearly as in broad daylight.

"I don't know," Rodrigo Paestra said.

Again Maria turned to the front. Then, not being able to bear it, she turned back to face him. She intensely wanted to look at him. The haggard expression he had had when he had looked at her had vanished. There were only his eyes now. And, over his eyes, the eyelids opening automatically whenever he raised his cigarette to his mouth. Nothing. Rodrigo Paestra had no strength left except to smoke. Why had he followed Maria this far? Probably just to be nice, a last polite gesture. Someone calls you and you answer. What was Rodrigo Paestra now? Maria devoured him with her eyes, devoured with her eyes this living prodigy, this black flower which had bloomed that night in the licentiousness of love.

He had split her head open with one shot of his gun. And his love was resting, in an improvised morgue in the town hall, dead at nineteen, still naked, wrapped in a brown blanket, identical with the one he had wrapped around himself on the roof. As for him, the other one, the bullet went through his heart. They were separated.

"What time is it?" Rodrigo Paestra asked.

Maria showed him her watch, but he didn't look at it.

"A little after two thirty."

His eyes looked at the wheat fields again. He was resting against the back seat and it seemed to Maria that she had heard a man sigh in the silence. Then the silence came back. And also the slow passing of time before dawn. Interminable.

It was cold. Had the warm wind blowing on the town before really existed? A gust that had followed the storm and had disappeared. The swelling, ripe wheat, tortured by the showers of the preceding day, remained motionless.

The cold that suddenly surged from the motionless air bit their eyes and their shoulders.

Rodrigo Paestra must have fallen asleep. His head was resting on the back of the seat. And his mouth was slightly open. He was sleeping.

Something changed in the air they were breathing, a pale light blew over the fields. For how long? For how long had he been sleeping? An onslaught began somewhere on the horizon, colorless, uneven, impossible to define. An onslaught began somewhere in her head and in her body a growing uneasiness, unrelated to the memory of any other, searching for its identity. And yet, and yet, the sky was clear and blue if you wanted it that way. It still was. Of course this was only an accidental light, the perfect illusion of a change of mood, happening through a sudden complaisance, coming from far away, from various strains and from the strain of that night. Perhaps?

No. It was dawn.

He was sleeping. Sleeping.

There still wasn't any specific color in the dawn.

Rodrigo Paestra was dreaming. He was so deeply asleep he could dream. Maria had her chin on the back of the seat, and was watching him. Sometimes the sky too, but always him. Very attentively. That is to say she was watching Rodrigo Paestra. Yes, there he was, sleeping soundly, flying over all his troubles with the wings of a bird. You could see it. He was carried well above his troubles, in spite of his new weight, and he consented unconsciously.

Maria was deprived of Rodrigo Paestra's perfectly empty glance while he was sleeping.

He had just smiled in his sleep. Above his slightly open mouth, she could swear that a smile had taken shape, a quivering smile, unmistakably like a smile of life and joy. Other words were banished from dawn.

Between his thighs, next to his sex, there was the shape of his gun. His blanket was on the floor. The car blanket next to him. It was useless

162

to cover him. Anyway she wanted to see all of him and forever. She could see him clearly. And that his sleep was sound, and good.

She had to avoid looking up at the sky.

It wasn't worth it. Dawn was rising upon him. The livid light had covered his whole body, little by little. His body had clear, obvious proportions. He again had a name: Rodrigo Paestra.

The time had come now when he would have been caught like a rat.

Maria spread out, a little like him, on the front seat, and she watched the dawn move over him.

Too late, the memory of a child came back to her. She pushed it away. While he was still dreaming just as he had dreamed the day before.

She still had to wait. And later, she would have to call him.

Then he became pink. A steady weariness blew over the countryside and over Maria. Peacefully, the sky took on color. She still had some time. A car going to Madrid drove by on the highway. Maria furtively looked at the sky, on the other side. The pink color that was on him did come from the sky. They had reached the time of the first departures. The car going to Madrid undoubtedly had come from the hotel. In one of the still dark corridors, stretching painfully after a bad night, Claire must have greeted the day that was rising on their love. And then, she fell asleep again.

He was sleeping. Maria got up and took the brandy out of the door pocket. Because of her empty stomach, the liquor came up in her throat, burning and familiar, with a feeling of nausea that woke her up. The sun. There was the sun on the horizon. All at once it was less cold. Her eyes hurt. He had been sleeping for nearly an hour. The sun swept over his body, entered his slightly open mouth, and his clothes began to let off a cloud of steam that looked like smoke. His hair let off the same smoke. Very tenuous smoke of an abandoned fire. He still couldn't feel the light. His eyes barely trembled. But his eyelids sealed in his sleep. He no longer smiled.

Wouldn't it be better to call him immediately, as soon as possible, so it would be all over?

Again Maria took the brandy, drank, put it back in the door pocket. She was still waiting. She hadn't done it yet. She still hadn't called Rodrigo Paestra.

And yet, it would be best if that moment in Maria's life, when Rodrigo Paestra would wake up in the Rover with this stranger near him in the wheat road, would be over as fast as possible. His memory would come back—predictably—a few seconds after he woke up. He would remain disconcerted just long enough to understand that he had been dreaming. Maria would have to decide to wake Rodrigo Paestra.

The sun was half off the horizon. Two cars, six cars went by on their way to Madrid. Again Maria took the brandy, took another gulp. This time she felt so nauseous she had to close her eyes. Then, afterwards, she began to call softly.

"Rodrigo Paestra."

He hadn't heard. His eyes trembled then sealed up still tighter. She was still nauseous from the brandy. She felt like vomiting. Maria closed her eyes so she wouldn't have to vomit and to look at him.

"Rodrigo Paestra."

She fumbled about to replace the brandy in the pocket and she let her head sink back onto the seat.

"Rodrigo Paestra."

Something must have moved in the back. Then nothing happened. He didn't wake up. Maria sat up and, this time, looked at him.

"Rodrigo Paestra."

His eyes had blinked. Maria, her nausea gone, started again. She took the brandy, drank some more. This gulp was bigger than the last one. Was she going to faint? No. It just prevents you from seeing, prevents you from speaking calmly, only lets you scream.

"Rodrigo Paestra, Rodrigo Paestra."

Again Maria buried her head in the back of the front seat.

It must have happened. This must have been his waking. A soft cry, a long moan had come from the back of the car.

When Maria turned he was already past the first moments of waking. He was sitting up on the seat and with rheumy, bloodshot eyes was looking at the wheat fields, his land of wheat fields. Was he surprised? Yes, he was still surprised, but just a little. Then his eyes wandered from the wheat fields. He was sitting up straight now, but no longer looking at anything. He remembered everything.

"I have to get back to the hotel."

He was silent. Maria handed him a cigarette. He didn't see it. She was holding the cigarette out to him, but he still didn't see it. He started to look at Maria. When she had told him that she would have to get back to the hotel, he had grabbed his brown blanket and his gesture had stopped abruptly. He had discovered Maria's existence. It was probably by seeing her that he had remembered.

She was trying not to breathe too deeply so as not to vomit. The last gulp of brandy at daybreak, probably, coming up in her throat like a sob that you have to keep holding in.

He was looking at her, looking at her, looking at her. An empty stare, inconceivably disinterested. What else did he notice looking at Maria? From what surprise, exactly, was he returning when he saw Maria? Had he noticed just then that he could expect nothing more from Maria, from Maria or anyone else? That with this dawn a new certainty was exposed which night had kept hidden?

"I have a child at the hotel," she said, "that's why I have to get back."

It was over. His eyes moved away from her. Again she held out to him the cigarette she had kept in her hand; he took it, and she lit it for him. He picked up the brown blanket from the seat.

"Listen," Maria said.

Perhaps he hadn't heard. She had spoken very softly. He had opened the door, he had got out, and was now standing next to the car.

"Listen," Maria repeated. "The border isn't very far. We can try."

He was standing in the dirt road and again he looked at his land of wheat fields all around him. And then he came back, he remembered, he closed the door. He remembered. In the same way, during the night, he had been willing to answer when his name was called. He had been gracious then. The sun was glaring and forced him to squint.

"We can try," Maria repeated.

He shook his head, as if to refuse, very slowly, he had no opinion.

"At noon," Maria said. "At noon I'll be here. I'll be back. At noon."

"Noon," Rodrigo Paestra said after her.

With her fingers, she pointed to the sun and opened her hands wide toward him.

"Noon, noon," she kept saying.

He nodded, he had understood. Then he turned around and looked for a spot where he could go, where he could settle down, in this wide, in this free expanse of wheat. The sun was completely above the horizon, and was hitting him full blast, his shadow was perfect, a long shadow on the wheat.

He could have found a spot to go to, where he could rest. He went off on the dirt road. Alongside of him, his blanket, which he held in his hand, was dragging. He was barefoot in his rope sandals. He had no jacket, only a dark blue shirt like all the men in his village.

He walked on the road, stopped, hesitated it seemed, then walked into the wheat field, about twenty yards from the Rover, and just dropped as if struck by lightning. Maria waited. He didn't get up.

When she got back on the highway, away from the humid clay of the wheat fields, it was already hot. It would get hotter still, until noon, inevitably, and would stay that way all day until sundown. She knew that.

With the sun on her neck, her nausea came back, throbbing. Maria fought off sleep, her hands gripping the steering wheel. Whenever she felt she had won, she would be engulfed again. However, she was getting closer to the hotel.

She passed the shop.

Then the garages.

There were already a few peasants. But very few cars going toward Madrid.

Just when Maria thought she could no longer fight off sleep, the memory of Judith got her to the outskirts of the town, then to the town. And then, the square.

The police were still there. The ones from the night must have been sleeping. These men, in broad daylight, looked discouraged. They were yawning. Their feet were muddy, their clothes crumpled, but they were still whistling throughout the town. In front of the town hall, wearily, they kept watch over the two victims of the day before.

The hotel gate was open. The young watchman had been replaced by an old man. There was room in the shed. The cars had been coming from the hotel. Maria left through the gate, took the street around the hotel where, during the night, she had met Rodrigo Paestra. She had some trouble walking because she had had so much brandy, but the street was still deserted and nobody saw her.

There was room in the corridor. Her nausea was so strong that she first had to lie down next to her child to gather enough courage to look around. The brown blanket was warm from Judith's body. Somebody had closed the doors leading to the balcony, so that the hall was still cool and quiet. And restful. Judith turned over, still happily sleeping. Maria rested.

They were still there, both of them. They were still sleeping. Two hours had gone by since she had left the corridor. It was very early.

166

Four in the morning. In their sleep, they had moved closer to each other, probably without realizing it. Pierre had Claire's surrendered ankle against his cheek. His mouth was brushing against it. Claire's ankle was resting on Pierre's open hand. If he closed his hand, that woman's ankle would be completely contained in it. Maria kept looking, but it didn't happen. They were sleeping like logs.

Six

"MARIA."

Maria woke up. Pierre was calling her. He was amused by such sleepiness. He was leaning against the wall and looking at her.

"It's ten o'clock," he apologized. "Everybody has left."

"Judith?"

"She's playing in the courtyard. She's all right."

The corridor around Maria was empty. The balcony window was open and the sun was shining obliquely into the corridor. It shone on the red, glaring ground, like the day before, and was reflected on Pierre's face. Maria felt nauseous again. She got up and then lay down again.

"One more minute, and I'll get up."

At the end of the corridor, waiters were already going back and forth carrying trays of cool drinks. The bedroom doors were open. Women were singing while they made the beds. And the heat was there, already.

"I told them to let you sleep," Pierre said. "But in a few minutes the sun would have been shining on you."

He looked at her insistently. She had taken a cigarette, she tried to smoke it, and threw it away. She smiled at Pierre through her nausea.

"It's hard for me, in the morning," she said. "But I'm going to get up."

"Do you want me to stay?"

"Wait for me in the dining room. When alcoholics wake up they should be alone."

They both smiled. Pierre left. Maria called him back.

"Claire, where is she?" Maria asked.

"With the child, downstairs."

When she managed to get up and reach the dining room, the coffee pot was steaming on Pierre's table. Pierre knew what Maria needed on

168

those mornings. He let her drink, drink all the coffee, without speaking. Then stretch, stretch, run her hands through her hair, and finally smoke.

"I feel better now," she said.

Except for two other tables, they were alone in the dining room, which was once more perfectly neat and orderly. The tables, all white, were already set for lunch. A large, brownish-gray canvas had been hung under the skylight that had been blue during the night, and was filtering the sun. Here the heat was bearable.

"You drank last night, Maria," Pierre stated.

She moved her hand over her face. It was through her hands on her face that she could feel, that she knew she had been beautiful, but had started to be less so. It was from the way in which she moved her hands on her face, without caution, that she knew she had accepted defeat forever. She didn't answer Pierre.

"It's a question of will power, again," Pierre went on. "You could drink less, at night at least."

Maria gulped down the rest of her coffee.

"Oh, that's all right," she said. "One unpleasant hour in the morning, and then it's over."

"I looked for you last night. The car wasn't there. The watchman told me that you had gone for a ride. I understood."

He straightened up a little, and this time he stroked her hair.

"Maria, Maria."

She didn't smile at him. For a moment he left his hand on her hair, and then took it away. He knew why Maria hadn't smiled.

"I'll take a shower," she said, "and then, if you want, we can leave."

There was Claire, holding Judith by the hand. They walked in. Claire was dressed in blue. She looked at Pierre first as she came in. From the moment she came in, her desire for Pierre was noticeable; it accompanied her like a shadow. It seemed as if she were shouting. But she was talking to Maria.

"You went off last night?"

Maria looked for an answer, in vain. She found herself exposed to Claire's gaze.

"They woke us up last night," Claire went on. "They thought they had found Rodrigo Paestra. Everybody was at the windows. What confusion! And we kept looking for you."

What did they do last night when they noticed she was no longer there? Once they noticed that she wasn't coming back, that the Rover wasn't coming, after the children had fallen asleep again, after the hotel had calmed down, first the corridor, and then little by little the whole hotel? Did they . . .?

"I was with the police," Maria said. "I drank manzanillas with the police. In the same café as yesterday."

Claire laughed. Pierre also laughed, but not as much as Claire.

Claire kept sighing, "Maria, Oh, Maria, Maria."

They loved her. Claire's laughter was not quite the same as usual. It was not impossible that it should have happened. That they should have been on the lookout for the Rover, leaning against each other, in each other's arms while waiting for her in the darkness of the corridor. Who could tell?

"Judith," Maria said.

She held her at arm's length and looked at her. A little girl who had slept well during the night. Blue eyes. The rings of fear had vanished from under her eyes. Maria pushed her away, away from her. He probably was in the wheat fields. He was sleeping. The shade from the stalks was frail and he had begun to feel too warm. Whom would you save, in the end, if you saved Rodrigo Paestra?

"She gobbled up a big breakfast this morning," Claire said. "A cool night and she starts gobbling."

Judith had come back to Maria. Maria took her, looked at her again, then let her go, nearly knocking her over. Judith was used to it. She let her mother look at her, then push her about to her heart's content, then she went off and walked around the dining room, singing.

"We shouldn't get to Madrid too late," Claire said. "Before night if possible. To get rooms."

Maria remembered, and left for the office. The bathrooms were available. The shower felt good. Some time went by like that. Maria looked at her naked body, all by itself. What would you save, in the end, if you took Rodrigo Paestro to France? He was asleep in an ocean of wheat. Water ran benevolently down her breasts and her stomach. Maria waited for time to go by, like the water, inexhaustibly. Of course, the findings would show extenuating circumstances. They would take into account Rodrigo Paestra's being jealous of Perez. What more could be done for Rodrigo Paestra than to take into consideration this jealousy which made him kill?

In the dining room only Claire was left waiting for Maria.

"Pierre went to pay the bill," she said. "And then we'll go."

"How beautiful you are," Maria said. "Claire, you are so, so beautiful."

Claire lowered her eyes. She tried not to, and then she said it.

"After they had looked for this poor man, just a short time after, cars started to leave. Impossible to go back to sleep. I mean it was difficult. But then—"

"What time was it?"

"It was still night, I don't know exactly. There was whistling all over town. There was a noise of falling tiles, over there, the wind I suppose. They really got into a state. We didn't fall asleep again until late."

"That late?"

"I think the sun was rising. Yes. Lying down, we could see the sky. We talked, Pierre and I, yes I think we talked until dawn."

Claire waited. Maria didn't insist. Judith came back. Claire loved Judith, Pierre's child.

"There will never be another storm," Claire told Judith. "You mustn't be afraid."

"Never?"

They promised. She went back to her exploration of the hotel corridors. Pierre came back. He was ready, he said. He had filled in the hotel forms. He apologized for making them wait. And then he was silent. Claire wasn't looking at him this morning. She lowered her eyes while smoking. They must not have been together, even before dawn, in the darkness of the corridors. Maria was mistaken. If they no longer looked at each other as they had the day before, if they avoided doing so, it was because they had confessed their love to each other, whispering, when the sky seemed red over the wheat fields and when the memory of Maria, poignant, loathsome because of the very strength of their new love, came back to them with the dawn. What were they to do with Maria?

"We still want to see San Andrea," Pierre said. "Three Goyas. If only not to be sorry later."

Some guests came in. Women. Pierre didn't look any more.

"I'm tired," Maria said. "I'll wait for you."

"What did you drink?" Claire asked.

"The brandy. I'll wait for you in the car. I'll feel better by noon."

They exchanged looks. They must have talked about that, that also last night, and once more hoped she would change her ways. And at the same time wished, and were satisfied, that she would stay busy away from them, but not with her new unhappiness.

They went down. The pleasant coolness from her shower disappeared and when Maria recognized the courtyard, her weariness came back, like a spell. It would take enormous strength to pull Rodrigo Paestra from his bed of wheat. She would have to tell them, thwarting their dawning desire, giving up Madrid where, at night, their love was to be fulfilled. Maria watched them load the car—she didn't help—and they laughed at having to do this small job which would have made Maria groan.

She sat in front, next to Pierre. In the back, without asking any questions, Claire folded the blanket that was lying on the seat. Maria saw her doing this but gave her no explanation. They made the trip through the city that Maria had made at night. It was eleven. Four policemen were still on guard in the square, exhausted, like Maria, from their night of searching. The church of San Andrea was on the square. As well as the town hall. The murdered bodies must still be there. Guarded.

"They didn't get him," Pierre said. He parked the car in the shade, opposite the café that had stayed open during the night. Again a church. Again three Goyas. Again a vacation. Why save Rodrigo Paestra, and from what? How would Rodrigo Paestra wake up this time, from what bad sleep? Pull him out of the wheat, get him into the car, while Claire's fierce desire was being thwarted. It was ten past eleven.

"Really," Maria said, "I'm so tired, I'm going to stay here."

Claire got out, followed by Judith. Pierre left the door open and waited for Maria.

"Ten minutes," he said, "come on, Maria, come along."

She didn't want to. He closed the door. The three of them walked over to San Andrea. They went in. Maria could no longer see them.

Noon would come and Rodrigo Paestra would understand that he had been abandoned. Maria closed her eyes for a moment. Did she remember? Yes. She remembered his eyes looking at the wheat fields without recognizing them, and also his eyes when he woke up, in the sun. When she opened her eyes two children were there, fascinated by the Rover. They weren't coming back. They must have seen something else, not only the Goyas, some primitive perhaps. Holding hands they were looking, together, at other landscapes. In the distance valleys could be seen through open windows, and woods, a village, a herd.

Woods in the twilight with charming angels, herds, a smoking village on a hilltop, the breeze blowing between the hills was like their love. A lake, in the distance, as blue as your eyes. Holding hands, they were looking at each other. In the dark, he told her, I never noticed this until now, your eyes are even bluer. Like this lake.

Maria felt like moving, like having a manzanilla in the bar right there, there, opposite the car. Her hands had started to shake and she could imagine liquor in her throat and in her body, as strong as a bath. If they didn't come back she would go in that bar.

They came back. Between them, Judith was skipping.

"There weren't just the Goyas," Pierre said. "You should have come."

Claire opened the car door. Maria stopped her. Pierre brushed against her.

"Last night," Maria said, "while you were sleeping, I found the man the police were looking for, Rodrigo Paestra."

Claire's face grew very serious. She waited a second.

"You were drinking again, Maria," she said.

Pierre didn't move.

"No," Maria said. "Just chance. He was on the roof opposite the hotel balcony. I drove him about eight miles from here, on the road to Madrid. I said I'd be back at noon. He lay down in the wheat. I don't know what to do, Pierre. Pierre, I really don't know what to do."

Pierre took Maria's hand. From the silence that followed her words, Maria realized she had been shouting.

"Please, Maria," he said.

"It's true."

"No," Claire said, "no. It is not true, I could swear it isn't true."

Claire pulled away from the car; she was standing straight, looking so majestic that Maria had to lower her eyes.

"I think he doesn't care whether we come or not," Maria said. "He just doesn't care. We don't have to go. I think I'd rather we didn't go."

Pierre tried to smile.

"But it isn't true?"

"It is. The town is very small. He was there, on the roof opposite the hotel balcony. One chance in a thousand, but it's true."

"You didn't tell us this morning," Claire said.

"Why didn't you tell us, Maria? Why didn't you?"

Why? Claire walked away from the car with Judith. She didn't feel like waiting for Maria's answer.

"By chance too," Maria said to Pierre, "the first time I saw him, you were with Claire on a hotel balcony."

Maria saw Claire coming back toward them.

"It wasn't until much later, when both of you were asleep, that I was sure it was him, Rodrigo Paestra. It was very late."

"I knew it," Pierre said.

People had stopped on the square. They were looking at Claire, who was walking slowly toward the Rover.

"I told you," Maria went on, "after we had finished talking. But you had fallen asleep."

"I knew it," Pierre repeated.

Claire was with them again.

"So, that's how it is, he's waiting for you?" she asked softly.

All of a sudden she had become very sweet again. She was close to Pierre, closer than ever. Threatening but discreet. Pierre was now paying attention to Maria's story.

"Oh! I don't know," Maria said. "I think he doesn't really care."

"Eleven-twenty," Pierre said.

"I really don't feel like going there at all," Maria said. "You do what you want."

"Where to?" Judith asked.

"Madrid. We could go in another direction."

Again the policemen were walking around the square, dragging their feet. It was already as hot as at noon, and they were exhausted. The streets were already dried out by the sun. Just two hours and there wasn't a drop of water left in the gutters.

"The car blanket," Claire said, "did he use it?"

"Yes. Oh! Before we do anything else I would like a manzanilla. Before anything else."

She leaned back against the seat and saw them look at each other. Then look around the square for a café that was open. They would always let her drink, they would always protect her in her desire to drink, always.

"Come," Pierre said.

They went into the café where she had been the day before. The manzanilla was ice-cold.

174

"Why did you drink the brandy?" Claire asked. "It's the worst thing for you, brandy, at night."

"A mad craving," Maria said.

She ordered another manzanilla. They didn't interfere. Pierre too was thinking of nothing but Rodrigo Paestra. He asked the waiter for a paper. On the front page there was a bad photograph of Rodrigo Paestra. The two other photographs also. Perez. And a very young woman with a round face and dark eyes.

"They had only been married eight months," Pierre said.

Claire took the paper from him, read it, and threw it on a chair. The waiter came up to them. He pointed at the police.

"Rodrigo Paestra was a friend of mine," he said—laughing—and he motioned as if to say that they would never find him.

"They didn't catch the man," Judith said.

Maria ordered another manzanilla.

Pierre did not prevent her from ordering. Ordinarily he would have. He let her drink a third manzanilla. He looked at his watch. Judith was sitting on Claire's lap and watching. The waiter left.

"You said noon?"

"Yes. He even repeated it. He said noon. But without believing it."

Pierre also had ordered a manzanilla. Maria was having her third. She smiled.

"It's strange and new," she said.

"Will you tell us, Maria?" Claire asked.

Maria smiled even more. Then Pierre intervened.

"No more drinking," he said.

He trembled slightly as he took the glass of manzanilla. Maria promised to stop. Claire had forgotten Rodrigo Paestra and again couldn't keep her eyes off Pierre. The sun had reached the arcade. The whole square was now moving into the midday calm.

"They were living the first days of their love."

Pierre took her hand and held it tightly. But Maria pointed at the town hall.

"His wife is there," she said. "And Perez with her. Decency demanded that they be separated in death."

"Maria," Pierre cried.

"Yes. I said: the border, perhaps. He didn't answer. What a mess!"

Around her, already, the loneliness brought on by the liquor. She still knew when she would have to stop talking. She would stop.

"It's a change though," she said.

The waiter came back. They stopped talking. Pierre paid for the drinks. Were they going to Madrid? the waiter asked. They weren't sure. They spoke about the storm. Had they been on the road yesterday? They hardly answered and the waiter didn't insist.

"Would you recognize the spot?" Pierre asked.

"I'll recognize it. But what about our vacation?"

"There's no choice," Pierre said, "if that is a question. You've placed us in a situation where we no longer have a choice."

He had said this without bitterness. He smiled. Claire was silent.

"Our vacation," Maria said, "when I mentioned our vacation, I was mainly thinking about you. Not about myself."

"We knew that," Claire finally said.

Maria got up. She stood in front of Claire, who didn't move. "It's not my fault," she whispered, "it's nobody's fault. Nobody's. Nobody's. That's what I meant. I didn't choose to see this man on the roof last night. You would have done the same thing, Claire."

"No."

Maria sat down again.

"Let's not go," she stated. "First of all, we won't be able to hide him, he's enormous, a giant, and even if we could, he cares so little about it, that we'd be doing something completely useless, even ridiculous I would say. There's nothing we can save of Rodrigo Paestra except his skin. Claire, you will get to Madrid. I won't move. Except to go to Madrid."

Claire was tapping on the table. Pierre had stood up.

"I won't move," Maria repeated. "I'll have a manzanilla."

"Twenty-five to twelve," Pierre said.

He left the café by himself and walked over to the car. Judith ran after him. Claire watched him go.

"Come, Maria."

"Yes."

She took her by the arm. And Maria got up. No, she hadn't had much to drink. She had been drinking a bit too soon after the brandy, but she'd be all right.

"I'll be all right," she told Claire. "Don't worry."

Pierre walked up to her. He pointed at Judith, who was already sitting in the back of the car.

"And Judith?" he asked.

176

"Oh! She's still so young," Maria said. "We'll just have to be a little careful."

They slowly drove away from the square. The town was quiet. Some policemen had given in to sleep and were lying flat on the balustrades.

"It's easy," Maria said. "You take the road to Madrid. There, straight ahead."

The road to Madrid. The biggest in Spain. Straight ahead, monumental.

This was still the town. A patrol was coming back, emptyhanded, in single file. They didn't look at the black Rover. They had seen many others since morning. The foreign registration plates didn't even make them turn their heads.

Not one of them looked at the Rover.

There was a garage. One garage. Maria had counted two.

"On my way out," Maria said, "I was worried. When I drove back, I was drunk. But even so I'm going to remember. There was another garage."

"The road to Madrid," Pierre said. "You can't go wrong."

The other garage. Pierre was driving nearly as slowly as she had during the night.

"Then some kind of a shop, quite large and isolated."

"There it is. Don't worry," Pierre said.

He spoke gently. He felt hot. Probably he was afraid. No one turned to look at Claire who kept silent.

The shop. It was open. An electric saw filled the hot air with its noise.

"Then, I think, some very small houses."

Low houses, children on the porches looking at the cars. They no longer wondered what time it was. It was any time before noon. Soon, after the houses, there was no other shade on the countryside but the fleeting shade of the birds.

The wheat fields weren't any help. No landmarks. Nothing but the wheat fields in the blinding light.

"I drove a long time through these fields," Maria said. "Eight miles as I told you."

Pierre looked at the mileage. He was figuring out the distance they had covered.

"Two more miles," he said. "Two more and we'll be there."

They stared at the landscape, swelling slightly toward the horizon.

The sky was evenly gray. Telephone lines were running along the road to Madrid as far as you could see. There were few cars because of the heat.

"Didn't the road turn?" Pierre asked.

She said she remembered a turn, yes, but she hadn't taken it. Then the road was straight up to the side of the road.

"Everything is going very well," Pierre said. "We're getting to the crossing. Look, there, on the left. Look carefully, Maria."

He must have been speaking so calmly because of Judith. Maybe because of Claire too. Judith was singing, rested and relaxed.

"He died from the heat, it's all over," Maria said.

The road was climbing slightly.

"Do you remember? Do you remember this climb?"

She remembered. The road was climbing very slightly, up to a crest that was probably hiding a fork, with one road to the left that they would see upon reaching the top of the hill, and more wheat fields, still more and more wheat fields.

"It's silly. It's stupid," Maria shouted.

"No," Pierre said, "not at all."

The other wheat fields. They looked less even than the previous ones. They were studded with enormous, brightly colored flowers. Claire was speaking.

"Around here," she said, "they've started harvesting."

Seven

"IT'S LIKE HELL," MARIA shouted.

Pierre stopped the Rover completely. Judith listened and tried to understand. But they stopped talking and she began to think of something else.

"Look again," Pierre said. "Please, Maria."

The side of the road went downhill on the left, straight to the bottom of the valley. There was no one on it.

"It's this road," Maria said. "The people who are harvesting are far away, half a mile on both sides of the road. They won't reach it before evening. You see, Claire."

"Of course," Claire said.

Maria now recognized the road perfectly, its gentle sweep, so gentle, its width, its original way of being buried in the wheat fields, and even its special light. She took the brandy from the car pocket, Pierre stopped her with his arm. She didn't insist, put the bottle back.

"He lay down in the wheat, waiting for noon," she said, "over there, probably"—she pointed to an indefinite spot. "It's so long ago now, where can he be?"

"Who?" Judith asked.

"A man," Claire said, "who was supposed to go to Madrid with us."

Pierre started the car. He slowly drove a few yards on the road to Madrid and then, still slowly, he turned into the side road. Two car tracks were noticeable, intertwined with those of carts.

"The Rover's wheels," Pierre said.

"You see, you see," Maria said. "The shade from the wheat must be down to nothing at this time of the day. He must be dead from the heat."

The heat was suffocating. The road was already dried out. The tracks of the carts and the Rover had been carved into it, until the next storm.

"Oh! How stupid," Maria said. "It was there. It's there."

It was a little after noon, just a little. The time agreed upon.

"Don't talk, Maria," Claire said.

"I'm not talking."

In the fields various spots stuck out, here and there, from the wide rectangles of wheat, staked out by dirt roads, each one gently sloping down to the valley. They watched the car that was coming toward them, they were wondering what the tourists were doing, if they had taken the wrong road. Standing, interrupting their work, all of them were now looking at the Rover.

"They're looking at us," Claire said.

"We're going to rest a little on this road," Pierre said, "since we didn't sleep last night because of the storm. There were no rooms in the hotel, remember Claire?"

"I remember."

Judith also looked at the workers. With her four-year-old experience she was trying to understand. Sitting on Claire's lap, she could see all the way into the valley.

Maria could now recognize the spot. In the hollow of the road, the heat didn't move and brought out sweat from every part of their bodies.

"Twenty more yards. Follow the tracks. I'll let you know."

Pierre moved ahead. The harvesters, still standing, watched them. This road led nowhere. It belonged to their fields. They were surrounding a large rectanglar area, in the center of which Rodrigo Paestra had lain down seven hours before. They had started harvesting at the bottom of the valley. They were moving up toward the road to Madrid, which they would reach by the end of the day.

The dirt road was getting more hollow, dipping beneath the level of the wheat fields. Only the heads, the still heads of the harvesters could be seen.

"I think you should stop," Maria said.

He stopped. The workers didn't move. Some of them would probably come over to the Rover.

Pierre got out of the car and made a friendly gesture with his hand, to the group nearest to them, composed of two men. A few seconds passed. And one of the two men answered Pierre's gesture. Then Pierre took Judith out of the car, lifted her, and Judith repeated the same greeting after him. When Maria thought of it later, she remembered Pierre's happy smile.

All the workers answered the little girl's greeting. The group of two men and, a little behind them, a group of women. Their faces changed: they were laughing. They were laughing, making faces because of the sun: like ripples on the water, that can be seen from far away. They were laughing.

Claire didn't leave the car. Maria got out.

"It's impossible for him to get out of the field now," she said.

Pierre pointed out to Maria several carts at the bottom of the valley. Half way down, between these carts and the road to Madrid, there were still more carts and horses.

"In half an hour," Pierre said, "they're going to eat in the shade of the carts. And, hidden by the wheat, they won't see us at all."

A voice from the car.

"In half an hour, we'll be dead from the heat," Claire said.

She again had Judith with her. She was telling her a story, while following Maria and Pierre with her eyes.

They had gone back to work. The wind that came from the valley, full of wheat dust, tickled their throats. And this wind was still balmy, it had blown through last night's storm.

"I'm going there," Maria said, "so I can at least tell him to wait, to be patient."

She slowly moved away, as if taking a walk. She sang. Pierre waited for her, in the sun.

She sang the song she had been singing for Rodrigo Paestra two hours before dawn. A worker heard her, raised his head, went back to work, failing to understand why tourists had stopped there.

She walked on mechanically and calmly, just as Rodrigo Paestra had, when he had left her at four in the morning. The road hollowed out so much that no one could possibly see her. Except Pierre and Claire.

What could Maria call the time that opened ahead of her? The certainty of her hope? This rejuvenated air she was breathing. This incandescence, this bursting of love at last without object?

Deep in the valley, there must have been a stream where the storm's luminous waters were still rolling.

She hadn't been mistaken. Her hope came true. Suddenly, on her left, the wheat opened up. She could no longer see them. She was alone with him again. She pushed aside the wheat and walked in. He was there. Over him, the wheat, naively, came back together. It would have done the same over a stone.

He was sleeping.

The colorful carts that had passed by him that morning in the rising sun had not waked him. He was where he had settled down, where he had dropped as if struck by lightning, when she had left. He was sleeping on his stomach, his legs folded, just slightly, like a child's, instinctively looking for comfort away from misfortune. The legs that had carried Rodrigo Paestra through his great misfortune, all the way to this wheat field, had, lonely and courageous, adapted themselves to his sleep.

His arms were around his head, and childishly abandoned like his legs.

Maria called out, "Rodrigo Paestra."

She bent over him. He was sleeping. She would carry that body to France. She would take him very far, her miracle, the storm murderer. So he had been waiting for her. He had believed what she had told him in the morning. She felt a desire to slip into the wheat next to his body, so that, on waking up, he would recognize an object of this world, the anonymous and grateful face of a woman.

"Rodrigo Paestra."

Half bent over him, she called very softly, wishing and at the same time fearing to wake him up. Probably Pierre and Claire could neither see nor hear her. Nor even imagine her.

"Rodrigo Paestra," she said very softly.

So strong was her pleasure at seeing Rodrigo Paestra again that she thought she was still drunk. Then she thought him ungrateful. He was there, waiting for her to come at the appointed time. Just as you wait for spring.

She shouted more loudly.

"Rodrigo Paestra. It's me. It's me."

She bent still farther and called him. This time closer, lower.

And when she got so close to him she could have touched him, she noticed that Rodrigo Paestra was dead.

His open eyes were staring at the ground. The spot around his head and on the blades of wheat, which she had taken for his shadow, was his blood. It had happened a long time ago, probably a little after dawn, six or seven hours ago. Next to Rodrigo Paestra's face was his gun, like a toy abandoned by a child overcome by sleep.

Maria got up. She left the wheat field. Pierre was standing on the road. He walked toward her. They met.

"There's no point in waiting," Maria said. "He's dead."

182

"What?"

"The heat probably. It's all over."

Pierre stayed motionless next to Maria. They looked at each other without speaking. Maria was the first to smile. A very long time ago, they had looked at each other in nearly the same way.

"It doesn't make any sense," she said. "Let's go."

She didn't move. Pierre left her, went toward the spot she had just left, where the wheat opened up. It was his turn to bend over Rodrigo Paestra. He took a long time to get back. But he walked back to Maria. Claire and Judith were waiting for them, completely silent. Maria picked up a grain of wheat, and another, held them, let them go, picked more and let those go again. Pierre was next to her now.

"He killed himself," he said.

"An idiot. An idot. Let's not talk about it anymore."

They stayed on the road, facing each other. Each one was waiting for the other to say a word that would serve as a conclusion, a word which didn't come. Then Pierre took Maria by the shoulder and called her.

"Maria."

From the Rover came another call. Claire. She had forgotten her. It was Pierre she was calling. Pierre answered, motioning. They were coming.

"And the man?" Judith asked.

"He won't be coming," Pierre said.

Maria opened the back door and asked Claire to sit in front. She would keep Judith with her in the back.

"He's dead," Pierre whispered to Claire.

"How did it happen?"

Pierre hesitated.

"Sunstroke, probably," he said.

He started the Rover and began to make a U-turn. It was difficult to manage. He had to drive up on the sides a bit because the dirt road was very narrow. Over his shoulder Pierre could see Maria, who had taken Judith in her arms and was wiping her forehead. She was doing this carefully, as always. Claire, in front, was silent. Maria didn't look at her beautiful neck outlined against the wheat fields.

Pierre had managed the turn. He drove up the dirt road and, while on it, moved slowly. Then came the road to Madrid.

"What are we going to do?" Claire asked.

Nobody answered.

"Am I thirsty," Judith said.

The road to Madrid. Monumental, straight, on and on. Again the harvesters must have looked up, in the fields, but they couldn't be seen anymore. Pierre stopped again and turned around, looking at Maria without speaking.

"There is no reason," she said, "absolutely no reason why we shouldn't do what we had decided to do."

"Exactly one-hundred fifty-two miles," Claire said. "We can be there before dark."

Pierre started to drive again. The heat was more bearable because of the speed. It blew away your sweat, made your head less heavy. Judith complained again about being thirsty. Pierre promised her they would stop in the next village. Twenty-nine more miles. Judith still complained. She was bored.

"She's bored," Claire said.

Then, well before the village, the road changed all of a sudden. First it climbed imperceptibly toward a spot that was very far away. Then it went down, in the same fashion, through a higher, rockier, lunar region. It didn't go down as much as it had gone up; then it became flat and straight again.

"We must have entered Castile," Claire said.

"Probably," Pierre said.

Judith once again cried that she was thirsty.

"Judith, if you cry," Maria said calmly, "if you cry . . ."

Judith cried.

"I'll leave you on the side of the road," Maria shouted. "If you cry, Judith, you'd better watch out."

Pierre went faster. Faster and faster. The Rover was leaving clouds of dust and gravel behind it. The air was torrid. Claire leaned back, looking at the road ahead.

"There's no point in killing ourselves," she said.

The wheat fields disappeared. All that was left were stones, heaps of stones, completely discolored by the sun.

Judith stopped crying, huddled against her mother. Pierre was driving faster and faster in spite of Claire's warning. Maria was silent.

"Mummy," Judith called.

"We'll get killed," Claire announced.

Pierre didn't slow down. He was driving so fast that Judith was tossed from one side to the other, from the back of the seat to her mother. Her mother reached out to hold her against her hip. And Judith stayed there, whimpering again.

"Pierre," Claire shouted, "Pierre."

He slowed down a little. They reached the end of the plateau and the road started climbing again. On the top, it became flat once more, but this time it was not going to go down again. At the end of the road, there was an amphitheater of mountains with round summits. As they moved ahead, other mountains appeared, strangely piled up. Now there were mountains on all sides, one on top of the other, some resting on others with their whole weight, white, pink or blue from the sulfides exposed to the sun, jostling each other madly.

"Mummy," Judith called again.

"Be quiet, that's enough," Maria shouted.

"She's afraid," Claire said. "Judith is afraid."

Pierre slowed down even more. In the rear-view mirror he saw Maria put her arm around Judith and kiss her, and Judith, who at last was smiling.

They were now traveling at a normal speed. They were only six miles from the village that Pierre had announced. There was a pause, the first since the mood that set in after they discovered Rodrigo Paestra's body in the wheat field, when time had started to rush forward.

"Our rooms," Claire said a little later. "Let's not forget to reserve them by phone before this evening. Yesterday we had planned to do this before three."

Maria let go of Judith, who had now calmed down. Maria became aware of Claire again, and of Claire's beauty which nearly made her cry. Claire was there, her profile outlined against the sky and the sulfurous and milky mountains on the horizon, which marked the progress of their trip and foretold its end that evening, in Madrid. Tonight, Pierre. She had been afraid earlier, when Pierre was driving so fast, that she would die while waiting. Now she had become thoughtful and her fear had been erased as she waited for a room, in Madrid, that very night in Madrid, as she waited to be coiled up against Pierre, that night, in Madrid, naked, in the warm moistness of a room closed to daylight, when Maria would be asleep in a lonely slumber brought on by liquor.

Could she see them already, in their white bed, in Madrid, that night, hiding? Yes, except for Claire's nakedness which she didn't know.

"I'll always love you, Claire," Maria said.

Claire turned around and didn't smile at Maria. Pierre did not turn. There was complete silence in the Rover. Claire had never shown herself naked to Maria. She would tonight, to Pierre. This was just as ineluctable as the coming of twilight in a while would be. She could read the fate of that night in Claire's eyes.

"Look Judith," Pierre shouted.

It was the village they wanted to reach. Looking like Rodrigo Paestra's, it moved quickly toward them. Pierre slowed down. His hands on the wheel were beautiful, supple, long, brown, uniquely docile from now on. Claire kept looking at them.

"There's an inn," Pierre said. "At the other end of the village."

The village was already enjoying a peaceful siesta. The inn was surrounded by pine trees, where Pierre had said it would be.

It was a rather old, immense residence, entirely shielded from the heat. There were many cars under the pine trees. A round terrace, looking out on the countryside, was empty.

They hadn't even noticed that it was already lunch time. Everybody was eating. Some of the people they had seen at the Hotel Principal. The recognized one another. Claire smiled at a young woman.

Judith discovered she was hungry and said so.

They felt unexpectedly at ease because of the coolness of the staggered, crowded rooms.

"Was it hot," Maria said at last.

They were shown to a table that looked out on the pine trees—they could see them through the blinds and discovered, next to the pines, a small olive grove. There was a path between them. Judith was brought some water. Judith drank and drank. They watched her drink. Then she stopped.

Maria was between Claire and Pierre. Surrounded by them. Even they had ordered a manzanilla. Judith was coming back to life and began to move about between their table and the entrance to the inn. Maria was drinking manzanillas.

"It's good," she said. "I think I'll drink forever."

She drank. Claire stretched out on the bench and laughed.

"As you like, Maria," she said.

She threw a quick, circular glance of happiness around her. The dining room was full. It was summer, in Spain. There were fruity food smells in the air about that time, every day, and they always made you feel somewhat nauseous.

"I'm not at all hungry," Claire announced.

"We're not hungry," Maria said.

Pierre smoked and drank his manzanilla. Ever since their trip had begun, he was silent, for long periods of time, between these two women.

Pierre ordered fried shrimp. Maria asked for good, tender meat for Judith. It was promised. They put Judith on a chair piled with cushions, the only one at the table.

"We could have arranged a good life for him," Maria began, "and perhaps I would have loved him."

"Who will ever know?" Claire said.

They laughed together, then were silent, and then Maria went on drinking manzanillas.

Judith was brought some acceptable meat. Then they brought the fried shrimp and olives.

Judith ate well.

"Finally," Pierre said, looking at his child, "finally she's hungry."

"The storm," Claire said. "This morning she was hungry too." Judith, well behaved, was eating. Maria was cutting her meat. She chewed and swallowed. Maria cut some more. They ate while watching Judith eat so nicely. The shrimps were fresh and hot, cracking under their teeth, smelling of fire.

"You will like this, Pierre," Claire said.

She had one in her mouth. You could hear her teeth biting into it. Again she was unable to escape her desire for Pierre. She had left her ferociousness behind, she was beautiful again, saved from the menace that Rodrigo Paestra had been, alive. Her voice was like honey when she asked him—her voice was completely transformed—whether he liked it, as much as she.

"They'll find him in a while," Maria said, "in about four hours. In the meantime, he is still in the wheat field."

"You know, to talk about it won't change anything," Claire said.

"I still feel like it," Maria said. "Must you stop me?"

"No," Pierre said, "no, Maria. Why?"

Maria drank some more. The shrimp were the best in Spain. Maria asked for more. They were eating more than they had thought they would. And, while Maria was giving in to her tiredness, Claire was coming to life like Judith, and devoured the shrimps. The same shrimps he was eating.

"We had hardly started playing, when the game was lost," Maria went on. "Lost games like that make you rationalize endlessly."

"It would have pleased me very much to save Rodrigo Paestra," Pierre said, "I must admit."

"It wasn't the sun, was it?" Claire asked.

"It was the sun," Pierre said.

Judith was no longer hungry. She was willing to have an orange. Pierre peeled it for her with great care. Judith followed this with envious attention.

They were no longer hungry. Green shade was seeping through the shutters and blinds. It was cool. Claire had stretched out again, completely, on the bench, where Pierre could see her. He wasn't looking at her, but how could he not be aware of her? She was looking toward the blinds and the olive grove, without seeing it. The reflection of the heat was still dancing in her eyes. Her eyes were violently awake, restless like water. Blue, like her dress, dark blue in the green shade of the blinds. What had happened in the morning at the hotel while she, Maria, was sleeping?

Maria half closed her eyes to see this woman, Claire, better.

But nothing could be seen of Claire except her quivering stare at the blinds. And all of a sudden, Maria's vigilance was discovered and had to stop.

Then Pierre suddenly got up, walked to the door, opened it—in a flash of light—and went out. Ten minutes went by.

"I wish he'd come back," Maria said.

Claire made a vague gesture: she didn't know where Pierre had gone. She stayed in the same position, her face toward the door, refusing to look at Maria. They were silent until he came back. He was smoking a cigarette that he must have lit on the terrace.

"The air is scorching," he said.

They made Judith get down from the chair.

"Where were you Pierre?" Claire asked.

"On the terrace. The road is deserted."

There was a little bit of manzanilla left in the jug. Maria drank it.

"Please, Maria," Pierre said.

"At last I'm getting tired," Maria said. "But this is my last one."

"We can't leave yet, in this heat, can we Pierre?" Claire asked.

She pointed at Judith. Judith was yawning.

"Certainly not," Maria said. "She must sleep a little."

Judith objected. Pierre took her in his arms and placed her on a large couch in the cool shade at the back of the entrance hall. Judith let him. Pierre walked back toward Maria and Claire. Claire was looking at him, all of him, as he came back. He sat down on the bench. They had to wait for Judith to finish her siesta.

"She's already asleep," he said—he had turned around to look at his child.

"We would have taken him to France," Maria went on. "Maybe he would have become a friend. Who knows?"

"We'll never," Pierre said—he smiled—"stop drinking, Maria."

"How tired i am," Maria said—she was speaking to Pierre—"it seems you can fight against anything except this kind of tiredness. I'm going to sleep."

Maria spoke gently. And Pierre was as used to her gentleness as he had been to her body. He smiled at Maria.

"It's a tiredness," he said, "that comes from very far, that has accumulated, and is made of all kinds of things, of everything. Sometimes it makes itself felt. Like today. But you know all that, Maria."

"One always overestimates one's strength," Maria said. "I think I'll sleep very well."

"You have always overestimated your strength," Claire said. They smiled at each other.

"It's the liquor," Maria said, "that's what it is. And afterwards, the distrust that one feels, but you wouldn't know."

"I don't know. But we can go on talking like this until evening."

"Oh no," Maria said, "I'm going to sleep."

She stretched out on the bench. Claire was opposite her.

Pierre turned around to look at Judith.

"She's asleep," he said.

"You'd think it feasible," Maria said, "but she's really too small for such long trips, and in this heat."

She had taken Pierre's place on the bench. There were many tourists stretched out like her. Some men were on the floor, lying on the rope carpets. The rooms were silent. All the children were asleep and people were whispering.

"I would have taken him traveling, a lot, again and again"—she was yawning—"and little by little, day by day, I would have seen him change, look at me, then listen to me, and then . . ."

190

She yawned again, stretched, and closed her eyes.

"No more drinking for you before Madrid," Pierre said. "No more."

"No more. I promise. I didn't drink enough to . . ."

"To what?" Claire asked.

"To be still more talkative," Maria said. "And to feel too desperate about Rodrigo Paestra's desertion. You know how it is, I was planning on starting a big project with Rodrigo Paestra. And now, now it has all collapsed before we even started. That's all. But I didn't drink enough not to admit it. Am I sleepy! I'm sleeping, Claire."

She closed her eyes. Where were they? She could hear Claire.

"Can we wake up Judith in another half hour?"

Pierre didn't answer. Then just one more time, Maria spoke.

"If you like. As you like. I could easily sleep until evening."

Pierre said he would call the National Hotel in Madrid to reserve three rooms. He was whispering. He went to call. Nothing happened. Claire must have been there. That sigh near Maria, that smell of sandalwood around her, that was Claire. Maria dreamed she was asleep.

Pierre came back. He had reserved three rooms for the night at the National Hotel in Madrid, he said. They were silent for a moment. Rooms in Madrid for the night. They knew that on reaching Madrid, Maria would want to drink and go from bar to bar. They would have to be very patient. Perfectly synchronized, they both closed their eyes. Shame prevented them from looking at each other in her presence, even if she was asleep. And yet they looked at each other, even though they couldn't. Then closed their eyes again, unable to bear the urgency of their desire. Claire said:

"She's asleep."

What silence. Claire softly stroked the rough linen covering the couch. As she continued to stroke it, she started scratching it with her nails. Pierre looked on, following the progress of Claire's caress, saw it stop abruptly, and painfully break loose from the couch and fall back on her blue dress. It was surely she who got up first and walked away from the table. That rustling of the air, hardly noticeable, that crackling of unfolding skirts, that slowness, that languid straightening out of a body, it could only be a woman. She would recognize among a thousand others those resinous whiffs, sweetened by perfume that had ripened on the skin and become adapted to its breathing, to its sweat, to its warmth in the shelter of her blue dress.

The smell of perfume around Maria subsided just as the wind does.

He had followed her. Maria opened her eyes, absolutely convinced. They were no longer there. At last.

Maria closed her eyes again. It was going to happen. In half an hour. In an hour. And then the coupling of their love would be reversed.

She wanted things to happen between them so that she too would be illuminated like them and enter the world she bequeathed them, since the day, in fact, when she herself invented it, in Verona, one night.

Was Maria asleep?

There were in this inn, in this residence shielded from the summer, a few openings onto the summer. There must have been a patio. Corridors that turn and die at deserted terraces where flowers, each day of that season, were dying too, while waiting for evening. During the day no one went through these corridors, or on the terraces.

Claire knew he was following her. She knew. He had already done so. He knew how to follow a woman he desired, from just the right distance so she would become a little more tense than necessary. He preferred them like that.

Here too, there was no one, because of the deadly heat of the countryside. Would it be there? Claire stopped, at the limit, as he wanted her, of the tenseness that came from his not having joined her yet, from his step, behind her, having remained calm and measured.

He had reached Claire. He had reached Claire's lips. But she didn't want to give them to him.

"We have an hour," she said, "before she wakes up. We can rent a room. I can do it, rent it, if it bothers you. I can't wait any more."

He didn't answer.

"I know her," she continued, "I knew she would fall asleep. Did you notice? After four manzanillas, she has reached that stage, she falls asleep."

He didn't answer.

"But did you notice it? Please. Did you notice it? Pierre?"

"Yes. Today she isn't sleeping."

She went up to him and pressed herself against him, from head to toe, from her hair to her thighs, entrusting her whole body to him. They did not kiss.

Liquor makes your heart beat more than usual. Such a long time before evening. Maria slightly opened her thighs where her heart, a dagger, was beating.

"Is it that I've already lost you?"

192

"My love. How can you? . . ."

She pulled away from him, moved away, farther away. He was alone. When she came back he was still in the same place, nailed to it. She was holding a key in her hand.

"It's done," she said.

Pierre didn't answer. She had gone by him without stopping. He had heard her say that it was done. She was moving away. He followed far behind her. Then she walked up a dark stairway. Even the maids were still sleeping. Hardly ten minutes had gone by since they had left Maria. She turned around on the stairs.

"I said it was for the siesta."

They reached the room they had to unlock. He did that. It was a very big room looking out on the olive grove. She was the one who slowed down suddenly, opened the window and spoke.

"What luck. Look."—and she added, loudly, "I couldn't wait any more." He looked, and while they both looked, he dared to start touching her. He kissed her mouth so she wouldn't shout any more.

The heat was still dazzling in the deserted countryside.

Was her heart beating in such an unreasonable way for the very last time? She half opened her eyes. They were no longer there. She closed them again. She moved her legs and put them back on the bench. Then she got up and, through the opened blinds, looked at the same olive grove, petrified by the heat. Then she lay down again, again closed her eyes. She thought she was sleeping. Her heart had become calm. She drank too much. Everybody said so, mainly Pierre. You drink too much, Maria.

The window was exactly in the middle of the wall. The grove was there. The olive trees were very old. No grass around the trees. They were not looking at the grove.

Pierre, stretched out on the bed, watched her take off her blue dress and walk toward him, naked. He would remember later that he had seen her come up to him framed by the open window, against the olive trees. Would he remember later? She had taken off her dress very fast and had stepped over it and here she was.

"You're beautiful. God, how beautiful you are."

Or perhaps they would not say anything.

Rodrigo Paestra's suicide in the wheat field, early in the morning, was foreseeable. He was uncomfortable, disturbed by the noise of the carts, and by the increasing heat of the sun; the presence, in his pocket, of a weapon that prevented him from stretching out, from falling asleep, made him remember a godsend he had absent-mindedly forgotten up to then: death. Maria was sleeping. She was sure of it. If she tried harder, she would dream. But she didn't try. She didn't dream. She was surprised by the sudden calmness that followed her discovery that she was awake. So she wasn't sleeping.

Pierre got up from the bed first. Claire was crying. Claire was still crying from pleasure when Pierre got up.

"She knows everything," he said. "Come."

Then Claire's crying subsided.

"You think so?"

He did think so. He was standing next to her, completely dressed, while she was still naked. Then he turned toward the window and repeated that they had to leave.

"You don't love me?" she asked.

Her voice sounded gloomy. He told her.

"I love you. I've loved Maria. And you."

Outside, the landscape had softened. He didn't want to know that she was getting up from the bed. The sun was less vertical. The shade from the olive trees had begun to grow longer, imperceptibly, while they were making love. The heat had weakened a little. Where was Maria? Had Maria been drinking herself to death? Had Maria's regal gift for drinking and dying led her into the wheat fields, far away, laughing, just like Rodrigo Paestra? Where was this other woman, Maria?

"Quick," Pierre said. "Come on."

She was ready. She was crying.

"You no longer love Maria," she shouted. "Remember, you no longer love Maria."

"I don't know," Pierre said. "Don't cry, don't cry, Claire. Already an hour since we left her."

She too looked at the landscape and immediately turned away from it. She put on her make-up, looking in the mirror next to the window. She was holding back her tears.

Maria, dead in the wheat fields? On her face a grin that had been stopped, laughter in full bloom? Maria's lonely laughter in the wheat fields. This was her landscape. Everything was leading back to Maria: the sudden softness of the shade from the olive trees, the heat which suddenly made room for the oncoming evening, the various signs which announced everywhere that the day had passed its prime.

194

Pierre was at the door, his hand on the knob. She was in the middle of the room. He said he would go down first. His hand was shaking on the knob. Then she cried out.

"But what's the matter? Pierre, Pierre, tell me."

"I love you," he said. "Don't be afraid."

The tourists had waked her. They all seemed in high spirits when they left. Judith was there, delighted, her hair still flat from the sweat of her siesta, in front of the main entrance, happily holding pebbles from the courtyard. Maria got up and Judith ran up to her.

"I'm hot," Judith said. And she went away.

They weren't there yet. You could still imagine the weight of the heat. There was a different kind of light in the inn. The blinds had been raised after their lovemaking.

"I'm going to give you a bath," Maria told Judith. "You'll see. In five minutes."

The head waiter went by. Maria ordered coffee. She waited, sitting on the bench. That's when Pierre arrived.

He came through the dining room. He was standing in front of her.

"I slept so well," Maria said.

The head waiter brought the coffee and Marie drank it greedily. Pierre sat down next to her, smoked a cigarette and didn't speak. He didn't look at Maria but kept looking at Judith, sometimes Judith, and sometimes the door. When Claire arrived, he moved back a little to make room for her.

"Did you sleep?"

"Yes," Maria said, "for a long time?"

"I don't know," Claire said. "Everybody has gone. I suppose it was for a long time. Yes." She added, "I'm glad you slept."

"You should have some coffee," Maria said. "For once it's good."

Claire ordered some. She turned toward Maria.

"While you were sleeping we took a walk in the woods behind the hotel," she said.

"And the heat was terrible?"

"Terrible. But you have to accept it. You know."

"I've reserved rooms in Madrid," Pierre said. "So we can leave whenever you want, Maria."

"I'll give Judith her shower. And we'll leave for Madrid after that?"

They agreed. Maria took Judith to the shower on the ground floor. Judith went along without objecting. Maria put her under the shower.

Judith laughed. Then Maria joined her under the shower. And they both laughed.

"How cool you look," Claire said when they came back. And she pounced on Judith and embraced her.

Outside it seemed at first that the heat had remained unchanged. But the mood wasn't the same. It was very different from the morning and its anguish. And now the approaching evening brought hope. The workers were back in the fields, harvesting the same wheat, and the pale red mountains on the horizon recalled the spent youth of the morning.

Claire drove. Next to her Pierre was silent. Maria had wanted to stay in the back with Judith. They moved toward Madrid. Claire was driving safely, just a little faster than usual. It was only in that respect that, outwardly, their trip seemed to have changed. There was no point in talking about it, since each one of them had accepted and understood this change.

They drove through Castile until the late hours of the afternoon.

"In an hour and a half at the latest," Pierre said, "we'll be in Madrid."

As they drove through a village, Maria said she wanted to stop. Pierre saw no reason why not. Claire stopped. Pierre lit a cigarette for her. Their hands met and touched. They now had precise memories.

The village was quite large. They stopped near its entrance, at the first café they passed. All the workers were still in the fields. They were the only customers. The café was very large and empty. You had to call to get served. A radio, in the back room, didn't manage to drown out the tireless lisping of the flies on the windows. Pierre called several times. The radio stopped. A man, still young, came out. Maria wanted wine that evening. So did Pierre. Claire wasn't going to have anything. Nor was Judith.

"It feels so good here," Maria said.

They didn't answer. Judith ran around the room and looked at the paintings on the walls. Harvesting scenes. Under a cart, children playing with dogs. A family, naively solemn, eating a meal in a wheat field, on and on, on all the walls, as far as you could see.

"Just looking at her," Pierre said, "you can tell it's getting less hot."

Maria called her and fixed her hair a little. She was thin, wearing nothing but a tiny bathing suit. She made faces as her hair was being combed.

"She will be as beautiful as you," Claire said.

"I think so too," Pierre said. "She looks exactly like you."

196

Maria pushed her back a little to see her better and then let her go back to the wheat on the walls.

"It's true that she's beautiful," she said.

Maria drank her wine. The man, behind the bar, was looking at Claire. Pierre stopped drinking. They had to wait for Maria to empty the carafe. It was a cheap wine, sour and warm. But she said she liked it.

"Tonight," she said, "we could go out. We'll register at the hotel, take a shower, change, and then we can go out, all right? I can leave Judith with a maid as soon as we arrive. All right?"

"Of course," Pierre said. Maria was drinking again. Pierre was watching the wine in the carafe go down. She drank slowly. They had to wait.

"But you're tired," Claire answered.

Maria pursed her lips as if the wine, all of a sudden, was not wanted.

"No, at night, never."

She motioned to the man behind the bar.

"Has there been any news of Rodrigo Paestra since this morning?" The man thought and remembered. A murderer.

"Dead," he said.

He raised his hand and placed an imaginary gun against his temple.

"How do you know?" Pierre asked.

"The radio, an hour ago. He was in a field."

"Already," Maria said. "I'm sorry I bothered you with this story."

"You're not going to start again, Maria."

"I knew it," Claire said.

Maria had finished her wine. The man had gone back behind the bar.

"Come, Maria," Pierre said.

"I had no time to choose him," Maria said. "He fell on me. At the border, we would have let him loose in the woods and waited for him, at night, on the banks of a river. Such suspense. He would have come. Had he spent all the time needed to reach the border without killing himself, he wouldn't have killed himself later, after getting to know us."

"Can't you try to forget him?"

"I don't want to," Maria said. "He takes up all my thoughts. It was only a few hours ago, Claire."

They walked out. Carts were already coming back from the fields. The ones who finished first. They smiled at the tourists. Their faces were gray with dust. There were also a few children, asleep.

"The Jucar valley is beautiful," Claire said. "Sixty miles to Madrid. We should be getting to the valley now."

Pierre was driving. Claire wanted Judith with her. Maria let her. Claire's hands were on Judith. After the village, Maria quickly fell asleep once more. They didn't wake her to see the Jucar valley, but only when Madrid was in sight. The sun hadn't completely disappeared yet. It was level with the wheat fields. They reached Madrid as planned, before the sun set.

"Was I tired!" Maria said.

"Madrid, look."

She looked. At first the city moved toward them like a mountain of stone. Then they noticed that this mountain was pierced with black holes bored by the sun, and that its rectangular shapes were spread out geometrically, at various levels, separated by empty spaces that swallowed up the pink light like a weary dawn.

"How beautiful," Maria said.

She sat up, ran her fingers through her hair, and looked at Madrid surrounded by a sea of wheat.

"What a shame," she added.

Claire turned around abruptly and, like an insult, uttered:

"What?"

"Who knows? Maybe the beauty."

"You didn't know?"

"I was sleeping. I just noticed it."

Pierre slowed down, he had to because Madrid was so beautiful even from that distance.

"The Jucar valley was beautiful too," Claire said. "You didn't want to wake up."

The hotel was full, like the other. But their rooms had been reserved.

They were able to get something to eat for Judith, who was very tired.

The rooms were still warm with the heat of the day. The shower was wonderful. Long, brisk, tepid because the heat had penetrated the city to the very depths of its water. Each one of them showered alone.

In her room, Claire was getting ready for her wedding night. Pierre, lying on his bed, thought of this new wedding made sad by the memory of Maria.

They had adjoining rooms. Claire, tonight, in the fulfillment of her desire, would not be able to scream.

Judith was asleep. Claire and Maria were getting ready, each for her own night. Memories of Verona came back to Pierre. He got up from his bed, left the room, and knocked at his wife's door. He felt an urgent taste for a dead love. When he walked into Maria's room, he felt enshrouded in his love for her. What he didn't know was the poignant magic of Maria's solitude, brought on by him, and of Maria's mourning for him that evening.

"Maria," he said.

She had been waiting for him.

"Kiss me," she said.

There was about her the irreplaceable perfume of his power over her, of his breach of love, of his wishing her well, there was about her the odor of their dying love.

"Kiss me again, again," Maria said. "Pierre, Pierre."

He kissed her. She moved back and looked at him. Judith was asleep. He knew what would come next. Did he know? She moved back toward the wall and kept looking at him, instead of coming closer to him with her usual lack of shame.

"Maria," he called out.

"Yes"—she too called out his name—"Pierre."

Her attitude was one of shame, her eyes lowered on her body. And there was even fear in her voice.

He moved toward her. He placed a finger on his mouth to signal her not to wake up Judith. He was upon her. She didn't stop him.

"Kiss me, kiss me, quick, please, kiss me."

He kissed her again. And again she moved back, very calmly.

"What can we do?" she asked.

"You're part of my life," he said. "I can no longer be content with a woman just for the novelty. I cannot do without you. I know it."

"It's the end of our story," Maria said. "Pierre, it's all over. The end of the story."

"Be quiet."

"I'll be quiet. But, Pierre, this is the end."

Pierre moved up to her, took her face in his hands.

"Are you sure?"

She said she was. She looked at him, horrified.

"Since when?"

"I just noticed it. Perhaps for a long time."

Someone knocked at the door. It was Claire.

"You're taking so long," she said—she seemed pale all of a sudden —"Are you coming?"
They went.

A man was dancing alone on the stage. The place was full. There were many tourists. The man danced well. The music took turns with his steps on the bare and dirty floor. He was surrounded by women, in loud, hastily put on, faded dresses. They must have been dancing all afternoon. The height of the summer with its overwork. Whenever the man stopped dancing, the band would play paso-dobles and the man would sing them into a microphone. Plastered on his face, he had at times a chalky laugh, and at times the mask of a loving, languorous, nauseous drunkenness that made an impression on his audience.

In the room, among the others, packed together like the others, Maria, Claire and Pierre were looking at the dancer.

THE AFTERNOON
of MR. ANDESMAS

TRANSLATED BY

ANNE BORCHARDT

I have just bought a house. A very beautiful spot. Almost like Greece. The trees around the house belong to me. One of them is enormous and, in summer, will give so much shade that I'll never suffer from the heat. I am going to build a terrace. From that terrace, at night, you'll be able to see the lights of G . . . There are moments here when the light is absolute, accentuating everything, and at the same time precise, relentlessly shining on one object . . .

Words overheard
during the summer of 1960

202

One

HE EMERGED FROM THE path on the left. He came from the part of the hill completely overgrown by the forest, rustling the small shrubs and bushes which marked the approach to the plateau.

He was a small reddish dog. He probably came from one of the hamlets on the other slope, beyond the summit, about six miles from there.

On this side the hill fell away sharply toward the plain.

When he had emerged from the path, trotting briskly, the dog suddenly slowed down as he advanced along the precipice. He sniffed at the gray light which bathed the plain. On this plain there were crops surrounding a village, this village, and numerous roads leading from it to a Mediterranean sea.

At first, he didn't see the man who was seated in front of the house —the only house on his route since leaving the distant hamlets on the other side—and who, like him, was staring at this same bright empty space, crossed at times by flocks of birds. He sat down, panting from fatigue and from the heat.

During this breathing spell, he became aware that his solitude was not complete, that it was being undone behind him by the presence of a man. The very slight and very slow squeaking of the wicker armchair on which Mr. Andesmas was seated followed the rhythm of his labored breathing, and this singular rhythm did not fool the dog.

He turned his head, discovered the man's presence, and pricked up his ears. No longer tired, he examined him. The dog must have known this plateau in front of the house ever since he was old enough to wander over the mountain and find his way about on it. But he could not have been old enough to have known an owner other than Mr. Andesmas. This must have been the first time a man had been there, in his path.

Mr. Andesmas did not move, nor did he show any sign of hostility or friendliness toward the dog.

The dog did not study him for long, in this contemplative way. Intimidated by this meeting and finding himself forced to bear the burden of it, he lowered his ears, took a few steps toward Mr. Andesmas, wagging his tail. But he gave up very quickly, his efforts not being repaid by any sign from the man, and he stopped short before reaching him.

His fatigue returned, he began panting again and took off through the forest, this time heading for the village.

He probably came to this hill every day, looking for bitches or food; he probably went all the way to the three villages on the west slope, every day, and made this very long journey in the afternoon in search of some windfall.

"Out for bitches, or garbage," Mr. Andesmas thought. "I'll be seeing this dog again; he has his habits."

The dog would need water, one would have to give this dog water here, make this a refreshing stop on his long trips through the forest, from one village to another, as much as possible ease his difficult existence. There is that pond about half a mile from here, where he can also drink, of course, but bad, stale water, choked with weeds. That water must be green and sticky, heavy with mosquito larvae, unhealthy. This dog, so eager for his daily pleasures, should have good water.

Valérie would give this dog something to drink whenever he passed by her house.

He came back. Why? Once more he crossed the plateau overlooking the precipice. Once more he looked at the man. But although, this time, the man gave him a friendly greeting, he again did not come close. Slowly he left, not to return that day. With a stroke of color, he had cut through the gray space where the birds flew. Yet so discreetly had he picked his way over the sandstone rocks along the cliff that the dry scraping of his nails, in the surrounding air, had conveyed the memory of a passage.

The forest was dense and wild. It had few clearings. The only path which crossed it—the dog took it, this time—bent very sharply beyond the house. The dog turned the corner and disappeared.

Mr. Andesmas raised his arm, looked at his watch, saw that it was four o'clock. So, while the dog had been passing by, Michel Arc was already late for the appointment they had made together, two days before, on this plateau. Michel Arc had said that a quarter of four was a good time for him. It was four o'clock.

When his arm fell back, Mr. Andesmas changed positions. The wicker armchair creaked more loudly. Then, once again, it breathed regularly around the body it held. The already blurred memory of the reddish dog faded away, and Mr. Andesmas was left alone with the oversized bulk of his seventy-eight years. When motionless, this bulk stiffened easily, and from time to time Mr. Andesmas shifted it, moved it a little in the wicker armchair. This way he could bear the waiting.

A quarter to four, Michel Arc had said. But it was still the warm season, and siestas probably lasted longer during summer in this region than elsewhere. Mr. Andesmas, for his part, always took exactly the same siesta, always for his health, in summer and winter. That is why he remembered other people's siestas, deep Saturday siestas under the trees of village squares, or amorous ones, sometimes, in bedrooms.

"It's to build a terrace," Mr. Andesmas had explained to Michel Arc, "a terrace that will overhang the valley, the village, and the sea. On the other side of the house, a terrace would be useless, but this side calls for one. Although I'm prepared to spend what it will take to make this terrace beautiful, large and solid, I would like as a matter of principle, of course, and you must understand this, Mr. Arc, I would like an estimate. Since this terrace is something my daughter Valérie wants, I am willing to make a considerable financial sacrifice. But an estimate is still indispensable, you understand."

Michel Arc understood.

Valérie is going to buy the pond where the dog had rested. That's agreed upon.

There was no other building in the forest besides the house Mr. Andesmas had just bought. With its yards, it took up the whole surface of the highest of the plateaus which formed a succession of terraces, on the slope of the hill, leap by leap, down to the plain, the village, and to the sea, so calm today.

Mr. Andesmas has been living in the village for a year, ever since he had reached an age sufficiently advanced to give him an excuse to stop working and wait for death, doing nothing. This is the first time that he has seen the house he had bought for Valérie.

> *When the lilac blooms my love*
> *When the lilac blooms forever.*

In the valley, somebody sang it. Perhaps siesta time was coming to an end? Perhaps, yes, it was coming to an end. The singing certainly came from the village. Where else could it be coming from? Between this village and the house, newly acquired by Mr. Andesmas for his child, Valérie, there were, in fact, no other buildings.

None other, none but yours. And this one, because it belongs to you, is hereafter exempt from the fate of any other, of some other which, just as well, instead of yours, might have created this white accident of quicklime in the pine forest. "I bought this house," Mr. Andesmas had explained to Michel Arc, "primarily because it is the only one of its kind. Around it, look, the forest, nothing but the forest. The forest, everywhere."

The road ceased to be passable about a hundred yards from the house. Mr. Andesmas had come by car up to the point where the road ceased to be passable, a clearing with level ground where cars could turn around. Valérie had driven him, then she had left. She had not got out of the car, she had not gone up to the house, had not expressed a desire to. She had suggested to her father that he wait for Michel Arc and then for her. In the evening, when it had cooled off—she hadn't said at what time —she would come to get him.

A few days earlier, they had talked together about this road and the possibility of owning it all the way up to the pond, of making it a private road, except for Valérie's friends.

Mr. Andesmas' friends were no longer alive. Once they had bought the pond, nobody would come through any more. Nobody with the exception of Valérie's friends.

In the heat of the road, she had sung softly:

When the lilac blooms my love

He was now sitting in the wobbly wicker armchair he had found in a room inside the house. In the heat, energetically, as if the heat were nothing, she had sung!

When the lilac

He had reached the plateau with difficulty, walking carefully, as she had advised him, taking his time. She would have sung the same way in the coolness of an evening or a night, in other places, somewhere else. Where wouldn't she have sung?

206

While climbing he could still hear her. Then the noise of the car motor had murdered her song. It had grown weaker, fainter; later snatches had still reached him, and then nothing, nothing more. Once he had reached the plateau, nothing more could be heard of her or her song. It had taken a long time. A long time also to settle this body into the wicker armchair. When this had been done, no, really nothing, nothing could be heard of Valérie, or of her song, or of the noise of the car motor.

Around Mr. Andesmas the forest rises motionless, around the house as well, and all over the hillside too. Between the trees there are heavy thickets which swallow up every sound, even the songs of Valérie Andesmas, his child.

Yes, it was certainly that. It was the village waking up from its siesta. From one Saturday to the next, summer was passing. Dance tunes floated all the way up the plateau, sometimes several at once. It was the workers' weekend rest. Mr. Andesmas never worked any more. It was up to the others to rest from their incredible labors. Only the others, from now on, from now on. Mr. Andesmas waited for them. Waited for them to be ready.

The white square was crossed by a group of people. Mr. Andesmas saw only one part of this square. His desire to see all of it was not strong enough to make him get up and walk the ten steps separating him from the ravine where he could have seen it, and seen, too, behind the row of green benches, still empty because of the heat, Valérie's black car.

It was a dance.

It ended.

Behind Mr. Andesmas, at the edge of the quiet pond overgrown with duckweed and shaded by enormous trees, could there be children at this time of day, playing at catching frogs and innocently subjecting them to slow tortures, roaring with laughter? Mr. Andesmas had given much thought to the youth of this pond, ever since the dog had come by, who must drink there every day, and ever since he had decided to make it completely private, except for Valérie, his child.

A series of very brief, dry, crackling noises suddenly surrounded him. Wind blew over the forest.

"So, already," Mr. Andesmas said aloud. "Already . . ."

He heard himself speak, he started, and fell silent. Around him, in

207

soft succeeding waves, the whole forest bent over. This was, from then on, an exceptional spectacle in the life of Mr. Andesmas. The whole forest bent over, but differently depending on the height of the trees, their slant, the more or less heavy load of their branches.

Mr. Andesmas did not yet move to look at his watch.

The wind died down. The forest again took up its silent pose on the mountain. It wasn't evening, but only a chance wind, not yet the evening wind. Down below, however, the square was filling up more and more every minute. Something was happening there.

I owe it to myself to talk to Michel Arc, Mr. Andesmas thought clearly. I'm hot. My forehead is covered with perspiration. He must now be over an hour late. I wouldn't have thought that of him. To make an old man wait.

It was a small dance, like every Saturday at that time of the year.

The melody, taken up now by a phonograph, rose from the main square. It filled the emptiness. The same one Valérie had been singing lately, the one he heard her sing as she walked through the corridors in their house; the corridors were too long, she said, and she got bored going through them.

Mr. Andesmas listened to the tune, attentively, quite contented now, and his waiting for Michel Arc became less pressing, less painful. From Valérie he knew all the words of the song. Alone, and never again able to make his ruined body dance, never again, he could still recognize the appeal of dancing, its irresistible urgency, its existence parallel to its design.

Sometimes, finding them too long and becoming impatient, Valérie dances in the long corridors of the house, most of time as a matter of fact, Mr. Andesmas remembers, except during her father's siestas. The pounding of Valérie's bare feet dancing in the corridors, he listens to it every time, and each time he thinks that it is his heart which is racing and dying.

Mr. Andesmas settled himself to wait for a man who did not keep his word, patiently.

He listened to the dancing tunes.

From his lost youth this was left him, this much: he would at times move his feet in his black shoes, keeping time. The sand of the plateau was dry and lent itself well to this game with his feet.

"A terrace," Valérie had said. "Michel Arc claims that it's essential to have one. Far away from you. But I'll come, every day, every day, every day. The time has come. Far away from you."

Could she be dancing in the square? Mr. Andesmas does not know. She had really wanted this house very much, Valérie. Mr. Andesmas had bought it for her as soon as she had expressed the wish. Valérie says she is reasonable. She says she never asks for anything she doesn't need. Just the pond, she had said, and after that, I'll never ask you for anything again.

This is the first time that Mr. Andesmas has seen this house bought by him for Valérie. Without seeing it, just because she wanted it, he had bought it for her, for Valérie, his daughter, a few weeks before.

As the whole wicker armchair creaked, Mr. Andesmas examined the place chosen by Valérie. The house was small but the land around it was flat. One could easily enlarge it on three sides whenever Valérie expressed the desire.

"My room, you'll see, will open onto the terrace. That's where I'll eat my breakfast, in the morning."

Valérie, in her nightgown, will therefore soon be looking at the sea, to her heart's content, from the moment she wakes up. Sometimes the sea will be calm, as it is today.

When our hope is here every day
When our hope is here forever . . .

Every twenty minutes, approximately, the melody begins again with greater and greater force, more devastating, strengthened by its regular repetition. And then the square dances, dances, dances, all of it.

Sometimes, the sea would be foamy and sometimes, even, it would disappear in the fog. At times it would also be purple, swollen, and there would be storms that would frighten Valérie from the terrace.

And Mr. Andesmas is afraid for his child Valérie, for his love of her rules without pity over his declining fate; afraid she will be frightened by the storms to come when, waking up, on this terrace over the sea, she finds them raging in all their fury.

There must be lots of young people in the village square. On the banks of the pond, deserted, even by that gadabout dog, weren't there flowers in full bloom which tomorrow would be fading? Valérie should go to her pond and look at her flowers. A short cut would take her there, in a minute. One could undoubtedly buy this pond, for very little. Valérie was right to want it for herself. Valérie, it seemed, still laughed at frogs swimming across the surface of ponds, didn't she? Valérie, it seemed, still thought it was funny to hold them in her hand? still laughed at terrifying them like that? Mr. Andesmas no longer really knew. Even if the age for torturing them had passed, wasn't she still amused by them in another way, by holding their life locked up in her hand and by their terror? Mr. Andesmas no longer knows at all.

"Michel Arc," the girl said, "asked me to tell you that he'd be here soon."

Mr. Andesmas hadn't seen her come. Could he have dozed off as she was approaching? He discovered her all of a sudden, standing on the plateau, at the same distance as the reddish dog. If he had dozed off, was it while she was approaching or even somewhat earlier?

"Thank you," Mr. Andesmas said, "thank you for coming."

The girl, at this respectful distance, examined the massive body, imprisoned in the wicker armchair, the massive body she was seeing for the first time. She must have heard them speak of it in the village. Below the very ancient, smiling and bare head, the body was richly covered with beautiful dark clothes, meticulously clean. You could see the immense shape only vaguely, it was very decently covered by these beautiful clothes.

"So, he is going to come?" Mr. Andesmas asked in a friendly tone of voice.

She nodded that he would come, yes. She was already so tall that it was only because of the improper way she stared at him that Mr. Andesmas realized she was still a child.

Beneath her black hair, her eyes seemed light. Her face was small, rather pale. Her eyes slowly became accustomed to the sight of Mr. Andesmas. They left him and surveyed the surroundings. Did she know the place? Probably. She must have come here with other children, and even as far as the pond—that pond where soon she would no longer be coming—she must have come. There, no doubt, before, the children of this village and those of the distant hamlets behind the hill must have met.

She was waiting. Mr. Andesmas made an effort, moved in his armchair, and took a franc piece out of his vest pocket. He held it out to her. It was also the way she came up to him and very simply took the coin that confirmed his impression that she was still a child.

"Thank you, Mister, Mr. Andesmas."

"Oh, you know my name," Mr. Andesmas said softly.

"Michel Arc, he's my father."

Mr. Andesmas smiled at the child by way of greeting. She smiled a polite little smile.

"What should I tell him you said?" she asked.

Taken by surprise, Mr. Andesmas looked for something to say, and found this.

"It's still early, after all, but if he could come soon, it would be very kind of him."

They both smiled at each other again, pleased with this answer, as if it had been the perfect one the child had been waiting for and as if Mr. Andesmas had guessed it by wanting to be nice to her.

Instead of leaving, she went to sit on the edge of the terrace-to-be and looked at the chasm.

The music was still drifting up.

The child listened for a few minutes, and then she played at taking the hem of her dress—a blue dress—pulling it down over her folded legs, lifting it again and pulling it down again, several times.

And then, she yawned.

When she turned toward Mr. Andesmas, he noticed that her whole body started, briefly, and that her hands flew apart and dropped the franc piece.

She did not pick it up.

"I'm a little tired," she declared. "But I'm going down to tell my father what you told me."

"Oh, I have plenty of time, plenty of time, why don't you rest," Mr. Andesmas begged her.

When the lilac blooms my love

Together, they listened to the song. With the second verse, the child began to sing also in a thin, uncertain voice, her head still turned toward the chasm of light, completely forgetful of the old man's presence. Although the music was loud, Mr. Andesmas listened only to the childish voice. At his age, he knew how not to make his presence bothersome, ever, to anyone, particularly children. Turned away from him, marking the rhythm like a schoolgirl, she sang the whole song.

When the song was over, a clamor arose. Just as, every time it ended, there were shouts of men and girls reveling in it, happy. They requested it a second time, but it didn't come back. Silence, near silence, strangely took hold of the square, laughter and shouting almost stopped,

211

having run their course, exhausted, overwhelmed by their own flow. Then the child whistled the tune. It was a sharper, slower whistling than it should have been. She probably wasn't old enough to dance yet. She was whistling, with strained application, badly. It pierces the forest and the listener's heart, but the child doesn't hear herself. Valérie whistles in the corridors, wonderfully, except during her father's siestas. Where have you learned to whistle so well, my little Valérie? She cannot tell.

When she had reached the end of the song, the child scanned the village square, for a fairly long time, then turned toward Mr. Andesmas, this time without fear. On the contrary, she had a happy look. So, then, perhaps she was calling for a compliment that didn't come? Perhaps she hadn't forgotten this old man's presence as much as one might have thought? Why such joy? The happy look lasted, fixed, then suddenly it faded into an immobile and unjustified solemnity.

"You whistle well," Mr. Andesmas said. "Where did you learn."

"I don't know."

She looked at Mr. Andesmas questioningly, and asked:

"Shall I go? Shall I go down?"

"Oh, take your time," Mr. Andesmas protested, "take all the time you want, why don't you rest. You've lost your franc piece."

Perhaps she was intrigued by so much concern. She picked up the coin, and once again examined the impressive bulk which seemed thoroughly at rest, squeezed into the armchair—in the shade of the white wall of the house. Was she hoping to find some sign of impatience in those trembling hands, in that smile?

Mr. Andesmas tried to find something to say to distract her from this spectacle, but finding nothing, he remained silent.

"But I'm not that tired, you know," the child said.

She turned her eyes away.

"Oh, you have all the time in the world," Mr. Andesmas said.

Smiles no longer registered naturally on Mr. Andesmas' face. Except when Valérie would appear in the frame of the French door which opened on to the garden, and when an uncontrollable, animal-like joy would break through, crisscrossing his whole face, Mr. Andesmas only smiled when he seemed to remember that social conventions called for it, and he could only do it with difficulty, pretending just enough to give the impression of being a good-humored old man.

"You have all the time in the world, I assure you," he repeated.

The child, standing up, seemed to be thinking.

212

"Then I'll go for a walk," she decided. "In case my father comes, I'll go back with him by car."

"There's a pond, over there," Mr. Andesmas said, his left arm pointing at Valérie's future forest.

She knew that.

She walked off toward the top of the hill, where the reddish dog had come from. She walked awkwardly on her skinny, nearly shapeless legs, bird's legs, while the old man looked on, smiling with approval. He watched her until he could no longer see anything of her, nothing, not one speck of her blue dress, and then once again he found himself in the state of abandonment whose disconcerting vastness she had only emphasized through her appearance, no matter how discreet.

On the sunny plateau her dress had been very blue. Closing his eyes, Mr. Andesmas recaptures the exact shade, while he already has difficulty recalling the color, reddish, of the dog who preceded her.

He is suddenly sorry he encouraged her to leave. He calls her back.

"And what is your father doing?" he asks.

While up until then she had acted disgusted, but respectful, before so much old age, she now becomes insolent. A shout comes back, piercing, exasperated, from the forest.

"He's dancing."

Mr. Andesmas' waiting began again.

Oddly enough it was at first calmer, more patient than a moment before.

He stares at the chasm of light. At this altitude the sea is almost the same blue as the sky, he notices. He stands up to stretch his legs and to have a better look at the sea.

He stands up, takes three steps toward the chasm, filled with a light already turning yellow, and he sees as he had expected, beside the green benches of the village square, in the shade of the trees, Valérie's black car parked.

And then he walks back to his armchair, sits down again, again considers his bulk, in the dark clothes, sunk in this armchair, and it is while he is preparing to wait still longer for Michel Arc, and, also, for the return of the child, an expected, foreseen return; it is then, during this interlude, that Mr. Andesmas will know the terrors of death.

Having sat back sensibly, ready to accept Michel Arc's delay, reduced by his own choice to a complete indulgence of any slights to

213

himself, at the very moment when the memory of Valérie returns to him even though she is so near—her black car is there on the white rectangle of the square—Mr. Andesmas knows the terrors of death.

Was it from having watched the child walk on the path, her frail way of stepping on the pine needles? from having imagined her solitude in the forest? her somewhat frightened running toward the pond? from remembering her submissiveness, that devotion to the duty her father had imposed upon her to inform this old man whose sight had sickened her, a devotion which had in the end marvelously exploded into insolence?

Mr. Andesmas believes he is overwhelmed by the longing he feels to love this other child and by his inability to have his feelings follow this desire.

When he recounted this episode in his endless old age, he claimed it was from the moment the little girl started off toward the top of this deserted hill, from the exasperating daintiness of her walk which was taking her to the pond where he knew Valérie would no longer go alone, that he felt this desire that day. That day, he wanted one last time to change his feelings in favor of this child who was going to the pond, with an intensity as brutal, as urgent, he said, as the desire, the mortal passion he had felt, years ago, for a certain woman.

But while he wants this so much, he suddenly recalls the smell of Valérie's hair when she was a child and his eyes close with suffering at this impotence, the last in his life. But is it the forest which hides in its depths, flowers he hasn't seen and which a breeze carries to him? Is it the enduring perfume of this other child who has gone, which he hadn't noticed when she was there?—now the memory comes back to him of the scented magnificence of his child's hair, and how, in advance, the infernal memory of a blondness which soon, in this very house, will perfume the sleep of a still unknown man.

An insinuating heaviness slowly penetrates Mr. Andesmas, it takes hold of his limbs, of his whole body, and slowly reaches his mind. His hands become lead on the arms of his chair and his head grows remote to itself, gives in to a despair never experienced before, at the thought of going on.

Mr. Andesmas tries to struggle and to tell himself that this very long wait for Michel Arc, without moving, in this heat, he must admit, is disastrous for his health. But it doesn't help. The insinuating heaviness penetrates still farther, deeper, more and more discouraging and unknown. Mr. Andesmas tries to stem it, to stop its intrusion within him, but it engulfs him more and more.

It now rules over his whole life, settled there, for the time being, a prowler asleep on its victory.

The whole time it is there and sleeping, Mr. Andesmas tries to love that other child whom he can no longer love.

The whole time it is there and sleeping, Mr. Andesmas tries to confront the memory of Valérie who is there, down below, in the white square, and who has forgotten him.

"I'm going to die," Mr. Andesmas said aloud.

But this time he does not give a start. He hears his voice in the same way he heard it say that the wind was rising, awhile before, but it does not surprise him since it is the voice of a man he does not recognize, a man unable to love that child at the pond.

He sits there not loving this child whom he would love if he could, and he is dying from not being able to, of a fictitious death which does not kill him. Someone else loves her, to distraction, who is not he but who he might be and who he will not be.

He waits for the passing of his intense surprise at discovering that he is not dying from believing so strongly that he is dying. Filled with this impossible desire to change his feelings, to love differently, he looks at the trees with all his strength, begging himself to find them beautiful. But they are of no help to him. He imagines that other child, so delightful, who is watching, without being able to see it at the edge of the pond, the imperceptible growth of the grass forcing its way toward daylight, but she is of no help to him. His preference for Valérie, his child, still remains shining and indescribable. That was it.

"That man, how rude he is," he continues.

In vain. Oh, how he tries to get back into this long wait to which he has relegated himself long before and which he can so conveniently call his despair! Oh! let Valérie's blondness roam the world, let the whole world look dull, if it so desires, next to so much blondness, why should one think about that? Mr. Andesmas thinks. At the same time knowing that one cannot think about it. And, if it were thinkable, why think about it with this crushing pain and not tenderly? Mr. Andesmas goes on thinking, knowing that he is lying, that one can only attempt to think about it with terrible pain.

This young, hatefully young pain lasted, Mr. Andesmas claimed. How long? He was never able to say. But long enough for him to become, in the end, its willing prey. And his mind, never a threat in his life but always, on the contrary, praised as one of the best possible minds, it, too, put up with this deviation from its normal course.

Mr. Andesmas agreed never to know any other adventure but the one of his love for Valérie.

"Why wait for Michel Arc, who won't come this evening anyhow?"

He had spoken aloud again. No question, he was speaking aloud. And it seemed to him that his voice was questioning. He answered himself without fear because, next to the discovery of Valérie's universal blondness, what comparable fear, actually, could he experience?

"Who would actually do it," he answered himself. "Who, in my place, wouldn't get angry?"

He ventured a glance toward the left, toward the path down which that other betrayed child should soon be coming, and he stayed that way, sitting straight in his wicker armchair, while that child did not come back from the pond and the afternoon reached its full measure of yellow, soft sunshine.

It was in this position that Mr. Andesmas fell asleep.

. Mr. Andesmas claimed later that he had, that afternoon, been the victim of a discovery—a penetrating and empty one, he said—which he had not had time to make in the course of his life, and which, probably because of his age, tired him more than it should have, but which he felt was nevertheless a very common one, he said. For convenience and perhaps also because of his failing vocabulary, he called it the understanding of his love for his child.

He went on with his speech, of which Michel Arc was the main target, but he never knew exactly what this speech had been. Strong and violent words were pronounced on the plateau during the period that followed his gain of wisdom. He heard them.

Having just tasted the delights of this funereal feast at which he would have devoured his own entrails in a fear that went unbearably beyond the strength he had left, and probably because of this fear, Mr. Andesmas laid the blame for it on Michel Arc's negligence.

After which he collapsed into drowsiness facing the soft, yellow light of the chasm.

216

In certain places in the valley, above the already-watered crops, there were fine mists which this soft, yellow light of the chasm dispelled with more and more difficulty.

This day in June was monotonous, perhaps, but of a rare perfection. How long did this respite of Mr. Andesmas last? This also he was never able to say. He said that he dreamed, as long as it lasted, of ridiculous satisfactions related to his previous talks with Michel Arc about the estimate for Valérie's future terrace, facing the sea of all seasons.

Actually, this respite was brief, just long enough to let the little girl play near the pond and return. Then she was coming back from the top of the hill.

Until the last moment of his life, Mr. Andesmas remembered the arrival of this other child.

In the forest, at first from far, then closer and closer, the ground was struck by the tapping of a step. But this step, so light on the dry leaves of the path, did not go unnoticed in Mr. Andesmas' sleep. He heard her. He recognized a human presence, which he placed on the southern side of the hill; he even told himself that the child was coming back from the pond, but he thought she was still far from the plateau and that he had time to sleep a little more, and instead of getting ready to greet her, he fell asleep again, so deeply that he soon no longer heard her at all, even when she was a few yards from him.

The child returned. Mr. Andesmas, plunged in this beneficent sleep, probably still had his head bent in the direction of the path through which she was to come back from the pond.

Did she look at him in silence for a moment? He did not know. Nor how long her walk had lasted. Or this sleep.

"Hey, Mister," the child said very quietly.

She softly kicked the sand on the plateau.

When he opened his eyes, Mr. Andesmas recógnızed upon him the immaculate rudeness of a stare already seen. She had come very close to him, not like the first time, and in the sun he saw her light eyes better. He realized he had forgotten her.

"My, oh my, I fall asleep all the time, everywhere, everywhere," Mr. Andesmas apologized.

The little girl did not answer. She examined him all over with an insane, insatiable, curiosity. This time, Mr. Andesmas tried to meet her gaze. But he did not succeed.

"Michel Arc hasn't come, you see," Mr. Andesmas went on.

The little girl frowned and seemed to think. Her eyes left Mr. Andesmas and tried to find something behind him, on the white wall, to discover something they wanted to see and didn't see. Then, her face suddenly expressed an overwhelming brutality, a revulsion at some nonexistent vision. She was looking at a dream and she was suffering. This dream she was looking at could not be seen.

"Sit down, rest," Mr. Andesmas said softly.

Her face relaxed a little. But her eyes did not recognize the old man when they rested on him again. However, she obeyed. She sat at his feet and put her head against the leg of the armchair.

He counted his breaths, forced himself to make them deeper to harmonize them with the calm of the forest and the calm that had taken hold of the child.

Very slowly, she raised toward Mr. Andesmas a narrow, long, dirty hand, displaying the franc piece. She spoke without turning her head.

"I found this on the path," she said.

"Oh, that's fine, that's fine," murmured Mr. Andesmas.

Had he really seen her just before? Her forgetfulness must be fleeting, must crush her for short moments, only to release her again.

She remained silent, her head against the leg of the armchair, in the shade of the wall.

Did she close her eyes? Mr. Andesmas could not see her face; only her motionless, half-open hands. In her right hand was the franc piece. So much stillness was choking Mr. Andesmas.

When the lilac blooms my love
When the lilac blooms forever

She didn't move while the song lasted. When it stopped, she raised her head and listened to the laughter and shouting coming up from the village square. The laughter and shouting stopped, but she remained as she was, her head raised. That was when Mr. Andesmas moved in his armchair.

The child burst out laughing:

"Your armchair, it's going to break," she said.

She stands up and he recognizes a child he has already seen.

"I'm fat," he says. "This armchair wasn't made for me."

He too laughs. But she quickly becomes serious again.

"My father hasn't come yet?" she asked.

218

"He's going to come," Mr. Andesmas says hastily. "He's going to come, you can wait for him if you like."

She stands there, but reasonably, trying to decide what she prefers to do with her time, orphaned all of a sudden by this father who has forgotten her. Her eyes remain wild, also abandoned, but by this frenzy which just before had carried her away as she was crossing the forest. She raises her hands to her face, crosses them over her mouth, and rubs her eyes as she probably does when washing.

What game had she played near the pond? It was dried mud that had dirtied her hands. She must have dropped the coin after holding it out to Mr. Andesmas. That's right, her hands had fallen empty, alongside her dress.

"I'm going," she says.

Then suddenly Mr. Andesmas remembers what Valérie had told him:

"Michel Arc's oldest daughter is not like the others. Michel Arc thinks his daughter is not like others. It isn't so serious, they say. At times, she forgets everything. Poor Michel Arc, whose daughter is not like the others."

She didn't seem in a hurry to go now that she had decided to do so. Perhaps she felt secure near this old man? Or, equally indifferent to being there or elsewhere, did she prefer to wait for a better idea than the one she had had, of going back?

"Shall I tell my father that you'll wait for him much longer?"

She smiled. Her face collected itself completely. Cunning filtered into her smile as she waited for Mr. Andesmas' reply, and Mr. Andesmas, his cheeks glowing, shouted merrily:

"Well, as long as it's light, I'll wait for Michel Arc!"

Does she hear the answer? Yes. She hears it.

As she is leaving, she sees the franc piece in the gray sand of the plateau. She looks at it, bends down, and once again takes it and shows it to Mr. Andesmas. Her eyes do not wander off.

"Look," she says. "Someone may have lost it?"

She laughs again.

"Yes," declares Mr. Andesmas. "Keep it."

Her hand, ready to close, does so with a click.

Again she grows dreamy, distracted. She walks up to Mr. Andesmas and holds out her left hand, the one that does not hold the coin.

"Later I'll be afraid," she says. "I'll say good-by now."

Her hand was warm, rough from the mud of the pond. Mr. Andesmas

219

tried to hold it in his but she slipped away, restless; she had the flexibility, the softness of an uprooted weed, even in her motions. She held out her hand reluctantly, she did it like a very small child, in a dread understood and accepted.

'Maybe Michel Arc won't come until tonight?"

She pointed at the chasm where the dance was going on.

"Listen," she said.

She stayed like this, in this rapt gesture, incomprehensibly. Then the gesture collapsed without reason, or was it that the dance had stopped?

"What did you do at the pond?" Mr. Andesmas asked.

"Nothing," she said.

She left, without making a mistake, by the path the reddish dog had taken, steadily, slowly. Mr. Andesmas made a gesture as if to stop her but she noticed nothing. Then he straightened, looked for a way to detain her, a way to express himself, and, too late, he shouted:

"If you see Valérie . . ."

She answered something after having already disappeared behind the turn in the path, but she did not come back.

Mr. Andesmas heard whistling.

He falls back in his armchair. He tries to disentangle from the silence of the forest the words the child has spoken, but he does not succeed. Did she say she didn't know Valérie? Or that Valérie knew very well that her father was waiting for her? Or something else that had nothing to do with the question he had asked?

The echo of the childish voice floats for a long time, insoluble, around Mr. Andesmas, then, none of its possible meanings having been retained, it moves off, fades, joins the various shimmerings, thousands of them, hanging in the chasm of light, becomes one of them. It disappears.

Again Mr. Andesmas finds himself alone. Alone waiting for a man without a sense of time. In the forest.

Some day they would have to chop down many trees in this forest, pull out bushes, ravage part of this shapeless denseness, so that air could sweep into it, free, through immense clearings, and at last disrupt this monumental undergrowth.

The weather is so clear that one could see him, if one wanted to, from the village square. His shape is outlined on the site of the future terrace of his daughter, Valérie. Everybody knows about this forthcoming construction. They know he is waiting for Michel Arc. As usual he is dressed in a dark suit. Yes, they can see him, distinguish this dark spot formed by his body squeezed into the wicker armchair which stands out against the whitewashed wall of the house he has just bought for his daughter Valérie. This spot grows darker and larger every minute as time goes by, and his presence on the bare, sunny plateau becomes increasingly undeniable. It is so sandy on this side of the mountain; yes, Valérie must be able to see him, this father, if she wants to see him, as he waits for Michel Arc. Others can too. He is there, exposed to their eyes, and everyone knows it can only be he, Mr. Andesmas. The purchase of the hill has caused quite a stir in the village. The land bought in Valérie Andesmas' name by her father covers a hundred and ten acres of forest. They have both been living in this village, in the heart of this chasm, for a year, ever since, it is said, he decided to retire from the business that had taken up his time, having the means to do so, and even more than the means. With this child. Just because of her wish, a few weeks before, he bought her this side of the hill up to the edge of the pond. He was going to buy the pond.

"Ah! That Mr. Arc, ah, that man," Mr. Andesmas says.

He has grown used to his own voice.

With difficulty he half rises, drags his armchair a little farther forward, closer to the edge of the plateau so he can be seen more easily from down below. But he does not look into the chasm. They are still dancing, if the singing is any sign. He prefers to look at his body spread out in the armchair—more spread out than while the little girl was there —and dressed in this beautiful dark material. His belly rests on his knees, wrapped in a vest of the same dark material chosen by Valérie his child because it was good cloth, a neutral color, and because a heavy-set man would be more comfortably and safely hidden in it.

Idle, and alone, Mr. Andesmas examined with boredom what had finally become of him. Still nothing came from the path. From where he was now, he could have seen again, if he had wanted to, Valérie's black car, parked.

But, he related, he had been unable for a moment either to look at this black car of Valérie's, or to think about the child. These memories surrounded him, linked one to another, in a coexistence which, for a long moment, had made them one in his mind. He knew that he could contemplate neither Valérie's blondness nor the other betrayed child's madness without being equally terrified. Mr. Andesmas did not even look at the trees which also, so innocently, partook of this same inconceivable fate, to exist that afternoon.

Mr. Andesmas looked at himself. And at the sight of himself he found some comfort. It filled him with a secure, irreversible disgust. It was, that evening, the equivalent of the only certainty he had ever known in the course of his life.

It is the wind coming up. It is never Michel Arc.

Time passes, and Mr. Andesmas reaccustoms himself to waiting.

He can even cherish the secret hope that the child has not returned to the village, that she is still lingering near the plateau; he reaccustoms himself to the idea of her presence there, nearby, and he even hopes for it, and his desire to see the child reappear exceeds his desire to see Michel Arc and Valérie.

A franc piece, fallen from her hands, shines in front of him in the sand. She has again dropped it, again and again.

"She opens her hands and drops things, she doesn't know how to keep anything. Yet she has some memory. You can't really tell."

Mr. Andesmas makes an effort to get hold of the coin, then gives up. And instead of picking it up, he pushes it with his foot as far as possible from his sight. But it does not reach the little thickets alongside the plateau, as he would have liked it to; it travels a yard in the soft sand and remains there, half buried.

No, she won't come back today. She must have arrived in the village by now. She went down without difficulty, whistling at times, looking right and left, at the trees and the ground—her legs, so frail and deft, carry her wherever she wants—gathering things, pebbles, or leaves, which for her, only her, for an instant have an obscure interest that captivates her. Then she opens her hands, drops her possessions.

"Yet sometimes she remembers having forgotten."

Was she afraid during her walk? Did she run once or twice? Did she take the wrong path?

"No, the paths, she knows them better than her brothers and sisters, who have all their wits. Why? You tell me."

At what moment did she remember she had forgotten the franc piece? If she did remember? Then, yes, she would have had to stop on the path, find herself alone on that deserted path, and with sharp regret must have wondered whether she shouldn't go back to the old man. But she decides against it in the obscure foreknowledge of her madness, she

222

does not make this childish, irrational move, and, on the contrary, she continues on to the village.

Mr. Andesmas made an effort, threw some sand on the franc piece which he wanted completely out of his sight. He could no longer see it. He sighed deeply, as he did after any effort.

He feels somewhat calmer again. If he goes down early enough this evening, there's a chance of his seeing this child again on the village square.

Mr. Andesmas had forgotten that Valérie often speaks to him about Michel Arc's daughter.

But he never goes to the village square. What then?

He sighs, then reassures himself. He'll manage to find the child. He'll ask Valérie for a way to find her. He'll give her back her treasure. The wait for Michel Arc is relegated behind this other wait, to give back to the child this treasure she had perhaps forgotten.

What an unexpected turn of events, Mr. Andesmas thinks, what a new and final responsibility! Would she remember him? Yes. She had looked at him so much just before, that if he proved himself with enough friendliness she would make an effort to remember. That rich, idle, very old man whose daughter is Valérie, you know? Yes. She had called him by his name when she arrived on the plateau.

"She doesn't understand what others understand, and yet she knows and remembers certain things. Whatever she feels like, one might think."

Shouts of pleasure rose up from the valley. Then dance music drowned them out. It was a waltz with lyrics. Ah, let them dance, let them dance, as much as they want, they shouldn't feel they have to suffer, as long as they're dancing, and stop soon because of an obligation to me.

Is it after arriving in the square, thinking she still possesses that franc piece, torn between the desire for a bag of candy and the obligation to inform her father that Mr. Andesmas would wait for him until dusk, that this child notices she has lost her treasure? That the memory of what she forgot comes back to her ?

She makes her way toward the square, she is so docile, so docile, then through the dancers. There is her father who dances so well. Does she keep herself from crying with regret?

"Mr. Andesmas said he would wait for you as long as there's light."

"That's right, good Lord, that's right!" Valérie exclaimed.

Isn't it, rather, as she wanders around the square in search of a bag of candy, that she notices that once again she must have lost the franc piece which she had found near the old man?

Does she cry, in a corner, at being that forgetful?

He will know this evening. This evening. He has to know.

"That's right, good Lord!" Valérie cries. "How late it is."

No, the child must not have forgotten the errand her father had asked her to run. She must have looked for the franc piece in the dust of the square. People look at her with pity. Is she crying?

Then, through the dancers, she went up to Michel Arc. The errand is done.

"He has nothing better to do after all," Michel Arc says.

"But he knows nothing about that forest. It's painful to wait."

No. The child did not remember the errand. The forgotten franc piece, the terrace. She is crying, alone. Her father is dancing with blind pleasure. She is crying, where? Who sees her cry, who?

Mr. Andesmas' waiting once again finally grows calm. The sun was still high. Since he had said so, he would wait until evening. He knows the little girl has forgotten the old man.

What could he do but wait? Wait for Valérie's car. He laughs. He is imprisoned in the forest by Valérie—his child.

From being on this plateau such a long time, he ended up knowing the instructions he would give Michel Arc, concerning the shape of the terrace, its dimensions. Their meeting would be short. In a few words he would tell Michel Arc what he thought should be done, up to what point the railings should go on the plateau.

The terrace will be a half circle, with no angles, it will come within two yards of the chasm of light.

When Valérie wakes up, her blond hair is so mussed that it falls over her eyes. It will be through the foliage of her blond hair that, from her terrace, upon waking, she will discover the sea, this child of Mr. Andesmas.

Had the sun turned? Apparently, Mr. Andesmas noticed. A beech tree, a few yards away from him, swept him with its noble and impressive shade. This shade began to mingle with the shade of the whitewashed wall.

When the lilac blooms my love
When our hope is there every day.

A very young voice was singing, slowly. The song lasted a long time. It was played twice in a row.

When it ended, the joy was less violent. Some laughter, and it died down.

Did Mr. Andesmas fall asleep again, after the song?

Two

YES, HE MUST have fallen asleep. The shade from the beech tree now covered the whole site of the future terrace. Mr. Andesmas found himself protected by it without at all remembering having noticed any of its progress.

Yes, he must have fallen asleep again, once again.

Now, from the village square, nothing can be seen of him any more. The shade from the tree is denser than the one from the wall, it covers a vast expanse and he is in the middle of it. It was useless for him to have moved closer to the precipice a moment before. Never again, from now on, never again.

The proof that he has slept is that he can distinguish this sleep from the other, the one that preceded it, disentangle these dreams— wonderful and torturing—from the other ridiculous ones that preceded them, and finally remember that he had discovered the little girl's mad eyes under a blazing sun, as well as the image he had of how she must have dirtied her hands on the muddy edge of the pond.

Without a stir, the shade kept spreading without his noticing it, while he felt surprise at having once again surrendered to sleep.

"It will probably take me several days," Mr. Andesmas says, "to recover from the strain of such a wait."

These phrases, spoken aloud in the solemnity of his loneliness, rendered Michel Arc's offense more serious. Thus, Mr. Andesmas, in order to make this trial more bearable, was trying to lie to himself as to the length and the consequences of Michel Arc's delay.

Thus he waits, pretending not to be able to understand Michel Arc's rudeness toward him.

Once again, in a soft, polite voice, he tells this lie to himself.

"I don't understand. It isn't right of Mr. Arc, it isn't fair to make an old man wait for hours, as he is doing."

He stops speaking, somewhat ashamed. He lowers his eyes, then slowly raises them, examining in bewilderment the site of the terrace-to-be.

"How can he allow himself to do something like this?"

One of these days, on this terrace, wearing a sumptuous, light-colored dress, Valérie would be gazing down this path, at this time of the evening. Under this beech tree which would extend the benefits of its shade to anyone who might be here at this hour, in the future, in this same season, Valérie would be waiting for someone to come. It would have to be here, in effect, that this waiting of Valérie's would soon take place.

Mr. Andesmas makes this reflection calmly. He moves back farther on the plateau until he can no longer see anything of the village.

In the square, which he can no longer see, the dancing stops.

No one is coming yet.

But Mr. Andesmas, who had claimed he could not bear waiting this way for such a long time, is becoming more and more adjusted to the wait. His strength returns with coolness of the late afternoon. So much so that he kicks the white sand on the plateau with his feet, thinking thus to express his anger. He smiles at dirtying his shoes and at his strength, ridiculous from now on. But it is a way for him to make the hours pass, like any other hours, like those which pass during other afternoons when he waits for dinnertime in his garden.

A wind blew over. The beech tree trembled. And in its rustling, the arrival of a woman took place, which escaped the notice of Mr. Andesmas.

She stood in front of him and spoke to him.

"Mr. Andesmas," she began.

For how long had she been looking at him, she too, while he played in that way with his feet in the sand? Probably a very short time. The time she had needed to come from the path and walk up to him.

Mr. Andesmas rose slightly from his armchair and bent forward.

"Mr. Andesmas, I'm Michel Arc's wife," she said.

She had rather long, straight black hair, which fell a little below her shoulders, light eyes which Mr. Andesmas recognized as being the little girl's eyes, very large, larger perhaps than the little girl's. She too wore canvas shoes and a summer dress. She seemed taller than she probably was, because of her slenderness.

She stood facing Mr. Andesmas.

"This contractor you're waiting for," she repeated once more, "I'm his wife."

"I see," said Mr. Andesmas.

She sat down at the edge of the plateau, very straight, her head turned toward the armchair.

She seemed by nature reserved, neither sad nor depressed, but this rigidity of her body and the expressionless intensity—carried to perfection—of her eyes on the old man arose from a desire to censure, which could have been misleading to anyone but Mr. Andesmas. Except when her eyes closed for a few seconds, weary of looking at nothing, one could have thought they were that way, vacant. But when her eyes closed, she was beautiful in such a different way, she was so beautiful—that was when her eyes came back to life in the dark night of their eyelids—that Mr. Andesmas understood that Michel Arc's wife was not this woman standing in front of him, that she must have been different, and he feared he would never know her.

Would he ever know the one who had been Michel Arc's wife?

"You go out very little," she said; "I've never seen you."

She pointed at the hill.

"This is high up. I'll rest a little."

Laboriously, Mr. Andesmas raised himself from his armchair and moved aside.

"Please," he said.

The woman examined the empty armchair, hesitated a moment, then refused.

"Thank you, but I'm all right here."

Mr. Andesmas didn't insist. He fell back heavily into his armchair. The woman stayed where she was, seated at the edge of the plateau, her head this time turned toward the chasm. She was outside the reach of the tree's shade, still in the sun, like her child. Like her child, too, she didn't talk. Even though it was likely she had come to bring a message from her husband to Mr. Andesmas, she said nothing. But then, how could one know if she hadn't just come to be silent there, near this old man, rather than elsewhere? If she had not chosen this spot, this witness?

Panic-stricken at again having to break so much silence, Mr. Andesmas hunted for words. His hands, clutching the arms of his chair, made the wicker stir with slight continuous cracklings which she didn't hear, still turned toward the chasm of light.

228

The square cannot be seen any more from where Mr Andesmas has retreated forever. Apart from a few unidentifiable sounds coming from the village, but which could be coming from any other village, the valley is now calm.

Mr. Andesmas, making a polite effort, extricates himself slightly from his armchair, and finally succeeds in speaking to the woman.

"Is Mr. Arc going to come this evening?"

She turned sharply. He was certain she had found it superfluous to give the reason for her coming.

"Of course, that's why I came," she said, "to tell you. Yes, he's coming this evening."

"Oh, you had to go out of your way," Mr. Andesmas said.

"No, not at all," she said. "It isn't so far. And there was no choice."

The song again rises from the chasm of light.

It is still a phonograph. The song varies in loudness. It fades and grows distant. The woman listens to it attentively whether it is far or near. But is she listening to it?

Mr. Andesmas sees nothing of her but the black and silky sheet of her hair spread on her shoulders, and her bare arms which, joined by her clasped hands, hug her knees. No, she is probably only looking, not listening. Mr. Andesmas thinks he can tell that she is watching this side of the village square, the side with trees and benches, the one he saw after the departure of the child for the pond.

"Are they starting to dance again?" he asks.

"No, no, it's over," she says.

Mr. Andesmas relaxes a little. Her voice had been even, flat, when she had answered.

An event was taking place, Mr. Andesmas knew it—which he called their meeting, much later. This event was taking root painfully in the arid stretch of the present, but it was necessary, nevertheless, that it should happen, and that the time it took should pass as well. Mr. Andesmas' surprise was hardly fading at all, of course, but it was fading all the same, it was growing older all the same. Mr. Andesmas claimed to know it from the fact that, little by little, the slight cracklings of his wicker armchair occurred less frequently and he soon only heard around his body the reassuring ones, in time to his labored breathing.

But then something happens that baffles him at first, then frightens him. One of the woman's shoes falls from her foot, from her raised foot. This foot is bare, small and white next to her sunburned leg. Since the woman is still outside the stately shade of the beech tree, or rather the shade hasn't yet reached her, her foot seems even more exposed than it would have in the shade. And her strange attitude seems even more evident: she doesn't budge, doesn't feel that her foot has lost its shoe. Her foot is left bare, forgotten.

Mr. Andesmas, in contrast to the preceding moment, felt then the urgent necessity to break into the woman's thoughts. He remembered. A little girl had come by. And couldn't the memory of this little girl play a role here, between them, breaking down their separation? About this child, who wouldn't agree?

"Had the little girl gotten back to the village when you left?" Mr. Andesmas asked in a friendly tone of voice.

The woman hardly turned. Her voice would have been the same if she hadn't stopped talking since her arrival. But her foot remained bare, forgotten.

"Yes," she said. "She told me she had seen you. It was quite a while after she got back that I felt I should come to tell you that Michel Arc would be still a little later than he had thought. He had said that he would be half an hour late. An hour had gone by when I left."

"An hour?"

"An hour. Yes."

"She hadn't mentioned any time, just a delay, without any details."

"I thought so," she said. "She must have forgotten. You too, it seems."

The sea became a large, perfectly smooth metallic surface. It was useless to hide from oneself that slower, more stretched-out hours were giving way to others, regular like the first hours of the afternoon.

"I have time, you know." Mr. Andesmas. said.

"The child said so to her father. And even that you would wait as long as it was light."

"That's right."

He added timidly, still making the same effort to pull her out of her thoughts even if it was going to hurt: "The child found this on the path. Then she forgot it. I can give it to you. I'll give it to you right away, later I'm afraid I might not think of it. Here."

The franc piece the child lost is buried in the sand. He takes another one from his vest pocket and holds it out into space. The woman does not even turn around, her eyes still glued to the chasm.

"It doesn't matter," she said.

She added:

"Since she didn't mention it to me, she must have already forgotten it. She is still very childish, more than she should be. But it isn't at all serious, it will go away someday."

Mr. Andesmas put the new franc piece back in his pocket. His bulk moved in the armchair, crumpled up in it. Again the armchair creaked.

The woman changed position. She unlocked her arms from around her knees; without looking she found her shoe with her foot and put it on.

"Of course," Mr. Andesmas said, "it isn't serious, not at all serious." She didn't answer.

Mr. Andesmas said that he was afraid at that moment that she would get up and go back to the village, but that if she had done so, he would have asked her to stay. Even knowing that she would never be able to satisfy his avid curiosity about her, he wanted her near him, that afternoon. Near him, even interminably silent, he wanted her near him, that afternoon.

If he saw her later, during the years that went by between these moments and his death, it was only by chance, when he rode through the village streets in a car. Never did she recognize him, or deign to recognize him.

Instead of leaving, on the contrary she stays there and talks, always in this even voice, and her words are revealed from a long interior monologue, she lets them escape at times and whoever cares to hear them.

"The music hasn't started again for some time," she says, "so the dancing should be completely over, even in the streets around the square where people sometimes dance because of the heat. They must have left already, but they're taking their time, they are coming up slowly. You have to wait a little longer."

"Oh, I have time," Mr. Andesmas repeats.

"I know," she says. "Everybody knows."

The spontaneous way in which Mr. Andesmas had reassured her, as well as the gentleness of his voice, softened the firmness of her resolve. The spectacle she was offering this remarkably courteous old man would be forgotten forever.

Her voice became somewhat languid. She repeated what her child had said a moment before. But she spoke to the empty chasm.

"I'm going to wait a little; if he comes, I'll go down with him."

She hides her head in her arms, and for a few seconds her hair covers her face.

"I'm a little tired."

Not only the similarity of their expressions but also her childish tone of voice would have indicated, to anyone who might have seen them one after the other as Mr. Andesmas had, that she was the mother of this little girl without memory of her sorrows.

"Why not wait, why not rest a little more," Mr. Andesmas said, "before going down."

"I have five children," she said. "Five. And I am still young as you can see."

She opened her arms wide, in an embracing gesture. Then her arms fell down and she again took up her stiff, haughty position, in the sun of the plateau.

"Oh, I understand, I understand," Mr. Andesmas said.

Perhaps the conversation could go on like this, on the basis of the children, of this aspect of her life as a mother; perhaps it could move in this way, cheatingly, along the byways of the present hour.

"The little girl is the oldest?"

"Yes."

Mr. Andesmas went on in a chatty tone of voice.

"Shortly before her, well, a good twenty minutes before her, a dog came by. A dog, how can I describe him? A reddish dog, I think, yes, reddish brown. Does this dog belong to your children?"

"Why are you asking me that?" she asked.

"Well, like anything else," Mr. Andesmas said, crestfallen. "I've been here since two o'clock and I've only seen this dog and the child. So I thought that perhaps . . ."

"Don't try so hard to talk," she said. "This dog belongs to no one. He follows the children. He's harmless. He doesn't belong to anyone in the village, he's everybody's dog."

The shade of the beech tree was moving toward her. And while they were both silent and while she was still stiffly and with fascination examining the village square, Mr. Andesmas saw, with growing apprehension, that this shade from the tree was approaching her.

232

Suddenly surprised by the coolness of this shade, realizing that it was later than she thought, would she leave?

She notices it.

She sees, in fact, a change taking place around her. She turns, tries to see where this coolness, this shade is coming from, looks at the beech tree, then at the mountain, and finally, earnestly, at Mr. Andesmas, seeking from him a final assurance that she still seems to be waiting for, that she wants to believe is definitve.

"Oh, it's really late," she sighs. "How could it already be so late, with the sun like that."

"And even if Mr. Arc doesn't come tonight," Mr. Andesmas says cheerfully, "I'll come back, perhaps tomorrow or at th⸗ end of the week, what does it matter?"

"Why? No, no, he'll come I assure you. What surprise me was how easily time just goes by. But I know he'll come."

She turned back toward the valley, then again to Mr. Andesmas.

"Especially in summer, especially in June," she adds.

Mr. Andesmas had noticed it.

"Anyway, didn't Valérie promise you that he'd come?"

Mr. Andesmas didn't answer right away. Throughout his life, it had always been easy to take him by surprise. And the slowness of his movements and of his speech, which had increased with age, caused the woman to misunderstand.

"I asked you, Mr. Andesmas," she went on, "if Valérie hadn't promised you that my husband would come this evening?"

"It's Valérie who brought me here," Mr. Andesmas finally said. "Yes, she is the one who made the date with Mr. Arc. Yesterday, I think. For the last year she has been taking care of my appointments."

The woman rises, moves closer to Mr. Andesmas, abandons her observation of the valley, sits down, there, almost at the old man's feet.

"So, you see," she said. "You have to wait longer."

Mr. Andesmas took the woman's rebuke to heart. She came even closer, hauled herself toward him while sitting, like an invalid, and her voice was as loud as if she were talking to someone who was deaf.

"And you trust Valérie?"

"Yes," Mr. Andesmas said.

"If she told you that he had promised her he would come, believe me, it's only a matter of patience. I know him just as you know Valérie. He'll keep his word."

Her voice suddenly became more womanly, it emerged from a well of gentleness.

"You see, when he makes life difficult for people, it's because he can't do anything else. It's when it is beyond his power to do anything else. It's only in this case that he could wrong you. That's how he is, without any ill will, but sometimes it happens that he can't help looking as if he had ill will."

"I understand," Mr. Andesmas uttered.

"I know you understand. Isn't Valérie like that?"

She was completely curled up. Her slenderness was covered by her hair and her arms. She said with an effort:

"Who, in such a case, wouldn't act that way? Who? Neither you years ago, nor I today."

Mr. Andesmas recounted later that he was tempted—but was he sure about his past, this old man?—to be cruel to this woman so as to protect himself from the cruelty that she, he knew it, would show him. But was this the right, the real reason? Wasn't it rather because this woman, who a moment before had been so fiercely resolved not to let any of her feelings show, was now sitting at his feet so dejectedly, in such complete surrender of her whole body; dominated by her feelings which had suddenly become so tyrannical that they crushed her, there, in front of him, the wife of Michel Arc?

In the old days, when his strength would have allowed him to subjugate her in this way, the old man remembered he would have done so.

He was cruel. It was he Mr. Andesmas, who was the first to bring up Valérie again.

"Do you know my daughter Valérie?" he asks her.

"I know her," she says.

She straightened, calmly raised herself up out of her silence. She spoke about Valérie as she had spoken about Michel Arc a moment before. Mr. Andesmas' cruelty hadn't reached her.

"I've known her for a year," she stated. "You came here a year ago, didn't you, nearly to the day? It was a Monday. An afternoon in June. The first time I saw Valérie Andesmas, your child, was on the day you arrived."

She smiled from deep in her well of gentleness at the memory of that afternoon.

Mr. Andesmas also smiled at the thought of that afternoon.

234

There they are, together, facing the memory of Valérie a year before, a child.

Smiling, they do not speak.

Then, Mr. Andesmas asks her:

"Your little girl must be about the same age now as Valérie was last year?"

She graciously objects to this remark:

"Let's not talk about my little girl. It'll take her a long time to grow up, a long time."

Again she is back in last year's month of June which Valérie passed through as a child.

'People said that you had already been here, long before, years ago. They said that you had just retired from business."

"Well! That was quite a few years before," Mr. Andesmas says, "but she wanted to live near the sea."

"First you bought that big house behind the town hall, then you bought land. And then this house. And more land. They said that you had already come here years ago with Valérie's mother."

Mr. Andesmas lowers his head, suddenly overcome. Does the woman notice?

"Am I mistaken?"

"No, no, you're not mistaken," Mr. Andesmas says weakly.

"You're very rich. That was known very quickly. And people came to sell you land. They say you buy carelessly. You're so rich that you buy land without looking at it."

"Rich," repeated Mr. Andesmas, in a murmur.

"One can understand and admit it, you know."

He buries himself a bit deeper in his armchair and gives a grunt. But the woman goes on, imperturbably.

"You're going to buy the pond too?"

"The pond too," Mr. Andesmas murmured.

"So Valérie will have a large fortune at her disposal?"

Mr. Andesmas agrees.

"But why are you talking to me about my money?" he sighs.

"It's about Valérie that I'm talking to you," she says smiling, "you're mistaken. Why are you buying so much land, more and more, in this completely careless way?"

"Valérie wants to own the whole village."

"Since when?"

"A few months ago."

"She won't be able to."

"She won't be able to," Mr. Andesmas repeats. "But she wants to."

The woman put her arms around her knees again and delighted in pronouncing the name.

"Ah, Valérie, Valérie."

She sighs with pleasure, deeply.

"Ah, I remember it as if it were yesterday," Michel Arc's wife continues. "The moving vans stayed in the square all night. They had arrived before you. No one had seen you yet. And the next day, when I was standing at my window as I often do, looking at the square, it was close to noon, all at once I saw Valérie."

She gets up suddenly and stays there, standing, very close to Mr. Andesmas.

"It was just before school let out, I remember. I was watching for my children. Valérie appeared in the square. I was probably the first one to see her. How old was Valérie then?"

"Nearly seventeen."

"That's right, yes. I was afraid I'd forgotten. So she crossed the square as I was telling you. Two men—they saw her after me—stopped to look at her walking by. She walked, the square is wide, she walked, crossing it, crossing it. She walked endlessly, your child, Mr. Andesmas."

Mr. Andesmas raised his head and along with the woman he contemplated Valérie's walk, a year earlier, in the light of the village square, when she didn't yet know the splendor of her bearing.

"Indifferent to the stares?" Mr. Andesmas asked.

"Oh, if you only knew!"

The tune burst forth in the chasm of light.

Just when one might have thought they were no longer dancing, they were dancing again.

But neither Michel Arc's wife, nor Mr. Andesmas, remarked upon it.

"Indifferent to the stares, as we were saying," the woman went on. "We were looking at her, the two men and I. She pushed aside the curtain of the general store. We no longer saw her during the time she was in there, and yet not one of the three of us moved."

The shade of the beech tree now reaches the chasm. It begins to sink down into it.

"In the general store," Mr. Andesmas repeated.
(He started laughing.)
"Oh, I know!"

"Because of the moving vans that had stayed in the square all night, I knew that the people who had bought that big house behind the town hall were going to arrive, any day. Already the name Andesmas had been mentioned. You had bought that house a few months earlier. Everybody knew that the two of you were alone, a child and father, already old, they said."

"Very old, they said?"

"Yes, in the district they were saying that you had had this child very late, from a late marriage. But you know, seeing Valérie so tall, so blond as you know, I didn't immediately make the connection between your arrival and her existence. Such boldness, I told myself, how beautiful she must be."

"Ah," Mr. Andesmas moaned, "I know, I know."

"How beautiful she must be, I told myself, but is she as beautiful as one can imagine from her walk, from her bearing, from her hair?"

She takes her time, desregarding the old man's waiting. Then she goes on in a voice that has become clear, loud, almost declamatory.

"The curtain closed on her hair. And I asked myself who in the town had brought her, who would join her any minute, now. The two men also seemed astonished and we looked at one another questioningly. Where did she come from? We kept asking ourselves what man owned this blondness, and only this blondness, since we had not yet seen her face. One just couldn't imagine so much useless blondness. Well? She took a long time to come out."

She comes closer, sits down right next to the old man and this time they look at each other but only while she is speaking, exactly.

"Then," she said, "she finally reappeared. The curtain was moved aside. We saw her as she crossed the whole square in the opposite direction. Slowly. Taking her time. Taking the time of those who were looking at her, as if it had been owed her from time immemorial, without realizing it."

"Without realizing it," Mr. Andesmas repeated.

Once again they were banished into that moment when she had seen, completely, fully, forever, the beauty of Valérie Andesmas.

She stopped talking. Mr. Andesmas had sunk back into his armchair.

Again, from crackling of the wicker armchair under his hands, he noticed that he was trembling.

"Mrs. Arc," he asked, "if this house has been for sale so often, as I have been told, there must be a reason?"

She smiled, nodded.

"You certainly say anything that comes into your head," she said.

She added, suddenly, seriously:

"But there must be a reason, I suppose, yes."

The forest fills with sunlight. All its shadows drown in the chasm of light, too long now for the hill to contain them.

"I have known none of the owners of this house," she says, "but it's true that it passes from hand to hand regularly. There are houses like that, everyone knows that."

She explores its surroundings very quickly and, again, looks at the chasm of light.

"It's isolation probably, in the end," she says.

"In the end, it's possible."

"Because," she goes on, "at first, couples, for example, might enjoy it!"

"Ah, probably, probably," Mr. Andesmas murmurs.

"And also this light, in summer, so harsh."

"It isn't any more now," he says. "Look."

It isn't any more. The mist rises thicker, from the woods and the fields. The sea is softly multicolored.

"Michel Arc had planned to buy it, you see, at the beginning of our marriage," she continues. "But your predecessors were living in it. Afterward, Michel Arc no longer mentioned it. I only saw it once, three years ago when I took the children to the pond. In the summer."

"Nobody had thought of a terrace? This is the first time."

"Oh, not at all, Michel Arc had thought of it."

"Only he?"

"The others? How would I know? Even though you might think, when you see this plateau, that it calls for a terrace, why had no one thought of it before you? If you know why, tell me, Mr. Andesmas."

"Money?"

"No."

"Time?"

"Well, perhaps, Mr. Andesmas, time to build it before leaving this house because of its isolation which, as we were saying, becomes unbearable in the end. Don't you think so?"

Mr. Andesmas does not answer.

She turns.

For a brief moment she at last sees this bulk, abominably final. He no longer is even tempted to express himself. And at that point, she probably feels a certain interest in so much past existence. Mr. Andesmas realizes this from her half-closed eyes which linger on him. Later he said he had recognized this to be the woman's greatest virtue, this ability at such a moment, even for just a few seconds, to forget about herself and take an interest in his immense, cold and burned-out life.

"Her mother left you," she says very softly, "and she has had other children since by different men? There was a law suit?"

Mr. Andesmas nods.

"A very long, very expensive law suit?" she continues.

"I won, as you can see," Mr. Andesmas says.

She again gets up slowly, moves still closer to him. She touches the arm of the chair and, leaning, stands there looking at him.

They are very close to each other: if she were to fall forward, her face would land against his.

"You had great hopes for her probably?"

He feels upon him the smell of a summer dress and of a woman's loosened hair. Nobody ever comes so close to Mr. Andesmas any more, except Valérie. Is the closeness of Michel Arc's wife more important than what she is saying?"

"I had no ideas on the subject," he says in a very low voice, "not yet. You understand. No ideas. That's why I may perhaps seem helpless to you."

He adds in a still lower voice:

"I no longer know anything of what I knew before I had this child. And, you see, since I had her, I have no ideas about anything any more, I know nothing but my ignorance."

He laughs, at least tries, as he has come to laugh now, falsely.

"I am really astounded, believe me, at such a possibility in life. The love for this child that outlives my age, my old age!"

The woman straightens up. Her hand lets go of the armchair. Her tone becomes sharper, but barely.

"I wanted to talk to someone about Valérie Andesmas," she says. "I assure you that you can put up with this inconvenience."

"I don't know," Mr. Andesmas complains, "I don't know if I can."

"It's better. No one has talked to you about her and now she's grown up, it's better."

The shade had now spread over the whole plateau. It was already part of the hill. The shade of the beech tree and of the house had toppled over completely into the chasm.

The valley, the village, the sea, the fields are still in the light.

Flocks of birds, in ever greater numbers, fly out of the hillside and wheel wildly in the sunlight of the chasm.

The shade overtakes this house more quickly than those in the village. Nobody had thought of it yet, neither Mr. Andesmas nor Valérie. But the woman notices it.

"Valérie will lose one hour of light here, compared to the village," she says.

"Mr. Arc hadn't told me that, you see."

"Did he know it? Even when we thought of buying it for ourselves, he didn't mention it," she adds, "ten years ago."

"What hurts is to see the sun so close, there."

"One has to be here the way we are to notice it. Otherwise who would think of it, beforehand?"

She takes several steps on the path, comes back, then sits down, as if reluctantly this time, a few yards from the old man.

"Valérie makes me suffer a great deal," she says.

She spoke in the same tone of voice about the disadvantages of the house, so that one might think the whole world in her eyes suffers from a contagious disorder, but only from that.

The sweetness of a recent past which contained a jumble of Valérie Andesmas crossing the village square, and what followed, and her suffering too, are equal aspects of this disorder.

Again she moves away toward the path with this walk which is the same as her little girl's a while before, light, a little off balance, only her legs moving, effortlessly, beneath her straight body. And once more, even in the very depths of his old age, Mr. Andesmas is still able to perceive, dimmed, dying, but recognizable, the reasons one might have had for loving her. She is a woman who cannot help welcoming into her whole body her moods, whether fleeting or lasting. These moods might be languid, gentle, or cruel; the ways of her body would immediately follow in their image.

When she comes back from the path, her walk is sleepy and careful, extraordinarily childlike—deceptively so—and one might imagine that she had been tempted, during the moment she was alone on the path, to escape from the calm disaster she was living. Just as her child might have been tempted.

It was when she had not yet come back that Mr. Andesmas understood he would have liked to see her again and again, until evening, until night, and that he began to dread Michel Arc's arrival, which would prevent him from seeing her.

He smiles at her.

But she walks by him without looking at him. As she passes on the windy plateau. She pulls the wind behind her. She speaks about it.

"It's windy. It must be even later than I thought. We have been chatting."

"Ten past six," Mr. Andesmas says.

She sits back down in the place she had just left. Still far from him. Has she noticed this? Or has she noticed it before?

"Valérie's car is no longer in the square," she announces.

"Ah! You see," Mr. Andesmas exclaims.

Once again, the song rose up, ravaged by the distance. The phonograph was turned down earlier than the time before.

"Then I think they won't be long in coming," she says. "Both of them are very decent and charming."

"Ah, aren't they though," Mr. Andesmas murmured.

She gets up again, again goes toward the path, comes back again, still possessed by this occupation, the passionate listening to the forest noises coming from the path. She comes back, stops, her eyes half closed.

"You can't hear the car coming up yet," she says.

She listens again.

"But the road is steep, longer than you'd think."

She glances absently at Mr. Andesmas' motionless bulk, buried in his armchair.

"You are the only one I can talk to about her, do you understand that?"

She goes away, comes back, goes away again.

Does she realize that Mr. Andesmas never takes his eyes off her? Probably not, but even if she knew, this look would not distract her from listening to the forest, to the valley, to the whole countryside, from its most remote horizons up to this plateau. The total impossibility with which Mr. Andesmas is confronted of finding something to do or say to lessen, if only for a second, the cruelty of this frenzy of listening, this very impossibility chains him to her.

He listens like her, and for her, to any noise that might signal an approach to the plateau. He listens to everything, the stirring of the closest branches, their rustlings against one another, their jostlings, sometimes, when the wind increases, the muffled bending of the trunks of the huge trees, the gasps of silence paralyzing the whole forest, and the sudden and successive waves of its rustling by the wind, the cries of dogs and chickens far away, the laughing and talking all mixed into one conversation by the distance, and the singing, and the singing.

> *When the lilac*
> *. . . my love*
> *When our hope . . .*

Sharing one outlook, they both listen. They also listen to the strangled sweetness of this song.

The wind mussed her hair each time she came back from the path. It blew more often and a little stronger. Tirelessly, each time she returned toward Mr. Andesmas, she would push her hair back with her hand and hold it like this a few seconds, and her bared face became the face of past summers when, swimming next to Michel Arc, she must have been told that she was beautiful, like that, for him, Michel Arc.

Once, the wind is strong enough to blow all her hair onto her face and, tired of having to make this mechanical gesture once more, of pushing it back, she does not do it. She no longer has a face, or eyes. Instead of moving forward on the plateau, she stands there, on the path, waiting for the end of the gust that mussed her hair.

The gust ends and once again she makes that sensible gesture. Her face reappears.

"So much blondness, so much, so much useless blondness, I thought, so much idiotic blondness, what could it be good for? Except for a man to drown in it? I didn't immediately realize who would to the point of madness love to drown in that blondness. It took me a year. A year. A strange year."

242

The shade starts to overtake the fields, it approaches the village.
More numerous, exuberant shouts rise from the valley.

The path remains empty.

"People are in the streets," she says.

"You were telling me, Mrs. Arc," Mr. Andesmas says hastily, "you were telling me that the curtain of the grocery had been pushed aside."

"And the car isn't there any more," she went on. "And they aren't dancing any more. And it's already too cool to go to the beach."

She comes up to the old man, slowly. And slowly, she speaks.

"The curtain was pushed aside. I have time, I have plenty of time to tell you. Yes. The curtain was pushed aside. And she crossed the whole square again, unconcerned. I already told you. I could tell you again. She appeared. The bead curtain covered her, she freed herself from it. And that day I heard the almost deafening noise, which I was to hear thousands of times, of the bead curtain falling back after her. I could also tell you how, like a swimmer, she pushed it aside, her eyes closed for fear of hurting herself with the beads, and that it was after she had gone through the curtain, in the sunlit square that she opened her eyes, with a slightly embarrassed smile."

"Oh, I see, I see," Mr. Andesmas exclaimed.

The woman went on even more slowly.

"And, taking her time, she crossed the square."

The song began again.

She listened to it without speaking, attentively.

"So," she said, "that's the most popular song this summer."

She starts moving toward the path again, comes back again, and then, giving up this maneuver, she sits down like a lump right where she is. She leaves her hair to the mercy of the wind, her idle hands stroke the earth.

"Beauty, we all know it," she says, "starting with ourselves. In love, we are told, how beautiful you are. Even when mistaken, who doesn't know what it is to be beautiful and the peace you feel to hear it said, whether as a lie or not? But Valérie didn't, Valérie, when I first knew her, as unbelievable as this may seem, was still very far from guessing how sweet it is to hear this said, how longed for. But without knowing it, she was yearning for it, she was wondering who, some day, would come to her, speaking these very words, for her."

"She crossed the square," Mr. Andesmas says, "you had gotten to that."

"She was already grown up, Mr. Andesmas, your child was already grown up, I assure you."

There was a lull in the village.

Her mouth half open, dazed by her own intensity, she stops talking —her eyes are following Valérie's black car on the road along the sea. Mr. Andesmas also sees this car.

She is the one to start talking again.

"It took me a year," she goes on, "to unravel the enormous problem posed by the wonderful blondness of your child. One year simply to accept its existence, to admit it as a fact: Valérie's existence, and to overcome my fright at the idea that she was still being offered without any reservations, to whom? To whom?"

Valérie's car is no longer visible.

The road along the beach leads deep into the pine forest beyond it at the foot of the hill, but to the east, where it is still sunny.

The car has gone beyond the turn-off for Valérie's house.

Again she starts pulling her hair back into place after each gust of wind. Mr. Andesmas watches her gesture as much as he listens to her words. This gesture remains the same as the one Michel Arc's wife must have made always.

"She knew it, she already knew it, in her heart, what you were saying. . . ." Mr. Andesmas moans.

"One doesn't know it by oneself. No, she did not know it."

Mr. Andesmas raised himself from his armchair and whispered:

"But she knows it, she knows it."

The woman mistakenly thought this was a question. She answered.

"You shouldn't ask this horrible question," she said. "Tomorrow, or tonight, perhaps she will know it?"

Severely she examined the shapeless bulk of Mr. Andesmas.

"Did you see her car go along the beach, Mr. Andesmas?"

"I saw it."

"Then we are in the same boat, both of us, at this moment which is perhaps the very one when she will find out."

Very quickly she is somewhere else, crucified on that sunny square Valérie was crossing.

"The first walk across the square," she said, "that morning, of

244

Valérie's, so blond, as you know, even you, her father, that walk followed by strange eyes, she didn't pay any attention to it, certainly, and yet she says she remembers it. She claims she raised her head and saw me."

"But you couldn't not have known that Valérie was my child," Mr. Andesmas wailed.

"After she had left the grocery, but long after she had gone, I understood that Valérie was a child. But only afterward. After having thought about it."

"She walked out with? With?"

"Yes!" she cried.

A long, deep, rumbling laugh shook Mr. Andesmas' body. And she, she burst into a loud laugh that stopped halfway in its flight.

"With candy!" she went on. "She was looking at no one, at no one, in spite of what she now says, just at the bag of candy! She stopped a second. She opened the bag and took out a piece, unable to wait any longer."

She looks at the pine forest in which Valérie's car has been swallowed up.

"That is how, afterward, I remembered her as a child. How old was she exactly?"

Mr. Andesmas said it again.

"Over sixteen. Almost seventeen. Two months short. Valérie was born in autumn. In September."

Mr. Andesmas is overwhelmed with words, he trembles from this unaccustomed flow of words.

"She was still a very little girl because of your love. But you didn't know that very soon, and no matter what you did to prevent it, she would be old enough to leave you."

She stops talking. And in this silence, brought on by her, the graceful memory of an old suffering slides into Mr. Andesmas' heart.

"But this other little girl, yours?" he moans.

She does not take her eyes from the pine forest which hides Valérie's car.

"Let her be," she says.

"Where is she? Where could she be?" Mr. Andesmas cries out.

"She's there," she says slowly. "There. She thinks she's lost something, she's looking in the square. I can see her. She's there."

Her eyes leave the forest, wander over the plain, move closer to the village.

"I recognize her by her blue dress."

She points toward a spot Mr. Andesmas can no longer see.

"There," she says. "She's there."

"I can't see her," Mr. Andesmas complains.

The graceful memory of his old suffering hardly stirs within him, hardly more than the memory of the inconsolable regret for a love glimpsed and, barely seen, stifled, and with thousands of others, forgotten.

Its grief is borne only by the very old flesh of this destroyed body. That is all. This time his head is spared the trouble of having to suffer.

"She won't find anything," Mr. Andesmas says. "Nothing."

Can she really see her child, who in the sun and the dust of the square is looking for her memory?

"While she is looking," she says, "she's not unhappy. It's when she finds that she's upset, when she finds what she is looking for, when she remembers clearly having forgotten."

Slowly she turns her head, seized again by the spectacle of the pine forest and the sea. The forest keeps its secret. The sea is empty.

Mr. Andesmas loses sight of her as suddenly as he had noticed before.

As though she is chilly, she suddenly clasps her shoulders.

"Little by little day after day, I started thinking about Valérie Andesmas, who would soon be old enough to leave you. You understand?"

With slow steps she moves closer to the chasm, not waiting for an answer from Mr. Andesmas. He is afraid she will let go of her shoulders, he thinks that once she has let go of her shoulders, nothing will keep her from going a little farther toward the chasm. But she lets go after turning back to him again. Mr. Andesmas' fear at seeing her move toward the chasm is so violent that he could have believed that his age, right then, inadvertently, was receding from him.

"Are you asleep, Mr. Andesmas? You're not answering me any more?"

Mr. Andesmas points to the sea. Mr. Andesmas has forgotten the child forever.

"It is not as late as you think," he says. "Look at the sca. The sun is still high. Look at the sea."

She does not look, shrugs her shoulders.

"Since they'll come anyway and since the later it gets the closer the time comes when they'll be here, why worry?"

Laughter exploded somewhere on the hill.

The woman freezes, like a statue, facing Mr. Andesmas. The laughing has stopped.

"It was Valérie's laugh and Michel Arc's," she cries. "They were laughing together. Listen!"

She adds, laughing herself:

"At what, do you know, can you imagine?"

Mr. Andesmas raises his stiff, neatly cared-for hands in a gesture of ignorance. She comes toward him walking like a weasel, she seems very gay all of a sudden. Does he wish she would leave now? He imagines the plateau deserted once she has left and so when she moves close to him, he listens with all his strength.

"You know what? It's by giving her candy that I got to meet her. A sweet tooth, hasn't she, Valérie?"

"Yes, a sweet tooth!" Mr. Andesmas admits.

He smiles, incurable, at this memory.

"I'm the one," she says, "who taught her to escape during your siestas."

Mr. Andesmas leads her on.

"Was it necessary?"

"Yes. She could still hardly bear leaving you alone at your age. The only time it was possible was siesta time, your long siestas."

"This house?"

"Michel Arc showed it to her during a walk."

"The terrace?"

"It would be an idea, he told her. It would be nice to have a house, so high up on the hill, with a terrace where you could see good weather coming, and storms, where you could hear every sound, even those from the other side of the bay, in the morning, in the evening, at night too."

"They didn't laugh just now as you claimed," Mr. Andesmas says. "We didn't hear the car drive up."

"If they come by way of the pond, it's such a long walk that they

247

would have left the car much farther down, and that's why we wouldn't have heard it. It doesn't matter actually, we'll know soon enough."

Again laughter exploded from another part of the hill. She listens. "Some children perhaps?" she asks. "It's over by the pond."

"ʌes," Mr. Andesmas declares.

Her good mood dies away. She comes back close to the armchair, very close.

"What do you think?" she asks very softly. "Is it worth our waiting longer? A while ago I took advantage of your confidence. I told you I was sure they would come, but it isn't true, I'm not sure of anything."

"I can't go back down by myself without running the risk of dying," he says. "My child knows this."

"I hadn't thought of that," she says.

She laughs at this joke, laughs. He laughs with her.

"I told this to your little girl. I'd wait for Michel Arc as long as there was light. There is still a lot of light."

"And she told him."

"Well then. There you are."

She sits down at the foot of the armchair like that little girl a while before. One might think she no longer expects anything to happen. She closes her eyes.

Her hair lies against the wicker of the chair, caressing it.

"She refused what I would give her, candy at first," she says. "As you had taught her. Even candy. Many times."

She repeated, wearily:

"Many, many times. Sometimes it made me feel almost discouraged."

She turned to him, stared at him from very close, and Mr. Andesma lowered his eyes. Who would ever again look at Mr. Andesmas, except, at some trying time, this woman, and, a moment before, that child?

"You look as if you weren't thinking of anything any more," she added softly.

"She's my child," Mr. Andesmas whispered. "Her memory is inside me, even in her presence, always the same and it fills me with laziness so that I can't even think."

"And yet you listen to me."

"You're talking to me about her. Was she running off to your garden, during my siestas?"

"When it wasn't too hot to stay there, yes, it was to our garden."

"I didn't know anything about it. But it makes no difference to me now, whether I know or not."

"You certainly are talking a lot all of a sudden," she said, smiling.

"When I wake up, Mrs. Arc, at my age, from these old man's siestas you are talking about, from a sleep thick as glue, with my memories I know that it's a very common joke to believe that it is useful to have had such a long life. I can still imagine Valérie's mornings and evenings, I can do nothing about it. I think that I shall never reach the moment in my life when the image of Valérie's mornings will have left me. I think that I shall die with all the weight, the heavy weight of my love for Valérie on my heart. I think that's how it will be."

She felt a burst of tenderness for him, such as she hadn't felt once until then.

"But Michel Arc is a wonderful man," she said. "Don't worry."

"I don't think I do," Mr. Andesmas said, "although perhaps you're right, I might worry without knowing it. Everything gets to my mind in such a confused way that, rather than being worried, it may be that I'm happy to be with you like this, feeling I can trust you."

"Make an effort, keep listening to me," she begged. "I swear I know Michel Arc better than anyone. You'll see him in a little while. Make an effort to know him better, I beg of you. You'll see what kind of man Michel Arc is."

"I believe you," Mr. Andesmas said absent-mindedly.

The woman found herself deprived of his attention and grew anxious.

"You're going to fall asleep, Mr. Andesmas, if I keep talking about him?"

"I don't know," Mr. Andesmas said, still absent-mindedly. "How sweet to think of her in that walled garden during those siestas, hidden in that garden during my sad sleep."

"Listen!"

The hill was once again perfectly silent. The shade was spreading over the edge of the sea.

"I thought I heard something," she said.

Mr. Andesmas claimed that it was from that very moment that he grew weary, that he began to break away from her, even from her, this woman, the last who would come close to him.

"Ah, I don't remember that she left me so often at siesta time, you see."

"But she would come back before you woke up, Mr. Andesmas. She would start to look at her watch, always, ten minutes before you got up. And she would leave, running to your garden, and very gently close the gate behind her, and run on to your room. Come, come now, Mr. Andesmas, what are you imagining?"

"I would have noticed, at least once, just once."

Sadly he shook his head. So did she. Both of them shared the same pity for Mr. Andesmas' situation.

"I believe you now," she said. "You have no memory left. You no longer have any memory."

"Oh, leave me alone," Mr. Andesmas cried all of a sudden.

When the lilac blooms my love
When the lilac . . .

She listened to the song, indifferent to Mr. Andesmas' angry sadness.

"I still have a memory," she said, "the memory of that man, Michel Arc, for whom we are waiting. But some day I'll have a very different memory from this one. Some day I'll wake up far removed from any memory of this moment."

She added, in a sudden about-face:

"I have made this my duty. Are you listening?"

He had been listening.

"Yes, yes," he said.

"Ah, I can already feel them move into my life, those other men, tens, hundreds of them, new ones, ah! Who will rid me of his memory, and even of the memory of this moment I'm living through here in front of you, this difficult, nearly unbearable moment, but which I bear anyway, as you can see, thanks to your courteous presence. Then, I'll be ashamed to have talked to you like this, to have confided to you these temporary difficulties. You'll be dead perhaps?"

It was his turn now to bend his head and look at the chasm.

"I have the impression that you, too, are saying just anything," he grumbled.

She turned, facing the chasm that Mr. Andesmas was looking at and shouted about her presently belonging to Michel Arc.

"Some day, some day, another man will come to me and under his eyes I'll feel the signs of a first desire, that heaviness, that warmth in

250

my blood, that I will surely recognize. The same thing will happen. No other man will be able to come close to me then, I won't be able to bear any, not even him, Michel Arc. In the same way that he . . ."

Mr. Andesmas cut her short.

"Valérie crossed the square, the bag of candy in her hand. And then?"

She seemed shocked for a second, then her listening to the forest covered over her amazement.

"Don't you know any more how she crosses squares?" she asked off-handedly. "You have to be told this?"

Mr. Andesmas laughed.

"Well!" he said, "I probably don't know too well any more."

"Others will soon know even better than I, and with a fresher memory. All you'll have to do is ask them."

"Calmly, indifferent to the heat?" Mr. Andesmas insisted.

"Yes, but how can one explain it to you?"

"It's true she's nice and calm, my little Valérie," Mr. Andesmas said.

She probably is now convinced that she is in the presence of a man who no longer matters.

She leaves him, goes toward the path, sits down, and talks to herself, her back to him.

"Oh, how difficult," she says, "how difficult it is to describe such a simple suffering, a suffering of love. What a wonderful relief it would have been to meet someone to whom I could have talked about it! How can one describe anything to an old man who has left all his troubles behind him except that of having to die, and that only?"

"Come back over here," Mr. Andesmas begged. "You're mistaken. Nothing else, nothing else matters to me, except that you still talk to me. Please come back."

She obeyed reluctantly, came toward him.

"We were so faithfully united," she said, "by day and by night, so exclusively, that sometimes, ashamed, we felt sorry to see ourselves so childishly condemned to being deprived of other encounters, more daring even than ours."

Mr. Andesmas raised his hand with authority and held it out to her She refused to take that hand.

"Valérie," said Mr. Andesmas, "Valérie."

"She went by," she told him, sounding bored, "in the way you know

251

she had of walking across squares, a year ago, across the squares and down the streets along her way. Blond. Her hair in her eyes, always. Busy sucking that candy, looking at the other candies, sorry not to have all of them together in her mouth at once."

An immense, set smile had spread over Mr. Andesmas' face.

"She has always been like that, my little Valérie."

At the bottom of the hill, from the exact direction they would have to take to get there, there was the purring, swelled by the echo, of the motor of a car.

The woman took the old man's hand and shook it.

"Hey, it's Valérie's car, this time!" she shouted.

Mr. Andesmas didn't stir.

"As old, as crazy as you may be, you have to accept it, Mr. Andesmas. Listen! The car is stopping "

"You're making up stories," Mr. Andesmas said.

The car stopped.

There is a moment of silence. And then a dual pounding of the earth can be heard still from the exact direction where it should happen if Michel Arc and Valérie Andesmas or two other different people were coming.

"Your love for Valérie has to get used to being far from her happiness. Our estrangement, yours and mine, has to be perfect, incomparable. Do you hear me, Mr. Andesmas?"

Mr. Andesmas' smile still lingered on his face. He always remembered this face—his own—torn and paralyzed by this smile that he could neither justify nor stop.

Mixed with the dual pounding of the steps was the sound of muted, reserved laughter, without any mockery at all, and yet without gaiety, but which, like Mr. Andesmas' smile, would not stop.

The woman listened for them, then moved closer to Mr. Andesmas in a frightened, animal-like impulse.

"I didn't recognize that laughter," Mr. Andesmas said. "I'd say it's the laughter of children going to the pond."

"They're coming!" the woman said hurriedly. "They have different laughs from the ones we know, this is their new laughter. When they are together that's how they laugh, I know it! Listen! How slowly they're walking. They're coming grudgingly. How slow they are!"

"What a bore!" Mr. Andesmas whispered.

The woman drew away from Mr. Andesmas. With exaggerated

252

motions, she roamed back and forth on the plateau, extravagant, disheveled, wringing her hands, recklessly walking along the edge of the precipice. But Mr. Andesmas, occupied only by his attempt to erase this paralyzing smile from his face, was no longer frightened.

The shade has reached not only the edge of the sea but the sea itself, almost entirely. Mr. Andesmas believes he has waked from an enormous siesta, several years long.

"How will they learn about it?" the woman went on. "That's the only thing that remains to be seen."

She searches for words and states calmly:

"The only thing that will completely escape us."

Only a thread of light was left between the horizon and the sea. Mr. Andesmas was still smiling.

"How will they tell each other? Now that the whole village knows, everyone, and everyone is waiting for that moment."

"I couldn't care less about what you're saying," Mr. Andesmas says. "But go on talking, please."

"There are only a few minutes left before they get here, look how late it is."

"They don't know anything?" Mr. Andesmas asks at last.

"No. Nothing. This morning, still nothing."

"Not my child Valérie either?"

"No. Neither Valérie nor Michel Arc."

When the lilac blooms my love

"Listen! It's Valérie singing!"

Mr. Andesmas did not answer. Then she walked back to him one last time, took his hand again, and shook it.

"After she had crossed the square, do you want to know how we met? I am suffering terribly, I have to tell you. You're so old, can't you hear everything?"

"It's your little girl coming back again," Mr. Andesmas said. "It was she: I recognized her voice."

"They'll be here in a few mintues," the woman implored. "I won't tell you anything more than what is necessary. I beg you."

"I won't listen to anything any more," Mr. Andesmas warned her.

She spoke anyway, her hand on his, in turn shaking it and stroking it, during the few minutes left before the dazzling appearance of the others, in front of the chasm filled with an evenly faded light.

Selected Grove Press Paperbacks

E732   ALLEN, DONALD & BUTTERICK, GEORGE F., eds. / The Postmoderns: The New American Poetry Revised 1945-1960 / $9.95

B472   ANONYMOUS / Beatrice / $3.95

B445   ANONYMOUS / The Boudoir / $3.95

B334   ANONYMOUS / My Secret Life / $4.95

B415   ARDEN, JOHN / Plays: One (Serjeant Musgrave's Dance, The Workhouse Donkey, Armstrong's Last Goodnight) / $4.95

B422   AYCKBOURN, ALAN / The Norman Conquests: Table Manners; Living Together; Round and Round the Garden / $6.95

E835   BARASH, DAVID, and LIPTON, JUDITH / Stop Nuclear War! A Handbook / $7.95

B425   BARNES, JOHN / Evita — First Lady: A Biography of Eva Peron / $4.95

E96   BECKETT, SAMUEL / Endgame / $2.95

E781   BECKETT, SAMUEL / III Seen III Said / $4.95

B78   BECKETT, SAMUEL / Three Novels: Molloy, Malone Dies and The Unnamable / $4.95

E33   BECKETT, SAMUEL / Waiting for Godot / $3.50

B411   BEHAN, BRENDAN / The Complete Plays (The Hostage, The Quare Fellow, Richard's Cork Leg, Three One Act Plays for Radio) / $4.95

E417   BIRCH, CYRIL & KEENE, DONALD, eds. / Anthology of Chinese Literature, Vol. I: From Early Times to the 14th Century / $14.95

E368   BORGES, JORGE LUIS / Ficciones / $6.95

E472   BORGES, JORGE LUIS / A Personal Anthology / $6.95

B312   BRECHT, BERTOLT / The Caucasian Chalk Circle / $2.95

B117   BRECHT, BERTOLT / The Good Woman of Setzuan / $2.95

B120   BRECHT, BERTOLT / Galileo / $2.95

B108   BRECHT, BERTOLT / Mother Courage and Her Children / $2.45

B333   BRECHT, BERTOLT / Threepenny Opera / $2.45

E580   BRETON, ANDRE / Nadja / $5.95

B147   BULGAKOV, MIKHAIL / The Master and Margarita / $4.95

B115   BURROUGHS, WILLIAM S. / Naked Lunch / $3.95

B446   BURROUGHS, WILLIAM S. / The Soft Machine, Nova Express, The Wild Boys / $5.95

E793   COHN, RUBY / New American Dramatists: 1960-1980 / $7.95

E804   COOVER, ROBERT / Spanking the Maid / $4.95

E742   COWARD, NOEL / Three Plays (Private Lives, Hay Fever, Blithe Spirit) / $4.50

B442	CRAFTS, KATHY, & HAUTHER, BRENDA / How To Beat the System: The Student's Guide to Good Grades / $3.95
E869	CROCKETT, JIM, ed. / The Guitar Player Book (Revised and Updated Edition) / $11.95
E190	CUMMINGS, E.E. / 100 Selected Poems / $2.95
E808	DURAS, MARGUERITE / Four Novels: The Square; 10:30 on a Summer Night; The Afternoon of Mr. Andesmas; Moderato Cantabile / $9.95
E380	DURRENMATT, FRIEDRICH / The Physicists / $6.95
B342	FANON, FRANTZ / The Wretched of the Earth / $4.95
E47	FROMM, ERICH / The Forgotten Language / $6.95
B389	GENET, JEAN / Our Lady of the Flowers / $3.95
E760	GERVASI, TOM / Arsenal of Democracy II / $12.95
E792	GETTLEMAN, MARVIN, et. al., eds. / El Salvador: Central America in the New Cold War / $9.95
E830	GIBBS, LOIS MARIE / Love Canal: My Story / $6.95
E704	GINSBERG, ALLEN / Journals: Early Fifties Early Sixties / $6.95
B437	GIRODIAS, MAURICE, ed. / The Olympia Reader / $5.95
E720	GOMBROWICZ, WITOLD / Three Novels: Ferdydurke, Pornografia and Cosmos / $9.95
B448	GOVER, ROBERT / One Hundred Dollar Misunderstanding / $2.95
B376	GREENE, GERALD and CAROLINE / SM: The Last Taboo / $2.95
E769	HARWOOD, RONALD / The Dresser / $5.95
E446	HAVEL, VACLAV / The Memorandum / $5.95
B306	HERNTON, CALVIN / Sex and Racism in America / $2.95
B436	HODEIR, ANDRE / Jazz: Its Evolution and Essence / $3.95
B417	INGE, WILLIAM / Four Plays (Come Back, Little Sheba; Picnic; Bus Stop; The Dark at the Top of the Stairs) / $7.95
E259	IONESCO, EUGENE / Rhinoceros & Other Plays / $4.95
E496	JARRY, ALFRED / The Ubu Plays (Ubu Rex, Ubu Cuckolded, Ubu Enchained) / $9.95
E216	KEENE, DONALD, ed. / Anthology of Japanese Literature: Earliest Era to Mid-19th Century / $12.50
E552	KEROUAC, JACK / Mexico City Blues / $5.95
B394	KEROUAC, JACK / Dr. Sax / $3.95
B454	KEROUAC, JACK / The Subterraneans / $3.50
B479	LAWRENCE, D.H. / Lady Chatterley's Lover / $3.95
B262	LESTER, JULIUS / Black Folktales / $4.95
B351	MALCOLM X (Breitman, ed.) / Malcolm X Speaks / $3.95
E741	MALRAUX, ANDRE / Man's Hope / $12.50

E697	MAMET, DAVID / American Buffalo / $4.95
E709	MAMET, DAVID / A Life in the Theatre / $6.95
E712	MAMET, DAVID / Sexual Perversity in Chicago & The Duck Variations / $5.95
E801	MARIANI, PAUL / Crossing Cocytus / $5.95
B325	MILLER, HENRY / Sexus / $5.95
B10	MILLER, HENRY / Tropic of Cancer / $3.95
B59	MILLER, HENRY / Tropic of Capricorn / $4.95
E789	MROZEK, SLAWOMIR / Striptease, Tango, Vatzlav: Three Plays / $12.50
E636	NERUDA, PABLO / Five Decades Poems 1925-1970. Bilingual ed. / $8.95
E364	NERUDA, PABLO / Selected Poems. Bilingual ed. / $6.95
B429	ODETS, CLIFFORD / Six Plays (Waiting for Lefty; Awake and Sing; Golden Boy; Rocket to the Moon; Till the Day I Die; Paradise Lost) / $7.95
E807	OE, KENZABURO / A Personal Matter / $6.95
E687	OE, KENZABURO / Teach Us To Outgrow Our Madness / $4.95
E359	PAZ, OCTAVIO / The Labyrinth of Solitude. Life and Thought in Mexico / $7.95
E724	PINTER, HAROLD / Betrayal / $3.95
E315	PINTER, HAROLD / The Birthday Party & The Room / $6.95
E299	PINTER, HAROLD / The Caretaker The Dumb Waiter / $4.95
E411	PINTER, HAROLD / The Homecoming / $4.95
E606	PINTER, HAROLD / Old Times / $4.95
E641	RAHULA, WALPOLA / What The Buddha Taught / $6.95
B438	REAGE, PAULINE / Story of O, Part II: Return to the Chateau / $3.95
B504	RECHY, JOHN / City of Night / $5.95
E930	RECHY, JOHN / Numbers / $5.95
E806	ROBBE-GRILLET, ALAIN / Djinn / $4.95
B133	ROBBE-GRILLET, ALAIN / The Voyeur / $2.95
B207	RULFO, JUAN / Pedro Paramo / $3.95
B138	SADE, MARQUIS DE / The 120 Days of Sodom and Other Writings / $12.50
B313	SELBY, HUBERT / Last Exit to Brooklyn / $2.95
E763	SHAWN, WALLACE, and GREGORY, ANDRE / My Dinner with Andre / $5.95
	SILKO, LESLIE / Storyteller / $9.95
B456	SINGH, KHUSHWANT / Train to Pakistan / $3.25
B618	SNOW, EDGAR / Red Star Over China / $8.95
E785	SRI NISARGADATTA MAHARAJ / Seeds of Consciousness / $9.95

GROVE PRESS, INC., 196 West Houston St., New York, N Y 10014